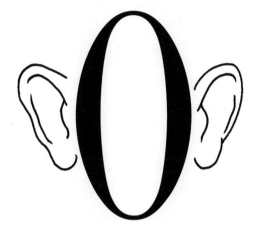

★ A PRESIDENTIAL NOVEL ★

Simon & Schuster
New York London Toronto Sydney

Simon & Schuster
1230 Avenue of the Americas
New York, NY 10020

First Simon & Schuster hardcover edition January 2011

SIMON & SCHUSTER and colophon are registered trademarks of Simon & Schuster, Inc.

For information about special discounts for bulk purchases, please contact Simon & Schuster Special Sales at 1-866-506-1949 or business@simonandschuster.com.

The Simon & Schuster Speakers Bureau can bring authors to your live event. For more information or to book an event contact the Simon & Schuster Speakers Bureau at 1-866-248-3049 or visit our website at www.simonspeakers.com.

Designed by Nancy Singer

Manufactured in the United States of America

10 9 8 7 6 5 4 3 2 1

Library of Congress Cataloging-in-Publication Data.

O : a presidential novel / Anonymous.
1st Simon & Schuster hardcover ed.
   p. cm.
   1. Obama, Barack—Fiction. 2. Presidents—United States—Fiction. 3. Political fiction.
I. Title: A presidential novel.
   PS3600.A1014 2011
   813'.6—dc22   2010045141

ISBN: 978-1-4516-2596-7
ISBN: 978-1-4516-2598-1 (ebook)

FOR K AND R

★ ACKNOWLEDGMENTS ★

I want to acknowledge with appreciation all those at Simon & Schuster who read an early draft of the manuscript and offered many intelligent suggestions to improve it, including Aileen Boyle, Jofie Ferrari-Adler, Jonathan Karp, Molly Lindley, Ben Loehnen, Alice Mayhew, Priscilla Painton, Michael Szczerban, and Brian Ulicky. Special thanks to Kate Ankofski for her excellent line editing. Many thanks, too, to my encouraging agent. Deepest apologies and gratitude to my family and close friends, few of whom understood why I was behaving more peculiarly than usual, but worried about me nonetheless. And I'd like to express my admiration for friends and colleagues who've worked conscientiously on campaigns and in the White House because they believed in their cause and their candidate. I apologize for the occasional exaggerated abuse. I kid because I love.

Finally, for their generous friendship, I want to thank K and R, to whom this book is affectionately dedicated.

★ CAST OF CHARACTERS ★

O'S TEAM

O, president of the United States.

Cal Regan, Democratic Party insider and manager of the president's reelection campaign.

Mick Lowe, Cal Regan's best friend and deputy manager of the O campaign.

Avi Samuelson, senior White House adviser and chief political counsel to the president.

Walter Lafontaine, a Chicago lawyer who served as an aide early in O's political career.

Tess Gilchrest, a volunteer on O's campaign.

THE OPPOSITION

Tom Morrison, a retired four star general, former governor, and the Republican aspirant for president in 2012.

Sandy Stilwell, veteran political operative and Tom Morrison's campaign manager.

THE POLITICAL ELITE

Maddy Cohan, a young reporter for *Body Politic,* an upstart Washington news website.

Allen Knowles, a California billionaire and major donor to O's campaign.

Bianca Stefani, founder of *The Stefani Report,* a liberal advocacy and news aggregating website.

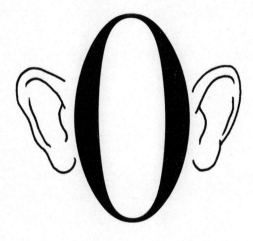

It was nearly eleven o'clock at night, and the president of the United States seemed to be enjoying himself. Friends and aides clustered in desultory conversations, keeping an eye on television screens, waiting, waiting, waiting for someone to call New Mexico or Colorado or Washington. The vice president circulated among them, trying to lighten the mood with his manic cheerfulness, winning a few forced smiles. The First Lady sat quietly and responded politely when someone addressed her but said nothing that would reveal emotion. Tomorrow, depending on the outcome, witnesses would recall her demeanor as either serene or stoic. Her daughters, excited and playful for most of the evening, were now tired and responding to solicitous adults by shaking and nodding their heads.

But O was lighthearted: reacting in mock horror when a reliably Republican state was called for his opponent; teasing aides that their incompetence had cost him another victory; imitating the pundit chatter on television; making faces at his daughters when he caught their eye; telling the voluble vice president, who had just repeated to the president's brother-in-law an off-color joke featuring the former governor of Alaska, the Prince of Wales, and an Eskimo guide on a moose hunt, "Speak up, I don't think the press heard you downstairs."

When he caught Cal Regan observing him from across the room, O winked at him and shrugged his shoulders, as if to say, "Worrying won't make a difference now. We might as well have fun." As O turned his attention to another guest, Cal recalled the day, six years ago, when they had first met.

Cal didn't put much faith in first impressions. They were what good candidates did best: they gave you a glimpse of intelligence, empathy, an even temperament. They tried to avoid making second and third impressions. When they did, they usually lost.

But no one had ever made as favorable a first impression as O. He had none of the tics of affectation: no self-satisfied smile, extravagant repetition, prolonged eye contact. His qualities were immediately apparent and finely balanced—shrewdness and sincerity, elegance and informality, watchfulness and daring. His glamour seemed effortless, his intelligence reassuringly mature.

"They tell me you're a smart guy, but not much of a risk taker," he said as Cal settled into the seat O had motioned for him to take. O, in shirt-sleeves rolled to his elbows, sat on the couch opposite him and stretched out his legs on the coffee table.

"I suppose that depends, Senator."

"On what?"

"On what I'm risking."

O gave him a friendly grin to indicate he had expected the answer. "There you go," he said. "That's not the first question a risk taker asks."

"What question is that?"

"What could I do with the reward?"

Cal had agreed to the meeting reluctantly. When Avi Samuelson had tried to recruit him a month earlier, Cal had put him off. He had already decided to join the front-runner's campaign and had met with her several times. They had discussed the job he wanted, deputy campaign manager. No formal offer had been made at the last meeting. But a week later a chair had arrived at his office, an inexpensive, oak-veneered Windsor reproduction, with a note signed by the candidate: "There's a seat for you at our table."

Samuelson persuaded Cal not to sign on with her until he had met O. "He wants to talk to you because I told him he should," Samuelson had explained. "So, hotshot, if you keep playing hard-to-get, don't worry about disappointing him. I doubt he gives a rat's ass. But *you* should."

So, on a cold February afternoon in 2006, Cal had gone to see the handsome, eloquent young senator everyone hailed as the party's newest rock star, but who in Cal's opinion was a little too new, too young, too liberal, and too black to be elected president of the United States.

O had explained why he thought he had a chance.

"Most of the country isn't just ready but desperate for change. And Democrats, especially disaffected Democrats who usually can't be bothered to get involved, are pissed off and motivated."

Then he asked Cal what the front-runner had that made her election plausible.

"That," Cal had answered. "The national mood. Even with her history, her unfavorables, the country is so freaked out they're willing to overlook it. She'll also have the most money and endorsements, the ones that matter: the unions, the governors."

"Will she?" O asked, and then answered his own question. "Certainly in the beginning."

The front-runner's gender wasn't a handicap, O asserted. Nor was her undeserved reputation for meanness and deviousness insurmountable. Her problem was that she wasn't a change. She was familiar.

"Change means new this time," he explained. "And a black man with a Muslim name and a different way of doing things is about as new as it gets."

He asked Cal if she thought she was owed the nomination; not to test him, but because O hadn't decided whether his opponent was running out of a sense of entitlement, and believed Cal would have an informed opinion that could help him make up his mind. Cal recognized the genuine curiosity behind the question and admired it.

"No, she's too experienced and too smart to believe that. I think she feels she's lucky the country's in such a bad mood that she has the opportunity to reintroduce herself."

O paused for a moment to consider Cal's response, before nodding in agreement. Then he stood up to indicate the brief interview was over. He asked Cal to talk to Samuelson again before he made a decision. "Call me, too, if you need more convincing. The risk is worth the reward."

O opened the door for him and put a hand on his shoulder.

"Do you know what all losing campaigns have in common?"

"What's that?"

"Candidates who thought they were lucky."

Spring 2011

★   CHAPTER 1   ★

Another day glided to a pleasant finish as Cal Regan walked the four blocks from his office to Lucille's Bar and Grill. He let his mind idle for a few minutes to enjoy the fragrant, warm April evening and the scent of the beautiful young woman who brushed by him and smiled when he caught her eye.

At thirty-four, he was impressively accomplished: he'd been a prodigy on Capitol Hill, where in six years he had risen from summer legal intern to chief of staff in the office of a Senate luminary famous for spotting and nurturing political genius; executive director of the Democratic Senatorial Campaign Committee in the election that returned Democrats to power; deputy manager of the president's campaign (responsible for, among other things, placating and gently disappointing major donors, party VIPs, Hollywood celebrities, and useful reporters); and a deputy again, to the head of the president-elect's transition team.

He had expected and was offered a coveted position on the White House staff, assistant to the president and director of the Office of Congressional Relations, where his practiced manner with sensitive egos could help assuage any distress caused by the president's aloofness and his chief of staff's brusqueness. He had turned it down, pleading the urgent need to settle a lingering student loan debt. In truth, he had correctly estimated that his market value at the time would not be increased by the position, and had decided to acquire wealth immediately. He had remained useful in various ways to his White House patrons in the expectation that he would return to public service in the second term, in a more prestigious capacity.

Two weeks after news of his availability caught the attention of Washington's most prominent deal makers, he was made a partner in the preeminent Democratic law firm of Hanson, Strong LLP, and de facto head of its government relations practice. Even the most illustrious of his new partners valued his connections and talent, and regarded him with a mixture of relief and regret. They understood that his smiling presence in the richly appointed partners' library would assure the firm's continued mining of wealth from politics, just as it signaled the beginning of a quiet end to their own days of supremacy among Washington's permanent elite. Thus it always was, they graciously conceded to themselves: the old must give way to the new.

Another, less valuable partner would serve officially as the firm's director of government relations, sparing Regan the necessity of registering as a lobbyist—a distinction that could complicate his future plans. Both men understood the arrangement to be the kind employed in a city where appearances were more important than titles. Both knew who would be giving orders.

Regan had signed a new client today, an important one: the country's newest software billionaire, a man much like himself who winked at the fussy guardians and moldier conventions of both their businesses, and paid them just enough attention to encourage them to get out of his way. Cal was flattered that his client recognized they had much in common. And now, as young, influential, handsome, and almost wealthy Cal Regan made his way to Lucille's, he had few cares worth bothering about.

He entered unnoticed and, reaching the bar, placed a hand on his friend Michael Lowe's shoulder. "Mick" to his friends, and "Mickey" when Regan was in an expansive mood, Lowe was short and muscular, the effect of habitual weight training that had caused one observer to describe him as "a squared-off fireplug of a guy." He kept his hair cropped so short that people incorrectly assumed he was anticipating baldness. He had a menacing look and an incongruously soft, high-pitched voice, for which he compensated with the extra ridicule he used when defending his opinions.

Lowe and Regan were genuine friends rather than "Washington

friends," those utilitarian, affectionless acquaintanceships prevalent in the nation's capital. They had been close since Regan had hired him to run opposition research at the Democratic Senatorial Campaign Committee, and had recommended him for a bigger if less specific job in the '08 campaign. Lowe had made his reputation by expertly sowing mayhem: conjuring from minor and ambiguously related facts in an opponent's record hints of possible scandal, and whispering those hints into the right reporter's ear. Regan had been the first to recognize his gifts, and Lowe was beholden to him.

Mick Lowe was a Cal Regan guy. They enjoyed each other's company and valued their alliance. They looked out for each other. Lowe had recently opened his own public affairs shop, offering full-service consulting to corporate and political clients. He and his partners relied on Regan to recommend them to his clients, particularly clients whose competitors enjoyed unnecessarily positive reputations. Regan knew he could turn to Lowe for almost any favor anytime he needed one.

Lowe turned to greet Regan with a "Hey, man," and nodded his head to indicate the table where Madison Cohan sat with her colleagues. Her familiar throaty laughter was distinctly audible over the din of the crowd. She saw them look at her and gave Regan a smile and a little wave. He returned the acknowledgment as casually as he could, careful not to appear delighted to see her.

Maddy Cohan always managed to make him self-conscious, causing him to premeditate every reaction to her, even simple gestures of greeting. Few people had this effect on him, and it irritated him. Were it not for the fact he was in love with her, he would have disliked her.

"She's got something," Lowe alerted him.

Mistakenly assuming it a reference to her sex appeal, Regan offered a crude reply: "Yeah, a great ass, the not-so-secret secret to her charm."

"Still pining?"

"I never want what I can't have, Mickey."

"Is that so?"

Lowe knew his friend had a romantic interest in Maddy Cohan that had begun the moment she had introduced herself to Regan during the last campaign. She had been a very junior reporter, not long out of journalism school, when she walked up to Regan after a press conference and asked to take him to lunch. Senior staff on a presidential campaign seldom have the time or curiosity to sit down to an unscheduled lunch with a reporter no one has ever heard of before, but Regan had smiled and said, "Sure, give me ten minutes," and gone to fetch his coat. A few days later, he had instructed Lowe to give her the first look at some opposition research the campaign had just finished.

"Why should we give it to a kid working for a fucking website start-up," Lowe had asked, "instead of the *Times* or *Post*?"

"What do you check first thing in the morning now? The *Times*? *Post*? Or that fucking website start-up?" Regan had answered.

"*Kansas City Star.*"

Lowe was a K.C. native. He had no intention of ever returning to his hometown, but he remained a sentimental booster of its attractions, especially its lackluster professional sports franchises.

"And after you find out the Chiefs still suck?" Regan teased.

"My horoscope."

Lowe had talked briefly to Maddy a few minutes before Regan arrived and had gotten the sense she was working on a story about the president's reelection campaign, which had recently opened its headquarters in Chicago. She had only asked if he had heard anything from Chicago. But Mick Lowe prided himself on his ability to detect reporters' ulterior motives even when they were disguised in seemingly innocent questions, or attractively packaged in the person of Maddy Cohan.

"That's it? That's all she asked?" Cal queried him. "I think that's called a conversation starter, Mickey, you suspicious bastard. Is there news from Chicago?"

"Yeah, it's still fucking snowing. I don't know, but she does. It's not what she asked but how she asked, with that superfly smile of hers."

Neither Mick nor Cal was close to Stu Trask, the veteran strategist whom the president had asked to manage his campaign, but they weren't adversaries either. Trask had come on board late in the last campaign. He had done work for several of the candidates competing for the nomination and had sat out the primaries. After O had clinched the nomination, Trask was one of the first calls Avi Samuelson, the president's closest advisor, had made. He and Trask had worked together early in their careers in several losing campaigns, and friendships formed in failure often outlast those made in happier circumstances.

When Trask arrived in Chicago as a senior advisor without portfolio, he was shown deference by staff who had worked for the campaign since its unpromising beginning and had learned how to avoid Avi Samuelson's displeasure. Regan had been careful to treat Trask respectfully, but neither man had been genuinely impressed by the other. Regan wasn't surprised Trask hadn't sought his advice as he assembled his headquarters or thought to include him in semiregular discussions with outside advisors, and he wasn't troubled by it either. Everyone, including Stu Trask, knew the campaign's command center wasn't in Chicago but in Avi Samuelson's West Wing office—just a few feet from the president's— where Cal Regan was a frequent visitor.

Regan finished his drink and, on the pretense of good manners, went to say hello to Maddy Cohan. Lowe trailed after him.

"How are you, Maddy?"

"I'm well, Cal. You? You know Jeanne and Tim, right?"

Jeanne and Tim Sears, Maddy Cohan's close friends and former colleagues, had left journalism a few months after they married. Jeanne had crossed the divide to work as communications director for a newly elected Democratic senator from her home state. Tim had traded the cachet of working for the latest multimedia venture for a living wage, shorter hours, and an office with windows at a midsize public relations firm. Neither regretted the decision.

Maddy motioned for them to sit down, and Regan pulled a chair next to hers.

Tim Sears greeted him with the information that they were now sharing a client.

"Who's that?"

"I understand you just signed or are about to sign Allen Knowles. He's my account at Fenwick."

Knowles was the client Regan had signed that day. He wasn't sure which annoyed him more: that someone who had been in PR for less than a year was the lead on a major account, or that Sears knew he had signed Knowles before Regan knew that Sears had.

"Great. We'll be working together, then. Look forward to it. Did I hear you're changing beats, Maddy?" Regan asked, surmising that if she was working on a Chicago story, she would be leaving Capitol Hill, where she'd been assigned after the election, to cover the campaign.

"Where'd you hear that?"

"Can't remember, offhand. Gossip I picked up somewhere. Back to the glamorous life of campaign reporting, I heard."

"Well, you know more than I do, then. Will hasn't decided, or he hasn't announced anyway, who we're rotating to the campaigns. I'm happy on the Hill, really. People talk to reporters there."

Will was Willem Janssen, Maddy's editor, who had left a promising career at a newspaper of record to start *Body Politic* with financing from a bored billionaire and a plan to make his new venture irresistible to Washington insiders by accelerating the news cycle from a day to an hour with hypercoverage of everything said or done by anyone with political credentials. His success at monetizing Washington's self-obsessive nature had marked him as a potential savior of political journalism. He was much disliked by editors and reporters still working for newspapers with cratering ad revenue, and who felt demeaned chasing stories his reporters had broken first or, in the opinion of some disgruntled critics, "invented."

"Who doesn't talk to you, Maddy?" Lowe mischievously offered. "You're as well sourced as they come."

"Well, you never made much of a habit of it, Mick. I think I'm still waiting for you to return a hundred or so of my calls."

"I'm the strong, silent type, Maddy. But my love runs deep."

"More like the use 'em and lose 'em type. Your love is entirely transactional."

Jealous of her attention, Regan cut short their teasing. "Let's get back to discussing your plans for the future. Are you gonna cover the reelect?"

"Why the interest, Cal? Aren't you too busy getting rich to worry about who's covering the campaign?"

"Simply expressing an interest in your career."

"Cal, when did you start taking an interest in careers other than your own?"

This stung him. He did not want to appear just another self-important, cynical Washington operator. Not to her. Were he to confess he'd been hurt by the remark, she would assure him she had just been teasing. But in Regan's experience, people revealed more of their real opinions in jest than in gentler conversation. He felt an urgent necessity to make every effort to improve her opinion of him, and wouldn't leave the table until he was certain he had made good progress toward that end.

Ninety minutes later, only Cal and Maddy were still there. The Searses had relatives visiting the next day, and Lowe had made his own excuses when he saw his presence had become superfluous. They remained there another two hours, talking quietly about themselves: families and old friendships; their simplest pleasures, rarely indulged anymore; early ambitions long abandoned and vague aspirations to other, more virtuous occupations. He showed her a picture of his recently acquired sailboat. She showed him a picture of a towheaded three-year-old, her niece. Progress was made.

★ CHAPTER 2 ★

Walter Lafontaine asked the bartender to turn up the volume so he could hear over the busy airport noise the clip he would watch several more times that day after he arrived in Chicago.

The object of Walter's attention was Tom Morrison, presently the class of the Republican field of presidential candidates, who was just finishing another well-delivered speech. The scion of a prominent Philadelphia family, Morrison graduated twenty-first in his West Point class and first at Ranger School; completed postgraduate work at Yale University; deployed on his first combat tour as a corps commander; was awarded a fourth star prior to assuming control of the United States Central Command; had a brief private sector career as CEO of one of the largest defense contractors in the country; and served one term as governor of the state where his company was headquartered, the first Republican to hold the office in twenty years.

"Tom Terrific," the sobriquet assigned him by jealous fellow officers during his swift ascent to a theater command, was now employed by rival campaigns. Walter Lafontaine never referred to him by any other name, except in playful moods when he called him "Tommy Terrific" or "Tommy Too Fucking Terrific." The speech clip finished playing and the ensuing cable chatter quickly turned to another subject. Walter paid for his bourbon and walked to his gate. On his way, he daydreamed again of becoming the instrument of Tom Terrific's destruction.

Walter Lafontaine had been born in St. John the Baptist Parish, Louisiana, three weeks before his father, Andre, decamped for parts unknown, leaving behind his wife and infant son, a mortgage in arrears, and a photograph of himself playing the accordion. The instrument had vanished with his father, alerting his mother, Geraldine, not to expect Andre's return. Seven weeks later, after receiving a welcoming reply to a letter she had hastily written to her brother, Geraldine and Walter boarded a bus for Chicago and a new home in desolate Englewood on the city's South Side, where absent fathers were common and children who reached adulthood without criminal records or unplanned pregnancies were considered overachievers and a credit to their mothers' perseverance.

Walter loved his mother, and he remembered as one of his two proudest moments the April afternoon seven years ago when he had given her the keys to a bungalow on South Calumet Avenue in Chatham, Englewood's more prosperous neighbor. The other was the day his friend had been elected president of the United States.

How quickly they had become inseparable! "Where's Walter?" was the familiar first question from the impatient young organizer to his welcoming committee of skeptical neighborhood matriarchs. Walter, who was never as punctual as Geraldine wished, would turn up for the meeting a few minutes later, with a "Hello, Mr. O," and a grin and good manners for the ladies, who wished he were their son and babied him.

Walter was a local darling in those days, and O a handsome stranger, shiny and exotic, paying a brief visit to their neglected world on his way to becoming someone. They were gracious to O, and thought it possible he would remember them, or a composite notion of them, after he had gone. They would be part of his story. But Walter was part of theirs. He was one of their blessed children, the ones who didn't get hurt or messed up, who proved an Englewood mother with no husband could teach a child how to slip past the statistics and become a man without having to hurt a soul.

Walter remembered the day he met O as his first comprehension of elegance. There was nothing extravagant about him. No strutting. No flash. He was all poise and balance. There seemed nothing false, nothing imitated. He was slender and square-shouldered. The two young men he arrived with were in jeans and sneakers. O was at ease in a white button-down shirt, sleeves rolled to his elbows and striped tie loosened, gray slacks and slightly scuffed black loafers. He had come to organize voter registration teams, but the volunteers began at once to instruct him. Talking over one another, interrupting, complaining, they gave Englewood's usual greeting to outsiders.

Walter watched O absorb the initial confusion, letting it run on for a bit while he nodded, as if someone were making sense. Then he held up his hands and said, "All right. I hear you. I hear you. We've got one job to do, and twelve different ways to do it or not do it. So how are we going to register more voters in Englewood so that Englewood helps elect people who won't forget about Englewood? I want to hear your ideas, and talk about a few of my own, if you don't mind listening."

Walter loved him from that moment. He loved how he projected authority without insulting anyone, how he disregarded their babbled protests without appearing dismissive, how he bent them to his purpose without seeming to bully or condescend.

Inspired, Walter played his practiced role of quick and willing student. When registration sites were discussed, he promised that a dozen local businesses, fast-food restaurants mostly, would be willing to offer their premises. He said he had already talked to the owners, and made a mental note to reach at least half of them before the day was over to make sure they wouldn't make a liar out of him. When deputy registrars were proposed, he shouted a "Yessir!" when his name was mentioned. Everyone smiled at his mother in acknowledgment of his good-natured enthusiasm, a rare attribute for an Englewood teenager.

Three weeks later, he turned in more signatures than any other Englewood registrar. Notice was taken and praise offered when Walter, wearing a white shirt and tie, unexpectedly turned up at a meeting in Washington Park. He asked to join O's ten-person staff. "I'll do a good job," he promised. Remembering the effect the boy's enthusiasm had on the others at their first meeting in Englewood, O indulged him.

"Yeah? And which job is that?"

"Any one you give me, Mr. O."

"Aren't you in school, Walter?"

"I got two months left before I graduate. But I'm done at three every day and can work as long as you want me to after."

"I couldn't pay you anything. Not much anyway."

"That's all right. I'd be doing it for the cause, Mr. O, just like you."

He slipped an arm around the boy's shoulder and said, "Walter, you are the cause." Then he gave him a card with an address on it and told him to meet him there the following Monday afternoon. By the summer, Walter was always at his side. *My cheerleading squad,* O thought, as Walter's exuberance roused another group of disorganized volunteers from inertia, got them clapping and laughing and listening. His protégé, Walter presumed, having heard the word used to describe the disciple of a famous activist from another time.

O included Walter in his frequent basketball games. O's style was crafty and smooth. He let the game come to him and played for the win. He had a decent jumper. He could get to the hoop, often on a fake-right, drive-left move that he would finish with a reverse layup. But he looked to pass more than he did to score. And he seemed more pleased with himself when he dished a no-look or behind-the-back for an assist. When Walter had the ball he was reluctant to give it up. He saw only the hoop, not the players. He'd put his head down and drive the lane no matter how many taller men were in his way, and as often as not, he'd turn it over or have it smacked back into his face by a laughing defender.

"Jesus, Walter, who do you think you are?" O would tease him. "Muggsy Bogues? It's not one-on-one, man. Take it easy. Pull up and shoot a jumper. Or try passing it once in a while."

More African Americans and Hispanics voted in Cook County that year than in any previous election. Much praise was lavished on O as the attractive public face of the county's most successful voter registration drive in memory, the young man from somewhere else who had bet his future on the battered hopes of the city's disadvantaged. He belonged to Chicago now. Walter believed Chicago would belong to O, and sooner than anyone expected.

One night at supper, not long after the election, Walter told Geraldine he planned to work for the mayor someday. "Not Daley, Mama. Mr. O. He's gonna be the mayor someday. I know it." *And I'll be there, too,* he told himself.

City hall might have been O's destination. He had considered it. But grander opportunities soon came his way. O's successes didn't surprise him. He never saw them, as others did, as an impressive run of unusually good luck. He believed in himself. The good timing observers complimented him on was the product of his confidence that he could exceed expectations at anything he put his mind to, which allowed him to glimpse possibilities in faint chances. And if he failed, he assured himself, he would still do better than predicted and increase the probability of success next time.

O had anticipated a clear field for an open seat in the state senate. But he showed little concern when several more established names unexpectedly competed for it. He simply cleared the field himself by sending Walter and a few others to scrutinize signatures on his rivals' ballot petitions and identify enough irregularities to file successful challenges with the Board of Elections. A few patrons advised him it would be imprudent to begin a political career by disqualifying opponents rather than defeating them. *I did defeat them,* he thought to himself, before politely dismissing the concern, *whether they accept it or not.*

He offered Walter a small stipend to work part-time in his district office on the condition that Walter continue a full course load at Illinois Tech, where, with O's help, he had enrolled three years before. Walter hadn't needed the encouragement, but he was glad of it nonetheless. Nothing gratified him more than O's demonstrated interest in his future. Two years later, however, he was reluctant to accept his patron's advice that he apply to Tech's law school, preferring to begin a full-time career in service to the man whose friendship and future success would, he felt certain, be a greater advantage to him than a law degree.

"You don't need a lawyer, Mr. O. You are a lawyer."

"It's not for me, Walter. It's for you. A law degree opens up a lot of doors. Time's gonna come when you'll need to start taking care of your mother instead of her taking care of you. And you won't be able to do that working for me right now. There's not a living in it. Not even for me."

"It'd be good enough for now, wouldn't it? You're not planning to stay in Springfield forever?"

"No, not forever. But nothing's likely to happen in the next few years. And if I do something else it's more likely I go back to practicing law than run for another office. I've got family relying on me, too. And who knows, huh? Maybe I'll be on the lookout for a sharp young associate to work with. Somebody from Englewood, maybe. Somebody who takes good care of his mother."

Walter didn't believe O had any intention of leaving politics. After all, he was just getting started. But whatever O became, Walter intended to be his most dutiful follower, and so he went, as bidden, to law school.

By the age of twenty-six, Walter was an associate at a prominent Chicago firm with an extensive civil rights practice, and at liberty to volunteer assistance to the Cook County Democratic Party, particularly to one of its most promising junior state senators. The arrangement continued for several years to the satisfaction of everyone involved. As O flourished, so did Walter.

When O entered a crowded primary for a vacant U.S. Senate seat, Walter was granted a leave of absence to serve as his personal aide. He was seated in the VIP enclosure, cheering himself hoarse, the night O delivered the speech to the party's national convention that made his reputation as the most promising politician of his generation. He got drunk on election night out of elation when the returns, as expected, indicated a lopsided result in O's favor. He understood when O explained he would need Walter to remain in Chicago rather than move to Washington, and hinted that another campaign might occur sooner than expected.

Harder to take was the decision, conveyed to him by the manager of O's presidential campaign, that Walter would not be given the position he had assumed was his. Someone from the D.C. staff, someone not from the South Side, not even from Chicago, had been asked to be the candidate's personal aide. "Jesus, Walter, you're too old to be the body man. O wants you here," he had been told, with no further explanation. He was made one of several deputies to the campaign's political director, and was assigned responsibility for organizing Illinois, which was, obviously, a minor concern. All other deputies had multiple states in their jurisdictions. It was hard for Walter not to feel it as an insult. But after a couple of weeks of feeling depressed, and despite a few episodic recurrences when he tried and failed to assume other responsibilities, Walter did as he was told with as much cheer as he could muster.

The worst blow arrived a month after the night Walter had stood among the multitude and wept copiously as his friend was declared the president-elect of the United States. "The greatest night in the history of America," Walter had shouted to a Chicago reporter of long acquaintance.

A few minutes were all he had. The president-elect's time was a carefully managed resource and often scheduled in quarter-hour increments. Avi Samuelson had made passing mention of Walter's expectations, and had promised to take responsibility for disappointing him. But O had insisted on delivering the news himself. "He'll take it better coming from me," he explained. "He usually does."

Walter listened disbelievingly as O, affecting his familiar attitude of solicitous older brother, encouraged him to see the bright side in the bewildering estrangement proposed. "Walter, you're thirty-five years old. If you want to come to Washington, we'll find you something. But right now it wouldn't be anything worth your time. My best advice is to stay here and make some money for the next couple, three years. I'll need you here for the reelect anyway. Wait for the second term, and we'll find you something better than we could give you now. I promise."

In the meantime, Walter would be well compensated for his loyalty and hard work. Samuelson, who had just that week finalized the sale to his partners of his interest in their profitable consulting firm, had made Walter's employment there a condition of the president-elect's continued favor and the generous retainer his former partners anticipated from the Democratic National Committee. They hadn't flinched when the salary and title suggested exceeded their initial assessment of Walter's value.

For the first time in their association, Walter felt too drained to protest. He was so incapacitated that when Mrs. O entered the room, he failed to recognize her presence as the signal for him to depart. He sat there a few moments longer, trying to discern the reasons for his hard fall from grace, before concluding what he feared would be his last intimate conversation with the man whose affection he cherished. It was she who impressed upon him the finality of the decision, when she instructed him, "Be sure to wish your mother Merry Christmas for us, Walter, and we'll see you both at the inauguration."

O walked Walter to the door, affectionately rubbing the back of his head as he told him again not to worry. He was still needed and appreciated. Everyone was just looking out for his best interests.

How that could be was a mystery to Walter. It seemed to him it had been a long while since anyone had given his interests any consideration at all. He had no need for an income greater than he could earn as a member of O's staff. He lived frugally. His mother was comfortably situated. Everyone knew he had no plans to start a family of his own.

He was still mystified when he returned to Chicago from the inaugural celebration, without receiving a personal word from the new president and First Lady. The memory of his sorrow and listlessness in the months that followed still pained him occasionally. He had never determined the cause of his estrangement from O or the precise moment when their fates had begun to diverge. No one had ever hinted to Walter that his presumption of a familial relationship with the president had made the First Lady uncomfortable, to the point where she considered it a more serious transgression than it was.

In time, Walter's tendency toward optimism returned and he recovered much of his vigor and natural exuberance. While he would never take anything for granted again, he believed he could yet redeem himself by once more proving to be indispensable to the cause. He had been greatly encouraged in that hope when Stu Trask called him last March— at the request, Trask said, of the president—and advised him to begin making arrangements to work full-time for the reelection campaign.

The president would officially announce his candidacy in the fall of 2011. But the campaign's leadership had been chosen, and its new headquarters in Chicago's Loop was already occupied and quietly staffing up.

Much of the political class had instinctively thought the physical establishment of a campaign so early in the year had been a mistake. He was running unopposed in the primaries except for a couple of fringe candidates who thought they could get a little free publicity for their various grievances. He could have easily set up an operation in the DNC and not opened a headquarters until the fall. Doing so this early exposed every administration decision to the taint of campaign politics.

Republicans, of course, had been making that charge since he had been inaugurated, but now the press would be more receptive to the criticism. But the president's political team had played by different rules from the beginning, deriding conventions as anachronisms, and had succeeded beyond anyone's expectations. The general acknowledgment of their prowess gave even Republicans pause to wonder if there was not some hidden advantage to starting so early.

In fact, the decision was based on nothing more complicated than the conviction of the president and his advisors that most Americans didn't care. Voters had assumed all along that the president would run for reelection. As long as the press focused their 2011 campaign coverage, as they surely would, on the crowded Republican field, few voters would even notice that the president had a campaign headquarters.

The campaign wouldn't run an ad or do an official candidate event other than the president's reelection announcement until after the 2012 State of the Union address. In the meantime, it would build the most prepared, tested, and lavishly resourced reelection campaign in the history of American politics. As soon as it became clear who the Republican nominee would be, they wanted to make him feel instantly and completely besieged.

Trask had hinted, or so it seemed to Walter, that this time he would be given the authority appropriate for a man of his experience and talents and long friendship with the president. Yet on the day he reported for duty full of plans, which he had outlined on a legal pad in order of the priority he thought they deserved, he had received little encouragement from Trask and no specific assignment. The older man had seemed distracted in their conversation that morning, and had dismissed him with the promise that they would talk again after he'd had time to consider Walter's ideas.

Taught by previous disappointments not to let his intentions wait on events, Walter decided he would on his own initiative assume an important function in the president's reelection. For the time being he would mainly concern himself with discovering the means to destroy Tom Morrison before the Republicans chose him as their nominee. Everyone knew the other Republican aspirants would prove less of a threat in the general election.

He picked up a hard line at headquarters to call the DNC and ask for the early research book on potential vulnerabilities in General Tom Morrison's background. "Stu Trask wants me to look it over," he reassured the reluctant staffer, who had never heard of Walter and hung up the phone wondering why Walter couldn't just examine one of several copies that had been sent to the campaign. The next day Trask was asked in an e-mail from the DNC chairman's chief of staff to confirm he wanted a copy delivered to Walter Lafontaine. Trask responded by e-mail, "no longer necessary," and made a mental note to call Walter into his office that afternoon and sternly warn him never to invoke his name for anything unless he had been so instructed. But, distracted by the controversy about to engulf him, Trask forgot.

★ CHAPTER 3 ★

O ran through his grievances as he dressed. They'd be waiting for him downstairs, and he intended to confront them before they could draw him into discussing their plans for his day.

How many weekends had it been now? The last five? Five consecutive weekends in the White House. His wife and kids had spent the last three Saturdays at Camp David. They no longer bothered to argue with him, their objection conveyed only by his wife's disapproving look as he kissed his daughters good-bye. What was there to argue about? It's not like he didn't want to go. Christ, he was desperate for a few unbothered hours; turn his mind off for a bit, hit some golf balls. A few drives off the practice tee and some chipping and putting were as close as he could get to playing eighteen these days. After all that grief he had taken last fall, staff had managed to make him feel guilty about it. It was too much to ask for a few hours outdoors on the weekend, the only time he felt normal, out of the bubble. He had insisted from the beginning that his White House wasn't going to fall into that trap. "The American people don't give a shit," he told his staff, "if the president takes his wife out for dinner or shoots some hoops or wants to spend a Sunday afternoon walking in the sunshine and joking with friends without agents smothering him, reporters shouting at him, and you guys crawling all over his ass." CEOs can golf. Cabinet secretaries can golf. Four-star generals can golf. Members of Congress can golf any goddamn weekend they please. But if the president plays a round or two on the weekend, the press totals them up, checks the genders and campaign contributions of his foursomes, and runs stories about America's golf-crazy president next to reports on that week's casualties in Afghanistan.

One midterm election postmortem included a quote from a defeated House Democrat listing all the problems the party had failed to overcome. They included the typical complaints—the slow economic recovery, stubbornly high unemployment, the war, the bills that didn't pass, the bills that did pass, the White House not doing enough, the White House doing too much, blah, blah, blah. Then he ended the litany with the observation, "and it sure didn't help when people worried about losing their jobs, losing their houses, losing their kids in this endless war turned on their televisions every day and saw the president playing more golf."

Avi Samuelson had showed it to him and said nothing while O read it. He knew not to belabor the obvious and let his crooked half-smile convey his message. *What are you gonna do? I know it's bullshit, but attention must be paid anyway.*

O had suppressed the urge to rant out loud. Droll sarcasm was his preferred medium when displeased. *Thanks very much. No concession prize for you, buddy. No embassy in a nice, quiet country to make you feel you're not a complete loser. It's back to selling real estate or whatever the hell you did before the voters of East Jesus sent you to Congress. Funny, I don't remember you whining when I invited you to play.*

"Okay. I got it. I hurt the economy when I play golf. I guess I'll work eighteen hours on Saturdays and Sundays, too. Maybe I can get a second job on the weekends. Show folks I'm having just as tough a time as they are. Would that make everybody feel better?"

Samuelson had responded with a "beats me" shrug of his shoulders as he withdrew, leaving the offending clipping with the president. "He isn't happy about it," he told a colleague, "but he gets the picture."

Samuelson shared O's ironic, big-picture sensibility. He was the message guy, in charge of protecting the president's brand from the corrosion of politics and the distortions of the media—and from the president himself, when the occasion required it. During O's rise to national prominence the older Samuelson played the who-are-you-trying-to-kid, severe but protective big brother, forthright to the point of discourtesy when he thought O's behavior was incompatible with his image as a practical idealist, a levelheaded agent of change. After the inauguration, Samuelson had become less of a scold and more circumspect in reproaching the president. Rather than the "you're screwing up" warnings he had once summarily delivered, he typically relied on nonverbal expressions of disapproval: the blank stare and slow, audible exhalation of breath through his nostrils when O paused a rant for his senior counselor's reaction. O knew Samuelson cared as much as he did that the world viewed his presidency and him as he wished to be viewed; as he wished to be.

At eleven o'clock today, for the second consecutive Saturday, O would meet with Democratic leaders in the private residence rather than the Roosevelt Room, where such gatherings usually convened. The informality was intended to contradict reports of discord and suspicion between the White House and Democrats in Congress. He would listen again as they seconded and occasionally contradicted one another about where they needed to focus their attention in the new Congress. There would be no notable accomplishments. They all knew that. The Republicans had had a good election, finally, but the Democrats could set some traps for them. Galvanize the base by forcing cloture votes on a few judicial nominations. Maybe get a few small things done. Some kind of middle-class relief package, with a couple of little tax breaks in it. Republicans wouldn't be able to block that. Something for small business, too, maybe the tax credit for new hires the president had campaigned on. "Nobody gets too worked up about the deficit when the government gives money back to them," the House Democratic leader would wryly note. If they really went on the offensive, they might try to make the banks swallow limits on credit card interest. They hoped Republicans would try to stop that.

They wouldn't say anything today they hadn't said in several meetings before the State of the Union. As he knotted his tie that morning, O resolved to disappoint them. He would not offer tepid reassurances today and nod sympathetically as they anguished about their predicament. Not this time, he told himself as he left the room.

He would delay by fifteen minutes the national security briefing that typically began his day and explain he wished to discuss something first. A firm but dispassionate analysis would serve best. If he appeared piqued, they would dismiss the argument as early morning crankiness. "Our most important asset," he would remind them, "is my ability to lead." Although Samuelson wouldn't dispute the predicate, he would ask him not to interrupt until he finished.

"And, guys, I'm tired. It's been two months since the State of the Union. We're nine months out before the Republicans start to choose their nominee. And I'm already starting to feel worn out. By this time next year, I'll be exhausted. By the general election, I'll be our biggest liability. I don't intend to let that happen.

"The election won't be decided by how many weekends I spend working in this office. It won't be decided by how many hours I don't spend on the golf course. It won't be decided by how many days I spend hand-holding the leadership.

"The election will be decided by the answers to two questions. Did I, as promised, change Washington? And do a majority of voters approve of that change? We passed health care. We saved the economy from depression. We lost seats anyway."

He did not need to mention the slow recovery and jobless numbers that had kept rising through the first quarter of last year and were still stubbornly high. They all understood this central fact of their predicament. They had inherited a mess, and voters didn't care. They hadn't made the mess go away fast enough.

"But the economy continues to improve and unemployment will come down," O insisted. "Even if we don't do another thing, even if I play golf every day and take the whole summer off, we'll have the easier argument next time."

His aides knew this. But they also knew the White House still had to make its case. White Houses on autopilot don't *appear* to be in charge. They get the blame when things go wrong and none of the credit when things go right. And they lose.

"I'm not suggesting we phone it in for the next two years," O added, anticipating their objection. "What we need now is to do a better job of showing voters we're trying to change Washington. And how do we do that?"

Samuelson cleared his throat as he considered his response, but O waved him off and continued.

"Changing Washington doesn't mean we have to do the impossible. It means not doing the predictable. Hunkering down is predictable. Playing by rules most people outside this city think are asinine is predictable."

O knew they couldn't change Congress. They couldn't make Republicans play nice. They couldn't change the news cycle. They couldn't stop the phony conflictmongering. But they could change how they reacted to it.

"What's the most unpredictable thing we can do?" he asked rhetorically. "We can ignore all that crap and be the adults. That's what we said we'd do."

He paused to emphasize that he had finished laying the basis for the instructions he would now issue.

"So, guys, we're not going to keep me chained to this desk every weekend. As soon as I can this afternoon, I'm going to Camp David, and next Saturday, I'm going to Andrews to play eighteen holes of golf. It's nonnegotiable."

O then began to explain his plans for the meeting with the leadership. He wanted them to take another crack at climate change legislation. But they wouldn't call it that. They wouldn't mention cap and trade, which struck many voters as a remedy in search of a problem, and many others as such a personally expensive solution that they would rather live with melting glaciers and hotter summers. O would propose a new jobs bill, a clean technology jobs bill. They wouldn't talk about it as part of a "green economy." It would be the new economy, the economy that would create millions of new jobs, the economy that would keep America on top. Republicans would complain about the government interfering in the market, that O was picking winners and losers. O didn't care, and neither would voters, he felt certain. Creating jobs that paid well impressed voters. Quoting Adam Smith didn't.

He wanted to do more on education, too. More merit pay for teachers and more limits on tenure. Democrats would resist it. The unions wouldn't like it. But parents would. Congress wouldn't pass it, but he could campaign on it. "When we win, we'll pick up seats in the bargain," O told them. "They'll bitch today and thank us later."

O's closest aides had heard this speech or one like it more than a dozen times. But it still impressed them. O's reluctance to submit to the sillier conventions of politics was one of the qualities that had first attracted their interest.

He had a talent for distinguishing genuine threats from distractions that could become threats only if they diverted him from his central message. But recognizing the folly of something doesn't guarantee a candidate won't take the bait anyway. And O fell for it, usually out of pique, too often for Samuelson's comfort. He was thin-skinned, and Samuelson told him so, bluntly and frequently, and warned he wouldn't win a primary outside of his own state if he didn't start practicing what he preached. O knew Samuelson was right and promised he would stop getting angry in public about things that didn't matter and that he couldn't do anything about. "But you're going to have to let me vent to you," he warned. "Or I won't be able to help myself."

"He's a dream candidate in most ways," Samuelson had remarked to his wife after they had lost a primary they'd expected to win, and O's had been the coolest head in the room during the following day's strategy meeting. "He's so vain about keeping his shit together. That's a good thing. His hide isn't tough enough yet, but he knows it and he's getting better. And when he loses it, he gets mad with himself when he's done getting mad with the unlucky bastard who pissed him off."

Like O, Samuelson knew a president's public image was fixed, for better or worse, in his response to moments of crisis. If he appeared prepared and confident in adversity, then the public would be reassured by his insistence on preserving some normalcy in his private life. They would see it as evidence that he wasn't unnerved by his responsibilities, and reject criticism of it as another irrelevant Washington obsession. Had the previous president not appeared so diffident after Katrina or paralyzed by Iraq, few people would have cared that he liked to spend time riding his bicycle at his ranch or couldn't utter a coherent sentence without a script. O never appeared surprised by events or irresolute in adversity. Privately, however, he was not always as he appeared.

There were moments when he was uncertain of how to proceed, when the politics of an issue looked dangerous no matter which decision he made. He had agonized over the decision to send more troops to Afghanistan, pulled in opposite directions by disagreements among his advisors. The situation there seemed close to hopeless, he thought, although his generals assured him an acceptable outcome could be achieved if he committed the necessary resources. His national security advisor was more skeptical, but not adamant one way or another. The vice president, who could be rather pedagogical when discussing national security matters, felt strongly that the generals were in error, and nothing could be achieved that was worth the cost proposed. Many Democrats in Congress noisily agreed with the vice president's view. Samuelson didn't like what he had seen in the polls: a strong indication that public support for the war was nearly exhausted. O would have preferred to begin winding the whole thing down. The thought of overriding his generals appealed to him. He imagined future historians writing approvingly of his self-confidence and his conviction that a well-informed intellect was more important in a chief executive than experience.

But he had campaigned on a promise to strengthen the commitment to Afghanistan. Were he to reverse his position, it would be difficult to convince the public he had been sincere, and it would increase people's apprehension, despite their own doubts about the war, that he did not have the stomach for the bloodier work of being president. His generals and secretary of defense argued that were he to maintain the current force in Afghanistan or only slightly increase it, they couldn't answer for the consequences, intimating he could expect any increase in casualties to be blamed on his refusal to send reinforcements. Full and immediate withdrawal was not an option. No one argued it was. Chaos would immediately ensue in Afghanistan and Pakistan, and it would shatter the confidence of allied nations in Washington's willingness to do the hard things they refused to do.

His frustration over his dilemma threatened to crack his composure. He was impatient over small impositions on his time and truculent in minor disagreements with staff. He became animated in his irritation over leaks to the press as his warring advisors sought to recruit reporters to their side of the conflict. He feared nothing more than losing control of his own destiny, and for a time he worried he was doing just that. It was then that the president's golf game began to be discussed by his chief of staff and closest counselor, after a Republican critic had enlivened an otherwise unremarkable cable interview with the accusation "When the going gets tough, the president goes golfing."

Samuelson began to worry that when a decision was finally made, someone on the losing side of the argument wouldn't merely leak his dissatisfaction to the press, but would paint a picture of an anxious and insecure chief executive. To his relief, nothing of the sort happened. The president's uncharacteristic behavior was a confidential and soon forgotten curiosity. And though he disagreed with the decision, Samuelson marveled over how O had managed to play for time without looking indecisive in public but, rather, commendably deliberative. And when he had finally made up his mind, the public's impression that he had carefully considered all options made it easier for him to sell his decision to those who were disappointed by it.

Successful politicians are often suspected of harboring a duality in their personalities. O was frequently a subject of speculative psychoanalysis, a favorite pastime in Washington, which suggested such a diagnosis. Much of it was merely idle dinner party conversation. In other instances, essayists subjected the president's character to their scrutiny. Some concluded he possessed the facility of a first-rate intellect, the ability to hold two opposing ideas simultaneously. Others were convinced he suffered from a mild form of the disorder popularly known as split personality. "Good O and bad O," they explained. O mocked these pedantic attempts to explore his psyche, noting that the analyses were rarely qualified by an observation that would have occurred to less insightful readers: human nature contains contradictions. Individuals can be generous at times and selfish at others, audacious in some situations and cautious in others; and people who tended to be idealists were occasionally susceptible to bouts of cynicism. That didn't make them strangers to reason or their personalities particularly complex.

Avi Samuelson understood that the risk-taking side of the president's personality was less audacious than assumed. O acted boldly when he perceived few disadvantages to doing so, when failure would pose no more than a temporary inconvenience. But when an adverse outcome threatened more serious injury, he was sensibly reluctant to take the risk and adroit at explaining his cautiousness as a public service. More than once, he had reversed or, more charitably, "redefined" a position he had previously proclaimed as principled by identifying a more effective way to advance the principle in question.

"He's no less calculating than any other politician," Samuelson had once reassured a colleague who considered cynicism an indispensable political virtue. But most politicians calculate only a proposed action's probability of success, and if they conclude the odds favor failure, they reject it. The president, however, grasped the limitations of that assessment. The odds of success or failure were a secondary consideration. Far more instructive was his assessment of whether the rewards of success substantially outweighed the consequences of failure.

O was neither innately audacious nor cautious, Samuelson concluded. He just took a longer view than most politicians. If a tactical victory could advance his strategic interest and failure not destroy it, he would act boldly. If it didn't work out, he moved on without cursing his fate or shifting the blame onto an unfortunate subordinate. He had strategic focus, which Samuelson believed only the most exceptional political intellect could sustain through the strain of a long campaign.

The meeting with the leadership exceeded expectations. "A real lovefest," Samuelson later characterized it to his personal assistant. "I thought he was gonna sneak a cigarette after."

"We're on the same page, Mr. President," the Senate whip assured him. "Jobs should be our first priority. They should be our only priority. Nothing else matters." All the participants pitched in with ideas of how to package the legislation and sell it. The House leader suggested the president unveil it at a specially convened "jobs summit" with industry leaders who stood to benefit most from the legislation. Several presidential jobs summits had previously been convened with great fanfare and had, disappointingly, failed to encourage public confidence or have a positive impact on the economy beyond a minor and temporary boost to the Washington hospitality industry. "Maybe you should hold it outside Washington," the leader added. "Maybe in coal country."

It was generally agreed that money to finance the jobs bill could be found, although most refrained from identifying specific reductions to offset the new expenditure. Some cuts would obviously have to come out of the defense budget, they acknowledged. They would leave it to the Office of Management and Budget to identify precisely where, as long as it didn't affect spending on any major weapons system. Defense companies were notorious for spreading the wealth they accumulated by manufacturing the nation's state-of-the-art weaponry among dozens of congressional districts and the campaign coffers of influential members of Congress. While no one suggested it, the idea had occurred to all of them that were O to wind down America's involvement in Afghanistan, the savings would cover the new spending.

Minutes after the meeting concluded, the Democratic leaders marched together to the North Lawn of the White House and proclaimed to the bank of television cameras assembled there that they and the president were in total agreement on the most important responsibility of the new Congress: "putting Americans back to work." They hoped Republicans shared their concern for the unemployed, although their facial expressions suggested they had doubts on that score.

Not long after his guests had departed, the president, accompanied by a single aide and two Secret Service agents, walked briskly toward the South Lawn, where a marine helicopter was waiting to fly him to Camp David. He was less satisfied with the outcome of the meeting than the others had been. Members of Congress often put him ill at ease when they became excited about something he said. He was never quite sure they had understood him correctly. But on the whole, he was pleased there hadn't been any arguments and relieved he had managed to salvage part of his weekend. And at that moment his mind was pleasantly occupied with plans to enjoy it. There were enough daylight hours left to practice his swing and putting. He would spend the evening watching a movie or two with his wife and children. On Sunday, they would do something outside together. A warm spring day was forecast. Maybe a hike, he thought, and then another hour or so on the practice tee.

His reverie was interrupted by his personal aide, who put a hand on his shoulder to get his attention. When the president turned around, he saw Avi Samuelson awkwardly jogging toward them. Little of the ensuing conversation could be heard by its witnesses. Samuelson had to shout in the president's ear to be heard over the noise of the helicopter. He needed the president's immediate attention. O looked at his aide as if he was going to say something. Then he shook his head and turned around to walk with Samuelson back to the Oval Office.

★ CHAPTER 4 ★

The third ring of his cell phone roused Cal Regan to semiconsciousness. He waited for it to stop. Then, prompted by her scent lingering in the bed linens, he turned to reach for her. He found only the comforter drawn back, and the impression her body had left on the sheet and pillowcase. Exhausted, their limbs still entangled, waiting for their heart rates to slow, they had smiled into each other's eyes and slipped into drunken, fitful sleep. Or at least he had. Did she sleep? Had she ever slept in his bed? He couldn't be sure. She was never there in the morning. Between his last conscious moment and the early hour when he would rise, she would gently untangle herself from his embrace, dress, and slip away, leaving him to awake to the sensations of hangover and disappointment and stir discontentedly in his empty bed as he recollected spent pleasures.

He had joked with her about it once, hoping to draw her out. "Why the vanishing act all the time? Seeing someone else?"

"Do you feel used?" she teased. "I'm sorry. Next time I'll leave a note. 'Thanks for the good time, sailor.'"

"I'll buy you a toothbrush, make you coffee, scramble some eggs. We can stay in bed. Read the papers."

"Aw, so sweet. Do you miss me when you wake up? Sorry, baby, I'm a busy girl. A busy, busy girl."

He thought he looked haggard in the medicine cabinet mirror. It could have been the effect of the late night and heavy drinking. But maybe it was a symptom of the strange emotion he was experiencing—something more than disappointment. Someone more accustomed to the vicissitudes of love might have recognized it as a form of grief.

Another Sunday to put to some less enjoyable use. Thousands of couples were snug in their beds, naked, warm, luxuriating in the first rays of what promised to be a sunny spring day. Cal Regan was alone in his bathroom, fumbling with a bottle of aspirin, shouting, "Who the fuck calls at this hour on a Sunday?"

It was Avi Samuelson.

"We need to talk to you about something today. How soon can you get down here?"

"Down where? The White House?"

"No, Miami. Yes, the fucking White House. Where do you think we work?"

"It's just, uh, it's Sunday morning. Thought you might not be in the office. Give me an hour? I just got up."

"Make it thirty minutes."

"Okay. What's going on?"

"See you in thirty."

"Who's *we*?" Regan wondered aloud as he hurriedly showered.

Samuelson's assistant met him in the West Wing lobby and escorted him up a staircase to the West Sitting Hall, where the president had met with the leadership the day before. Cal Regan had never before been invited to the First Family's living quarters. For that matter, he had never been invited to a meeting with the president in the Oval Office. He tried not to gawk as he passed through the Central Hall toward a room with an elaborately carved lunette window, where Samuelson, several other aides, and the president of the United States were waiting. Regan had the impression they had been there a while, and had exhausted whatever subject they had gathered to discuss. The president, sunk into an oversize armchair, looked tired.

"Good to see you, Cal. Sorry for the short notice," the president offered. "As you can see," he added sourly, "we don't have anything better to do on a Sunday morning than work. We've got an issue, a personnel problem."

O asked his press secretary, Rick Noth, to provide the background. It was Noth's call to Samuelson the day before that initiated a hectic eighteen hours of investigation and planning that culminated in the meeting now under way.

A reporter whom Noth trusted had called to inquire into "a rumor making the rounds" that Stu Trask "had a situation." The reporter didn't know what kind of "situation" Trask was rumored to have, but it wouldn't have become a rumor if its implications were harmless. The reporter was looking to break a story, a story he knew other reporters had been working on longer than he had. He was not calling for comment but for information. He had hoped that if the White House was looking for a reporter who could be trusted to break the story in a way that minimized damage to its interests, the press secretary, with whom he had a long and friendly relationship, and who was the subject of two flattering profiles the reporter had authored (which had dealt at length with the subject's quick wit, strategic mind, encyclopedic knowledge of sports trivia, and exceptionally close relationship with the president; the description "almost like a member of the First Family" had been used in both profiles), would recommend him for the job.

This kind of inquiry was known colloquially in the fraternity of press flacks as a "shit sandwich." Noth knew that when a reporter doesn't have the story and the press secretary doesn't know the story—hasn't heard a goddamn word about it until that very call—there is no good way to respond. Had he given a simple "No comment," it would have implied there was something to comment on. So would "I'll get back to you on it." He could try to knock it down with a disdainful comment about Washington rumormongering. But if the rumor was true, as Washington rumors often were, and its public disclosure imminent, he would soon look like an imbecile or a liar, possibly both. A nonresponse employing feigned outrage and self-deprecating humor would permit the most ambiguity. "Is this what you're interrupting my weekend for? Don't you know my wife will have my ass for a grape if I don't get to my kid's soccer game in ten seconds? I'll call you back later." But the technique had been overused by scores of flummoxed press secretaries. It would have registered as a transparent dodge and indicated the tantalizing prospect of a possible cover-up in the planning stages. It's a problem that has no perfect solution, and thus, it was one of the few occasions when Noth considered resorting to honesty, as long as the reporter solemnly agreed the conversation would be strictly off the record. After frantically searching his mind for alternatives, that was what Rick Noth decided to do.

"Just between us, all right? Can't even tell your editors for now, okay?"

The reporter, sensing that his temporary discretion would earn him a scoop, agreed, and Noth made a painful admission that any press secretary would be loath to confess.

"This is the first I've heard anything of the kind. Gimme some time to figure out if there's anything to it. If there is, and if we decide we have something to say about it, I'll give it to you first. Deal?"

"Deal."

After hanging up, Noth had made straight for Avi Samuelson's office to ask, with more than a trace of irritation, what was going on with Stu Trask, and why no one had bothered to inform him about it before he started getting press calls. Samuelson confessed, "I have no fucking idea what you're talking about."

"Well, I just got a call from Rich Fox asking me about his 'situation,'" Noth retorted.

Samuelson began his investigation with a call to Trask's cell phone, but it went straight to voice mail. His next call went to Trask's assistant, who answered but was unable to provide any information about her boss's whereabouts. "I don't know where he is, sir. He seems to be off the grid today. He's getting a lot of calls and not returning any of them." Samuelson's curiosity became alarm, which was soon followed by panic. He grabbed his BlackBerry and e-mailed Trask a curt "Call me ASAP," and then told his assistant to find Trask's home phone number and call it. No one was taking calls at the Trask residence either.

"Jesus, what the fuck is going on?" a suddenly irate Samuelson shouted at his assistant, who did not feel she was in a position to provide him with a satisfactory answer. Samuelson was not by nature an excitable man. But in the profession of politics, nothing had greater value than access to pertinent information in what was suspected to be an emergency situation. To be deprived of it, even for a brief time, could frighten the steadiest hand. "Let's call Phelps and see if he knows anything," Samuelson suggested.

"He got married last week," Noth pointed out. "He's still on his honeymoon."

"I don't care if he's halfway through a blow job. Just call him," Samuelson insisted. Noth patiently explained that the honeymooning Phelps, the campaign's director of communications, was almost certainly not receiving press calls on the Caribbean island where he might have been enjoying fellatio. And had a reporter somehow managed to interrupt his idyll with an alarming question, Phelps would have immediately called Noth for guidance. In an attempt to assuage the disappointed Samuelson, Noth offered to call Phelps's deputy, Chris Ryan. Ryan was cheerfully available, but he, too, was mystified as to the whereabouts of Stu Trask, and the only information he could offer them concerned two calls he had received from reporters, one of them Rich Fox. They had asked to talk with the absent Trask and had refused to share with Ryan the subject they wished to discuss. "It's a personal matter," they had both explained.

"What the hell has that guy done?" Noth wondered aloud after hanging up with Ryan. Samuelson drummed his fingers on his desk, his heavy-lidded eyes almost closed, and imagined various worst-case possibilities that might answer Noth's question.

Both men were relieved to have their speculation interrupted by Samuelson's cell phone, its caller ID indicating Stu Trask was finally returning a phone call. The president's counselor drew a deep breath before answering. He did not want to sound on edge or intimidating as he began his careful inquisition of the man he suspected would soon be known as the president's former campaign manager.

"Stuart, we're getting some calls here, and I understand you are as well, suggesting you've got some kind of personal problem. Do you know what they're referring to? Because we don't have a clue." Samuelson was surprised by the anguished reaction his question provoked.

"Oh God, I'm sorry. I'm so sorry. I thought I had more time to get a handle on it."

"What are we talking about here, Stu?"

"I was going to call you, I swear, Avi. I just thought I had more time. It's not what you think. I'm not that kind of person. I'm not a freak. I didn't know until later."

"Stu, Stu, calm down. I don't *think* anything. We're totally in the dark here. Okay? You've got to walk us through this from the beginning. You didn't know what?"

"That she was in high school."

Samuelson paused to look up at Noth, who was standing a few feet away and could not hear Trask's end of the conversation, roll his eyes, and mouth "Holy shit." They were perilously close to the category of worst case.

"Stu."

"Yes, Avi?"

"Who is *she*?"

She was an eighteen-year-old call girl. When she wasn't working, she lived with her mother and two sisters in a three-bedroom ranch in Melrose Park, and attended East Leyden High School in Franklin Park. She met Trask after he had called an escort service and described the kind of girl he would like to meet that evening in the bar of a hotel near O'Hare Airport. Two hours later, a girl, stunningly close to his stated preference for "a blonde, very fit, on the younger side, cheerleader type," introduced herself as Brittany. Trask introduced himself as Andrew, his middle name. An hour and a half later, she departed with seven hundred dollars of his money, and his promise that he would "like to make this kind of a regular thing." Over the course of several months, their "regular thing" became a source of comfort to Stu Trask, "a release from all the bullshit," as he described it to Samuelson, who told Trask he wasn't interested in his fragile state of mind or the "bullshit" he sought release from: the unhappy state of his twenty-two-year marriage, which, for all its unhappiness, had managed to produce four children.

Six weeks ago, Brittany had seemed upset to Trask. When he asked about the cause of her unhappiness, she mentioned her frustration with the escort service that employed her. She told the sympathetic Trask she was trying to save enough money to go back to college, which due to an unspecified family misfortune she had been forced to leave two years before. However, she was obliged to pay sixty percent of her earnings to the escort agency, leaving her barely enough to cover her rent and other living expenses. Trask assured Samuelson he was "not a stupid man" and had suspected this might simply have been a ruse to encourage a generous tip. But she put him at ease when she proposed that he no longer use the service to arrange their dates, and that they exchange cell phone numbers "like a real couple."

Four days later, Brittany called his cell phone for the first time and informed him she didn't intend to resume her college career. She was, in fact, barely eighteen and a month shy of graduating high school. She asked Trask for ten thousand dollars, a sum she felt certain could be provided by the fifty-three-year-old Stuart Andrew Trask, formerly of Chevy Chase, Maryland, but currently residing in a rented brownstone at 1241 North Astor Street on Chicago's Near North Side, with his wife, Beverly, and two of his daughters, Lilly and Audrey, while he worked as campaign manager for the president of the United States. Were he to refuse her request, she would inform his wife of their relationship. Were he to call her escort service to complain about the extortion, she would inform his wife. "I'm just taking a little initiative here, Stuart," she explained. "It's not *that* much money. And, frankly, I think you know I'm worth it."

"Did you pay her?" Samuelson had asked him.

"No, I didn't," Trask assured him. "I'm not a fool. I hung up and immediately called her agency. The woman I spoke to apologized, said she understood and that she'd have it taken care of."

Whether the proprietress of Elle Escorts for Discriminating Gentlemen was sincere in her assurance was unknown. What was known was that when Stu Trask came home from work eight days ago, a little late and perhaps a little drunk, Beverly Trask, who appeared more than a little drunk herself, was waiting for him with a photograph of a naked, very fit, on-the-younger-side cheerleader type and a note that said "This is the high school senior your husband is fucking when he tells you he's working late."

A noisy row ensued, overheard by several of their immediate neighbors, who also witnessed a number of Trask's possessions being thrown from an upstairs window. Trask had been living in a hotel since. Four days ago, his assistant gave him a message from a reporter for a Chicago-based news website that specialized in celebrity gossip. He didn't respond. The next day, he received a call from a *Chicago Tribune* reporter, which he did take, and which concerned an alleged spousal abuse incident that had recently occurred at the Trasks' home, according to several unsolicited tips. Trask feared the press calls that followed were of the same nature, although he wasn't certain, because he hadn't answered any of them.

"What did you say to the *Tribune*?"

"I denied it. I never laid a hand on Bev."

"Did she hit you, Stu?"

"No. She threw some things at me, but she missed."

"Did you tell him anything else?"

"I told him I loved my wife, and there was nothing to report."

"Anything else?"

"He asked me why I was living in a hotel."

"And you said?"

"None of your business."

"That's it?"

"Yes."

"Okay. Don't do or say anything for now. Let's try to figure out who knows what, and how much damage we're looking at."

"Avi."

"Yes."

"I think he might have talked to Bev."

"Just stay put. I'll call you back in a little while."

Samuelson tried to push from his mind for the time being the question of what Beverly Trask might have said to the reporter, and hustled to intercept the president on the South Lawn before he boarded the helicopter for Camp David. His lumbering half trot, half brisk walk emphasized the urgency of his mission and the considerable time that had passed since he had regularly exercised.

Well into Saturday evening, Samuelson, Noth, and several trusted subordinates labored to get a clear picture of the situation. Samuelson talked twice more to Trask: the first time to gather more information, and the second to explain, rather curtly, the plan they had conceived to limit the potential damage from his indiscretion. He also very reluctantly placed a call to Beverly Trask, after she refused to talk to her husband, to ask as delicately as he could what, if anything, she had said to the *Tribune* reporter. She assured him she had offered nothing more than an ambiguous "Why don't you ask Stu about that," although her icy brusqueness—and her unsolicited disclosure that she and her daughters intended to return to Chevy Chase at the end of the school year—caused him to worry that she had not been entirely forthcoming about the conversation.

When they agreed their inquiries had yielded all that could be ascertained at present, they decided on a course of action and briefed the president. O offered to break the news to Trask himself, but was dissuaded by the others, who assured him the courtesy was unnecessary and would only put the president in an awkward situation were Trask to divulge to him, in a misguided attempt to apologize, the reasons for his misadventure.

The short version Noth provided to Cal Regan was a model of factual economy.

"At two o'clock eastern this afternoon, pending an assurance of Beverly Trask's cooperation, the campaign will release a statement announcing Stu's resignation from the campaign for personal reasons. We also think it's best to include some kind of vague acknowledgment of marital discord to cover us in the likely event that the hooker is discovered. Right now, we're thinking about something along the lines of 'The Trasks have asked for understanding and privacy in this difficult time as they seek to protect their family from recent strains on their marriage.' That will obviously invite further press interest, but probably not much more than there would be anyway. We're going to give Rich Fox the statement thirty minutes before release, and if the situation with the girl is discovered, we'll background him that staff, acting on the president's instruction, demanded Stu's resignation as soon as we discovered there could be a problem like that and advised him to report to authorities any illicit activity that might have caused his predicament. That's pretty much where we are right now."

Regan assumed he had been invited to offer an opinion on the proposed plan or perhaps to help refine the draft press release. The president, however, immediately made clear the actual reason he had been asked there.

"Cal, we'd also like to include in the release an announcement that you've agreed to replace Stu. Rick, can we call him the campaign manager if we haven't officially announced I'm seeking reelection?"

"You've acknowledged in several interviews right after the State of the Union that you expected to run for reelection. Everyone referred to Stu as your campaign manager. So, yes, I think we can say he has agreed to serve as campaign manager, when there is officially a campaign to manage."

"Well, that's what we'd like to do, Cal, if you're agreeable."

"We want as much news as we have to report included in the first story," added Noth.

"Congratulations," offered Samuelson sardonically.

Cal would have to call Hanson, Strong's senior partners shortly before the announcement was made. They wouldn't be happy about not receiving notice, but they would understand he couldn't refuse a direct request from the president or negotiate different terms. Nor would they want him to. His value to the firm increased as his value to the president increased. The next few hours would be consumed in conference with Samuelson, discussing the current state of the campaign, its fund-raising goals for the year, and the challenges he would have to focus on during his first few months on the job. The president would join them for part of the discussion. As soon as he had a chance, he'd call Lowe and ask to meet him for dinner tonight.

Cal had been drawn to politics by its improvisational nature, its surprises and sudden detours, the way fortunes could change overnight and new opportunities present themselves without warning. He had experienced, he thought, everything there was to experience in campaigns, and yet the profession always managed to find a way to thrill him again. He loved it. At that moment he felt a surging sense of well-being, of poise and potency. *My God,* he thought, *I'm a lucky son of a bitch.*

In the flush of his success, the only thought he spared for the unlucky Stu Trask was a reflection on the incongruity of the image of the dour and homely Trask—sad-eyed, stooped, balding, and emaciated but for a small paunch—and his fateful weakness. *Christ, how old is he? And out there in the night chasing teenage hookers. Jesus.*

He left the White House three hours after the statement had been released in Chicago. He wanted to change out of his suit before he met Lowe for dinner. He had turned his cell phone off. He wouldn't have anything to say to reporters on the record or on background for a few days. He felt his BlackBerry vibrating with a rush of e-mails, and when he checked it he saw that the first message was from Maddy Cohan. "Thx for the tip. WTF?" *That's what you get for not sticking around,* he thought. The second was from Allen Knowles, whom he had planned to call the following morning.

His partners were quick to congratulate him. He would be missed, and his sudden departure would inconvenience the firm, they acknowledged, but he wasn't to worry. They were accustomed to disruptions of this kind, and the president's reelection was, of course, as important to the partners of Hanson, Strong as it was to the progress of the country.

Some of the clients he called reacted uncertainly to the news and wanted an assurance he would still be involved to some extent in the firm's management of their accounts. Regan promised them the firm would keep him "in the loop" for the duration of the campaign, and that he had every intention of returning to Hanson, Strong after the election.

Allen Knowles, however, was enthusiastic, applauding the decision as "good news for you, and good news for the president." The billionaire was a novice in the world of politics and unfamiliar with its discretions. He betrayed his naïveté by asking Regan, "How did what's his name, the guy you're replacing, screw up?" and received a dismissive "I think it was just a family issue" in reply.

Knowles also expressed an interest in becoming "a bigger player" in the campaign than he had been in the last one. "I assume the best thing I can do is get you guys more money, right? But I don't want to do it half-assed. So let your finance people know I want to be as helpful as they'll let me. I'm happy to come to Chicago to discuss it," he offered. Regan thanked him and promised to be in touch as soon as he settled in. "Make sure you do," Knowles urged him.

"I will," Regan assured him.

"Hey, Cal, before you go, I wonder if you could do me a favor."

"Sure."

"I understand there's going to be a vacancy on a presidential advisory committee, the telecommunications one—NSTAC, I think it's called."

The National Security Telecommunications Advisory Committee is one of dozens of panels established by executive order to provide the president with expert counsel from outside the ranks of government on almost every issue that could possibly concern him. It was created by President Reagan in 1982 to solicit the views of industry leaders on how to protect the nation's communications networks from attack by foreign enemies and acts of God. One of its members was the retiring chief executive of a telecommunications company that had recently merged with another; his leaving would create the vacancy Knowles hoped to fill.

Knowles had made his fortune when his company, Gabriel Tech, had cornered the entertainment industry market for encryption software and was aggressively seeking new opportunities in other lucrative markets. A recent focus of its efforts and capital was a joint venture with a leading defense contractor to develop the next generation of cybersecurity software for the military's communications networks. Although they were competing with several other firms for the contract, Knowles was confident Gabriel Tech and its partner currently had the advantage. One of their competitors occupied a seat on the NSTAC, and to maintain their advantage, Knowles thought it advisable that he occupy one as well.

"If it's not a big deal, I'd like to join it. But I'm not really sure how you do that. Do you think you could help?"

"I'll see what I can do," Regan promised.

CHAPTER 5

Every spring, in a hangar-size subterranean hotel ballroom filled to capacity, journalists and their invited guests fête one another's notoriety and steal glances at surrounding tables while the president of the United States and a professional comedian vie to amuse them. The latest modifications to Washington's political hierarchy are registered at the White House Correspondents' Dinner and the various pre-parties, after-parties, after-after-parties, and brunches that have proliferated in its spreading social wake. Invitations are highly coveted.

The sponsoring news organizations assemble their guest lists with ruthless attention to proving their own surviving prestige in the perpetually shuffling order of the Washington ascendancy. Rarely are reporters more competitive than when they recruit table companions for the dinner from the ranks of the powerful, the glamorous, and the sensational. A few invitations are reserved for executives of important advertising accounts. One might be bestowed as a reward to a dependable if undistinguished source. Many, however, are used to lure a conspicuous quantity of the year's most celebrated or controversial names from Washington and Hollywood. Status in Washington is measured by an invitee's perceived proximity to the president or to a major presidential candidate. Hollywood guests are ranked according to the frequency with which their striking good looks have graced the covers of *People* magazine or *Us Weekly*. A scandal, preferably of a sexual nature, confers instant cachet on an invitee, and gives a leg up to the host in the race for the distinction of most-talked-about guest list, awarded by *The Washington Post*'s Style section.

0

Cal Regan's prominence in the new generation of Democratic Party insiders and his reputation as confidant to the president's most powerful advisors earned him several invitations to the dinner and to the most selective of its associated parties. He had accepted NBC's before his selection as the president's new campaign manager was announced. His subsequent elevation in stature was a welcome surprise to NBC's Washington bureau chief, who, at the moment, was seated to Regan's right and working in tandem with the network's senior White House correspondent, seated to Regan's left, to entertain Regan with questions they knew he wouldn't answer honestly.

The White House reporter attempted his usual trick of asking one question to get an implicit answer to an unasked one. "Cal, if you were Morrison's guy, what would you be most worried about?"

Regan supplied a stock answer with an air of studied indifference. "I'd be worried about running against an incumbent who was elected on a promise of change and delivered on that promise."

"So, you think Morrison is probably their nominee?" the reporter quickly countered, smiling at his own cunning.

Regan smiled back and easily turned the question into an opportunity to raise the opposition's disadvantages. "Not necessarily. I don't know and don't care who they pick. Whichever one of them survives will have the same challenge. Voters will be sick of hearing what Republicans are against, and want to know what they're for. But they're not *for* anything."

Temporarily forgotten in his hosts' solicitousness was their interest in the radiant young actress in taffeta across the table from them, who was brushing bread crumbs from her cleavage. One of Hollywood's most bankable stars, she had been an early and enthusiastic supporter of the president in the last election. She was also known to have a keen if episodic interest in the nourishment of Third World children. She had recently testified before two congressional committees on the plight of a famine-struck country in sub-Saharan Africa and posed for pictures with several excited members of the committees, who displayed them prominently on their office walls. Regan was distracted by her presence

8

and appeared to his hosts to be insufficiently interested in their conversation. "The guy's a little full of himself, isn't he?" the bureau chief later remarked to his White House reporter.

"Yeah, and they're still running against the last president," the reporter sniffed. "I guess no one's told them he won't be on the ballot again."

"Regan, Cal Regan. I sat at your table," he reminded the actress, who looked a little put out when he approached her as she fended off admirers in the predictably rococo drawing room of the French Embassy, where the most discriminating after-party was under way.

"Oh, sorry, from NBC, right," she replied.

"No, I was invited by NBC. I don't work there. I work for the president. On the reelection campaign. I'm the manager," he explained.

"What do you manage?"

"The whole thing, the president's reelection campaign. I'm the campaign manager."

"Oh, sorry, wow. Big job, huh? Good for you."

Vexed by her apparent lack of interest in his professional achievements, he tried to steer the conversation to hers. "Yeah, I guess you could say that. I didn't get a chance to tell you at dinner—since our hosts decided to interrogate me—but I'm a big fan. Saw you in the film with Jake Gyllenhaal. Very impressed."

"Oh, yeah? And what impressed you about it?"

"You d-did, y-your performance," he said, his stuttered reply caused by a sudden and unwelcome high school memory of the lovely Ellen Robicheau mocking him for asking her out.

"What about my performance? If I remember correctly, I was completely naked in it. Is that what impressed you, Mr. Regan, Cal Regan?"

Jesus, he thought as he pondered his escape from further embarrassment, *I guess she only breeds with her own kind.* "No, your acting, your acting impressed me."

She leaned a little closer to him and whispered into his ear, "Really? My acting? I'm flattered. What was the title?"

"The title?"

"The title of the movie where my acting and not my nudity impressed you."

With that, Cal Regan remembered who and where he was—the campaign manager for the president of the United States at a party in Washington, D.C., where his presence mattered more than hers—and excused himself. "Well, nice to meet you. Hope your stay in the nation's capital isn't too disagreeable."

"Thank you, Mr. Regan, Cal Regan, I hope so, too," she replied as she wondered, not for the first time, *Why does every dickhead preppie in Washington think I'm an imbecile and an easy lay?*

As he left the harrowing encounter in search of friendlier companions, the first face he recognized was that of Bianca Stefani, who was bustling toward him at speed. *Christ, I should have stayed in Chicago,* he lamented. Over Bianca's left shoulder, he saw Maddy Cohan, standing with a small group of friends, look at him and laugh. He didn't know if she was amused by his imminent confrontation with Bianca Stefani or by his failed attempt to engage the interest of the actress.

Bianca Stefani was standing so close as she spoke to him that he felt her copper-colored coif stiffly brush the side of his face. He never knew whether her practice of standing in intimate proximity to whomever she was speaking was supposed to be part of her charm or whether it was a habit she picked up because people had difficulty understanding her heavily accented English. Whatever her purpose, the effect it produced on Regan was claustrophobia, and he hoped their exchange would be a brief one.

"Caleb, you haven't forgiven us for that little thing? It was nothing personal, darling, really, just a little pinch, no? I'm very fond of you, you know. It was really a message for the White House. We don't want them to take us so much for granted."

Bianca was the founder of the eponymous *Stefani Report,* the news-aggregating, occasionally muckraking, blogger free-for-all website that became in the last campaign the cybernewspaper of record for leftist activists, intellectuals, and dilettantes from Williamsburg to West Hollywood. The "little thing" to which she referred was a post she had penned herself the day after the White House announced Cal Regan would replace Stu Trask.

"The choice of Caleb Regan to run the president's reelection campaign is the latest example," she wrote, "of how the progressive candidate elected on a message of hope and change has become another president captive to the reactionary and corrupt culture of Washington."

Regan had a friendly relationship with Stefani during the last campaign. He had regularly returned her calls and responded in kind to her flattery and exuberant affection. He had made sure Mick Lowe gave her the occasional juicy item that more reputable reporters would have taken weeks or months to confirm, and that the press office shared with the reporter she had assigned to the campaign the kind of insider accounts of decision making usually reserved for the *Times* or *Post*. He had even agreed to be the honored guest at a party the *Stefani Report* had hosted at the convention, where he had offered a warm and not noticeably insincere tribute to the "citizen journalism invented by the *Stefani Report* as an antidote to the conventional wisdom that too often affects campaign reporting."

Stefani's affections, however, were infamously changeable, as scores of her former intimates and benefactors complained. Today's dear friend would become tomorrow's villain, as she took advantage of every opportunity within her grasp to spice the airwaves with her Mediterranean drawl and plant her quicksilver personality in the consciousness of the political class. She had arrived in the United States young and penniless, and within a year became a courtesan to the wealthy and powerful in the highest strata of New York society. "She has a great talent for friendship," smitten patrons would observe to puzzled profile writers who charted her progress up the greasy pole. Many of them would eventually have cause to reconsider the compliment.

She left New York to replicate her success in the less elegant circles of Washington politics, attaching herself as hostess and muse to the restive young conservatives who claimed power in the mid-nineties, intent on destroying the moral assumptions of liberalism. When they had exhausted their energy for idealism and cared only to entrench themselves as a permanent governing class, the protean Stefani pulled up stakes for Los Angeles, where she suddenly and improbably reinvented herself as a tribune of the poor and progressive, and a scourge of conservatives, militarists, and corporations who savaged the environment, starved children, and slaughtered the innocent. She founded *The Stefani Report* with financial backing from new Hollywood friends.

With only a handful of paid staff, and a growing stable of unpaid reporters and bloggers drawn from the ranks of the liberal intelligentsia, hipsters, and entertainment industry idealists between projects, the website quickly captured the fancy of angry progressives everywhere in the second decade of Republican supremacy, and it began intimidating professional political reporters, worried over yet another assault on their relevance and dwindling resources.

She reacted indifferently to accusations of disloyalty and opportunism from cast-aside friends and benefactors. "I'm loyal to my principles," she sniffed, "and I've always had a questing soul."

Cal Regan, according to Bianca's mass e-mailed broadside, was "a talented political operative who decided to cash in and become another Beltway bandit lobbying for special interests at the expense of the people's hopes. Just the kind of old political insider trading this president was elected to change."

Apparently, Hanson, Strong, despite its close affinity with the Democratic Party, included among its many corporate clients "some of the worst polluters in America, and two health care insurers that paid people like Caleb Regan to deny Americans a real public insurance option." Bianca always included in her liveliest posts a nonnegotiable demand for some remedial action that the objects of her tirade would likely refuse. In Regan's case, she had demanded the president reverse himself and choose another campaign manager, someone who would inspire progressives to work as hard for his reelection as they had for his election.

"I'm not a lobbyist, Bianca," Regan protested.

"Of course you are. Just because you're not registered doesn't mean you don't use your political connections to protect your clients' interests. I don't think they hired you because you're a fabulous litigator."

Before he could object, she grasped both his hands in hers and tenderly assured him of her continued affections. "Don't be such a sensitive soul, darling. Avi isn't going to fire you just because we had our little say. You know, I'm very fond of you. And we want you to succeed. We're on the same side. We all have our passions, and you mustn't take them personally."

Regan knew Bianca had but one abiding passion: her own notoriety. All her other enthusiasms were as inconstant as her friendships. But political alliances aren't love affairs. They're not conceived in passion, and they're not sustained by affection. He didn't care if she was fond of him. She almost certainly wasn't. Not because she believed him to be the apparatchik of the corporate criminal class she had accused him of being, but because her relationships were transactional: temporary bargains made of compatible interests.

Bianca and her website, despite the occasional excess of ideological purity, affected the enthusiasm of Democratic activists and commanded attention from the rest of the media. Regan was and would remain the president's campaign manager. Their alliance was necessary.

"Darling, when are you moving to Chicago?" she asked.

"Already have," he answered.

"Wonderful, I'll be there next month to give a speech. Let's have dinner."

"I'll look forward to it."

One more drink and I'm off, he told himself, and was relieved to see the actress was no longer stationed at the bar, crushing the self-esteem of potential suitors.

"So, how'd you make out?" Maddy said.

"Make out with who?"

"With the actress. With Bianca. With any other girlfriends here."

"The actress and I discussed her interest in famine relief. Bianca and I discussed my moral turpitude. What happened to your little gang of admirers?"

"Two of them went to try their luck with Ms. Famine Relief. The others are around somewhere. Buy me a drink?"

"Sure. Are you sticking around for a while?"

"I don't know. Wanna make me a better offer?"

"What do you have in mind, Maddy?"

"Something your actress friend apparently didn't."

Autumn 2011

★ CHAPTER 6 ★

Newcomers to his campaign were always initially uncertain how to address him. Governor? General? Which distinction did he prefer? They all eventually settled on "sir," emulating the practice of veteran aides. No one called him Tom except his wife, Margaret, his fellow general officers, and friends of long standing. The other Republican candidates addressed him as General, heedless of the advantage their deference gave him or too intimidated by his commanding presence to attempt an equalizing familiarity.

They resented him, of course. How could they not? The hero, Thomas Irwin Morrison, square-jawed, straight-backed, irresistibly perfect, trespassing in their profession, threatening the ambition they had schemed and sacrificed all their adult lives to achieve. Their initial expectation that he, like other retired officers who had attempted it, would find politics maddeningly offensive to his sense of dignity and order had been dashed by the natural aptitude he possessed for its arts, which became apparent in his election and successful tenure as governor. He was a skillful political communicator and seemed to enjoy campaigning. He had none of the awkwardness of a professional officer struggling to ape the counterfeit emotions of politicians and translate the language of military leadership into the populist jargon of politics.

While other candidates exaggerated the least of their accomplishments, he made few explicit references to his impressive military résumé. He didn't need to, as it was featured in almost every news account of his candidacy and praised by every speaker who introduced him to an audience. He stressed the accomplishments of his single gubernatorial term and his experiences in the private sector. He had a strong command of domestic policy and explained his views concisely and coherently. He had a talent for declaring his support for positions that were broadly popular with the voters with arguments that appeared insightful and principled.

The confident authority he projected reminded voters of his military service. Yet it did not seem to them an acquired quality of rank, but natural to a man of his ability and character. An attractive public image that appears authentic to a candidate's nature is the most prized attribute in politics, and is admired by voters above all other qualities. Morrison possessed it, and his rivals suffered in comparison.

His affability and courteousness in several candidate debates made their gentlest criticism of him look unreasonable and indecorous. His dignified forbearance in the face of provocation was a welcome contrast to their pettiness. He often complimented his opponents, observing that this one or that one had "made a great point, much better than I could, I'm sorry to say," and qualified accounts of his accomplishments with self-effacing references to minor mistakes that had preceded success and to his dumb good luck in having a "great team that made me look smart." Voters thought it showed a becoming modesty in a man who had more reason to be boastful than did any of his self-important opponents.

Unlike the other candidates, he never referred to the president by his last name. He always called him "the president," and he tempered his criticism of the man whose job he coveted with frequent praise for his intelligence, good intentions, inspirational message, and "wonderful family."

"I'm not running for president to tear anybody down," he repeatedly claimed. "I'm running to help Americans build a better future. This election is too important for candidates to waste everyone's time insulting each other." The other Republican candidates all agreed and were careful to describe any criticism of the general as an "honest policy difference." As there were few genuine policy disagreements among them, they had to invent a few. They had no other outlet for their growing hatred of him.

The president and his aides were more dispassionate in their assessment of their likely opponent. He was a talented and attractive candidate, and his campaign, while yet to be fully tested, appeared disciplined and well financed. He was a legitimate threat, and he had their professional respect. They would need their best game to defeat him, and they would have to begin early. His appeal wouldn't be easy or inexpensive to destroy.

The Rotarians of Derry, New Hampshire, also recognized Morrison's appeal, although none of them were interested in calculating the cost of destroying it. Rather, as they consumed the last bites of their lemon meringue pie, which had followed their usual lunch of baked chicken and rice at the Marion Gerrish Community Center, they were pleased Morrison had arrived at the conclusion of his remarks without sounding as rehearsed and insincere as the other presidential candidates who had recently entertained them. None of them played with the flatware or indicated they were uninterested as Morrison briefly mentioned America's most notable accomplishments from the end of World War Two to the present, and characteristically claimed only a minor role in a few of them.

"I know how lucky I am to have played any role at all in our country's history," he confessed. "My greatest dream as a boy was to go to West Point, and to someday serve my country in difficult circumstances. That dream came true, and I've never expected a greater privilege. But I can't sit back and watch this country accept second best. I just can't."

Without seeming angry or distraught, he spoke of his concern that America might be entering a period of decline.

"There are many things to admire about our current president, and I take no pleasure in saying this, but he doesn't seem to know where to lead us anymore. He's settling for less than Americans expect of their president and less than we expect of ourselves. And his policies make it harder for us to build an American future as great as our past. With all due respect, we need to make a change."

He wouldn't play the usual campaign games, he promised them. "Our situation is too critical for that kind of nonsense. I'm just going to tell people where I hope to lead us and how I intend to do it, and then trust your judgment to make the right choice. No one ever went very wrong in this country by trusting the judgment of the American people."

No one in the audience thought the speech eloquent. There weren't any perorations that burst at the crest of a steadily building tempo. No lines would be remembered and chanted by supporters. But no one had remained seated when he finished. All were on their feet and applauding more enthusiastically than New Hampshire Rotarians were known to do for the many candidates who interrupted their lunches every four years. Many of them were relieved that Morrison's style had been so relaxed. Candidates who spoke to them as if they were addressing an audience of thousands always made them feel uncomfortably conspicuous and afraid to finish their meals. "Who was he shouting at?" they often wondered to one another. Despite his conversational style and modest artistry, Morrison had conveyed sincerity and dignity. "Guy seems to know who he is," one Rotarian observed to another. "Kinda refreshing, isn't it?" came the reply.

There hadn't been a teleprompter or written text in evidence, and his audience was impressed that Morrison had been so coherent, speaking, as he promised them he would, "from the heart." Had the reporters who covered the speech not heard him deliver nearly identical remarks on many previous occasions, they would have believed so, too. They were no less impressed, however. As far as they were concerned, a well-received speech that appeared unprepared and unrehearsed was as remarkable as one that actually was extemporaneous. "O couldn't have done it," they agreed. "Take his prompter away and he can't remember who he is."

Several hours later, on a chartered plane en route to a Houston fund-raiser, Morrison removed from his briefcase a binder containing the speech he had given from memory that afternoon and began to make a few notes in places where he thought he had not connected with the audience. It was his practice to do this after every speech, and to discuss with his speechwriter before the day was finished where he thought the text could "stand a little more zip."

Margaret would join him at the fund-raiser and was already waiting for him at their hotel. They wouldn't be able to leave the event until eight o'clock, and both would be tired. But they would have a couple of hours' private time before exhaustion drove them to bed. Theirs was a close and trusting marriage. In every endeavor he had undertaken, with the exception of his time in combat, he had relied on her for advice and encouragement. It had been a week since they had last been together. While they spoke on the phone as often as a dozen times a day, they reserved discussion of important matters, especially those that concerned the family, for moments when they were alone together, holding hands and drawing strength from each other's cheerful, plucky certainty that no problem in life lacked a solution.

Tonight, they would surely discuss again their son, Alex, the youngest of their three children, and the weakest. He was seventeen and chronically in trouble at school. A year ago, they had decided to take him out of the prep school where he had courted expulsion on several occasions with offenses that were mostly typical teenage pranks, though a few had been inexplicable and inarguably odd. On one such occasion, he had crawled out on the slate roof of his dormitory and recited several verses of a song that had achieved modest commercial success for a recording artist with a nasally voice that was distinctive and, until recently, underappreciated. "I thought it was funny," was the only explanation Morrison could get out of him.

He had never been noticeably interested in the military, beyond a natural curiosity about his father's war experiences. Morrison had never encouraged his son to follow in his professional footsteps. It made no particular difference to him what vocation his son aspired to, he frequently insisted to Margaret, "as long as he grows up to be useful." Nor did Alex appear to sympathize with those of his peers who opposed the wars in Iraq and Afghanistan. They had never heard him offer any view on the subject. His interests were childish enthusiasms for science fiction and computer games. They weren't aware of any others.

He had a temper that erupted quickly over small provocations and was not easily soothed by his parents' entreaties or subdued by their firm discipline. He was a handsome boy and naturally athletic. He had played Little League baseball for two summers, and his coaches had been excited by his potential. But he had refused to play a third season and declined all other invitations to participate in organized sports. He formed few friendships, which his parents attributed to the family's frequent relocations. They knew army life was hard on children that way. The friends he did acquire were always younger than he was, and were more minion than peer.

Tom Morrison did not fit the stereotype of the autocratic military father. He wasn't especially demonstrative in his affections, but neither was he cold and taciturn. He seldom lost his temper with his children. When it was necessary to discipline them, he never did so angrily or without explaining his reasons. He praised their accomplishments appropriately and encouraged them to be independent and self-confident. Although the demands of his career often necessitated long absences, he was an attentive father when he was home.

Margaret, too, was a conscientious parent. Their two daughters, Courtney and Eleanor, both now at college, had flourished in their care and were attractive, sensible, and popular young women. The Morrisons were at a loss to understand the cause of their son's peculiar and often disagreeable personality. They thought his separation from them might have aggravated his tendency for self-indulgent behavior, and they had enrolled him in a day school near their home. But they soon received reports from teachers that he was an indifferent student, and aloof. "He's kind of a loner," one had informed them, "and I know he's smarter than he pretends to be."

They hoped the disorder would naturally right itself in time, and if it didn't, they felt confident they would eventually discover its remedy. The boy had the security of a stable and loving family. He was good-looking and intelligent. He could be popular if he would only behave sociably. There was no reason they could discern for his failure to govern himself.

A year ago, when Tom and Margaret spent a weekend at their summer home discussing whether he should run for president, they had identified only one concern that argued against it: the effect it might have on Alex. As he was the governor's son, his misbehavior at boarding school had aroused the interest of local reporters and had been kept out of the papers only after Tom and Margaret separately placed calls to editors to plead for their son's privacy. They worried that the national press would be less sympathetic.

In the end, they decided the excitement of a presidential campaign might work to arouse the boy's enthusiasm. They agreed Alex would travel with his father in the summer. Things had gone well; Alex had shown interest in the campaign and, in Tom's opinion, a little more maturity. Margaret suggested Alex return to the campaign trail as Tom's personal aide the summer after he graduated from high school, and that he postpone attending college until after the election. And although Alex had reverted to bad form once he returned to school, they had not thought it necessary to alter their plan. They assumed, of course, that Tom would be the Republican nominee. Nothing would be taken for granted, but they felt good about their prospects, and even more so that the campaign would prove a tonic to their son.

That evening, alone in their hotel suite, Tom and Margaret reassured each other that theirs were blessed lives, and that their decision to seek the presidency would prove as providential as had every important decision they had made together. It was the right thing to do, they reasoned, for their family and the country. Neither could imagine anyone better prepared for the responsibilities of the presidency or more dedicated to America's interests. If it was not Tom's destiny to lead the country, why had the opportunity so unmistakably presented itself?

The other Republican candidates—two sitting governors, one former governor, two United States senators, and a once widely respected former member of the House of Representatives who was getting on in years—were experienced politicians and fine individuals. But none was capable of the inspirational leadership that had distinguished Tom's long service to the country. And although neither mentioned it to the other, both Morrisons doubted any of the other candidates possessed his reserves of courage and patriotism either. They could have chosen to enjoy their prosperity free of the inconveniences of public life. But that would have struck them both as selfish. The country needed them. They tried not to be publicly judgmental about the character of the incumbent president, but they believed his celebrated political talents disguised an immature and irresolute nature.

O's vacillation on Afghanistan had seemed as dishonest as it was tortured. Morrison suspected he had arrived at the right decision only after searching desperately for an assurance that the wrong decision would prove a greater threat to his reelection. And he had been revolted by the way the president's political aides, not one of whom had served in uniform, had excused his indecisiveness by suggesting to the media the inexperienced O was determined not to be intimidated by hawkish generals into surrendering his constitutional authority and doubting his own informed judgment.

Morrison kept to himself his conviction that O was a weak man and that, like other weak men, he resorted to vanity to hide his insecurity. This was only Morrison's second campaign, but he possessed the instincts of a veteran campaigner. The polls indicated that independent voters had lost confidence in the president and were persuadable by arguments that criticized his policies and his competence. They were disappointed in O. They did not, however, hold his character in contempt and were repulsed by suggestions they should.

Republican activists were scornful of the man they considered dangerously liberal and morally unfit to occupy the office of president. Unlike several of his Republican rivals, Morrison refrained from personal insults that would have suggested he shared their disposition. He knew his appeal to Republican primary voters resided in the contrast between his and the president's life stories and political convictions, his personal rectitude, and, most important, the voters' judgment that he had the best chance of defeating O. He did not need to compromise his appeal to swing voters by indulging the base's appetite for red meat. He never let on that he, too, disdained the man they reviled and hoped would not just be defeated but consigned to ignominy in history's account of his presidency.

"Tom, could we be happy," Margaret had asked him, "knowing the country should be in better hands and refusing to do something about it?" She always knew the right questions to ask, he thought. He had known from the moment he recognized he had fallen in love with her that she would prove invaluable to his career. He often said in public that the best proof of his judgment was his decision to ask her to marry him, and the best proof of his good luck was her acceptance. He knew other officers had resented his success and tried to impede his progress by intimating that his talent for public relations exceeded his aptitude for command. He never doubted himself. Not as long as he had Margaret's support. There wasn't an officer in the army, not a person in the world he had ever met, who had better instincts about people or better judgment in difficult decisions than Margaret. "I wouldn't know what to do without you," he often told her. "Sure you would, Tom," she invariably replied. "You'd always do the right thing. You don't know how to do otherwise."

In less than four months, ninety thousand highly motivated Iowa Republicans, representing twenty percent of all registered Republicans in the state, would brave the state's famously harsh winter winds to attend their precinct caucus and vote their preference for the presidential nomination. Local party officials would release the results to thousands of anxious reporters, who would promptly proclaim a winner, using the awful weather conditions as a metaphor to describe the failure of the various losing candidates. A week later, New Hampshire Republicans and voters unaffiliated with either party would vote in the state's primary to either endorse the selection of Iowa Republicans or, as they often chose to do, contradict it.

According to all recent public polls, Tom Morrison had a substantial lead in both states, although his margin was lower in Iowa, where evangelical Christians harbored some doubts about the general's affinity for their views on the issues that most concerned them. He had governed a state where social conservatism had little public support. And while he had pledged his opposition to abortion and gay marriage, he didn't emphasize those positions to their perfect satisfaction, and they thought they detected a disquieting discomfort with the language and arguments he employed to defend their causes.

Social conservatives always worried they would be taken for granted by the party after the election. Their experience with Republicans who had relied on their support in close elections but neglected their priorities once in office made them suspicious of all candidates, and uncertain as to whether an inherently sinful country could ever produce a righteous leader. Wasn't it better, many evangelicals argued, to keep their distance from all aspiring Caesars and their own souls free of contamination by the duplicitous bargains that politics always involved? But temporal power, however transitory, is intoxicating even to the virtuous. And every four years, in Iowa's abstruse and clannish Republican caucuses, evangelicals had power and found hard to resist the elaborate attention they received by exercising it in their exacting scrutiny of the candidates who courted their support. They weren't convinced Morrison was trustworthy, and their doubts offered the best and perhaps only opportunity for his opponents to discredit him.

His rivals knew their tactics would have to be subtle. There was nothing in Morrison's public record or private life they could use to aggravate the suspicions of social conservatives. But there was little in his record he could cite to reassure them. As a northeastern governor, Morrison had had little opportunity to engage their issues. They were not much in dispute in his state. For the time being, the other candidates would stress in their public statements, mail, and paid advertising their own long records of public support for the rights of the unborn and the sanctity of heterosexual marriage, and hope they would contrast favorably with Morrison's comparatively timid and recent defense of those causes. They would attempt in debates to engage him in discussions that would emphasize their greater familiarity with the vocabulary and reasoning of social conservatives. They would have their supporters whisper confidentially, in offhand conversations in scores of small gatherings of the faithful, their worry that Morrison's views were more likely expedient than sincere. If Morrison still retained the advantage in the final weeks before the Iowa caucuses, they would have to consider more aggressive tactics.

Conventional wisdom held that the top three finishers in Iowa retained a chance at securing the nomination. The others were finished even if they refused to acknowledge it. It was generally assumed, however, that were Morrison to win Iowa, he would be the favorite. And were he to follow his success in Iowa by winning the New Hampshire primary, he would be unstoppable.

Campaign reporters hoped the race would last longer. Were it to be settled in New Hampshire, they would have little of genuine interest to cover, and their bylines would make few appearances on the front page until the parties held their national conventions at summer's end. The president's advisors were divided in their opinions. Regan hoped the Republicans would produce a presumptive nominee early, giving the Democrats ample time to use their financial advantage to, in Mick Lowe's words, "kick the shit out of the four-star son of a bitch until it looks like a mercy killing." Samuelson preferred that Republicans take their time. He believed it was to the president's advantage to appear above the fray and focused on the people's business for as long as possible. The president agreed with him, although he assumed an early result was most likely.

Even though he knew it wouldn't happen, he still wished the Barracuda, as he called her, would join the Republican race.

His aides had joked during the midterm elections that the Tea Party's support for the most controversial and ill prepared candidates in Republican primaries would lure her into seeking the Republican presidential nomination. "What could we do to help her?" Rick Noth had asked O and Samuelson, not quite in jest.

"Improve our karma," Samuelson had answered.

O knew they wouldn't be that lucky, but he had let himself imagine such a contest. On a Saturday afternoon two weeks before the last election, he had watched her speak to a rally of her faithful. There she was, baby on her hip, thick hair piled up high, chin out, defiant, taunting, flaunting that whole lusty librarian thing, sweet and savory, mother and predator, alluring and dangerous.

Intrigued as he was by the prospect of personal encounters with her, more intriguing still was the notion of running against the darling of his harshest critics—those who saw him as an overeducated and pampered snob who didn't love his country. He would have had to struggle not to patronize or demean her. He would have had to pretend she was a person with serious ideas worth detailed rebuttal no matter how ridiculous they were, no matter how incomprehensible the syntax she used to convey them. But he could not possibly lose to her. Despite her big crowds, despite how fervently they adored her, no one with negatives as high as hers could be elected president. And by defeating her, he would be defeating the myth, even if it were only a personal triumph that would not outlive his presidency. But he wasn't going to have that opportunity, so he no longer allowed himself the pleasure of fantasizing an ideal opponent. He would beat whomever they picked, whenever they picked him.

Cal Regan didn't share O's accommodating view of the Republican contest. If Morrison was going to be their opponent, he preferred to get after him as soon as possible. But almost any other candidate would be easier to defeat. And if an opportunity to trip up Morrison before he secured the nomination should unexpectedly present itself, it would be professional malfeasance not to take advantage of it. He had no idea if they would be so fortunate, but if they were, he would make the most of it. Cal Regan was always ready to be lucky.

★ CHAPTER 7 ★

Evelyn Cohan had always worried her daughter's restless ambition would be the cause of much unhappiness in her life. Maddy had been a precocious child. She had excelled at everything—schoolwork, sports, friendships—and yet no success ever gave her more than a moment's satisfaction before she became anxious about some other pursuit. She would weep in frustration when someone, even a close friend, achieved a distinction that had eluded her, and she could manufacture the most fleeting and unconvincing pleasure only when the honor was hers.

"You have to let yourself be happy, Maddy," Evelyn urged her. "Life is hard on people who expect something better than happiness."

"I am happy, Mommy," she insisted. "I like my job, my friends. I like my life. I'm just happier when I'm busy than when I'm sitting around thinking how happy I am."

"Honey, sometimes you have to keep still for a minute to know if you're happy or not."

Her father had divorced Evelyn when Maddy was six years old, and was never much of a presence in the lives of his children. Evelyn worried his example had made Maddy distrustful of male love. In high school, boys had fought for her affection. Maddy told Evelyn she thought them ridiculous. Being the object of their lust seemed nothing more to her than a humorous predicament—being fumbled at and rubbed against by boys who grunted pledges of love at an age when acquiring a driver's license was a triumph and a sudden blemish a catastrophe.

She had never had her heart broken. Evelyn didn't think she had ever had a crush on anyone. Tim Kerry had been Holy Family High School's quarterback and the most popular boy in school, and he and Maddy had dated exclusively their senior year. But Evelyn suspected Maddy had acquiesced to the relationship only because Tim was considered by her girlfriends to be the school's biggest catch. Just before she left for college, Maddy informed him matter-of-factly that they had better break things off now, so neither of them would feel guilty about seeing other people, and she had been surprised and uncomprehending when her sensible proposal upset him.

Maddy called her mother regularly and reserved thirty minutes every Sunday at noon, after Evelyn had returned from mass, to listen good-naturedly as her mother tried to investigate her sex life.

"All you ever talk about is work. You never talk about your love life or if you even have one. You always tell me you're dating, but you never mention a boy's name. The last boyfriend I knew you had was in high school. If you have one, I'd like to know who he is. I'd like to meet him. I'd like to know he makes you happy."

"I'm twenty-eight, Mommy. Old enough not to need a boy to make me happy, and young enough not to worry when one doesn't."

She never mentioned Cal Regan to her mother. She was reluctant to acknowledge their "situation" to even her closest friends. Her best friend, Jeanne Sears, in whom she had confided a few details, wasn't certain whether the acknowledged indiscretions were the beginning of a real relationship or an impulse surrendered to once or twice after a night of flirting.

Maddy hardly knew herself. It certainly wasn't love. Barely an infatuation, she thought. There was a sexual attraction strong enough to risk the predicament of sleeping with someone on the other side of a professional divide. She enjoyed his company. They shared a sardonic sense of humor, and she liked teasing him. She didn't think there was much else between them worth the complications and responsibilities emotional intimacy would impose.

She really wasn't certain he was a man worth caring for. He could be so full of himself. She had been surprised at first by his desire to become more involved. They had fallen in bed together late one night, both of them inebriated, and apart from his unexpected attentiveness as a lover, he had given her no reason to suspect he had an emotional as well as a sexual attraction to her.

She had a hard time picturing him as a romantic. His dating habits had been filler for gossip writers, who could always fill a hole in their columns with the latest doe-eyed model or voluptuous actress seen on his arm at the cancer ball or Kennedy Center awards. He was good-looking, influential, and well on his way to being wealthy, and everyone believed his female companions were chosen to advertise his good fortune. She didn't know what to make of him now. He must realize how ridiculous sentimentality made him look. Was he playing at being hurt by her off-handed manner? Why bother? They had given each other what they both wanted. And as far as she was concerned, it was good enough to excuse the occasional repeat performance. She didn't need to be seduced. She preferred he not try to be endearing. It didn't suit him.

Cal Regan, being the kind of man Maddy Cohan took him to be, agreed. And it was disconcerting, to say the least, for him to find he was not behaving like himself. The arrangement should have been perfectly agreeable to him. A satisfying romp every now and again, no obligations or expectations. It hardly mattered whether he said thank you. Their nights together were never prearranged. She did not ask for them to be. If they were in the same location at the end of an evening, and available, and so inclined, they went to his apartment and exhausted their desire. "Fucking perfect," he insisted aloud to himself when he deliberated their situation.

He meant to restore the balance in his life that she had upset. It shouldn't be difficult. He was in Chicago most of the time. He resisted the urge to call her. He saw other women, even tried his luck with a few who weren't obviously susceptible to his charm.

But he couldn't stop stray thoughts of her from distracting him. On Monday, he had spent a half hour longer than necessary going over the quarterly budget because his mind kept recalling her sitting astride him, her hair brushing the side of his face, her nipples barely touching his chest as she bent to kiss him. Yesterday during a live cable interview he had lost his train of thought in the middle of an answer; something he had just said had amused the interviewer, whose husky laugh, the effect of the cold she was suffering, had reminded him of Maddy's. He had to ask her to repeat the question, which must have made him look like an idiot, since he had already answered it in part. At lunch with Mick Lowe, he had suddenly broken their companionable silence with the announcement "I'm too busy for this shit." "For lunch?" a puzzled Lowe, his mouth full of flank steak, had asked in response.

No more inventing reasons to go home on weekends, he vowed to himself. He would stay in Chicago, except when summoned to D.C.

They had to consider the career implications of their situation as well. Were Maddy's editors to learn of her "situation" with Regan, she would not be allowed to cover the election, and not just the president's campaign, but the campaigns of his Republican challengers. She would expose the paper to credible charges of bias by rival campaigns no matter how scrupulously she avoided showing favoritism.

Romantic attachments between reporters and staff were not uncommon, especially those formed on the campaign trail between junior staffers and young reporters in the traveling press corps, who spent late night after late night drinking in the same hotel bars before retiring to rooms that were often located on the same floors. As long as the couples were discreet, the impropriety was usually ignored. But an affair between the president's campaign manager and a senior reporter for *Body Politic* could not be overlooked, even if it had begun before the campaign, when neither party's occupation had posed a clear conflict of interest. If her boss, Will Janssen, learned of it, he wouldn't deliberate for a moment before informing Maddy she would not be reassigned to the presidential campaign. She would continue to cover Congress and the reelection campaigns of several of its members, a decidedly unglamorous beat in a presidential election year.

Maddy didn't intend to trade her byline's prominence for the pleasure of Cal Regan's company. Their situation couldn't continue much longer. Any day, Janssen could notify her she was being reassigned to the campaign. She would accept it with a clear conscience. What had happened between her and Regan would be in the past. They had been discreet. She didn't think Janssen had learned of it, although he was reputed to be one of Washington's most informed gossips. But since she would have taken the appropriate action before the affair became a professional impropriety, she would not be under an obligation to inform her editor of it. It would be a memory, not a conflict, and no one's business but hers. Their next evening together, which she presumed would be soon, would be their last.

She hoped Regan wouldn't pretend to be hurt by her decision. For the duration of the campaign, their relationship would be necessarily adversarial. She would want to know things that Cal Regan would not want her to know. That essential conflict between reporters and the people they covered was, under the best of circumstances, difficult to manage without resentments of a personal nature confusing things. She had had good sources in O's last campaign, not the least of whom had been Cal Regan. She hoped he would be again. She didn't imagine he could be genuinely offended by a decision that implied she preferred him as a source rather than as a lover. Cal Regan, of all people, wasn't the type to take offense at the obvious.

Will Janssen paid his reporters more than they had made at the papers he had pinched them from, and he expected them to earn it. At eight o'clock on the evening of his fifty-first birthday, he was still at his desk and, in a worsening temper, waiting for just one of his several reporters to confirm a single fact: that the president, in the presence of several members of Congress, had used a four-letter word beginning with *f*. The expletive in question, according to a secondhand source, who had heard it from a staffer to one of the members present at the meeting, was uttered in frustration by the president after he was informed a second-term Democrat from a swing district in southeastern Ohio would under no circumstances vote for the clean technology jobs bill that was still several votes short of passing the House. Despite a personal meeting with the president, several follow-up phone conversations, and a generous offer to relocate an FBI fingerprinting lab to his district, the congressman still insisted the voters in his district wouldn't tolerate any new federal spending, especially on windmills or solar panels or anything else that threatened the future of the coal industry.

This was the kind of story *Body Politic* prided itself on breaking. No one would ever have leaked the Pentagon Papers to it. High-caliber scandals, government misfeasance, and genuine political controversies were still the province of old media, and Janssen didn't care. *Body Politic* wasn't in business to win Pulitzers. It wasn't a national news organization. Most of its readership was located in Washington, D.C., and its tonier suburbs. It was, in essence, a trade publication, published exclusively for politicians, staff, government bureaucrats, consultants, lobbyists, journalists, and assorted hangers-on who made a living one way or another from politics.

Body Politic had built a profitable business model on the ever shrinking news cycle's appetite for any scrap of information that could be, with a little imagination, interpreted as news. And a presidential profanity, especially one beginning with the letter *f,* could be interpreted as a crack in the famous reserve of a young president besieged by a quarrelsome Congress and impatient electorate. The day had long passed when an exasperated president could assume the press would overlook an occasional lapse into human behavior. If the president said *fuck,* Washington wanted to know about it, and Will Janssen wanted Washington to learn it from him first.

Maddy Cohan had received the initial tip, and it was Maddy Cohan on whom Janssen now relied to find someone who had actually witnessed the indiscretion or, at least, someone who worked for someone who had witnessed it and could be induced to confirm it on background. No two-source rule need apply tonight. Just one credible, anonymous "Yeah, he said it," and it would lead the webpage and instantly enter the cable news bloodstream; and Will Janssen could join his irritated wife and a few close friends for a birthday celebration at his favorite Asian fusion restaurant.

And so, nursing a cold and with Janssen annoyingly hovering within earshot, Maddy Cohan plied her trade. At the moment, her attention was focused on the press secretary for the chairman of the Senate Budget Committee.

"Peter, please, c'mon. Everyone's heard about it. You know we're going to get it. Do me a favor, huh, so I can get home, eat some soup, and go to bed. Did your boss hear the president say *fuck*?"

She didn't like to be in the position of supplicant to sources who had no self-interest to serve by cooperating. None of those who had been in the meeting or their staff stood to gain anything from confirming the presidential outburst. There had been no Republicans present. None of the Democrats in the room had a grievance with the White House big enough to avenge by collaborating in the president's embarrassment. She had nothing with which to threaten or bribe her sources. She could only ask for help as a personal favor and acknowledge a debt to be redeemed in some unspecified way at an undesignated time. It was a weak hand.

There were, however, two things that worked to her advantage. She was quite popular with her sources (several of whom nurtured barely concealed crushes on her). And many of them shared a compulsion common in politics, a profession where power and knowledge were thought to be synonymous. They often found hard to resist an opportunity to prove they knew something others would like to know.

Pete Mitchell was attracted to Maddy, and he was an impulsive show-off. Which of these attributes succeeded in loosening his tongue was open to speculation, and this didn't really concern her once she had overcome his initial resistance.

"Okay, Maddy, if I give you something, it's from a source with first-hand knowledge of the meeting. It's not from a staffer to one of the members there. Right?"

"Right."

"And I want this quoted in full: 'During a friendly and productive meeting on the critically important jobs bill in the House, the president briefly expressed his disappointment with one member's unreasonable opposition to a bill that would create tens of thousands of jobs in some of the hardest-hit communities in our nation.'"

"That's it? Peter, I need you to say whether the president's brief expression of disappointment included the word *fuck*."

"C'mon, Maddy, you can imply it from the quote."

"I can't, Peter, unless you give me a quote saying I can imply it."

"Can you just say a source with firsthand knowledge confirmed it?"

"Of course."

"Okay, then do that."

"Peter."

"Yeah."

"You have to actually confirm it before I can write it. Did the president say *fuck* at the meeting?"

"Yeah, he said it."

"Thank you."

"You owe me."

"Yes, I do."

Will Janssen congratulated himself often for hiring Maddy Cohan. At considerable expense to his billionaire financial backer, Janssen had recruited several respected political reporters from the major papers and weekly magazines to give the paper immediate credibility. Maddy had not been one of them. She had only a year's experience as a reporter for a left-leaning online magazine that was in exigent circumstances after the dot-com bubble had burst and reduced the ranks of liberal billionaires eager to squander parts of their fortunes on advocacy journalism. He had not heard of her until a friend had sent him links to a few of her pieces and suggested he consider her for a staff position. He had been impressed by the quality of her writing, by the irony and acerbic humor that enlivened her copy. It was clever enough to seem edgy and fun to Washington sensibilities but calibrated to avoid making veteran reporters feel hopelessly out of date.

She had been charming, too, when he had interviewed her: sophisticated and playfully impertinent without a trace of nervousness or over-eagerness to please, and agreeably modest in her expectations. She had been offered a position that involved more research than writing. She might be tossed some incidental items that her colleagues couldn't be bothered with, but she could not expect her byline to make more than a few, unnoticed appearances. "Highly unlikely you'll get any time on the campaign," Janssen warned her.

But when *Body Politic*'s exhausted campaign reporters, who were expected to produce daily copy for the paper, as well as blog posts and videotaped interviews for the online version, had pleaded for time off to recover their wits, Maddy was ordered to relieve one of them for a few days. Her first time out with the O campaign, she became a favorite of the young male press aides who traveled with the candidate, and her stories were better written and more widely quoted than her predecessor's had been. Janssen worked her into the regular rotation.

Within a few weeks she had established fruitful relationships with obviously higher-pedigree sources in O's campaign, and in his rivals' campaigns as well. By the general election, she was Janssen's star reporter, with considerable liberty in her choice of assignments, a popular presence on cable television shows, and had been affectionately nicknamed "Zelig" by fellow reporters and campaign staff for her uncanny luck in being present at campaign events where something unexpected happened. A month after the election, she topped *Washingtonian* magazine's list of the brightest new lights in journalism. Cal Regan was quoted in the accompanying short profile, complimenting her fairness and work ethic.

She had gently rebuffed two recent overtures from television news executives who had generously praised her work and assured her theirs was the medium best suited to her talents. They hadn't felt it necessary to remark specifically on her physical beauty or the rather alluring timbre of her voice, which had excited their interest in the first place. "You have real presence on camera," one of them had noted, "real appeal." "Authority," the other had called it.

She was flattered and tempted, she admitted, and wished she were in a position to entertain their offers. But her services were committed to Janssen through the election. "I know these opportunities have a short shelf life," she acknowledged. "I'd love to revisit the issue next year if you're still interested. But I won't get my hopes up."

They made no attempt to encourage her hopes. There was a chance, they thought, she might reconsider her decision if they left her with only regrets. But they were certain Maddy Cohan would become a major television talent. Neither would be surprised if, while they were still in the business, she became the host of a morning show. They could even imagine her looking down on them someday—benevolently, they hoped—from the anchor's chair on the set of the evening news broadcast. Despite their reticence, they would certainly revisit the issue, at her earliest convenience, or sooner if it could be arranged.

Maddy, too, knew her days in print journalism would soon come to an end. There wasn't much of a future in it anymore. Television would make her rich and influential. Nothing wrong with that, she reminded herself. But it would have surprised her few detractors, reporters who felt cheated by blind fate as they watched her rapid ascent, that she wasn't thrilled by the prospect of moving to television. Experience had not extinguished the last embers of her schoolgirl infatuation with the image of the hard-nosed, good-hearted newspaper reporter. It was the only romance she had ever been completely captivated by. She knew she would miss it, even though she would be the first to joke there really wasn't much left to miss.

She believed a television career to be a prize for the accident of good genes rather than for distinguished journalism. And she had always been a little put off when too much attention was paid to her good looks. Not that you would notice: she kept those kinds of feelings to herself. Nor did it trouble her self-esteem to use her sex appeal to her advantage, not when all it sometimes took to get usable intelligence was a little familiarity, a brief grasp of a hand to accompany a greeting kiss, or a quick, encouraging smile when apprehending a lingering study of her eyes or a stolen glance at her cleavage. Were someone to call her little deceptions demeaning, she would ask, "Of whom?" She could keep her priorities straight. You'd never catch her pining for a handsome face or capitulating to oblivious desire at the expense of her professional discretion. Boys are boys. They demean themselves, if it can be called demeaning to behave as nature intended them to. It's a wonder, she often thought, that women had yet to control all professions that didn't require masculine strength. Nature had given them more advantages as competitors.

Cal and Maddy were intent on dissolving their attachment and prepared only for the other to grieve as they arranged their farewell. In Cal's living room, a fire was lit to dispel the gloom of hastening winter. Two bottles of the best wine Cal possessed were consumed too quickly for its quality to be finely appreciated. Their resignation to necessity brought with it an emotional calm they had never before experienced in each other's company, and an intimation of the privileged familiarity of a long-devoted couple. Neither wished to hurry their appreciation of such unexpected and luxurious contentment, suspecting that many years might pass before they experienced it again.

The next day, morning arrived late, the sunrise curtained behind the uninterrupted gray of the November sky, forbidden to intrude on their blissful sleep. Regan was the first to awake. Nearly ten thirty by his watch, and Maddy was still beside him, charmingly innocent in repose.

He had to catch a noon flight to Chicago. No, that was wrong. He didn't *have* to catch it. He was booked on it and was expected to be back in Chicago by one this afternoon. But that was a small matter, easily changed with little explanation. A reference to unspecified personal business would suffice. He could take the last flight tonight or maybe the earliest one tomorrow morning, although he would miss the Monday morning staff meeting. That, too, wasn't much of an inconvenience. It was Sunday. The holiday season was approaching. He was entitled to a little unscheduled relaxation.

The night had so pleasantly progressed to a different conclusion than either of them had intended that they had both thought it cruel to interrupt it with discussion of the impracticality of their relationship. Unnecessary, too. They weren't exactly in dire straits, Cal thought. How urgent was this, really?

They should probably discuss it today, but that might feel a little awkward. *Just play it by ear,* Regan instructed himself. *Don't rush it.* He was careful not to disturb her as he got up to make coffee. He wanted to have a cup ready to bring her when she awoke. As he spooned the last scoop into the filter, he suddenly remembered saying or, more accurately, grunting words in the throes of last night's passion that he had used very sparingly in his adult life. That really could make things awkward. No need to bring it up, was there? If she even remembered it, she would probably be no more willing to explore its intended connotation than he was. Or would she? No, she wouldn't. They'd both be uncomfortable in such a loaded conversation and impatient with the hesitation and obliqueness it would occasion. She might make a joke of it. She could be indelicate that way. God, he hoped not, even if he didn't want to admit that she could wound him.

How had the words escaped? Just exuberant bliss, he supposed, an expression of fleeting pleasure, not really a binding declaration. Funny, though, he had never impulsively uttered them before. On a few forgettable occasions, they had been required by partners who became petulant and regretful when their sexual generosity hadn't coaxed them out of him. That had obviously not been a concern with Maddy Cohan.

Forget it, he told himself again. *Just let the day be what it wants to be.* He got back in bed, and as he began to relax, she woke up and stretched herself, emitting a girlish squeal in the process, before turning on her side to nuzzle him. "I made you coffee," he announced.

"Hmm," she replied, still nuzzling. "How domestic. Can we stay in bed awhile?"

"Yes, we can. It's Sunday."

"No plans, Mr. Regan? No meetings? No plane to catch?"

"Tomorrow."

"Well, okay, then. Wanna make a fire? It looks cold outside."

"Sure."

"Then come back here. I've got plans for you."

CHAPTER 8

He couldn't trust them. Their brisk, detached manner and practiced ambiguity offended him. They hardly bothered to conceal their impatience. They didn't respect him. He had made sure her doctor and every nurse on every shift knew who he was: Walter Lafontaine, man of means, attorney and friend of the president. "I wrote my private cell number on the back," he told them as he handed out his business cards, so they would know he hadn't made up that stuff about being a senior advisor to the president's reelection campaign, and was so much in demand that he needed more than one cell phone. "Call me anytime, okay? If there's any change, good or bad, I want to know. Nothing's more important to me than that woman. The president understands that."

They never needed to call him. He was there every day. They had to chase him out at night. The nurses had been patient with him in the beginning; touched by his devotion to Geraldine even though he could be a little overbearing at times. But they had soon tired of his harassment. He had read up on the disease and pestered them with worried speculation about every change in her condition, real or imagined.

His behavior embarrassed Geraldine. She didn't want him bothering the nurses or the doctor, telling them their business like he did. "Leave them be, Walter," she urged him. "I'm not the only sick woman in this hospital."

"That's right, Mama, you're not," he replied. "But you're the only sick woman in here who's my mother. And I don't want them taking their sweet time getting you better. I don't want them forgetting you got a lawyer in the family who's gonna keep 'em on their toes."

Geraldine knew it wasn't necessary to keep them on their toes. What could be done for her was being done. She had been diagnosed with myelodysplastic syndrome, MDS, a hematological condition. Her bone marrow wasn't producing enough red blood cells.

Her treatment had begun three weeks ago, following a blood transfusion (the blood supplied by Walter), and Geraldine had withstood its immediate side effects, mostly nausea and muscle pain, as well as could be expected. It was too early in the therapy, which would continue for six months, to take much comfort from her initial resilience to its toxicity. But Dr. Ketchum was satisfied there was no indication yet of the worst possible side effects: damage to the heart and central nervous system.

Yet Walter had to struggle to keep up his normally cheerful confidence, so heavily did he feel the responsibility for urging her to risk the aggressive treatment. He was comforting, even lighthearted as he held the bedpan while Geraldine vomited, and when he rubbed her neck and legs to relieve their deep, persistent pain, smiling and making jokes to lessen her embarrassment. But when she slept, and there was nothing for him to do, he couldn't suppress the creeping dread that he had caused his mother's suffering. His only defense was to badger the nurses and the doctor and find fault with their care for her.

Tormenting him as well was the realization that no one seemed to mind his absence from the campaign. Nor, for that matter, had his mother's illness elicited his colleagues' interest beyond the expected expressions of sympathy. "Take all the time you need, Walter," Cal Regan had told him. "We'll manage without you until she's better." Walter had hinted to Regan that a call from the president would certainly lift her spirits. But no call had yet come.

Long before Geraldine's diagnosis, Walter had been embarrassed by the campaign's continued disregard of his services. He had again been made a deputy to the political director, and was given no more real authority than he had possessed in the last campaign. He was included in senior staff meetings but excluded from the smaller, daily conferences with Regan and his top deputies, where important questions were debated and decisions were made, and he had never been asked to join the calls with Washington, where Samuelson dictated strategy. He was given tasks that should have been handled by the political director's personal assistant: setting up meetings with the regional political directors; issuing directives to the field he had played no part in deciding; responding to minor complaints from grassroots organizers who were worried Chicago wasn't paying sufficient attention to their concerns.

Anyone could have done his job, and the recognition of his dispensability distressed him and convinced him the "Washington professionals," the self-important hired guns who had taken charge of O's campaigns, would never respect those who had been with him from the beginning.

Regan would have been surprised to know Walter resented him. He believed he had been unfailingly courteous to the legacy staffer, for whom the president, according to Samuelson, had a soft spot. He had told Curtis, the new political director, to keep him busy and make him feel "part of the team," and had himself pretended to welcome Walter's frequent, unscheduled visits to his office. He had listened patiently to Walter's ill-conceived and enthusiastic suggestions about where his skills could be put to some better use. He had, at Walter's urging, told Lowe to include him in a couple of meetings where gaps in their opposition research were discussed, but to make clear Walter understood the invitation didn't confer any specific responsibility to remedy the deficiency. He had even talked to the press office about starting to prep Walter to do the occasional afternoon cable or local TV interview, spots they typically filled with B-list surrogates and young D.C. political consultants no one had ever heard of. He had just told his assistant to contact the White House Office of Presidential Correspondence to have a get-well note for Walter's mother signed by the president. What more could he be expected to do to keep happy and occupied a former errand boy for whom the president felt sorry? He was the campaign manager, and a little busy to be concerned with a minor personnel matter.

Walter was determined not to be as trusting as he had been in the last campaign, and he saw these offers for what they were: small gestures intended to placate him. "They think I'm nobody," he told himself, "except that the president likes me."

0

During the long hours spent at his mother's bedside, frustration turned to anguish. He would never be valued, never trusted, never noticed as long as he was dependent on the goodwill of people who thought they had invented O, who believed they were the ones who had first glimpsed his potential and rescued him from the amateurs. He did not know what he could do about it. He wasn't sure O hadn't come to see things the same way. "There's not one of them who cares if I come or go," he despaired.

Seeking to regain his balance, he vowed, "Well, I'll do it alone, then, and they can just sit back and watch." And then he would look at his dozing mother, wasting away before him, and feel himself slipping back into despondency. He had never felt the world could defeat him until now. Not many who had grown up where he had, in the squalor and hopelessness of Englewood, could say that. And it was because of the woman who had made him feel every day of his life that he was special, and wouldn't be imprisoned by the pitiless gravity of the lost world into which he had been born. Now he could be losing her, too.

"Hope can survive without others believing in you," he had heard O tell a roomful of Englewood mothers. "But not if you don't believe in yourself." Walter wasn't sure he believed that anymore. How could he have believed in himself if others hadn't? If Geraldine hadn't encouraged him to? If O hadn't noticed him? How would he believe in himself now, if he had lost them both? Who isn't forlorn who has only dead memories to encourage him? The past proves nothing in this world. There's nothing to believe in that lasts. The sun doesn't know you when it rises, gives you the day to get its attention, and forgets you when it sets. You can only try to fool it before it makes a fool of you.

"I need to go take care of a couple of things," Walter informed Geraldine. "Try to sleep some more, Mama. I'll be back before they bring your dinner." He drove to a bar near his apartment and ordered the first of several drinks. It occurred to him others would think he was sulking. *Drowning my sorrows, they'd probably say. Maybe I am. Maybe I'm just another drunk nobody today. But they don't know who I'll be tomorrow. They won't see me coming.*

Fortified by drink and resentment, Walter considered the opportunities available to a man who had given up on his past. Campaigns spend a lot of time trying to set expectations they know they can exceed. Walter was already there. Nobody expected anything from him. It wouldn't be hard to surprise them. And whatever he did, he would do it for himself. He was beholden to no one. Not O, not anyone. The president would benefit from it, of course. He couldn't expect any reward from O or Samuelson or anyone else. But that, too, was fine with Walter. He'd make sure the whole world knew what he had done. "I'll be hard to forget," he promised himself.

Geraldine opened her eyes to find Walter sitting in a chair in the corner of the room, his mouth slightly open, and staring vacantly out the window. He looked tired. She said nothing and pretended to be still asleep so she could observe him for a few moments without his knowledge. It was strange to see her son appear idle. He had always been so full of nervous energy that he could never sit still. In church, he was always the first to jump to his feet and shout an "Amen, brother," not because the spirit had moved him, she suspected, but because he was eager to break the monotony. He had to be doing something every minute, and if he wasn't, he was talking about doing something. He had a habit of bouncing his leg up and down while he sat listening to others talk as if he was struggling not to speak out of turn. She used to worry his impatience would get him into trouble. And he had got up to mischief now and then because he couldn't contain his excitement. But mostly he had used all that energy to hustle and scheme his way out of Englewood, to make something of himself, and she was proud and relieved he had.

In the morning, at Geraldine's insistence, he went home to shower and change before making an appearance at the campaign. He would put in a few hours, although he doubted there was work waiting for him that would take more than an hour to see to. He wouldn't initiate any of the schemes he had been turning over in his mind. He wasn't sure he still had those intentions, or any intentions at all.

He had been at his desk for less than half an hour when Cal Regan stuck his head in the door and asked him if his mother was feeling better. *Goddamn, that guy is irritating,* Walter reflected. *Feeling better? No, she's not feeling better. She doesn't have a cold, goddammit.* But he kept his irritation to himself. "She's holding up okay," he answered.

"Glad to hear it." Regan smiled at him. "How long will you be here today?"

"A couple of hours. I have to get back to the hospital this afternoon."

"Well, good. You know you can take as much time as you need, Walter. We can manage awhile without you."

"I know. Thanks."

"Stop by my office before you go, will you? I have something for you."

Walter was waiting for the elevator to arrive when he remembered Regan's instruction.

"There you are. The president asked me to give this to you," Regan explained as he handed him an envelope he had retrieved from a stack of papers on his desk. "For your mom."

So there wouldn't be a call. Just a get-well note some intern had produced and signed by autopen. Walter took the envelope, thanked him, and turned to leave.

"Hang on, Walter." Regan pointed at a chair and told him, "Sit down a minute, if you can.

"You know we've still got a few months before things start getting crazy around here, and we're about seventy, seventy-five percent staffed up already. So there's no reason for you to worry. It's probably the best time to have a family emergency—not that you can schedule these things, of course. But we understand your situation, and I'm sure the president wants us to make sure you have all the time, and anything else you need. So, if there is anything else we can do, just ask. And when you can come back full-time, let's get together to discuss your situation here. I want to make sure we're making the best use of you. Give that some thought, will you, and we'll talk again."

Walter supposed Regan had only been trying to be considerate. Maybe being irritating was just natural to him. Things hadn't gone so far that he felt his very presence at the campaign bothered people. He wasn't disliked, he knew that. They just didn't respect him. His mother's chemotherapy would last another five months, and if she survived it, and they let her go home, she would still be in need of care. He could spend all his time with her and be drawing a paycheck whether he earned it or not. Maybe it's one of those blessings in disguise, he thought.

On the elevator, he took the envelope with the presidential seal from his jacket pocket and read the note it contained. It had been handwritten by the president. A few short sentences offering the president's and First Lady's best wishes and encouragement. The last sentence read: *You let me know if Walter isn't taking good care of you, and I'll make sure he does.*

Well, at least that's something, Walter thought.

January 2012

★ CHAPTER 9 ★

At five o'clock eastern standard time, several calls were placed to a veteran Associated Press reporter. He took Mick Lowe's first. "We're not quite done weighing them," the reporter cautioned, "but it looks to be bigger than the last wave. He'll probably get over fifty. Right now, we have him at fifty-four."

Lowe's mordant wit made him a favorite of campaign reporters, and the reporter who had just given him the unwelcome though not unexpected news of Tom Morrison's New Hampshire triumph waited to be amused by his response. "Well, gosh, isn't that better than a kick in the head," Lowe said, borrowing one of the victorious Republican's much-mocked G-rated expressions. "I gotta go share the good news," he said before hanging up.

Exit polls often overstate the margins, but they could have been off by ten points, and Tom Morrison's victory in a crowded New Hampshire primary would still be hailed as a landslide. Morrison had been expected to win, but an outright majority was hard to come by in a seven-man field. In the metaphor of the moment, the already high-flying Morrison campaign was now burning rocket fuel.

More surprising than the size of his New Hampshire win had been the comfortable plurality he had won the week before in the Iowa caucuses. No one could remember the last time a Republican candidate in a competitive nomination contest had won both Iowa and New Hampshire. Iowa had appeared to all observers to be the best opportunity for Morrison's rivals to trip him up and stretch out the race. But he had managed to allay the concerns of social conservatives by doing nothing to damage his reputation as a model of personal rectitude, and was the candidate who had the best chance of beating the incumbent, whom they fervently wished would suffer a humiliating defeat in November.

New Hampshire voters had been so enamored of Morrison that they had declined, for the first time in decades, to overturn Iowa's verdict. When Morrison took the stage that night to make his brief victory speech, the image he presented to the nation shimmered with an aura of invincibility his campaign aides would modestly dispute on the record but avidly promote on background to every reporter within earshot.

Tomorrow, the first of Morrison's Republican opponents would end their campaigns and endorse him, hoping the all but declared nominee would appreciate his early concession to the inevitable and remember it as one of his many estimable qualifications when he got around to choosing a running mate. A few would hang on through the Michigan and South Carolina primaries because they assessed their chances of joining Morrison's ticket as negligible and were willing to risk further embarrassment for the slender hope that some unexpected calamity might suddenly befall Tom Terrific. After those primaries, their campaigns would be broke, and they would reluctantly and temporarily relinquish their ambitions, and privately pray for O's reelection.

The AP reporter provided the same information, along with his congratulations, to his second caller, the Morrison campaign's communications director, who received the news while standing in the candidate's hotel suite, where senior staff and a select group of the candidate's friends and family had gathered to celebrate the results. He passed the numbers on to Sandy Stilwell, the campaign manager, to give to Morrison, who was rehearsing his speech in one of the suite's bedrooms.

The Morrison campaign was Sandy Stilwell's third "presidential." He had run campaigns in 2000 and 2008 for candidates who had dropped out after failing to finish in first or second place in Iowa or New Hampshire. Many political consultants, having once experienced the excitement of working in a presidential campaign, acquired a lifelong obsession with it, and every cycle scoured the field for a candidate who would take them on and give them another shot at finally working for the winner. Stilwell was not one of them. After the 2008 loss, he assumed he was finished in presidential politics and wasn't upset by it. He was happily married, the father of four children, three of whom had begun their own careers and the youngest in his junior year of college; he had reached the point where he recognized that while he might not have ascended to the heights he had once hoped to, he had lived a prosperous, eventful, and mostly satisfying life. Unlike most of his peers, he had interests that had become more enjoyable than his work, and he didn't dread the thought of having enough time to pursue them more avidly.

He and his wife had a summer home in the Adirondacks, where in the brief vacations his career permitted him he indulged his admitted fondness for fly-fishing, and for the recreation few people outside his family knew he enjoyed: bird-watching. He had not planned to retire abruptly but to begin a gradual departure from politics over ten years: working for one or two candidates a cycle in an advisory capacity rather than a managerial one; spending more of his time on a few private-sector accounts; charging smaller retainers and taking on fewer responsibilities; and enjoying more than one uninterrupted week a summer waiting happily, with binoculars in hand, to hear the thrilling melody of the bashful Bicknell's thrush.

He was fifty-nine but looked older. Balding, round-shouldered, with a delicate, almost shuffling walk that suggested the careful exertions of an arthritis sufferer, he had the discernment to know the exciting part of his life was long past, and the wisdom not to resent it. He expected the 2012 presidential race would engage his professional interest, but he was content to remain a spectator. Were he asked for advice by colleagues working for the candidates, he would give it freely but not preferentially. He didn't have a favorite in the race.

He had not sought a meeting with Tom Morrison. Morrison had reached out to him. They had met three times when Morrison was looking for a campaign manager. Stilwell informed him in the first meeting that he wasn't interested in the job but was willing to offer his thoughts about the suitability of other prospects.

Their conversations, however, encompassed subjects other than staffing. Stilwell was impressed by Morrison's self-discipline and strategic mind, qualities common in military officers but which the few other candidates with military backgrounds he had known had not successfully adapted to the idiosyncrasies of political campaigns. Morrison admired Stilwell's seasoned intelligence, natural reserve, and his deliberative consideration of Morrison's opinions. Most of all, he appreciated Stilwell for not patronizing him, a grating weakness Morrison thought common among political consultants. Stilwell, he believed, had the qualities of an exceptional executive officer, someone who would offer sound advice on strategy and tactics but leave major decisions to the candidate and make certain they were executed competently. He would know who the boss was and not resent it.

In their third meeting, Stilwell had advised against choosing another consultant who had been recommended for the position. "I don't think he's the guy you're looking for," he advised. "He's aggressive, smart, a good conceptual thinker. But he can be a little impulsive and reactive. And he's not much of a manager. He likes to be on TV too much. You'd need an awfully good deputy for him if you picked him, and you shouldn't take anybody he suggested."

Morrison nodded in agreement. "No, you're probably right. He's not who I'm looking for. You're who I'm looking for."

Stilwell responded to the flattering declaration graciously and politely rebuffed it. "I'm too old for it, General, and too conventional. The game's passed me by. Too many new tricks in campaigns these days for an old dog to learn."

"Then I'm too old for it myself," Morrison countered. "You have experience, judgment, integrity, and self-respect. That's what I'm looking for. So do me a favor, think about it, talk it over with your wife, and ask yourself two questions: Should Tom Morrison be in the White House? And can anyone help him get there better than I can? If you answer yes to the first and no to the second, then you have a duty to your country to change your mind."

Now Sandy Stilwell stood in a crowded room looking at a page of hastily scrawled numbers that informed him he was working for the

Republican nominee, and quite possibly the next president. He noticed Alex Morrison leaning against the wall outside the candidate's bedroom and decided to let him deliver the news to his father. As Stilwell shared the news with him, the boy bounced on the balls of his feet and excitedly grabbed from Stilwell's hand the scrap of paper with the exit poll numbers. "How about that," he said as he read the numbers, adding for emphasis, "This thing is over!"

"Not quite," Stilwell cautioned. "But it's looking very good. Your dad is on his way to being the nominee. Now all we have to do is beat an incumbent president with a lot of money, talent, experience, and the powers of the federal government at his disposal. That won't be easy, Alex. But your dad is the right man for the job. Why don't you go give him the news with our congratulations."

The ecstatic Alex showed his father the numbers and embraced him. Morrison was touched by his son's excitement and the rare display of filial affection. He felt tears beginning to well and pressed his fingers to the corners of his eyes to avoid embarrassment.

He had expected the result the exit polls were predicting, and his mind had already turned to the immensity of the task still before him. He was not a man who bubbled with excitement when things went right for him. He told aides who had expected him to be euphoric after the Iowa win that he wasn't "the type who dances in the end zone after one touchdown in the first quarter of the game."

The near elation he felt this night wasn't in reaction to the size of his New Hampshire victory, but to the welcome change the campaign had seemed to work in Alex's personality. He and Margaret had been right to think it would. There wasn't a question in his mind that Alex could handle the responsibilities required of his personal aide. He had mentioned to Stilwell that the young man who currently served in that capacity should be promoted in the summer and Alex would replace him. For a father to work in concert with his son for a possibly historic cause was to Morrison's mind the finest gift a man could receive.

His campaign would have to come to grips with the new realities that awaited them. He had never run for president before. But he had made a careful study of the campaigns of previous nominees, Democrats and Republicans alike. He read press stories chronicling their daily ups and downs. He read a half dozen campaign books, which he had expected to read like after-action reports but which proved to be gossipy insider accounts that were mostly the collected grievances, conceits, score settling, blame shifting, and credit taking of campaign staffers, which he found distasteful, to say the least. But they were useful because they showed patterns of incompetence that were predictable even if the circumstances that caused them were not.

He noticed that every nominee's campaign, the losers as well as the winners, appeared at one time or another taken aback by the greater volatility of a general election. The enhanced scrutiny by reporters, who were determined to find or manufacture news every day, could seize on the most trivial occurrence—a meaningless slip of the tongue, a misinterpreted observation, a minor memory lapse—to disrupt the campaigns' plans and force their messaging to become defensive and disordered. Accustomed to the steadier rhythms of the primary season, campaigns could become disoriented by the accelerated pace of the general election. Decisions were rarely the product of considered judgment but merely the best guess a campaign could make on the spot. Keeping the initiative at all times was beyond the ability of the best-run campaigns. All were forced occasionally by circumstances beyond their control to be reactive and improvisational, and to rely on luck. The winning campaigns were those that steadied themselves the quickest after being knocked off stride by a contingency they didn't see coming, the ones that had the discipline to go back to the plan after they had lost a round.

Campaigns that experienced those moments during the primaries were quicker to recover from them during the general election. The press had praised Morrison's campaign for its discipline and message control. But Morrison knew they had yet to be really tested. There hadn't been a single moment of crisis during the primaries to cause them to second-guess themselves, and he knew this would put them at a disadvantage against an incumbent who had experienced many such moments and wasn't likely to have forgotten them.

He recognized, too, that their first test would come soon, while they were preoccupied with the organizational distractions imposed on the apparent nominee's campaign: negotiating his former rivals' terms of surrender; absorbing their donors and staff; tripling the size of headquarters staff; building state organizations, many of them almost from scratch; beginning to take command of the national party's operation; planning budgets and ad campaigns and fund-raising; and many other new responsibilities, all of which would have to be executed too hastily for the comfort of a thorough military planner like Morrison.

The Morrison campaign had been careful with its expenditures, and because they had effectively won the nomination so early, they had more money than expected for the initiation of the general election campaign. Nevertheless, their cash on hand was slightly more than a quarter of the money the president's campaign was sitting on, and the Democratic Party had outraised the Republicans by two to one. They would catch up eventually, but no one had any doubt the O campaign would make make maximum use of their initial advantage.

They assumed the onslaught wouldn't begin until the spring, and certainly not before the last of the losing Republican campaigns had formally surrendered. Morrison's campaign planned to buy in April as much radio and TV advertising time in several battleground states as they could afford to counter the coming attack. The timing would prove to be the first mistaken assumption of their campaign.

The president's campaign hadn't any intention of observing customs that had no tactical or strategic value. The longer they waited to exploit their advantage, the less of an advantage it would be. They had an immense pile of money now, and it was easily replenished. They would run two weeks of positive ads touting the president's accomplishments as a defense against criticism they were afraid to run on O's record. Then they would hit Morrison hard to drain his momentum and test him at a moment of vulnerability.

The press would squawk a little. Editorial writers would tsk-tsk the unseemliness of their quick resort to negative advertising. Reporters would gasp when they discovered the expense and scope of the first wave of ads. The president and his advisors would ignore their dismay. So, they believed, would voters.

They expected the press, once it recovered from its initial bout of the vapors, to be awed again by the ruthless professionalism of the president's campaign and begin to suspect his opponent was overmatched. The sentiment would creep into the daily coverage and become the shared wisdom of the gabbers on cable TV. And the notion that General Morrison was a capable military officer who proved to be a hapless politician would begin to break through to the voters.

"Give me one good reason why we shouldn't," Regan had challenged colleagues during a senior staff discussion two months ago. No one offered him one. It wouldn't have mattered if someone had. The White House had already approved the decision, and the buy had already been made.

"Holy shit" were the first words spoken by Frank Carelly, the head of the Morrison campaign's media team, when he learned of the size and timing of Chicago's planned ad buy in just one state, Colorado. He hung up immediately, called the media buyer for his agency and two other members of the Morrison ad team, and instructed them to find out where else the O campaign had bought time. He did the same, calling friends, acquaintances, and people who owed him a favor at dozens of local television stations in other battleground states. Within an hour, he had a rough idea of the scale of the buy.

It would commence six days after the New Hampshire primary and would be not much smaller in scale than the advertising campaigns conducted in the last two months of a general election. The buy was so extensive, there was very little good time still available for the Morrison campaign to purchase for the hastily produced and untested spots they would scramble to put up in response. After the first two weeks, only a single ad in the entire barrage would be positive, a thirty-second spot during the Super Bowl broadcast featuring the president wishing good luck to both teams and their fans.

It was scheduled to last six weeks, and the O campaign had plans to buy another two weeks if the first wave didn't inflict as much damage as expected. It would cost tens of millions of dollars.

The O campaign had tested every spot it intended to air, rewritten them, and tested them again. Morrison would be damaged severely, and the first test of his ability as a presidential nominee, and possibly the outcome of the race, would be decided by how well he recovered, if he recovered at all.

All the president's advisors would have preferred to have faced any one of the other Republican candidates. And O could still be sensitive to criticism he hadn't lived up to his image as the antidote to relentless partisanship. His experiences as president, however, had taught him there was little he could do to tame the thoroughly polarized political culture, which everyone involved—Congress, interest groups, the media—preferred remain that way. He had learned to live with the disappointment and play the game by his own rules.

His first rule, as the avid basketball fan often reminded his advisors, was "Take the shot the defense gives you. Shoot when they sag; cut when they overplay." They all believed that Morrison, in his first moments as the presumptive nominee, wouldn't be ready to present any defense at all, and they could take any shot they wanted.

After Sandy Stilwell had been told of the O campaign's advertising blitz by Carelly, who had seemed traumatized by the discovery, he called an emergency meeting of senior campaign aides to discuss "the shit storm coming our way" and how to respond to it. He had wanted to have a plan with at least three decision options prepared for Morrison before informing him of the O campaign's major offensive. Stilwell had never served in the armed forces, but he liked to use military metaphors whenever appropriate in consideration of his candidate's background.

He had already informed Morrison, who had taken a rare day off from campaigning following his New Hampshire victory, that something had come up, which he wanted to discuss with him tomorrow, "when I have a better idea what it is, and what we should do about it." Morrison was scheduled to fly to Michigan the next day, and Stilwell would meet him there. But ten minutes into the senior staff meeting, the candidate called to say he would be joining them.

He asked no questions as Carelly described what they knew. "It's huge and unheard of, a buy like this when our side still has contested primaries," the still-staggered media consultant exclaimed. "Every major market in every battleground state, a lot in prime time, national cable, niche markets, and a Super Bowl spot. I'd say it's almost half as big as a late October buy. On the bright side, I guess you can take it as a compliment. They think you're going to be tough to beat. If we push the idea, the press might even think it's kind of panicky on their part."

"That will be hard to sell," Stilwell countered. "More likely they'll see it as the privilege of a campaign with a mountain of cash to spend and a reputation for leaving nothing to chance. It's the same thing Clinton did to Dole, only bigger and earlier. They started in March, and by June, Dole was impersonating a corpse."

"Will all their ads be attacks?" Morrison asked Stilwell.

"We only know they're going up, we don't know their message," Stilwell answered. "My guess is they'll run some positives for a while, and then go mostly negative. It's not the image O likes to present, and he might be sensitive to criticism that he's gotten pretty cynical. But whether he likes it or not, O is already polarizing. He knows he's not going to win Republican votes like he did the last time. He's not going to win right-leaning independents. Like most incumbents, he's facing an election that's a referendum on him. They're probably not feeling too good about that right now. So they'll want to get us into the act. Make this a little less about them, and more about you."

Morrison had a habit, unnerving to some of his aides, of listening to them without seeming to be affected by what he was learning. "Jesus, you'd think we were just giving him the weather report," Carelly would later remark to Stilwell.

When they had finished briefing him on their discovery, Stilwell led a discussion of what they could do to counter it. Not much, was the unspoken consensus, and what they could do would have to be done by the candidate in his speeches and interviews. "We don't have the money yet to come close to matching it," Stilwell acknowledged. "We'll do what we can, where we can. We can go up in a few states with decent-size buys, but that's about it. We still have at least a couple of primaries to go, and we can use them to sharpen your message. Go right after him now. He's taken the country in the wrong direction. His economic policies have failed. Americans can't afford another four years of his mistakes."

Morrison excused himself as his aides discussed a general narrative for their response that could encompass several lines of attack, and he asked Stilwell to come to his home that evening and brief him on the plan.

"Well?" asked Margaret as her husband walked into the kitchen, where she and their eldest daughter, Eleanor, were waiting for him.

"The president has decided to speed things up a bit. He's going to start advertising before the primaries are over, and Sandy thinks it will be pretty negative."

"And what do they recommend we do about it?" she asked.

"They're trying to figure that out now. Sandy's dropping by later to fill me in. I'm not sure they're heading in the right direction, but I thought I'd leave them to work up something on their own. We'll see what they come up with. But I think this might be a mistake by the president's campaign, an overreaction I wouldn't have expected from them. I don't know that we need to get too worked up over it."

Stilwell arrived around seven that evening, while the Morrisons were eating dinner. He declined an invitation to join them. His wife had dinner waiting for him, he explained.

"Take a seat anyway, Sandy," Morrison instructed. "We can go over this now. I won't keep you long."

A subdued Stilwell proceeded to briefly summarize the campaign's planned response as the candidate, his wife, and their three children signaled their polite attentiveness with nods and smiles. The campaign had enough money to run "a credible ad campaign in four of the biggest battleground states," he informed them. "Ohio, Florida, Missouri, and Colorado. We can buy some national cable as well."

He had already instructed the media team to produce the spots and buy time on the same day the O campaign went up with theirs. The buy wouldn't be anywhere near as extensive as the other side's, but it would show the press they hadn't been caught completely by surprise or, at least, hadn't been rattled and indecisive in response.

The message Morrison's advisors had spent the afternoon crafting for him was an obvious one. Polls still showed the number of voters who felt the nation was headed in the wrong direction to be above fifty percent. "Blaming administration policies for the country's decline is the most productive line of attack," Stilwell recommended. "And we think you should concentrate most of your fire in the beginning on deficit spending and tax increases." The administration's health care and energy policies would follow. "We'll get some talking points to you in the morning," Stilwell promised, "and you should start making the argument right away."

When Stilwell had finished, Morrison allowed a little time to pass before responding, as he idly brushed a few crumbs from the tablecloth into the palm of his hand.

"I can see why that would make sense, Sandy," he admitted, nodding as he spoke. "But I wonder if we're not rushing too much into the kind of back-and-forth on this issue and that issue that voters hear all the time, and might tune out after a while."

Where is he going with this? Stilwell wondered, before interrupting him.

"Sir, you're about to be the target of just such an attack, a very large and sustained attack. They don't have anything to attack your character with. They can't make an experience argument. So they'll come after you issue by issue to create the impression that they and not you are on the side of the middle class. For now, we are limited in what we can do in response. And we think—all of us think—the best way to make sure the charges don't stick, given our current financial disadvantage, is to go on offense. Yes, voters are used to it, and they may well tune it out. But that's a good outcome for us. The other side will have spent a lot of money and not moved the ball downfield very far."

Morrison smiled at his wife to acknowledge that the argument Stilwell had made was one they had both expected to hear from him. As if on cue, she excused herself and the children.

There was a brief clatter of dishes being cleared, as Morrison reached for a three-quarters full bottle of wine and offered Stilwell a glass before pouring a small measure into his own. "Have a glass of wine, Sandy. I just have a few more questions, and then we'll let you get home to your family." Stilwell started to pick up where he had left off, but Morrison held a hand up to interrupt him.

"Sandy, what do you think of the president?"

"Excuse me?"

"What do you think of the president personally? What kind of man do you think he is?"

"Well, General, that's not a question I ask myself very often. Professionally, I have an opinion on what kind of candidate he is. I tend to leave character judgments about an opponent to others. In my opinion, he's a shrewd, disciplined, and talented candidate, with a shrewd, disciplined, and talented campaign."

"Well, he is that," Morrison conceded. "He certainly is that. But you see, I haven't been in this business long enough to break my old habits. And when I was just a voter and not a politician, I always thought I had a sense of the character of the candidates before I decided who to vote for. Now, that character judgment, if you want to call it that, was probably based in my perceptions of how good a campaigner they were. But the point I'm trying to make is that people don't go to the polls to pick the best campaigner for president. They think they're picking the best person even if their impressions of the man are completely shaped by his skills as a campaigner."

"Okay, what kind of man do you think the president is?" an intrigued Stilwell asked.

"That's just it. I'm not sure now. By going on the attack so early, so over the top, he seems to be a different candidate than he was the last time, and a different man. It tells me something has gotten to him and made him act rashly. In the last election, he was a very compelling character. He struck me as being very capable, very competent, and at the same time mostly sincere. He believed in himself. He believed in his talent and he believed he could do politics differently, *and* he could govern differently. That came through to the voters, who were tired of the incompetence of his predecessor and the petty back-and-forth BS of campaigns. They believed him. They believed he had the skills and the character to change things."

"General," Stilwell interrupted, "in the last election, O ran the biggest negative ad campaign against his opponent we've ever seen. And no one, no one in the press, none of the voters who were open to persuasion, held it against him or thought it said anything about his character."

"That may be true. But it didn't seem desperate then or a surprise. And it happened well after the story line for the election had already been set. Voters saw a bright, talented young candidate running a competent and innovative campaign, who said he could give Americans the kind of politics and government they wanted. The ads he ran were overlooked or rationalized as a fair response to attacks against him."

"And why do you think their decision to go after you now won't be perceived the same way, as an example of their professionalism?"

"Because it's the first political thing he's done that will get voters' attention. By political, I mean the first noticeable thing he's done as a candidate for reelection. Up to now, Americans have been judging his executive ability as the head of the government. And they haven't been very happy with the results. They don't think his policies have made anything better and they don't think he's changed Washington."

"Agreed. That's why it makes sense to hit his policies."

"Incidentally, yes. But that's not the big target. It's fine to talk about his policies not working or taking America the wrong way. They'll make the same claims about mine. And people will just assume we're both full of it. It's not our central message. Or it shouldn't be."

"What should it be, then?"

"What the voters have decided is he isn't as competent as they thought he would be. He might not be up to the job. It might be too big for him, despite the qualities they like about him. I do think they still like the guy. But this ad campaign of theirs could be seen as an admission of failure, and now, just like every other politician, he's focused on saving his skin. It's an attempt to make voters forget their worry that the president might be overwhelmed by the office, and start worrying about someone else. And that, Sandy, is what we need to suggest in terms of what I say, and what our ads say."

"That the president isn't who he promised to be?"

"No. He isn't who *we* thought he was."

"That sounds like you're blaming voters for their lack of discernment."

"I said *we,* not *they.* But I take your point. Change *thought* to *hoped."*

"And he isn't who we hoped he'd be, because he's acting like another politician? He's getting down in the mud with the rest of them?"

"Well, yes, but that's an inference, and we can probably let people infer it themselves."

"He's not big enough for the office?"

"Another inference they'll get themselves."

"He's what, then?"

"Incompetent. He's incompetent. People can like you a lot, but they won't hire you as their brain surgeon or accountant or president if they don't think you can do the job better than the next guy. Maybe he wanted to change Washington. Maybe he wanted to fix our problems. Maybe he wanted to run a smarter government. Maybe he wanted to avoid small-ball politics. But he couldn't do it. He's not who we hoped he'd be. He's not as good a president as he was a candidate. And he's given up trying."

Stilwell had spent his adult life scrutinizing the decisions of politicians to divine their strengths and weaknesses, and to develop messages to either beat them or elect them. He marveled at Morrison's intuitive grasp of distinctions that voters feel before they understand, a skill of incalculable value.

"So, how do you think we frame this message, exactly?"

"I'm still tossing that around. Give me some time. Tell the fellows to hold on to the time we bought for the ads but not to produce anything yet. Let's wait for them to start this fight, and for me to react to it along the lines we've talked about. Our ads should say the same thing I do."

"I'm sold," Stilwell declared. "I should get out of your hair now." As Stilwell stood up to leave, he promised Morrison he would place a call that night to Carelly, the campaign's anxious media director, who had first alerted them to the coming O advertising onslaught. "I'll call him off for now, and we'll talk about it more tomorrow."

"Good," Morrison responded. "One last thing, though, about Carelly.

He's a nice fellow, and capable enough, I suppose. But I thought he looked a little rattled today, a little excitable for a leader. I'd like you to find another guy to the lead the team. You don't have to fire him, but put somebody else in charge. Sorry to stick you with it on a Sunday night. But I'd like it sorted out before we start producing the ads."

Stilwell thought about arguing the decision but resisted the impulse.

"I'll take care of it," he promised.

★ CHAPTER 10 ★

"He's not easily provoked," Samuelson allowed. "I didn't expect him to be. But I'm not worried about their response. It's not big enough to have an impact."

The president motioned for his senior advisor to follow him to the patio outside the Oval Office, where in the dark he would smoke his third and last cigarette of the day. "It's not the weight behind his ads that concerns me," he explained after exhaling his first, satisfying drag. "It's how prepared he was for ours. No heat. No overreaction. Levelheaded and smart. He was appealing, just as voters are getting their first good look at him."

"It's too early to know that," Samuelson argued. "Give our spots time to burn in, and we'll see where we are. He won't hold up."

"Avi, he protected his brand pretty well, and I think he might have damaged mine a little."

O had seemed pensive all day, and uninterested in the usual crush and variety of White House business. Samuelson had suspected this was the concern that preoccupied him and was prepared to reassure him that nothing his opponent had said or could say would change the basic premise or the effect of their strategy. Morrison was as outgunned and outnumbered as he would ever be in this race, and it would have been political malpractice had they not exploited their advantages when they could inflict the most damage.

"Look, he's a good candidate," Samuelson calmly conceded. "We never thought he wouldn't be. He reacted as well as he could in the spotlight. But the spotlight won't stay focused on this, the press will move on.

Whatever good he did himself is temporary, and it won't change the fact that he simply doesn't have the resources to seriously counter our attack."

O's slight smile and level gaze gave the impression he had expected that argument and wasn't persuaded by it. "He didn't just perform well in the spotlight. He turned it on us, on me. And he did a pretty good job of making us look bad."

"That's not anything we didn't expect," Samuelson countered. "It's all he can do. We knew going in that the press would think we were playing too rough too early, and maybe we're more worried than they thought we were. We knew we'd go through the 'Gee, he's not the same hopeful, new-politics guy he was the last time.' We knew all that crap would happen, and Morrison would use it to his advantage. And we knew it wouldn't last longer than a week, because nobody in that business has an attention span longer than your average kindergartner. The Office of the President has the power to change the subject anytime we want. That's our greatest advantage, the one that lets us maximize all our other advantages. Jesus Christ, you could get another dog, and the press would forget about this and start begging for bulletins about how it's getting along with your other dog."

O laughed as he stubbed out his cigarette. Ridiculing the frivolousness of the press amused him almost as much as the behavior itself frustrated him. But he wasn't ready to yield the point and wished he hadn't limited himself to just three cigarettes a day. Even on a cold February night, he enjoyed being outside the Oval Office, outside all the stately apartments of the museum that was his home. He felt less burdened and constrained on the White House grounds than he did inside the mansion, where portraits of dead predecessors hung from the walls that had once confined them, warning him there could be no permanent escape from the life of a president, in office or out, alive or dead. He preferred to continue their conversation there, but he couldn't expect Samuelson to shiver in the cold for his pleasure. "Let's go back in, Avi," he wearily suggested.

Seating himself in a chair opposite the sofa where O sat, Samuelson picked up where he had left off. He believed that long before their ads had run their course, the favorable first impression Morrison had made would have been replaced with the one they wanted: a once reputable officer who spent too much of his retirement hanging out with rich people and advocating their interests over the needs of hard-pressed Americans.

The ads themselves were all a variation on that theme: isolating parts of Morrison's record as governor to suggest an excessive sympathy for the wealthy, and a disappointing indifference to the struggles of the middle class. They weren't over the top. Their tone was matter-of-fact, business-like, no ominous music or hammy voice-overs, which O loathed.

On such and such a date, Governor Morrison cut daycare assistance to working mothers, while cutting taxes for the top one percent of earners in his state, with a legislative record citation and a supporting quote from an outraged editorial writer. On another date, he raised the state gas tax and lowered the tax on "yachts and limousines." That kind of thing, a series of them, all starting with a title card that read, "Setting the Record Straight." In some, Morrison was referred to as a "millionaire and former governor," as if the words *millionaire* and *former* were synonyms for *disgraced*. Others acknowledged he had served honorably in uniform, before implicitly suggesting he had cashed in on his service after retirement by citing several cost and schedule overruns for equipment our troops desperately needed and contract disputes between management and labor during his tenure as CEO of Channing-Mills, which resulted in smaller pensions and less generous health care benefits.

Channing-Mills was the type of commercial entity many people have difficulty comprehending. With the vast and diverse scope of its holdings and extensive overseas business—an estimated book value that rivaled the GDP of small countries—it struck some people as less an American business than a stateless one or, perhaps, a state in itself. Such immense and murky enterprises were popularly believed to be run by secretive, powerful, and avaricious executives who had nefarious connections in the CIA and other intelligence agencies with unknown acronyms, who spent a lot of time in foreign countries and did not trouble themselves to adhere to the laws and mores of the country where their headquarters were located. Hollywood was always ready to bankroll cloak-and-dagger movies that played on those suspicions. And while the

O campaign did not overtly suggest in their ads that these fears were well founded, it nonetheless hoped the ads would trigger the paranoia reflex some voters had when it came to large corporations that sold guns and God knows what else to foreigners.

Samuelson did not mention he had been as surprised as O that none of Morrison's ads pushed back on the charges. Nor had Morrison addressed them in detail. His campaign had e-mailed a lengthy document to reporters, putting the incriminating items from his gubernatorial record in the context of larger policies intended to benefit a broader public interest. The tax cut for yachts, for instance, had been intended to increase sales for the state's numerous boat builders.

These facts had been included in most of the press analysis of the O ads, several of which were denounced as distortions by reporters assigned the responsibility for scrutinizing their claims. But the effect of that criticism on swing voters' perceptions of the candidates, if it had any at all, was negligible and soon forgotten.

The Morrison campaign made no rebuttal at all to the attacks on his business record beyond circulating a contemporaneous account in *The Wall Street Journal* explaining the circumstances that had necessitated the renegotiated labor contract. Channing-Mills's legacy costs had risen so rapidly that had they not been reduced, they would have forced the company to shutter plants and lay off several thousand employees. Workers had been compensated for the reduction in their benefits and pensions with shares of the company's stock.

Samuelson had anticipated a more vigorous response. He had expected that a weeklong exchange of recriminations would commence the moment their first attack aired. He understood the O brand would come under assault for being the first to go negative. But he knew, too— and the rest of the senior staff knew, and he was certain O knew—that if left unmolested, Morrison would start the race with the better brand. The unavoidable compromises and conflicts of governing had tarnished the president's reputation as a postpartisan conciliator. Repairing it would be harder to do, and less profitable than destroying Morrison's appeal as a modest military hero come to rescue America from the politicians.

They had to make him a politician, too; get him in a wrestling match and clutch him. "The plan is to bury the hero," Cal Regan had instructed the media team, "and kill the mercenary."

Regan liked the formulation so much that he repeated it the next time he spoke with the president.

"That's a good line," O agreed. "But I better never see it in print."

O had approved the strategy. The doubts he now harbored had nothing to do with the accuracy of the ads. Campaigns couldn't afford to have scruples about garden-variety misrepresentations of an opponent's record. Everyone did it, and Morrison's campaign would be no different. The first rule of politics is "Do unto others before they do unto you." And no need for a troubled conscience, O reasoned, as long as the creative license the ads took with his opponent's record conveyed an essential truth about him. Which is the more dishonest, a false image or the small exaggeration intended to expose it?

However distinguished his military career had been, Morrison was not in uniform now. Americans did not have a choice, as Morrison would have them believe they did, between a politician and an army officer. They had the same choice they always had: between two politicians, a Democrat and a Republican. Morrison had retired from the army. He had quickly made a fortune in business and then entered politics. Once elected to office, he had governed as a Republican. His policies had favored the wealthy over the less advantaged. The gap between the rich and the middle class and poor in his state had widened when he was governor. It was dishonest of Morrison to pretend he was a candidate who wasn't a politician. There's no such creature, however fervently the public might wish there were.

That was the truth O believed their ads exposed. Tom Morrison was a professional Republican politician with conventional Republican positions, and were he elected, his policies would harm the country. And this truth was the reason O must be reelected. He believed America could do better. Morrison liked it the way it used to be. That was the choice the country must make, between a progressive and a reactionary. And their ads had made that plain.

The doubts that now nagged him concerned the shrewdness of Morrison's response to their attack. He hadn't taken the bait. He had calmly redirected the public's attention to the argument he wanted to have. It's what O would have done were he in the same situation. It was what he had done in the last campaign.

O had studied the tape of the first interview Morrison gave after their first attack ad had aired. The anchor for the nationally broadcast morning show opened with a question that perfectly set up Morrison's response.

"Well, General, you seem to have gotten the attention of the president's campaign. Apparently they aren't going to waste any time coming after you. Are you ready for it?"

"Thanks, Matt, I guess I should be flattered. They tell me you have to expect this sort of thing in politics, and you shouldn't take it personally. I understand why the president and his team would do it."

"Okay, you don't take it personally, but *understand*? That seems a little generous, and, forgive me, a little blasé. Don't you think you need to take it seriously?"

"Oh, you can't let yourself get wrapped around the axle every time your opponent exaggerates or fudges the truth a little."

"What do you mean when you say you understand why they did it?"

"Well, that's what they're good at. And when you've sort of fallen down on the job like the White House has, you know, with respect to the things a president is elected to do—turn the economy around, help business create jobs, get the civilian side of the government to operate on a budget with some of the efficiency the military side manages to demonstrate—well, if you're them, you probably want to show off the one thing you're still pretty good at: running a political campaign."

The anchor, who had clearly been unprepared for the response, could only think to ask whether Morrison thought the American people would see it that way.

"I think they will," Morrison responded gently. "They've gotten pretty smart at figuring this stuff out for themselves."

Morrison's performance convinced O they had underestimated him. O expected him to be a disciplined candidate with a compelling life story.

He recognized and understood his public appeal. *Christ, I like him,* he confessed to himself.

Unchanged and left to run their course, the ads would probably blunt Morrison's momentum and the expected rise in his net favorables, as they were intended to do. But they would not improve O's own numbers or begin to repair the damage his image had suffered during his three years in office. On the contrary, they were an admission that the promise with which he had begun his administration, that he could elide the polarities of American politics, had vanished in the clashes and concessions of governing.

Idealism had capitulated again to the meanness of politics. He would have a harder time running again as who he was. So, for the time being, he would have to run on who he wasn't. He wasn't Wall Street's candidate. He wasn't the guy who would cut taxes for the wealthy and cut entitlements for the middle class. He wasn't trying to turn the clock back. He wasn't offering the same hands-off, heartless government that created the disaster he had been elected to clean up. He wasn't Morrison.

This shouldn't have been a surprise to a veteran of Chicago politics, where the transactional nature of governing is considered honest, and politicians pride themselves on their understanding that human nature can stand only so much improvement. But he had believed he could adapt his policies and style to some of Washington's institutions and subvert those that refused to bargain for his favor. He had lost the initiative within a year. He had pressed on too many fronts, had tried to leap too many hurdles at once, in the hope of accelerating the sluggish pace of a city that would not be hurried. Washington had undermined him not by faulting him for his attempts to circumvent some of its customs but for submitting to those he had thought it necessary to excuse. In the bargains made with congressional egos, and the resort to common practices that were necessary to produce budgets and reform health care, to remake energy and education policies and a dozen other initiatives, he had been defined by his tactics and not his purposes.

For all the barking from conservatives about his radicalism, O believed it had been his practicality and not his idealism that had changed the way voters perceived him. Yes, many had come to believe he was too liberal. But they had been receptive to the charge only after becoming convinced by every tale of backroom vote buying and back-scratching that he was not the idealist they had thought he was. *How can you govern a people who could be made to believe a president was too idealistic and too practical?* The question had an easy answer. *You don't. They govern you.*

He had been redefined and left to run for reelection as the figure the voters now took him for: the disappointment, the change who had become the incumbent. There was no choice but to define his opposition as a less attractive alternative: the defender of the privileges of the few at the expense of the hopes of the many. But it grieved him nonetheless to find himself in this situation. He would have to battle for nine miserable months to damage another man's reputation while mostly relying on events to improve his own.

O would refrain for several months from personally engaging in attacks or counterattacks. As soon as he did, he would permanently impair his ability as president to, in Samuelson's words, "change the subject."

O had never before liked to wait on events for support and had trusted his instincts and intelligence and art to seize his opportunities when they were ripe. But he wasn't impetuous and wouldn't rush his shot when a better one would soon be open.

For the time being, he would defend himself by sleight of hand. He would attract more favorable attention by picking easy fights with Republicans in Congress or unpopular interest groups, by commanding the world stage rather than inhabiting a campaign's shabbier venues, and he would wait on the growing economy, finally picking up speed now, to improve the public's opinion of his competence. Then he would engage directly, and the general would discover the real implications of his backhanded compliment that the president was good at running political campaigns.

His fortunes had changed in the last three years, and he was running a reelection campaign he once believed he would not need to run. So be it. One thing hadn't changed. He was still the country's best hope for progress, whether the country knew it or not.

Being president wasn't as satisfying an experience as he had expected it to be, and he doubted any president would have said otherwise. Its intrusions on his privacy were maddening, its demands exhausting, and the powers of the office fewer than popularly assumed. Enduring its frustrations without losing his sense of purpose was an accomplishment more difficult than his critics would ever understand. *Well, fuck them,* he thought. *Let the mouth breathers question my patriotism. My patriotism is more demanding than theirs. I don't use it to inflame people's prejudices. And fuck the professional left, too. Let's see them try to do what I've done. Let them try to make the history I'm making.*

Nine months, nine miserable months, and then he would have another four years, without the worry of another election constraining him, to make the progress he had promised. He wouldn't overload the system as he had done in his first term. But he wouldn't play small ball either. And what he couldn't get from Congress he would accomplish in part by executive order and regulation. It was possible, even likely, that by the end of his second term he would have nominated a majority of the justices to the Supreme Court, and the court's days of defending the interests of corporations and the Republican Party would come to an end. He would withdraw the last brigades from Afghanistan and his budgets wouldn't spare the Pentagon the spending cuts other departments had to suffer.

"We need to find something he won't ignore," he told Samuelson. "Something he can't resist arguing. Something that makes him look like a hypocrite when he takes shots at our record."

"We will," Samuelson assured him. "But he can't continue to ignore the spots we have up now. He'll have to push back on them a lot harder when they burn in. His numbers won't hold up, and he'll have to engage. He won't have a choice."

O gathered up a few papers on his desk to take with him to the residence. He and Samuelson walked together to the portico connecting the mansion to the West Wing, where they parted company.

As he took his second step toward the West Wing parking lot, Samuelson suddenly turned around. He thought he had heard the president say something. But O was still walking toward the mansion. It had probably been the wind. Or a sigh meant for no one in particular.

★ CHAPTER 11 ★

In Chicago, the president's campaign manager was wrapping up his day. He and Lowe had just finished dinner and were hailing cabs to take them home. They had spent much of the evening analyzing Morrison's response.

"What is it about that fucker," Lowe wondered, "that makes you want to slap his face?"

"Probably that grin he always keeps plastered on it," Regan suggested. "You could kick him in the nuts, and he'd probably smile when he said ouch."

"Maybe it's just me, but I think people will know it's bullshit," Lowe declared. "All that 'I understand why the president needs to do this' crap. Who the fuck talks like that? 'Hey, General, the president just called you a cocksucker. Any response?' 'Well, gosh, geez, for goodness' sake, imagine that. I'm sure the president doesn't really mean it.' Who doesn't see that and think, man up, motherfucker?"

Regan didn't share his friend's confidence in the voters' discernment. "If only they were all cynical bastards like you," he reminded him. Like O, Regan had been impressed with Morrison's performance that morning. Americans like to believe their presidents are more levelheaded under pressure than they are. And that's how Morrison had appeared, as if he assumed voters knew the truth was on his side and there wasn't any need to waste their time debating the matter. He had relied on the voters' assumption that politicians always lied about their opponents' records, and he disguised his counterattack as an explanation for why the president had lied about his.

It was an article of faith in Regan and Lowe's profession that campaigns had to run three or four positive ads before polls revealed voters had absorbed their message. It takes only one negative ad to get their attention. Why did campaigns bother to run any positive ads? Every campaign's advertising decisions are complicated by the same paradox. Voters are more receptive to negative ads, and they detest them.

In Regan's first campaign, the lead consultant, a veteran of many campaigns, had taken the time to impress upon the young Regan his insights on the profession. "In campaigns, you don't need a lot of experience to make the right decision," he had told him, "as long as you understand the pathology of voters. They're schizophrenic. They're as gullible as they are skeptical. They believe the worst and hope for the best. They don't trust us. They don't like us. And they rely on us to make up their minds for them."

The best message a campaign could communicate to voters excited one of their appetites and suppressed another. That's why Morrison's response had impressed Regan. It was pitch-perfect in its sensitivity to voters' contradictory impulses. He didn't defend himself from their attacks, he had counterattacked. But the voters couldn't tell he had. They thought he had simply given them a reasonable explanation for why the president was behaving in a way they didn't expect. *Oh, he's trying to distract us from paying attention to the real issues. That makes sense. He is a politician, after all.* O was pretty good at such feints as well.

Negative ads often used humor because voters were more likely to remember them if they were amusing, and less likely to be revolted. But the president's advisors, including Regan, had thought sarcasm, the kind of humor campaigns typically employed in their attacks, was a little beneath his dignity, for now, at least. They had decided on an analytical quality for the ads, using the legislation citations and third-party opinions to suggest an impartial statement of regrettable facts. The ads were less entertaining, but their volume would ensure they were remembered.

In a month they would do another poll. Regan would study the responses to the verbatims, where respondents were invited to describe the candidates in their own words, to gauge how much the spots had defined Morrison, and how much they had changed perceptions of the president. Often when campaigns used a lot of adjectives in their spots the same words would show up in the verbatims. But they hadn't used many adjectives in theirs. They had let the facts, as they interpreted them, suggest certain pejoratives to the voters. Regan wanted to see descriptions like "entitled," "rich," "not what he seems," and "doesn't really care about people like me" show up in Morrison's verbatims.

He expected to see fewer favorable descriptions of the president than their last poll had included. He wouldn't be too concerned if there were fewer references like "means well," "nice," and "fair." Presidents don't need to be seen as nice to win reelection, and such descriptions could be a signal of voters' concern that O might be too softhearted to be president. But he would worry if words like *negative, mean,* and *unfair* appeared frequently in the responses from moderates and independent voters. That would suggest a sea change was occurring among persuadable voters in their perceptions of the president. The likable, confident candidate of hope and change was becoming another brawling, lying politician.

They'd have to reassess if that was the case. They couldn't back off. Let Morrison catch his breath and he'll really take off, Regan believed. But they'd need another approach. Maybe a little softer. Maybe some humor. Or maybe find something bigger to hit him with. Something voters would expect them to be mean about. Something that would make voters mad.

Regan had no evidence to believe their attacks hadn't been modulated carefully enough to avoid inciting that kind of reaction. But he prided himself on being prepared to adjust when things didn't work out as planned. He wouldn't raise the concern yet with the White House. They'd think he was getting jumpy. O's world valued grace under fire and saved the sharpest derision for people whose nerves couldn't survive their first encounter with an unfavorable press. "Stop worrying about Washington," they'd say, and laugh. "Nobody's votes count here." In Washington, opinions changed as quickly as spring became summer. Washington was insular, arrogant, and infamously fickle. A consensus formed one day was undone the next when some celebrated blowhard issued a contrary opinion. "It's a moron bubble," Samuelson would bellow. "It's not Chicago."

Samuelson and other White House aides were not as dismissive of Washington in practice as they liked to protest they were. And neither was Regan. It was an emotional defense mechanism campaign operatives in both parties shared to keep control in their own hands and not in the hands of Washington opinion makers. And it didn't always work.

Regan understood that however flighty it was, a Washington consensus could inform voters' opinions. Some blog masquerading as a news service conjures from the daily detritus of insignificant political events a faux controversy. Cable repeats the story for twenty-four hours. A columnist for one of the major papers writes of its larger implications for the health of the republic. The broadcast networks pick up the ball, and with a single arched eyebrow an anchor invests it with more portentous meaning. Comedy writers mock it as an authoritative account of a politician's ineptitude, hypocrisy, or immorality. And the musing of a handful of gossipy Washington pedants becomes the informed opinion of millions of voters.

"You can't swim up a waterfall," Regan remarked whenever a campaign he was involved in tried to resist the narrative Washington had imposed on it, an old saw he had picked up from the consultant who had mentored him on his first campaign. He, Lowe, and Phelps, the campaign's communications director, would try to keep reporters focused on the campaign's preparedness for the general election and the confident execution of their strategy. Reporters could never resist a juggernaut story or fail to be impressed by any large enterprise that worked with a ruthless efficiency unknown in their profession.

News organizations commissioned their own polls, however. Were they to reveal the ads hadn't done as much damage to Morrison as expected, the narrative they had tried to divert would come cascading down on their heads. Critics would argue that going negative early, on such an unprecedented scale, had harmed the president's reputation. Morrison would have proved himself a confident and capable candidate, whose appeal to the voters had withstood a savage assault by a juggernaut that no longer looked like one.

Regan did not expect this to happen. He thought it unlikely Morrison could talk his way clear of the ceaseless barrage of negative messages, and the polls would only show the electorate had been quickly polarized: Republican voters firmly supportive of their candidate and outraged by the president's attacks, and Democrats excited in their support of the president. Swing voters would register new doubts about the Republican nominee even if they admitted to a slight disdain for the president's tactics. And the press would reluctantly acknowledge the O campaign's ruthlessness had succeeded.

Every talking head in Washington would issue the obligatory caution that it was far too early to make final predictions, reaching for their supply of tired sports metaphors to underscore the point. But the narrative would be set, and its assumptions visible just beneath the surface of the babbling brook of Washington punditry. The president's campaign was in control of the debate and would probably grind out a victory.

"Okay, say we take a hit for being assholes and Morrison's numbers hold up pretty well," Regan proposed to Lowe. "What do we do to change the subject?"

"Hit him again."

"With what?"

"Same stuff. New stuff. Whatever we got. We punch our way through. Nietzsche never ran a campaign," Lowe reminded him. "If a candidate survives an attack, it doesn't make him stronger. He's weaker. Maybe not as weak as we hoped, but his legs are getting shaky."

"He might have a lot of people's sympathy by then."

"Sympathy is what you get when you're terminal. You don't win elections because people feel sorry for you."

Regan had started to ponder new lines of attack before the campaign's first ad had aired. They would probably have to get more personal, he concluded. That would not be easily done. The media would profess to be shocked and revolted by the ads' viciousness, but their stories would betray their excitement that the race had begun with the president's campaign making the first serious mistake. And Morrison's character was hardly an easy target. Nothing in their research uncovered even the smallest hint of corruption or immorality. He had no known vices, and while such strict rectitude was, in Cal Regan's opinion, a vice itself, a dull and tiresome conceit, it would be hard to convince voters it was a disqualifying defect. They might have to invent one.

Regan told Lowe he wanted their researchers to get him "a plausible connection between the increase in Channing-Mills's share price and some policy decision Morrison made as governor." Morrison had put all his assets in a blind trust when he ran for governor. But Regan was certain the thousands of Channing-Mills shares he had received as the company's CEO still constituted the bulk of his wealth. *Fine, Mr. Terrific doesn't cheat on his wife. He doesn't get drunk. He'd never take a bribe. He doesn't even cuss. But everybody wants to get rich.*

It didn't matter how tenuous the connection was or who else had benefited from the policy. He didn't have to prove it. He just needed a fact he could use to make an argument.

★ CHAPTER 12 ★

"You're off the Hill," Will Janssen announced to Maddy Cohan, confirming the reassignment she had anticipated for months. "We're moving you to the campaign as soon as they break for Memorial Day."

"Which one?" she inquired.

"Both. You're our new chief political correspondent. Congratulations."

"No blogging?" she asked, with her hands clasped together and a wide-eyed expression that suggested it was more of a plea than an expectation.

"Yes, Maddy, you'll blog. Don't let the new title go to your head."

"Oh, don't worry, Will, I know what new titles mean around here. It means you don't want to give someone a raise."

"Is that so, smart-ass? As it happens, we *are* giving you a raise. Fifteen percent. Don't make me regret it."

"Any suggestions for a first assignment?"

"Yeah, make some friends on the Morrison campaign. You've got plenty on O's. Write a nice profile on Sandy Stilwell that his mother will want to put in her scrapbook. Then ask him for a sit-down with Morrison."

Janssen was right. She did need to cultivate sources on the Morrison campaign. She knew few of his senior staff. She had met Stilwell a few times. She had gotten a quote from him, critical of the previous nominee's campaign, for a postmortem she had written right after the last election. She didn't know him well enough to have an opinion on his abilities, but nothing he had said in their brief encounters had impressed her as particularly insightful. She knew Regan thought he was competent but unimaginative. "He's a plodder," he had told her. "He can stick to a budget. He'll make the right hires. He's pretty good at keeping message discipline. But he's not quick at adjusting to the unexpected. He isn't creative."

She could tell Regan had meant the criticism as a dispassionate assessment of his peer's abilities, and she was inclined to credit it as close to accurate. But she also had an instinctive regard for people who acted like adults in a business that seemed to attract an unusually high number of people who avoided maturity. Sandy Stilwell was an adult. He didn't seem the type who enjoyed politics like other people enjoyed gambling: because its risks were thrilling and its rewards immediate. He seemed to believe, in an undemonstrative sort of way, that elections were consequential events in the life of a country, and that however puerile and disingenuous campaigns could be, their purpose was important. She respected him and hoped he would come to respect her.

Now that Morrison was the nominee, his campaign would soon take on staff from the losing campaigns and the usual complement of veteran consultants who wait for a nominee to be chosen before making their counsel available to the new leader of their party. Maddy had good relationships with a number of them. But few, if any, would enjoy the confidence of the candidate and the campaign leadership, especially the old hands, who would soon be lumbering aboard the campaign. Their value as sources would be modest. The welcome most of them would receive would be polite but not genuine, and the attention paid to their advice would be courteous but not serious. Many of them would be invited to join the campaign simply to discourage them from making mischief by anonymously criticizing its decisions to reporters, which would probably be their only utility to Maddy Cohan. She would rely on a few of them, disgruntled by the campaign's insufficient deference to their views, to give her a good quote from a "campaign insider" savaging one or more of its operations.

She had, too, a problem that Janssen hadn't thought was necessary to raise. Morrison's people would not believe she was impartial. Her relationships with the president's campaign staff, which had the appearance of something approximating friendships, were known to the Morrison campaign, where, at best, she would be considered untrustworthy and, at worst, a shill for the other side. Morrison's communications team would warn everyone in the campaign's leadership to assume any inquiries they might receive from her would be informed by the most recent opposition research provided to her by the president's campaign.

She would need to do something soon to make a more favorable impression. An opportunity presented itself to her during a telephone conversation late that night with the person who posed the greatest threat to her reputation within the Morrison campaign.

"Big news. I've been reassigned. Back to campaign reporting. Yay. They're giving me a new title and like a hundred-dollar raise and everything."

Cal Regan offered his congratulations.

"Happy for me?"

"Yeah, and for me. I'll get to see more of you now."

"Hmm. Not sure how often. I'm the chief political correspondent now. Can't expect to go traipsing along with the rest of the herd. I need to keep some altitude. I'll probably drop in when the network anchors do."

"Good for you, and you'll get the same kind of nothing they get."

"Don't be mean. Besides, you, and by that I mean *we,* have to get to a whole 'nother level of discreet. They hate me enough in Morrison world."

"Who hates you?"

"I'm sure they all do. They think I'm sweet on you guys. Will told me I need to start changing their minds right away."

"And how are you going to do that?"

"Well, the first thing *we're* going to do is make sure our situation is, for the next nine months, on hiatus. You know we have to, right? It was risky enough, for both of us, when I wasn't covering the campaign."

"I thought you just said we had to be more discreet."

"Right, and by more discreet, I meant purely professional. Until November anyway. If we really have something, and I think we might, it will still be there in nine months."

"Maddy, I think that's a little extreme. I don't want to go nine months without seeing you."

"You'll see me. I'll just have all my clothes on, we won't be alone, and I'll be asking questions like a real grown-up reporter."

"C'mon. We can be careful. We've been careful."

"Not careful enough. I can't do my job and you can't do yours if we're worried we might hurt each other's feelings."

"Who says we need to?"

"Need to what?"

"Hurt each other's feelings."

"We will if we do our jobs right. Which brings me to the next thing. I need to talk to you or somebody on the campaign for a piece about these ads."

"What about them?"

"Kind of old-school, isn't it, for a postpartisan president? And Morrison impressed a lot of people with the way he's handled it."

Cal Regan felt the change as soon as she said it. In an instant, his anxiety over the end of their affair gave way to his instinct to defend the campaign and himself. And her choice had made clear to him the change in her affections. Hers was more than a decision to subordinate their relationship to her professional obligations. She would rather hurt him than fail to make herself a success. She was choosing to be a reporter to him, and, for the time being anyway, nothing else. He was angry, but recognized he would have done the same in her circumstances. He would do his job, too, whatever it meant for the future with her he had begun to imagine. And doing his job did not mean he had to help her do hers.

He responded to her question with the practiced indifference he would have used on a reporter with whom he wasn't in love. "I think we've said everything we need to about our ads, Maddy. You know we don't like to get into process stories."

"Uh, process or not, it's about the only story anyone is reporting at the moment," she countered, trying unsuccessfully to keep the note of dismay out of her voice.

"Yeah. I'm kind of surprised you're bothering with it. You're a little late to a crowded party."

"Cal, don't be mad. I need to do my job. And I need to be even-handed. Yes, I'm late to the story. I just got the assignment. And I want to, or least hoped I could, do something more with it than the usual they said, they said."

"Off the record, Maddy, I need to do my job, too, and I wouldn't be doing it very well if I encouraged reporters to write more process stories. Not good for the campaign, and not, I think, very relevant to voters."

"So you want to leave it like this? I can't sleep with you while I'm covering you, so you want to be a prick about it."

"No, Maddy, I'm not being a prick about it. I'm being the president's campaign manager."

"Fine, then treat me like you would another reporter."

"Then I might not take your call."

"Treat me like another reporter whose calls you do return."

"Okay. I'll give you this on the record. The president expects to run on his record. And Governor Morrison will have to run on his. That's the only point the ads make."

"C'mon. They're making him out to be some kind of Bernie Madoff type, for chrissakes."

"It's all on his record. His policies. His business decisions. If that conclusion is unfair, then why doesn't he defend them?"

"Were you surprised that he didn't? Off the record, were you impressed by his response?"

"On the record, no and no. It's what candidates do when they can't defend their record. That's it, Maddy. That's all I've got for you."

"Please don't be mad at me."

"I'm not. I'll see you later. Congratulations, again."

After he had hung up, he called Mick Lowe and told him to alert the communications director that Maddy Cohan was writing a story about the ads, and they weren't going to like it. "I gave her a response, but she'll be calling through her list for more. Tell him to give her the same response he gave everyone else. And I don't want anyone else talking to her. On the record or on background."

Regan had never confided his affair with Maddy to his friend. Mick Lowe hadn't needed him to confirm his suspicions. He had known for a while there was something between them. Their frequent chance encounters at social gatherings; each of them taking care not to pay too much attention to the other; their obvious distraction, allowing conversation to lapse and then resuming awkwardly when they noticed the quiet; their disappearing at the end of the evening without saying good night to the people with whom they had arrived—these were signs Lowe had silently observed for months.

Regan appreciated Lowe's hidden virtues and relied on them. He knew Lowe would have surmised the personal nature of his relationship with Maddy long before anyone else suspected it, and that he would keep the knowledge to himself until Regan invited his opinion. He knew, too, he could rely on Lowe to pay discreet attention to Washington gossip for any signs a rumor about the affair was gaining currency, and, if it was, to take tactful measures to quash it; if he couldn't, he'd inform Regan he had a problem.

Lowe knew Regan's instructions to him that evening signaled the affair had ended or had reached a difficult impasse. The campaign's communications director did not need Mick Lowe to tell him how to handle another story about their ads. He had responded to reporters' questions on the subject all week long, using language that had been agreed to in a meeting of senior staff before the ads had run. He wouldn't have any reason to go off script with Maddy Cohan. Nor would he need to remind other staffers not to respond to her. They had been cautioned in advance to refer any inquiries to the press office without comment, a warning that was probably unnecessary. O's world prided itself on its communications discipline and did not tolerate unsanctioned communication with reporters, even if it proved clever and effective. Staff lived in terror of being caught breaking the commandment. Lowe, in particular, seemed to have a sixth sense about the source of an unattributed quote, and he could be quite brutal in confronting suspects, telling one, "You run your mouth one more time without our say-so, and I'll kick your ass to the curb and call your mother to come get you." The object of his abuse had been a seasoned and well-liked consultant in charge of the voter micro-targeting operation, a prosperous forty-two-year-old father of three children, who hadn't talked to his aging mother in weeks and had quailed in the blast of Lowe's wrath like a twenty-year-old intern.

Lowe wondered whether the change in Regan's personal life threatened to impair his judgment more than the affair had. It was probably a wash for the time being, he concluded. Regan was obviously still infatuated with her and resentful over her apparent change of heart. He would be distracted for a while. Not at the top of his game. He might act a little weird, as he just had, in matters that involved her access to the campaign. His behavior might raise the suspicions of staffers who hadn't a clue why he would have such emphatic interest in making life difficult for a pretty, fair, and well-liked reporter, with whom he was believed to be on friendly terms. But the risk of the affair being discovered was now diminished, and Regan would get over the whole thing soon enough if Cohan had the good sense, which Lowe believed she did, to stay out of his sight until then. Lowe went to sleep that night reassured that a potentially serious problem for his friend and his friend's love interest was in the process of becoming a manageable one, a welcome development for all parties concerned whether they realized it or not.

Four days later, *Body Politic* announced Maddy Cohan's return to campaign reporting with a seventeen-hundred-word piece entitled "Morrison Steals from O Playbook." Using quotes from unnamed Democrats, on-the-record Republicans, and two flattered academics, as well as her own analysis, Cohan concluded that Morrison had deftly used the attacks against him to show voters a political personality that closely resembled O's in the last campaign.

The story immediately claimed Washington's attention, and its thesis was argued by pundits of varying degrees of intelligence on news shows of varying degrees of quality. Will Janssen congratulated himself again for being an astute judge of talent. Sandy Stilwell was impressed and pleased, which had been one of Cohan's objectives, and instructed Morrison's press secretary to schedule the lunch she had requested.

The president's team was angered. Samuelson personally conveyed to Janssen his frustration with the story's false assumptions. Cal Regan was furious with her. And Mick Lowe quietly sighed as he conceded to himself that the problem he had thought was nearing a satisfactory resolution might remain his concern a while longer.

After he let four of her previous calls go to his voice mail, Cal Regan answered the fifth one with "Nice work, Maddy. You must have made Morrison's Christmas card list."

"I guess that answers my first question," she replied. "You're still mad at me."

"I thought your story sucked, Maddy, as journalism, even though I'm sure it worked as a beat sweetener. It's not personal. Morrison is not this year's O, and it's ludicrous to suggest he is, based on a couple of TV interviews. Every challenger runs a change campaign. That's what a challenger represents. But change needs to be defined. The change Morrison wants is a return to the policies of the last administration. The president wants and will run on change that takes the country forward, not backward. He's had to spend a big part of his term cleaning up the mess caused by the policies Morrison would bring back."

"Well, that's surely a better argument than the talking point you gave me. Too bad you didn't make it when I asked you and several of your associates for a comment. I would have been happy to include it in the piece."

"We made the mistake of believing it would have been self-evident to an intelligent reporter."

"Oh, so you think I'm stupid now?"

She spat out the last remark angrily, and her face had begun to flush. She was genuinely offended now.

"That's bullshit, Cal. You don't like the piece. I get it. Then make an argument when it's being written. Why is it that only the O campaign thinks it was stupid or unfair or whatever you think it is? Most people thought it was at least an interesting take on the beginning of the general election."

"You ever wonder why stories like yours get buzz? Why no one else had thought to write it? Because it's a work of imagination, not reporting. You imprinted a stupid Hollywood psychodrama on the race when there are no facts to support it. Occam's razor, Maddy. The simplest explanation is usually the right one. Morrison wants to lead the Republican restoration, with all that means for people who don't have summer homes and big portfolios and well-paying jobs. But he doesn't want voters to know that. We *do* want voters to know it."

"I guess this isn't going to be a very fruitful conversation. I'm sorry I'd hoped it would be."

He had thought about what he would say to her when they eventually spoke. The invented scene always concluded with a wittier exchange than their actual conversation had produced thus far.

"Fruitful? What would make it fruitful for you, Maddy? If I surrender, and confess I thought the piece was just brilliant?"

"No. It would be fruitful or better or at least not unpleasant if we talked to each other as friends."

"If I recall, it was your decision we go back to being just reporter and campaign manager. So, as the president's campaign manager, I'm just doing my job, telling a reporter she wrote a piece about the race that could have been written by the other campaign, in the hope you'll do a better job next time."

"Well, thanks for sharing your time and opinion."

"You're welcome."

What he felt now, as he still held his cell phone in his hand and sank deeper in his chair, wasn't satisfaction. It wasn't remorse either. *Incomplete* was probably an accurate description. No, it hadn't been a very fruitful conversation.

He was careful not to admit to himself that his dissatisfaction was the result of his unrealistic expectations. He had imagined a triumph achieved with a remark so potent in its effect that she would call again a few minutes later to beg his forgiveness and tell him she missed him, and that nothing was more important to her than their shared happiness. He had let his mind wander into ridiculous fantasies. That really wasn't like him.

Sandy Stilwell was not given to fantasizing happy endings either. They had done as well as they could under the circumstances. They hadn't been knocked off stride right out of the gate or appeared unprepared for the attacks. The blowback against O's ads was livelier than he had expected, and more than Chicago had expected. And they had succeeded, so far at least, in holding the ground they wanted to fight on.

Pleased as he was, Stilwell began to worry that a false sense of security would settle in and breed overconfidence.

They, or, more accurately, their candidate, had responded well to the attacks. But they could claim nothing more than a small tactical victory that had generated some favorable press. They would have to fight every day, and with more than their candidate's speeches and interviews, to stick to their message and keep O from framing the debate. They couldn't be sure they had survived the attack. They had impressed Washington. But the ads were still running. They were reaching more voters than Morrison's message would. They wouldn't start polling to gauge their effect for another week, but Stilwell knew they would find the ads had done damage. He didn't know how much, but it was foolish to believe they would escape without any.

"We need money," Stilwell lamented to a colleague. The Morrison campaign had spent prodigiously early in the primaries in the hope they could secure the nomination in record time. They had assumed wrapping up the nomination early would leave them with ample time to replenish their treasury before the fight with O was seriously under way. That had been a mistake. Chicago had paid attention and exploited it.

They had to get on the air in all the battlegrounds in less than two months if they were to stay in the game. And their message would have to be as attractive and deceptively negative as Morrison had been in his response. We can do better, was Morrison's message. Better than what? The campaign had to explain that to voters as soon as possible. They had to get after the president's failures as Morrison had done without anger or hyperbole; by reminding voters of their disappointment with O's unfilled promise, but without appearing to take pleasure in it.

So Sandy Stilwell spent more time than he cared to with the finance people scheduling fund-raisers, developing direct-mail and e-mail solicitations, and pushing the Republican National Committee to start running ads much sooner than the committee had planned.

They would close the gap eventually. But how much damage would they suffer before they did? Low-dollar Internet donations were coming in solidly, exceeding projections, and Stilwell was frantically reworking the budget to devote as much of it to airtime as quickly as he could.

Raising large donations was a lot more labor-intensive. They were scheduling two and sometimes three finance events a day for Morrison, and they had him on the phone every spare moment, exhorting members of his finance committee to meet their targets ahead of schedule. But Stilwell believed it would take two months to be in a position to meet whatever else Chicago threw at them, and much of the money they were now diverting to advertising was coming at the expense of political operations. It would be the roughest two months of the election.

If they survived them, they would have a real reason to feel confident going into the conventions and the fall campaign. But if the president's campaign succeeded through the spring and summer in making the debate about Morrison, the Morrison they were inventing, the best convention ever might not give them a big enough bump to get out of the hole they would find themselves in by midsummer. They would enter the final, frenzied two months of the election on defense. And they would lose.

★ CHAPTER 13 ★

The president was writing notes to himself. He had rejected a speech his writers had been preparing for a month, and which he had twice revised before deciding to abandon it and write it himself. Writing rejuvenated him in low moments when he felt his influence and energy ebb, when another impasse proved insurmountable, another change in course was required, another facile debate had begun over who was to blame for Washington's manifest dysfunction. The solitary nature of the work, his schedule hastily reorganized and aides banished from his presence for a prescribed period, restored his autonomy. His gift for self-expression, still potent in its public effect, reclaimed his authority.

"The most successful speeches," he had once explained to a close friend, "aren't always the best written or the smartest. They're the ones you inhabit. You use everything—your movements, your breathing, your intonation, emphasis, cadence, everything—to do more than express emotion or an idea or argument, more than persuade an audience. You're transferring them to the audience, making them feel, think, see what you're feeling and thinking and seeing. If I seem bigger at the end of the speech, I want them to feel bigger. That's my gift. But to make it work, I have to feel all these things I want them to feel in the text itself. And you can't get that from reading it. I have to feel it as it's conceived, hear the delivery as I'm writing, anticipate the reaction, be moved by it myself."

In the exultant rush he felt when an audience erupted wildly, crying, roaring, chanting his name, at the conclusion of a speech that had worked perfectly, he knew the effect had been his achievement. "It doesn't matter how good your speechwriters are, how good a feel they have for your style," he told his wife. "They can never do that for you."

It had become common among the more familiar faces of the Washington commentariat to slight, subtly, his gift. They still recognized his artistry and polish; still gave it an approving if perfunctory nod in their observations of his speeches. But they weren't awed by it as they once had been. Three years in office, and countless speeches, press conferences, and various other public utterances issued and soon forgotten, had convinced many he had overrelied on his gift for public speaking. "The president thinks he can talk his way out of problems," one pundit had opined, expressing the general consensus of his peers. "He can't keep going to the well again and expect anything more than the same result he got the last time. Governing is making choices. Governing is forcing the action. Governing is what you're doing offstage, too."

For an opinion to gain the force of indisputable truth in Washington it need only be repeated often, and it stuck O with the burden and irritation of a talent dismissed as wasted because he used it.

Now, when the White House Press Office drew their attention to a forthcoming presidential address on a particular policy initiative, reporters considered it an admission that the White House didn't have any notion how to get the policy out of Congress, and they would smirk and raise their eyebrows at one another.

"You think it ever occurs to these fuckers," O asked Rick Noth, his press secretary, after reading another column scorning his rhetorical profligacy, "that a president can't order Congress to produce a bill? Next time they start bitching about how long it's been since I held a press conference, tell them we don't want to become 'overexposed.' Tell them we'll use the, uh, what the hell did he call it"—he paused to refer to the offending column—"oh yeah, tell them we'll use the 'president's arsenal of nonverbal methods of persuasion' to answer their fucking questions."

It had never occurred to them either that his every public address was not intended to be as memorable, as enthralling, as his best speeches during the last campaign had been, the ones that had first won over the press and encouraged forlorn Democrats to dream again. It wasn't possible to reach those heights anytime he chose, even if he wanted to, which he did not, because then the criticism that he had overused his talent would have been right; the magic would have become banal, losing its potency as it became familiar.

Most of his speeches as president were intended to define the policies and achievements of his administration and rebut Republican criticism of them. He was selling details, not dreams. Should he let Republicans bang away at his administration every hour of every day because the debate was too commonplace and uninspired for a man of his talents?

The speech O would give in four days would prove he hadn't squandered his talent but had held it in reserve for moments like this. Morrison was a good candidate. But he was a better one.

The venue was a domed football stadium at a university in the Midwest that seated seventy thousand people. There wouldn't be an empty seat, and a parking lot would contain an overflow crowd expected to reach five thousand. Supporters would be bused in from various locations within a two-hundred-mile radius. Several celebrity musicians had agreed to perform in advance of the president's remarks. They would finish the last of a five-song set as the president made his entrance and return to the stage five minutes into the thundering applause that would follow the president's speech, encouraging the applause to reach a new crescendo, and lead the massive assembly in singing Woody Guthrie's "This Land Is Your Land" as the president slowly made his exit.

Cable would cover the entire speech live. The broadcast networks would lead the evening news with reports from the event. Most of the White House and campaign senior staff would be in conspicuous attendance, giving the impression to Washington insiders of a conquering army on full parade on the eve of a call to arms.

To their surprise, reporters in attendance, including nearly all the most prominent political journalists of the day, would find themselves involuntarily captivated again by the spectacle of O inspiring a multitude to a delirious display of their faith in his promise. They would convey the excitement of the experience in their copy and stand-ups, with similes and adjectives that implied the president's psychological and physical transformation as he returned to the campaign trail. *Like a heavyweight champion . . . veteran Super Bowl quarterback . . . Triple Crown Thoroughbred . . . modern Caruso . . . returning to the stage . . . the field . . . the track . . . in perfect condition . . . peak form . . . great voice . . . a revitalized . . . reinvigorated . . . rejuvenated . . . reenergized president . . . recovered . . . reclaimed . . . recaptured . . . recalled the magic . . . mojo . . . excitement . . . possibilities of his last campaign . . . rallying . . . rousing . . . stirring . . . thrilling his supporters with a full-throated call to arms . . . inspirational appeal to their dreams of better politics and a brighter future . . . moving summons to the cause of a more perfect union.*

The speech would be credited as a triumph for the candidate. But hundreds of people and many weeks of planning and modifying would be involved in making certain it was. It would be a test of the campaign's logistics capabilities; its ability to conceive, market, and sustain a winning message; and the turnout proficiency of its communications networks, as much as it would be a test of the president's performance skills. And they would have to perform at that level and higher from that day to November. It was a commitment that put the campaign and the candidate on the hook for more. Once a campaign did an event like that, drew a crowd that size, and created that kind of explosive and contagious energy, smaller events with less excitement became signs the campaign was losing momentum. A repeat performance would be required at least once a month until the conventions. During the fall campaign, twice a week or more, O would have to speak with the same effect to crowds just as large.

He could not vacate his office, as he had the Senate in the last campaign, to meet the extraordinary demands on his time and energy. Every day imposed the same unmanageable burdens whether he was in the Oval Office or campaigning in Terre Haute. Every morning of every day he had to scrap for his reelection would begin with a national security briefing, and every hour after would be crowded with the other briefings, discussions, presentations, options to be examined, disputes to be settled that consumed a president's day.

Late in the last campaign, he had confessed to several close aides that he really didn't enjoy campaigning. What part? they had asked. All of it, he had answered. This time he would have to endure the indignities and exhausting demands on his person of a national campaign while exercising the enormous and numerous responsibilities of the office accurately described as the hardest job in the world.

"It's too soon," he had argued to Samuelson when the date for his first major campaign rally was initially proposed. "*Way* too soon. It's not even summer yet." He had anticipated waiting until the Fourth of July recess to start campaigning in earnest. "I'm the president. I'm on TV every day. I command as much attention here as I could campaigning. And once we start, everything I do as president will be criticized as a political move. It's not necessary to get out there. It's not necessary and it's not sustainable. Jesus, I'll drop dead from exhaustion before the convention."

This had been Samuelson's opinion, too, and the opinion of all his advisors. Part of their pitch to get his approval of the media strategy was that it would allow him to keep a strictly presidential schedule into the summer, while they fought the opposition from the air. But they had reassessed, though they had been loath to, when they observed the consensus forming in the press that Morrison was an exceptionally intelligent candidate with a winning message, and a campaign that was as skillful as the candidate. They scorned the consensus as predictable hyperventilating of an easily manipulated press corps. But they wouldn't ignore it.

"They're all ADD," Noth diagnosed, "but it's contagious." They didn't like being coerced into altering their plans. It put them all in ill temper.

"Let me make the case," Samuelson had pleaded, "before you reject it."

"You're not going to convince me."

"Maybe not. But let me try. Let's start with the obvious—a dissatisfied electorate. The country wants change now, as much as they did last time. You're the incumbent this time. Getting on the right side of a change election is gonna be a lot harder. Morrison's got the easier hand to play, message-wise anyway. Does it help us if you're in the country's face every minute of every day as the emblem of what voters want to see changed? Or is it better to be out there making the case that you're fighting powerful, entrenched forces that are trying to stop you from changing Washington?"

"Like it or not, Avi, I am the president. I'm the face of the government wherever I am."

"You're the face of change wherever you are, including Washington. And we need to remind people of that. Second point, it's still way too early to draw conclusions, but the first reaction to the plan to put Morrison on the defensive isn't what we want to see." (On Samuelson's order, the campaign's media consultant had recently finished conducting several focus groups of swing voters to gauge their reaction to Morrison's response to their ads. The results hadn't been encouraging. The adjectives most frequently employed were *considerate, thoughtful, believable,* and *confident.* Samuelson hadn't shared the results with the president. Nor had he informed him the campaign was doing the focus groups in the first place.)

"He's scored some points. He's new. A bored press gravitates to the new. They'll exaggerate his talent and his chances and his campaign's success to justify the expense of traveling with him, and doing more front-page stories on him. Early on, that could start a general narrative that's mostly from their point of view. We don't want to let that sink in."

"I thought the ads were supposed to prevent that."

"They were, and they will, but it will take time. Until we start to see numbers that show he's taken a big hit, they'll continue giving him props and build his momentum. We have to give them something head-turning to look at. We have to give them the once-in-a-generation-candidate thing. They've forgotten what that really looks like."

"I can do that without starting to campaign this early. And if we start this early, by the fall I won't be a once-in-a-generation anything. I'll be a worn-out, mistake-prone, inept candidate *and* president."

"The best way to beat back the idea that Morrison's in your class is for you to do what you do—do what he can't. Inspire people. And show them all this crap about a loss of intensity, a dejected base, isn't real. You're always going to disappoint people when you govern. It can't be avoided. But campaigning is different. Everyone is just waiting for you to give them the sign. Give them the sign."

"Once we start, we can't stop. It's too long a stretch to do two jobs, each of them impossible for sane people."

"We'd only need to do big events once a month until the conventions."

"But you'll have me on the road more than that."

"You're on the road a lot now."

"Not as much as I will be. Avi, explain in a sentence the one reason we need to change our plans. I can think of a lot of good reasons why we shouldn't. What's happened in the last few weeks that's already got us second-guessing ourselves?"

"Morrison turned out to be a better candidate than people expected. But not as good as you are."

They had four other conversations and repeated their same arguments before O finally relented, making his displeasure and helplessness known with a twice-uttered "Goddammit" and an abrupt exit from Samuelson's office.

"He'll be all right," Samuelson assured Noth. "He's a gamer. Now that he's accepted it, he'll make sure he blows the roof off the place. We have to make sure the event is worth the performance."

"You need to be on top of every piece of this, start to finish," Samuelson told Regan, who made sure he was, exhorting senior staff in twice-a-day meetings to make certain "everybody concentrates on pulling this together. We have a stadium to fill. Make sure every organizer hears from us ten times a day, and they communicate our instructions to their people to the letter. Treat it the same way as a convention. Make sure we have enough whips planted in every section. All signs look handmade. I don't want the cameras to find a single person who isn't cheering his ass off or about to collapse from overexcitement. I want the press panting when it's over."

Walter Lafontaine, who was helping organize the turnout operation for the speech, told Regan he was sorry he wouldn't be able to attend it. "My mother's not doing real well right now. I need to stay close by." Regan told him not to worry. "We understand, Walter. You'll be missed, but there'll be other speeches."

Walter said he appreciated it, but he didn't believe for a moment Regan was interested in whether he went to the speech or not. He was too worried about Geraldine to care much anymore how unimportant he was to the people to whom the president had entrusted his reelection. Regan would have been surprised to know how Walter felt. He liked the guy and assumed the feeling was mutual. He was quite certain he had done what he had been asked to do by Samuelson. "Make sure you take care of Walter. Don't just patronize him. Make sure he feels useful. That's what the president wants."

Allen Knowles, who was attending the speech along with many of the campaign's finance committee, called Regan to offer him a ride on his Gulfstream G550, which Regan declined. "I appreciate it, Allen, but the campaign would have to pay for it. We've already got a charter to take most of us there."

"Well, can I buy you dinner after we see the president or would the campaign have to pay for that, too?" The campaign had arranged for a brief reception after the event, so the president could thank his leading donors again and encourage them with flattery to redouble their efforts.

"Not unless you're coming to Chicago on your way home. No one's overnighting there. We're all coming right back as soon as the president leaves."

"Done."

"What's done?"

"I'll stop in Chicago on my way home and take you to dinner."

"That's awful nice of you, but not necessary. We'll have some follow-up work to do when we get back."

"I know you're busy. But listen, I want to get together and talk some business with you, campaign business and my business. Don't want to do it on the phone or at the campaign. So have your people give my people a time when you can get free for a few hours. Okay? You'll be glad you did."

"I will. Sorry things are so crazed right now."

Regan still admired Allen Knowles. He had been thrilled when he landed him as a Hanson, Strong client. He had personally asked Knowles to join the campaign's finance committee, and Knowles hadn't disappointed him.

"Jesus, he's a real earner, isn't he?" Regan remarked to Mick Lowe.

"He's already raised more than a half million for the quarter and signed up nine other zillionaires as All-Stars who've never bundled for anybody. I don't even know if they're Democrats."

All-Stars was the designation the campaign gave fund-raising bundlers who raised a million dollars or more for the campaign. "We ought to call them ambassadors," Lowe had suggested, "because that's what they think they're buying. And the ambassador who raises the most gets to be called secretary of state."

Knowles never asked Regan for much. The only thing he had asked for was a seat on that presidential commission, which Regan had managed to arrange without much difficulty. He didn't complain that his advice wasn't being taken or that he was unappreciated, like many big donors habitually did. "That guy's a real producer," Regan had remarked more than once. "And low maintenance. Why aren't more rich people like that?"

There was something about Knowles's manner that prompted a trace of skepticism about his intentions, but it was so imperceptible that it barely engaged Regan's curiosity. It might have been the impression Knowles gave in conversation that he wasn't really listening to you but trying to ascertain if what he had said to you had had the intended effect. There's nothing unusual about a little narcissism in a billionaire. Nor was it unusual for big donors to have their personal interests in mind when they generously supported a candidate. Regan hadn't met any who didn't. And he couldn't identify anything in Knowles's behavior that raised a more worrying suspicion. He felt just a slight unease for a second or two when he talked to Knowles at any length, and beyond recognizing these brief instances of disquiet, he hadn't given it any greater consideration. *Probably just something about rich people,* he told himself. *They're so self-assured, they make you feel like they're playing you even when they aren't.*

"You're on the plane," Janssen announced, after receiving the confirmation from the White House Press Office. "First time, right?"

It would be Maddy Cohan's first ride on *Air Force One,* where thirteen seats in a small cabin in the rear were reserved for the traveling pool of rotating reporters from all journalism disciplines: newspapers, wire services, magazines, television, radio, and photography. The rest of the press traveled from Washington to the speech on a less luxurious aircraft. The White House Correspondents' Association set the pool rotation every month, and it didn't often include a reporter from *Body Politic* on days when the president was scheduled to travel out of town. Reporters affected nonchalance about their presence on the president's plane, but since it was her first time on *Air Force One,* and she was amazed by her extraordinary luck to be so handsomely accommodated on the first occasion she covered O as president, Maddy wouldn't make much of an effort to hide how thrilled she was.

As part of the pool, and responsible for observing every public moment of the president's day, she would spend most of the time in several small, dreary holding rooms in reasonably close proximity to the better-appointed spaces the president occupied. She would travel in the motorcade several SUVs behind the presidential limousine. She would drink lukewarm coffee and check her e-mail two hundred feet from where the president enjoyed "twenty minutes of downtime," which consisted of at least thirty minutes of conversation with his aides, another quick scan of his prepared remarks, and five minutes to compose himself before making his way to the stage. She would watch the speech from the press pen on the floor of the arena. She would be cordoned off in a corner of the hotel banquet room where the president held a reception for his biggest fund-raising bundlers. And since the campaign's senior staff, as well as several top White House aides, would attend the speech and most of its related functions, she would almost certainly encounter Cal Regan.

She had not spoken with him since their difficult conversation following the publication of her story, in which he had, by her count, insulted her a dozen times. She assumed he had cooled down by now. But she had become angrier over the last few days, frequently recalling the most offensive remarks and his snotty, patronizing attitude. She did not think he would seek her out, and if he wandered over to chat casually with a few reporters in her vicinity, she didn't expect he would address her with anything more than a nod and a "Hi, Maddy." And he would get nothing more from her in return than a "Hi, Cal." Of course, it was possible he would attempt some conversation with her or to convey with a look that lingered a second or two longer than necessary that he was still angry or that maybe he had experienced a change of heart. Her anticipation of the scene was charged with a stimulating mixture of resentment, curiosity, and the recognition that she was not dreading it. She was rather looking forward to it, for reasons she would not admit to herself.

Regan looked forward to it as well, for the same unacknowledged reasons, when he saw the manifest for the president's plane. He and Maddy Cohan had similar personalities and enthusiasms. They were both the kind of people who intuited that difficult love affairs were often the most memorable ones.

Sandy Stilwell had discussed with the campaign's communications people how to bracket the president's speech with their message. On the evenings before and after the speech, high-profile Morrison surrogates would be dispatched to the networks. Local evening news shows in battleground states would be offered interviews with local Morrison supporters. Their talking points would be blast e-mailed to their entire press list in case the surrogates didn't make them as forcefully and repetitiously as hoped.

As they could not replicate, lacking their opponent's finances and organization, an event as large and showy as the president's, they would not schedule a speech for Morrison for the remainder of the week. They debated whether to make him available for interviews with the broadcast networks the evening of the speech. Morrison had told them not to bother. "I think we can let the president start his campaign without me butting in on the spot," he explained.

"He wouldn't show you the same courtesy," Stilwell observed.

"It's not a question of courtesy, Sandy," Morrison replied. "I'd rather we make our case on our time and not his. The story this week is the president began campaigning for reelection. Nothing we can do about that. I can only be a part of that story, *his* story. Let the moment pass. It's just a few days."

In the end it was decided that Morrison would not do any interviews that week and would keep a lighter schedule than usual. They would give the president the week. None of his advisors had recommended it. Most thought it unwise. Morrison had decided it himself.

"Next week," he advised Stilwell, "we'll get back in it." To inaugurate his return to the daily message battles, he agreed to an interview on one of the Sunday morning political shows. The following Sunday, he and Margaret would do their first joint *60 Minutes* interview, which would be taped, weather permitting, in the well-tended garden of their weekend home, which Margaret had invested many pleasant hours in creating. During the interview, Morrison would compliment his wife's imagination and industry as an amateur horticulturalist, as well as the president's talent for public speaking. "The president sure can give a good talk," he would smilingly acknowledge. "No doubt about that."

August 2012

★ CHAPTER 14 ★

Losing a contact lens in the men's room sink was the last thing Regan remembered doing. The rest of the evening's activities were, like his contact lens, lost due to his insobriety. He couldn't recall how or when he had returned to his room. He wasn't sure, but considering the mess he had made of himself, he doubted he had located it unaided.

The companion he thought had come to his room with him had either escaped or been a hallucination. There was no one with him now. Perhaps she had declined whatever slurred suggestion he had probably offered to encourage her. His hangover produced the symptoms of arthritis, the pain making his entire body tender: head, neck, back, and knees. Even his feet hurt as he padded slowly to the bathroom. The self-recrimination he now summoned was felt, too, as pangs of physical pain. *What a moron. Drinking shots. Like a fucking college kid.* With *a bunch of college kids. Christ, you are an idiot.* He thought he might vomit.

The evening had begun sensibly. He and Lowe and two other colleagues had sat down to a late dinner in the city's most popular restaurant after a day mostly spent in tedious disputes over the last unsettled items in the party's platform. They had all planned on retiring after dinner, but the wine that had been chosen was exceptional, and second and third bottles were ordered, when one would have seen them comfortably through the meal. Relaxed for the first time in days, and anticipating a busy week ahead, Regan had suggested a last drink in the bar after they had returned to their hotel.

A second round of drinks had arrived unrequested, their waitress identifying as their benefactors a group of young staffers clustered around the bar, where they had clearly been drinking for a while. Regan, in an expansive mood, waved at them and shouted an invitation to join them. Among their number were several quite attractive girls, in their early twenties, who seemed delighted by the opportunity to form a more familiar relationship with the campaign manager, with whom none of them had ever before exchanged a word.

After a third and then fourth drink, Regan welcomed the proposition offered by the most flirtatious of the young women, almost a dare, really, that they order shots of tequila. He didn't remember how many additional rounds were ordered. Quite a few, he suspected. He vaguely recalled Lowe urging him repeatedly to "call it a night," as well as making a rather too loud proposition of his own to the tequila enthusiast, and possibly some kissing and groping in the dimly lit alcove where the bar's restrooms were located. Whatever had been done or said must have been if not unwelcome, then unpersuasive, as there didn't appear to be any evidence that someone had shared the large bed from which he had been driven reluctantly by pain and the apprehension he would be late for the first of his many appointments that day. He was relieved more than embarrassed by his lack of success.

Moments after he had ordered bacon, eggs, toast, and a pot of coffee from room service, someone knocked on his door. More insistent pounding followed the first discreet taps. He struggled with a hotel bathrobe as he went to open it and repeated "Just a second" after his first attempt had been garbled by a catch in his throat.

"Hi, forgot something," the tequila girl, looking none the worse for wear, announced as she brushed by him, strode to the nightstand, and withdrew from its drawer a wristwatch. "Sorry, can't stay to play. Busy day for us worker bees," she explained. "I'll see you tonight, though. Are we leaving from here or going directly from the convention center?" she asked as she took a pill from a compact, deposited it on her tongue, and swallowed it without aid of water.

"Uh, here, I guess. I'll need to change before dinner," he replied.

"Great. You want me to come up here first?"

"We can just meet in the lobby."

"Suit yourself. Around seven?"

"Quarter after?"

"Sounds good."

He was still standing at the door, gawking stupidly, he thought afterward, as she passed him on her way back out, stopped, turned around, and abruptly kissed him.

"See you later, lover," she smilingly offered over her shoulder as she walked to the elevator.

He remained standing at the door for several moments after she had left, contemplating the surprising encounter and trying to retrieve a few more memories of the evening. *My God, I must have blacked out. I am* in *college. I don't even remember her name.*

"Tess."

"What?"

"Tess. Her name. It's Tess," Lowe repeated.

"And her last name?"

"No fucking clue. She works in Collias's shop. Want me to ask him?"

"No, thanks. You know I slept with her."

"Really? Who would have guessed that when the two of you were tearing the clothes off each other by the bathroom."

"Shut up. I just wish I knew if it was worth it. I can't remember a goddamn thing. Honest to God, I think I blacked out. Apparently, I invited her to Knowles's dinner tonight."

The admission prompted a snort of laughter and more sarcasm from Lowe, before he, not entirely in jest, offered the assurance that Tess, last name unknown, would probably make a favorable impression on Allen Knowles. "He doesn't seem the kind of guy who has a problem with intergenerational dating."

It was not her youth that bothered Regan either. She was past the age of consent, quite attractive, and obviously available on short notice, the only qualities usually required to arouse his sexual interest. But he had an informal and, until last night, inviolate rule about not sleeping with women who, in the management structure of whatever enterprise he was then employed in, would be considered his subordinate. And the greater his authority, the more necessary he believed such prudence to be. A single night's pleasure wasn't worth risking the potentially embarrassing complications that could ensue from the encounter if one party assumed a greater emotional commitment than the other.

Such things happen in campaigns, of course, and often between people who risk even more—their marriages, for instance. Though he had never been married, Regan believed his professional reputation was as dear to him as a marriage could be, and certainly worth the discretion expected of him. Not sleeping with junior staff or becoming excessively intoxicated in public—these were hardly intolerable proprieties for the president's campaign manager. And their violations weren't just regrettable lapses of judgment that excited gossip in the campaign. They could be, in certain circumstances and to certain reporters, considered newsworthy.

Regan would explain all this to Tess, who in their brief exchange that morning had impressed him as a sophisticated and self-confident person. He would have to discover her last name, and her job at the convention, so he could ask her to meet him for a quick drink before dinner earlier than they had agreed. He would ask Lowe to find the information for him. Lowe's discretion was worth the abuse he would take from Lowe's delight in his predicament.

There would not be a repeat of last evening's indiscretion. It wouldn't be in either of their interests for their mutual attraction to become a staple of campaign gossip. Relationships between senior and junior staff were too easily misunderstood and maligned. More important, a continued attachment (and he made a mental note to use such delicacy in describing their one night of inebriated passion) would distract their attention from the most important service either of them would ever give their country: helping to reelect the president. Certainly, he still wanted her to accompany him to the dinner. He would be disappointed if she now thought it best to beg off, but he would understand, of course.

"Sure," was all she had said in response to the suggested predinner drink. At six forty-five, he entered the bar where things had gotten out of hand the previous night, and saw that Tess Gilchrest had already arrived and taken the same seat at the table where they had introduced themselves to each other. Her last name had been provided to him by Mick Lowe, who had dryly remarked on the coincidence that it was spelled the same as that of a prominent campaign donor, Hank Gilchrest, presently under serious consideration for the post of ambassador to Great Britain, and "how about that, apparently his youngest daughter is also named Tess. Talk about a coincidence, huh?"

With this biographical information in mind, Regan vowed to take an even more tactful approach to the unpleasant but all the more urgent task of reaching an understanding with Tess Gilchrest that their new friendship could continue only platonically. He would show her as much consideration as if his intentions were quite the opposite, as if he were a love-struck suitor begging her favor. She was beautiful, and last night would always be a special memory for him, and he wished, oh, how he wished he could relive the experience (in truth, he wished he could at least remember it), but they both had obligations to the president and the country that necessitated this sacrifice. He wouldn't hold her to it, but it would surely ease his suffering if he knew this difficult decision had not cost him her affections, affections that he might, after the election, be allowed a chance to rekindle.

"Wow," was her first reaction after he had made his case, as delicately as planned. "You've got the whole chivalry rap really down, don't you?"

"Pardon me?"

"Don't sweat it, Cal. You can just file it under 'fun things that happen when you get shit-faced on tequila,' and forget about it. Honestly, it's not like we got married in Vegas or something. But I appreciate the effort. I really do."

"Well, I don't want you to think it was meaningless or, uh—"

"Or what? Casual? I think it was pretty much the definition of *casual*, don't you? And that's okay by me. I was just as drunk as you were."

Not sure if he was relieved or slightly insulted by her last remark, he continued to explain that unplanned campaign romances often cause complications of which he, of all people, had to be mindful. Again she dismissed his concern as unnecessary.

"Dude, *you're* making it complicated. No worries. You can go back to being my good-looking boss, and I'll go back to being one of a hundred errand runners, who's just thrilled you even know my name. I won't breathe a word that you're terrific in bed. Promise. I'd still like to tag along tonight, if that's okay. I know Allen. He's a friend of my parents, and I told my dad I'd see him tonight."

"Sure, of course. Did you tell your father that I'm taking you to the dinner?"

"I did. That's not a problem, for you or him. I think he's probably more worried Allen will try to have his way with me. It wouldn't be the first time." Regan almost asked her to elaborate on that last disclosure but restrained his curiosity. Tess Gilchrest was full of surprises, and they certainly added to her allure. But all that was likely to come from other disclosures was trouble, as their titillating effect could weaken his new-found resolve. Regan looked at his watch and signaled for the check. "We should probably get going. We don't want to keep Allen waiting. Tell your dad I'll keep an eye on him and make sure he keeps his hands to himself."

"Would it make you jealous if he didn't?" the surprising Tess Gilchrest asked in reply.

The dinner had been arranged in his honor. The engraved invitation announced: *A Salute and Thank You to Cal Regan*. Regan had initially discouraged the idea, pleading the unmanageable demands on his time, but Knowles had insisted. "We'll do it on the weekend before the convention officially starts. We'll invite a lot of the money people, and I think I could probably even get you some A-list celebrities, or B-plus, anyway, who like to think acting and politics are the same thing. Then you won't have to hassle with us for the rest of the week. We'll start it early and end it early. Deal? C'mon, someone always has a party for the campaign manager. Let me do the honors this time."

Regan was not opposed to being feted. On the contrary, he usually enjoyed being the center of attention. He had given Knowles the actual reason for his reluctance: he was too busy to take an evening off. Whatever free time he could scrounge now would be best spent on a decent night's sleep. There would be very few if any nights over the next two months when he would get more than four or five hours of rest. All presidential campaigns reach a point when every waking moment is an anxious one, when they consume every thought and burden every sense of the people involved in them, when they drain from even the hardiest souls any expectation of enjoyment. That time, the time when the campaign reached a level of intensity that threatened to overwhelm them, had arrived some weeks ago.

Thursday night, the president and vice president and their families would bounce on the balls of their feet and raise their arms in the air and hug one another and wave and jut their thumbs at the cheering crowd. Balloons would be batted around and stomped on, and confetti would be carried out of the stadium in hair and on shoulders to late-night parties and pub crawls. Staff would stare dumbly at the screens of their Black-Berries and iPhones, hurriedly scroll through the first wave of media commentary, and circulate among themselves early reports from the various focus groups that had been commissioned to react to the president's acceptance speech. They would wait anxiously for the overnight polls to confirm the president had received the expected good bounce out of his convention that would, if they were lucky, last a week. After they had congratulated themselves on a successful convention, those who remained in town would get quickly drunk and drop into an exhausted sleep before they returned to Chicago on an early morning flight; others, including most of the senior staff, would be hustled onto *Air Force One* to travel with the president and vice president to the small, picturesque Ohio town where they would hold their first postconvention event at eight o'clock in the morning.

For the next two months, they would experience the sensation of drowning. They would work twenty hours and more a day. They would bull their way, minute by minute, day after day, through an endless list of actions and decisions and discussions and reconsiderations and further discussions and allocating and reallocating of funds; through voter identifying and targeting and contacting and recontacting; through polling and focus groups and flattering and cajoling and cursing of donors and congressional leaders and party stalwarts who wouldn't lift a goddamn finger to help but would anonymously criticize their every decision if they were not consulted by someone with a title they respected. They would suffer through arguments and temper tantrums and a tired and cranky candidate and relentless badgering by reporters until it bored them. They would make ads, and remake them, and change the places and times and frequency they would air, and change them back and then change them again. They would follow schedules that were constantly revised and seldom kept. They would discover, debate, and respond to unexpected problems and minor scandals and misinformation and leaked information that was accurate but not the whole truth or wouldn't be true when they were done explaining it. They would survive mistakes by the campaign manager, by his principal deputies, by White House aides, by the communications team, by donors and geriatric politicos who hadn't worked in a campaign for decades but who still liked to see their names in print, by a cabinet secretary who was widely admired for her intelligence but given to making ill-timed and impolitic remarks, by the candidate, by the candidate's spouse, by the press, by the advance kid who was in charge of making sure the traveling press's luggage reached their hotel at a decent hour but had left the handsome leather overnight bag of a self-important and infamously vindictive columnist sitting in a dimly lit corner of the FBO in Charlotte, North Carolina.

They would rely on adrenaline, paranoia, coffee, Diet Coke, alcohol, Advil, Ambien, sarcasm, luck, and one another to get them through each day without losing their focus or their minds. Every now and again they would get drunk or laid or enjoy some other unplanned pleasure that would release them for an hour or two from the asylum, and they would regret it the next day, when a hangover or embarrassment or desire or weariness that numbed their senses became an additional distraction they had to medicate, shrug off, or curse.

Cal Regan had done exactly that, forgotten himself for a few hours in the unscheduled remains of a hectic Saturday. It happens. Instances of recreational irresponsibility are expected on campaigns. They are not expected, however, of the campaign manager. He had been stupid and lucky. No serious damage seemed to have been done. Rumors would swirl for a time through Tess Gilchrest's circle of campaign confidantes, and a few knowing looks might be furtively exchanged when he arrived at the dinner that evening with his sensational-looking and very young date. But she had made clear she expected nothing from him, and he needn't worry his lapse in judgment would cost him more than temporary embarrassment. "Looks like no harm, no foul," he later explained to Mick Lowe. "She's an unusual girl."

Relieved, and not normally given to introspection, Regan did not bother to identify a motive for his indiscretion. Had he done so, he might have concluded he had simply taken the opportunity to blow off a little steam between the end of the summer campaign and the start of the convention and the frenzied, perilous two months that would follow. He would have dismissed as absurd the suggestion that he had sought comfort to ease the pain of his separation from Maddy Cohan.

All things considered, the campaign was in decent shape. Better than decent, really. The president's reelection was not a certainty or as secure as they had once hoped it would be by this point, but Regan was confident they would leave the convention with a decided advantage over their opponent. The campaign, under his management, had made no grievous errors during the summer, nor had their candidate, and he did not think it was tempting fate to indulge in a little self-congratulation.

Their attacks through the spring and summer had not destroyed Morrison, and Regan now conceded it had probably been unrealistic to expect they could have. Morrison, as they had realized early, was a steady and intelligent opponent, and his campaign reflected his virtues. In the last general election, their opponent's campaign had been obsessed with the daily news cycle, making it overreactive and inconsistent, shifting from one attack to another, one message to another. Their opponent had been unpredictable, sometimes maddeningly so for O, who believed one of his greatest talents as a candidate was his ability to anticipate and preempt attacks. But in the final weeks of that campaign, holding a lead they knew was insurmountable, an atmosphere of celebration and self-congratulation had begun to pervade his campaign. It was not in O's nature to be exuberant in success nor to despair over a setback, and he often reacted to displays of either emotion by playing the detached analyst, and introducing a modestly discordant observation. One week before the last election, an uncharacteristically excited Avi Samuelson had called him to share the latest polls. "It's over," his advisor had pronounced. "Next Tuesday, you'll be the president-elect of the United States, and we'll all be geniuses." O had responded that his opponent "had defeated himself. Our only genius was to let him."

The remark had not been intended to chastise Samuelson for his boast or to disparage the talents and industry of his campaign staff and the pride that was their due. He just found it hard to resist displaying the intelligent scrutiny he always brought to his endeavors and the self-knowledge that informed it, and which he believed he possessed in greater measure than most people did. It was a paradox that did not confound him as it did others, that his modesty could be so prideful.

Luck had not favored them this time with an opponent who could be induced to defeat himself. Morrison was patient and disciplined, and shrewd in defending his reputation for competence and probity. He had not survived their attacks unscathed. Nor had he easily brushed off their attempts to make a vice of his virtues when they had started to concentrate their fire, as O had instructed, on policy positions that should trouble voters. It is all the more alarming, it was strongly implied, that his record as governor showed that with his military discipline and closed mind, Morrison could prove quite competent in imposing these unwanted policies on the country. A suggested tagline for one wave of negative ads, "Tom Morrison might be strong enough to lead America in the wrong direction, but why would we let him?" had been rejected as too wordy. More favorably considered was "Tom Morrison: Strong, maybe. Wrong for America, definitely." But Regan had worried that voters would consider strength such an admirable trait in a president that they couldn't be made to fear how he might use it. Regan wrote the tagline they eventually decided to use: "Tom Morrison, the wrong direction for America." In political advertising, avoiding subtlety is a safer bet than being artful.

Morrison had weathered it. But he had not, as it had once appeared he might, ridden his early momentum to a sustained lead in the polls. His unfavorables had grown slowly but steadily. He had had a good convention the week before theirs. His selection of a young and promising senator from a northern plains state, whose firmly conservative convictions were modestly expressed, had been widely praised as a solid choice for a running mate. Morrison's acceptance speech had been admired for its reassuring sincerity and dignity. The day after he had delivered it, he had gained his first lead in the polls. It had been a modest one, only four points—disappointing, really, the press had hinted.

It was all bounce, the O campaign insisted, and now it was their turn to showcase their candidate in the venue that best displayed his talents. They would recover their lead and add to it.

As long as O and the campaign made no serious mistakes in the next two months, the debates would be Morrison's only opportunity to overtake them. None of them worried O would manage worse than a draw in any of the three debates. They had been through them before, and they knew their man could handle them. Their self-assurance would not prevent them from sweating them out, of course.

The strain of their exhaustive preparations, the painstaking compiling of briefing books, the endless rounds of mock debates, the nagging worry they might have missed something—an unanticipated angle of attack, a small issue overlooked because no one had imagined how it could be interpreted to suggest bad judgment or ill intentions or a character flaw, or how it could expose a vulnerability that would leave their tired candidate momentarily perplexed and stuttering in the hot glare of the television lights while fifty million voters squirmed uncomfortably on their sofas—made debates, because they could completely alter the course of it, the most terrifying experiences in a campaign.

Morrison's campaign had been leaking for several days that their latest filing with the Federal Election Commission would show they were finally closing the resource gap, which had been narrowing throughout the summer, and they were confident they could compete dollar for dollar for the remainder of the campaign. No one doubted the claim was at least approximately true. Money always poured in during and after the conventions. No one on the president's team had expected they would enjoy such a pronounced financial advantage for the entire campaign. But Morrison would have to outspend them substantially to alter the trajectory of the race, which Regan was increasingly confident favored them, and no one in either campaign believed Morrison would ever have enough money to do that.

"We have the better candidate, the better record, the better message. And most of all, voters always respond better to the candidate who campaigns on a vision of the future and not some manufactured nostalgia for the past," Regan replied to a reporter who had asked him why they were not worried that Morrison, who was now running a little ahead of the president, might have as good a chance to win as the president had.

He could have added, but did not, that the race had been theirs to lose since June, when the unemployment rate, which had stubbornly remained above eight percent, had finally dropped below seven percent and was now approaching six. Consumer confidence was approaching levels last seen in 2005. "The country," the president's chief pollster had cheerfully pronounced, pausing for dramatic effect before he presented the results of their most recent battleground state polls, "is in a much better mood." It was a moment of relief verging on triumph that many of them had once worried they might never enjoy.

The country had not been in a good mood for three years. And everything they had done to improve it—a trillion dollars of government spending to arrest the slumping economy; subsidies to the middle class to obtain better health care insurance and a college education for their children, and to purchase automobiles; reregulating the banks and forcing them to provide better terms for troubled mortgages; tax credits for businesses that hired new employees; all that and more—had failed to assuage the public's anger that Washington had failed them in their hour of need.

Through the midterm elections that had cost the president's party its comfortable majorities in Congress and beyond, everything they did to alleviate the anxiety of the American middle class seemed at times only to exasperate the people more. It was as if they had expected O to turn the country around in his first month in office, and when he didn't, they hardened their hearts against him. They were skeptical about everything. Everything he had done, things no other president in modern times had managed to do, had been vilified by Republicans as an arrogation of power that stole by degrees the liberty and property of the American people. Comical and predictable, O thought, how Republican criticism had acquired no more subtlety or maturity than it possessed in the days when Republicans had huffed indignantly that Franklin Roosevelt was a traitor to his class.

What had surprised him was how easily their anger and obsessive distrust had influenced the people who stood to gain the most from his policies, the struggling middle class, the kind of people who had revered FDR. Why would they be more susceptible to fearmongering from Republicans than their grandparents had been during the Great Depression? It was baffling that they could not see the absurdity of these attacks from the very people who were most responsible for the economic predicament they were now in: the people whose fiscal policies had plunged the nation ever deeper into debt for the benefit of the wealthy and their own hold on power; the people who had mired the country in two wars of indefinite duration and incalculable expense because to them vengeance and machismo were the proof of American exceptionalism; the people who had sanctioned and cosseted the Wall Street pirates whose unregulated greed had caused the near collapse of the global credit system.

He had inherited this mess. He hadn't caused the events that had made Americans so anxious about their future and had so infuriated them with the inequities that followed in the wake of those events: the layoffs, the bailouts, the bonuses, the seemingly daily reminders they had been screwed, and that the people who had screwed them were laughing all the way to the bank. He had expected them to understand he was doing all he could, and urgently, to rescue the economy from the disaster the Republicans had let happen. Instead, many of them had been stirred into almost a mob mentality, impervious to facts and reason or even the memory of their recent experience with Republican incompetence, as evidenced by ridiculously contradictory complaints of socialism and favoring the interests of Wall Street over Main Street.

He had fought for more than a year to make certain they would have decent health care insurance, that people would never lose or be denied coverage because they had become sick or their children had preexisting conditions. And Republicans had managed to convince at least half the country he wasn't protecting them but taking something from them. He had been denounced for wresting control of the automobile industry from the idiots who had destroyed it, and providing the capital necessary to prevent its complete collapse and save tens of thousands of jobs. Had people been driven mad by the sudden economic downturn that had brought him to office? Was there ever a more impatient people? Did they expect it all to be repaired overnight? How could they take seriously, much less consider returning to power, the people who had caused it and were resisting his every effort to hasten a recovery?

There had been times when he had briefly despaired that he could not make people understand how unreasonable they were. But he would not panic. He did not like to wait on events, but accepted he had no other choice. And as the recovering economy belatedly began to be noticed by the voters, and each month brought new reports of increased job growth, the public was proving less susceptible to Republican lies and less appreciative of Republican opposition to his policies. Lately, they had begun to see in their polling evidence that independents, even some of those who usually voted for Republicans, were beginning to show a long-overdue openness to the idea that the president might have known what he was doing all along and had admirably stuck to his course while Republicans had barked and obstructed. That was O's interpretation anyway, as he saw his favorable numbers steadily improve, although he knew Americans weren't by nature a self-reflective or self-critical people.

In Cal Regan's opinion, voters were always the most lagging of economic indicators. But the recovery had gained sufficient steam far enough in advance of the election to work the sea change in public opinion that now gave them their advantage. They were finally in a position to play offense for the sake of scoring points and not just as the only defense available to them as it had been in the spring, before the country had come to its senses. He had come up with the theme for the fall campaign, "We've come too far to go back now." It had seemed the obvious argument to him, as one recent poll after another revealed the public's growing optimism, expressed, as it always is in political polling, by the rising number of affirmative responses to the question "Do you think the country is heading in the right direction?" For six years the majority of voters had answered the question firmly in the negative, striking terror into the hearts of any incumbent facing reelection. Now, a clear though not overwhelming majority were encouraged that the country had turned around. "Time to take credit," Regan asserted. "God knows we've taken enough of the blame. And time to make Tom Terrific accept responsibility for the fact that his party did everything it could to hold us back."

The president's speechwriters had been lukewarm to the line. "Speechwriters," Regan complained to Mick Lowe, "all think they're fucking Shakespeare, and everybody else in this business is illiterate." In truth, they had thought it, in the words of one, "a little uninspired," although the alternative they had offered—"Promises Made. Promises Kept"—had struck Regan as pedestrian. "Not only is it not about the future," Regan had complained, "but it invites Morrison and the press to remind voters of the promises that weren't kept. Maybe we should add, 'and promises we're still working on.'"

The dispute proved a brief distraction, however. Samuelson had liked Regan's suggestion, and so had the president, and thus the line would become the chanted mantra of a campaign on the move and would be featured in every form of campaign communication from the moment the president introduced it in his acceptance speech until Election Day. "How long do you think it will take Campbell to take credit for it?" Regan had derisively asked Lowe, referring to the president's chief speechwriter, Tim Campbell. "I'm sure he already has," Lowe had responded. "He's probably worked out the Latin for it and tattooed it on his ass."

Since the June unemployment figures were released the O campaign had believed that the environment they were running in would continue to improve and favor them. Swing voters were increasingly optimistic that the worst was finally behind them, and that the country, by which they meant the government, was doing reasonably well, even though ingrained cultural hostility toward government prevented them from saying so.

In this environment, Morrison, not O, needed to catch some unexpected breaks or do something to shake up the race. The need could cause him to take risks, maybe do something out of character for a man with his self-assurance and discipline. They could only hope. "What's it gonna take to make that fucker sweat?" Mick Lowe often asked after watching Morrison placidly respond to another reporter to whom Lowe had fed questions they hoped would provoke him. But all the O campaign believed they needed to do was protect their advantage, avoid catastrophic mistakes, and be patient. They weren't going to win by a landslide, but they would probably win. They had attained the enviable position when they could say to one another, junior and senior staff alike, "I'd rather be us than them."

It was only human for Cal Regan to wish they could blow the race out so they could all sleep a little longer and more soundly at night. But it was good to be in a position where you didn't need any more luck to win. *No need to tempt fate, buddy,* he cautioned himself. *Just win the fucking thing. No extra credit for beating the guy senseless.*

$\star$ CHAPTER 15 $\star$

"I think your whole approach has to change," the not-quite-A-list celebrity, who wore glasses without corrective lenses to affect a more intelligent look than nature had provided him, said. "Right now, you're trying to convince people to sacrifice something to fix a problem they're not convinced is a problem for them. Melting glaciers, it's one or two degrees warmer in the summer. They don't give a shit. They don't care what it means for polar bears. What's it mean for them? Maybe they think it could be a problem a hundred years from now. But they don't know anybody who'll be alive a hundred years from now. People are selfish. And you're not going to convince them there's some new economy waiting to be built on electric cars that's going to make them rich. Why should they pay higher utility bills or higher taxes so some hippie can get a job building windmills? You have to scare the shit out of them. Show them how their standard of living, not their grandchildren's, is going to suffer right away if we don't start doing something about it. Everything's going to get more expensive for them. Groceries, gas, air fares, retirement, Christmas presents for the kids, everything. Their employers are going to lay off people because their energy bills are too high or they're selling products to a disappearing market. You have to start blaming climate change for all the bad stuff they feel threatened by today. Then you'll get them to swallow the costs for doing something. There's no other way. You just aren't making it personal enough."

Regan had ceased trying to interrupt this long and emphatic exposition on the politics of climate change, which had just concluded with the criticism that the O administration hadn't scared people enough. For the last several minutes he had merely nodded in agreement until he could signal to his harasser he had gotten the message and there was no need to continue. "You make a lot of good points. I'm going to share them with the president." This was his standard ploy to change the conversation.

The dinner, five attractively presented courses and three well-chosen wines, delivered at appropriate intervals in a tastefully modern private dining room reserved for them at the very expensive restaurant on the top floor of Knowles's very expensive hotel, now approached its third hour and was becoming as tedious as Regan had feared it would be.

From the moment Knowles had greeted him with "Ah, our guest of honor has arrived," Regan had been pressed with advice, criticism, information, and occasional praise from the eighteen invited guests, not including Knowles and his personal assistant, a breathtakingly beautiful twenty-seven-year-old girl of Scandinavian origins, whose round-the-clock attendance on her employer would end with the arrival of Mrs. Knowles on Tuesday morning.

"My God, look who's here," Knowles had exclaimed upon recognizing Tess Gilchrest, who he had been told that afternoon would be coming, "the apple of Hank Gilchrest's eye, and mine!" An embrace followed, perhaps a little more intimate and lingering than usual, and explained by a reference to their long acquaintance. "I've known this young lady since she was breaking hearts in kindergarten," he had cheerfully boasted. And then, taking her face with both his hands, he asked after her parents. "They're great," she replied. "They send their love. They're coming tomorrow." Lowering her voice a little, she added, "And I bet the first thing they'll ask me is if you behaved yourself tonight." Knowles took the caution as playful flirtation, winking as he responded, "If I don't, they'll have themselves to blame, raising such an irresistible daughter."

Regan was used to being told his business, and to being lectured on how the White House should frame its policy arguments by people who had never run a campaign or worked there. He accepted it politely. Many successful people share the conceit that their genius for managing investment funds or selling software or making movies would be a welcome asset in politics. It was a bore, but being bored was a small price to pay for the money they raised or the glamour they lent the campaign. *And you never know,* he told himself. *The billionaire boring the shit out of you today might become your new fifty-thousand-a-month retainer tomorrow.*

It was not a sentiment shared by most political professionals, many of whom had at one time or another worked for candidates who had tired of making millions and decided to try their hand at politics. The self-funder disease, they call it, in reference to the common attribute of CEOs who are encouraged by the party to challenge a well-financed incumbent or run for an open seat in an expensive television market, not because the party thinks they are born winners, but because no experienced politician is willing to and no one thinks anyone else could raise enough money. Their wealth is recruited. Their possible political talent is a secondary consideration. But with their wealth often comes a presumptuousness that eventually causes professionals involved with the campaign to grind their teeth and question whether their generous and promptly paid compensation is worth the aggravation.

Typically, a grudging yes is the answer. Self-funding candidates pay better. They assume politics works just like their business. You pay the talent more than the competition offered. Money is the only reliable motivator. Winning bonuses, sometimes eye-popping sums, are often promised. As one veteran of several self-funded campaigns explained, "They really can be pains in the ass. They'll spend hours rejecting bumper stickers and yard signs. And, Christ, you can't tell them anything about message or ad strategy. But they're the best-paying pains in the ass you'll ever find."

For Regan, these purely transactional relationships were part of politics' appeal. And he never minded as much as others did the presumptions and interference of rich people, who, once they had invested in your campaign, expected a little deference in return. "Oh, he's a sinner, all right," he had once cheerfully conceded to Maddy Cohan, who had mocked the recent conversion to Catholicism of a Democratic congressman widely reputed to be a philanderer. "But doesn't the church welcome sinners? Or is politics their only route to redemption?"

"I don't care that he's a sinner," she had replied. "I care that he's a hypocrite. Don't you?" Not quite recognizing the earnest conviction behind the question, he had joked, "Only if he converts to the Republican Party."

A nonjudgmental attitude about, as he put it, "people who pay for the privilege of being assholes" had served him well so far, in politics, at Hanson, Strong, and as he patiently feigned interest in the unsolicited opinions of his companions at the dinner held in his honor. It also made it easier for Regan to like Allen Knowles, recognizing in his host and client the conniving heart of a mercenary, but recognizing, too, the peculiar honesty in the lack of pretense to virtue that made him a valued client and, more often than not, good company.

Knowles, as dozens of mostly flattering profiles observed, was a man of infectious energy and enthusiasm; a "charismatic corporate leader," as a bedazzled *Fortune* reporter had described him; a "boardroom swashbuckler," proclaimed another. Much of his biography, from his childhood to his thirties, was "shrouded in mystery, apparently by design." All that was publicly known about him that was not in doubt or disputed was his emergence from anonymity in Los Angeles in the mid-1990s, when he had acquired with venture capital from several obscure investors a small and struggling gaming software company he reorganized to develop antipiracy software for the new video format that would soon come to market, the DVD. He renamed the company Gabriel Tech, for a younger brother who had died in childhood, it was said. By 1999, he had a contract from one of the largest entertainment corporations. By 2001, he had contracts with the corporate parents of all the major studios and announced he was taking his company public. Gabriel Tech was listed on the NASDAQ a full year after the technology bubble burst. Its IPO made him a billionaire.

From there, the company began to develop encryption technology for other markets, and had since 2005 focused much of its attention on the defense industry, and the U.S. military's growing concern with threats to the security of its communications networks, primarily from China. Initially, he had intended to sell his software to the militaries of several foreign countries; none of them were enemies of the United States, but neither were they allies. When he declared his intention to Gabriel Tech executives, the company's lawyers informed him that existing export restrictions on dual-use technology forbade such sales. He showed neither surprise nor skepticism at the unwelcome news. "All right, then, we'll sell it to the U.S. military," was his immediate reaction. "What's the best defense contractor we can work with?" he asked his subordinates, none of whom had an immediate answer. "Well, figure it out," he charged them, "by the end of the day."

By his own admission, he did not have a background in science or technology. In the late eighties and early nineties, he had worked in sales for a software developer in San Jose. Although he was apparently an employee in good standing with the company, he was not, according to a former executive there, "on the management track." How he had managed to persuade investors to finance his purchase of Gabriel Tech is one of the many unanswered questions that gave his reputation its intriguing air of mystery.

In several press accounts of his life, he was described as the son of a car salesman and a stay-at-home mother, the second of five children raised in a well-kept one-story ranch in La Verne, a middle-class suburb thirty miles east of Los Angeles. He played varsity basketball for the local high school and attended the University of California, Riverside, where he majored in history and graduated summa cum laude from its College of Humanities, Arts, and Social Sciences in 1980. A partial scholarship had made it possible for him to earn an MBA in 1982 from Harvard Business School. He had married three times and had three children, two sons and a daughter, the two sons by his second wife, the daughter by his third.

Not all of these biographical details survived subsequent scrutiny, though many of them were believed to be accurate. He was thrice married. He had three children. He did, in fact, grow up in La Verne, and his late father had sold cars for a living. His parents had divorced when he was seven, however, and his mother, who had worked as a receptionist in the office of the family's pediatrician, was given custody of their four, not five children. The deceased younger brother, Gabriel, was in reality the family dog, a sheltie-Lab mix, who had succumbed to old age when

Knowles was still in high school. "A real charmer," Knowles had remembered. "I loved that dog. Best friend I ever had."

He had made the varsity basketball team in high school, but contrary to the perception promoted by Knowles's oft repeated boast—"I really had some hops back then; used to dunk on this guy who started for UCLA as a freshman"—he rarely played more than five minutes a game, just to give the starting small forward a little breather. He had attended Riverside but had not, it seems, actually graduated, summa cum laude or otherwise. The Harvard MBA was a fiction.

When confronted by a reporter with the fact that all his siblings were alive and not one of them answered to the name Gabriel, he expressed his befuddlement. "I don't know how that rumor got started. Someone must have confused me with someone else," he mused. "I never said the company was named for my brother." The explanation confounded several senior executives at Gabriel Tech, who remembered a tearful reminiscence of the lost brother in a toast offered at a company dinner to celebrate its going public. The discrepancies in his academic career were breezily confessed. "Oh, that. A little résumé padding when you're trying to get started. Get-your-foot-in-the-door kinda thing. Typical kid stuff."

Gabriel Tech's success discouraged any doubts about his entrepreneurial skills or competence as a chief executive. Although his familiarity with the idiosyncratic personalities of software engineers was limited to his occasional pestering of a few "mad geeks" at the San Jose software company for information that could help him "juice up" his sales pitch, he was widely regarded as an extraordinary judge of talent in that field. "Half the time, you wonder if he really understands his products," one competitor had anonymously volunteered to a reporter. "But he's got balls, and a hell of a talent for recognizing talent."

To the same reporter, Knowles had dismissed the second part of the compliment. "Anyone with an IQ above a hundred can recognize talent. If someone can do something I can't, and nine out of ten people can, they have talent."

When the reporter asked him, "Then *what* would you say your talent is?" he instantly replied, "I'm a great motivator of talent."

"And what makes you a great motivator?"

"The same thing that religions use to motivate."

"God?"

"No. The afterlife. I sell my people on the afterlife. Do you really think religions only use God to motivate their people? They use the promise of the afterlife. Heaven or hell. I know what my people can do. I know what they can achieve for themselves. The life they can achieve for themselves if they do what I know they're capable of doing. I talk to my people all the time about how their lives will change, their professional opportunities, their reputations, their self-respect, their place in history, their standard of living, their children's future. All that and more, if they just do what I know they can do, and do it faster than the competition. And if they don't, I'll make their lives hell."

Although he had not intended to give offense with his brief discourse on the practical similarities between theology and his leadership style, he had. The observation suggested the headline for the magazine profile, "Heaven on Earth: The Gospel According to Allen Knowles," and the theme for many deprecating sermons in many places of worship on many Sundays that followed its publication. In a subsequent interview, he conceded the remark had been foolish and inconsiderate. "I should have listened to my mother, who told me never to discuss religion with anyone but my pastor," he observed. Had she been asked, his mother would have been unlikely to remember imparting the caution to her inattentive and staunchly agnostic son.

After dessert, a fresh strawberry and marshmallow tart, had been gently placed before each guest and wineglasses were refilled, Allen Knowles stood to toast Cal Regan.

"I met this young man about four years ago, during the last campaign. He wasn't the guy in charge that time. But you could tell right away he knew his business, and it wouldn't be long before he would be running a big operation of some kind. I said to myself, there's a kid who's going somewhere. Not to get too sentimental here, but I think you could say I recognized a kindred spirit, a guy with big ambitions, and the nerve and talent to get after 'em. So I did what I always do when I'm really impressed with someone: I put him on the payroll." As guests applauded the businessman's expression of esteem, Regan smiled demurely and slightly bowed his head, and noticed Tess Gilchrest wink at him.

"And he did what a guy with his smarts and talent should do: he maximized his opportunity. He got me on the hook for a pretty fat retainer. I knew he was fleecing me a little, but you know what? He was worth it. Every penny. And you want to know how committed this guy is to the president? Well, I can guarantee you the president's not paying him anywhere near the money I was paying him, and he's getting a lot more for his money, too."

Knowles paused for a moment for his guests to laugh at his joke—which he had meant to be at his own expense, although Regan wasn't quite sure it hadn't been at his—before briefly paying homage to the president and the importance of the president's reelection.

"After all, what else could be so important that it could get a guy like Cal to work a lot harder for a lot less money?" He paused again for another murmur of appreciative laughter before closing his toast. "So here's to the president's campaign manager, Cal Regan; a man with the character to take a pay cut for the sake of the country, and the brains to know we'll all come out ahead on the deal."

When a few guests offered "Hear, hear," Regan wondered which of the tribute's possible interpretations they were seconding before he rose to thank Knowles for the dinner and the "very kind words, I think." To the other guests, he expressed his gratitude for the honor of their presence: "for your commitment to the president and what he's trying to achieve for America; for giving him your support and counsel, and helping give our country a government it can be proud of. Thank you for your patronage, but most of all, on behalf of the president and the country, thank you for your patriotism." It was a line he had used to good effect at similar gatherings, and was his preferred interpretation of Knowles's "come out ahead on the deal" comment.

Flattered and well fed, the hour approaching eleven, the guests thanked Knowles for his hospitality and began their leave-taking, offering Regan a last compliment or suggestion or pledge of further assistance as they shook his hand and patted his shoulder on their way out. Regan, too, with a nod to Tess Gilchrest, signaled his intention to leave as soon as he could politely withdraw. After he had dropped Tess at her hotel and made a last phone call to check in with Mick Lowe, he would be in his bed before midnight and enjoy, for the only time that week, more than five hours of sleep.

"Hang on a second," Knowles instructed him. "Let's have a drink before you leave."

"I can't, Allen, not tonight. I've still got a couple of calls to make and a six o'clock start tomorrow."

"Oh, c'mon, a quick one," Knowles pleaded as he released the hand of a departing guest. "I've got something for you that can't wait." The guest, whom Knowles had just bid good night, paused to consider whether he might himself stay for the proffered last drink and satisfy his curiosity about the "something" his host had that couldn't wait. But Knowles, seeming to sense the interest, discouraged it with a wave and a repeated "Good night, Tony." Regan, who was not compelled by curiosity to remain, knew from experience that another appeal would be pointless once Knowles had refused to be refused, and reluctantly he nodded his assent.

A few minutes later, Regan and Tess settled into chairs in the spacious sitting room of Knowles's hotel suite, while Knowles's assistant took a seat on the sofa opposite. Knowles, not bothering to ask their preferences, fetched a bottle of cognac and four snifters from a well-stocked bar and poured out a decent measure for each of them, before seating himself next to the assistant, whom he called Maj or Maja, Regan not quite catching whether the name ended in a vowel.

"Ladies, I'm going to talk a little campaign business with Cal, here," he announced. "I'm sure I don't need to ask you to treat anything you hear as privileged. Not the kind of stuff you want to gossip about with friends." Then, addressing himself to Regan, he asked for "the short version where you guys think you are. The way you guys see it. Not the way you explain it to the money."

Vexed not by Knowles's presumptuousness, which he was used to, but by the prospect that he could be detained for considerably longer than it would take to finish one after-dinner drink, Regan tried to put him off. "There isn't a short version. There's only a really short version. We're in good shape. The environment's a lot better than it was six months ago. The polls are good. We think we've contained Morrison. It's probably ours to lose. I couldn't tell you much more until a week or so after the convention, when we see the first numbers that don't have a convention bounce in them. I expect they'll be fine, but we'll have to see."

As Regan spoke, Knowles nodded, indicating not merely his agreement with the assessment but that the answer had been one he expected, though not the one he wanted. "I'm sorry, I should have been clearer. I wasn't asking for a general state-of-the-race briefing. I'd like to know where you guys are with Morrison. How do you plan to keep him contained?"

"Not sure I'm following you."

"Well, you went after him pretty hard right out of the gate. He seems to have survived it, though I'm sure you managed to hold him back a bit. I've seen all your ads. I know what you threw at him. I assume you're holding your best stuff in reserve, right?"

Regan explained that campaigns tried to budget their advertising in advance, but decisions about content and placement were usually made closer to airtime. "You want to be able to respond to changes in the race, unanticipated developments, an opponent's mistake, or something else you didn't see coming."

"I get that. But still, theoretically, you don't throw your best punch, your knockout punch, if you've got one, before the conventions, right? What I'm trying to figure out is if you guys have something you're gonna break out in case of emergency or if you don't."

Now Regan was curious. While the campaign would continue to have discussions about how to sharpen their negative messaging, they weren't holding in reserve any research that would deliver a knockout punch. Knowles's abruptness and the leading nature of his questions gave Regan the impression that Knowles knew something he did not.

"In my experience, Allen, nothing is ever guaranteed to knock your opponent out unless you have pictures. And, no, we don't have anything like that. We think we can continue to make a strong case that Morrison's election wouldn't be in the best interests of about ninety-five percent of voters. And considering that a majority of voters now think the country is headed in the right direction, we think we've got enough to convince them to stick with the president. Is there something you think we've overlooked?"

"I guess there is. Unless you're not telling me something because you think you can't trust me."

"No."

"Well, I guess I assumed you guys would have this. It's not exactly hard to find."

As Knowles began to explain, Regan glanced at Maj or Maja and then at Tess, and interrupted him. "Allen, before you go any further, why don't we stop for tonight and talk about it at some point tomorrow? I'm very interested, but it's probably not something that will interest our friends here. And I'd like Mick Lowe to hear it from you as well."

"Girls, that's Cal's way of telling you politely he doesn't trust you."

"It's not that, it's just—"

"Just what?"

"Late. It's just late to have this kind of conversation, and to ask the right questions about this information, if it's potentially as interesting as you indicate it is. So I think—"

Knowles, who for some reason seemed to have become irritated, cut him off again. "Right. Well, let me just give you my short version, then. Word in the industry is Channing-Mills is under investigation by the FBI for violating the Foreign Corrupt Practices Act. I figured you guys would have known that, since your candidate is the president of the United States and your opponent used to run the company. You and Mick can decide whether it's worth your trouble."

CHAPTER 16

"Can't be," Mick Lowe said, shaking his head for emphasis.

"I know," Regan agreed.

"There's no way we wouldn't have heard about it."

"I know."

They both felt certain an investigation wouldn't have escaped the attention of the White House or the press. But their skepticism allowed for a barely nurtured hope that perhaps some embarrassing incident had occurred during Tom Morrison's tenure at Channing-Mills that had attracted the interest of the company's competitors, and had been embellished with a speculative allegation of criminal misconduct.

Lowe would be embarrassed by the failure of the research team he had hired and supervised to discover a rumor about Morrison's past, even one that proved to be ridiculously exaggerated, and felt a professional responsibility to avoid appearing intrigued by the prospect. Regan's curiosity was less inhibited, owing to his appreciation of Allen Knowles as the kind of man who would have a practiced eye for evaluating incriminating rumors about a competitor.

"I didn't know Knowles had any defense business," Lowe admitted.

"He's got a joint venture with a defense contractor to develop encryption technology for the military," Regan explained.

"So, what's in this for him?"

"I don't know."

The short version Knowles gave him had been met with the same incredulity. "We *would* know about it, Allen, if it were true," Regan had insisted the previous night. "We would have known about it a long time ago."

But that had led to the offering of a longer version as Regan glanced at his watch, noticing the approach of midnight, and with each passing minute being made more uncomfortable by the presence of his attentive twenty-four-year-old date and the silent Maj or Maja. But he couldn't terminate the conversation then, not while a barely glowing ember of probably false hope existed. Could there be at the bottom of the almost-certain-to-be-untrue rumor about an FBI investigation some small, overlooked fact about the operations of a defense company that could, if discovered and properly presented, reflect poorly on the man who used to run it?

"You might be right. Could just be a rumor," Knowles had conceded. "A lot of Channing-Mills's competitors wouldn't mind seeing them in trouble with the feds. But it's really making the rounds."

"Well, what exactly have you heard?"

"The usual thing, winning overseas contracts the old-fashioned way by bribing the cousins and mistresses of various Third World thugs."

"Anything else? Was Morrison still CEO when the rumored bribery occurred?"

Knowles recounted for Regan all he had learned about the rumored circumstances that had led to the rumored investigation. When Morrison had run Channing-Mills, he had overseen the acquisition of Shield Holdings, a profitable but relatively small contractor. Most of Shield Holdings' business was in small arms and body armor. "Not really Channing-Mills's thing," Knowles observed, explaining that Channing-Mills's competitors thought it was an odd acquisition, especially since Shield Holdings had a reputation for beating the competition without "cutting their margins by coming in with the lowest bid."

Even more intriguing was Morrison's decision to retain the services of Shield Holdings' vice president for international sales, Victor Salazar, who was rumored to be a shady character. "No one believes that's just a rumor," Knowles added. "He's the kind of guy who always seemed to find the right local to put on the payroll. No one thought he would survive the acquisition."

But Salazar had stayed on at Channing-Mills and remained in charge of Shield's small-arms overseas trade. He didn't leave the company until after Morrison had left to run for governor. Early retirement had been the official explanation, but few people believed it, and the industry began to buzz with gossip that the Justice Department was close to indicting Salazar. Knowles had first heard about it then, from a senior executive in a defense company Knowles neglected to name.

"This must have been what, seven, eight years ago?" Regan asked.

"Two thousand five, yeah."

"And he hasn't been indicted. So, obviously, they weren't close or they decided they didn't have enough to charge him or they never had a case in the first place. After seven years, you'd think they would have tried, convicted, and sentenced him. He'd probably be out on parole by now."

"Fair point. But sometimes these things get dropped and picked up again, when the feds get ahold of some new information. Or maybe unloading Salazar was part of an informal agreement Channing made, a 'We'll save you the trouble and get rid of the guy' thing, only the deal didn't happen until Morrison left the company. I understand cases like that are hard to prove unless you've got something on tape, caught someone in a sting. But it begs the question, why didn't Morrison get rid of the guy when he ran the company? I doubt his successor knew something about him that Morrison didn't know. Like I said, Salazar didn't exactly have a sterling reputation."

Regan entertained the supposition that Victor Salazar was, as widely rumored, dirty, and that Justice had investigated him. But they would have investigated him for things he had done before Channing-Mills acquired his company. And for whatever reason, Justice hadn't indicted him, and he thought it was unlikely Salazar was still under investigation. He had left Channing-Mills less than two years after the merger. Knowles conceded he hadn't heard an allegation that Salazar had violated any laws while he was at Channing-Mills, which, if he knew he was under investigation, he wouldn't have risked. And there wasn't proof Morrison knew of or condoned the practices that Justice at some point might have been investigating.

"Look, I just assumed you guys already knew about this," Knowles repeated. "Maybe there's nothing to it. You guys will know better than I do whether it's worth your trouble. But, as I said, Salazar's reputation wasn't a secret. Everyone in the arms export business knew what kind of guy he was. And Tom Morrison would have known it when he bought the company and decided to keep Salazar in the same job."

In the car, Regan had impressed on Tess his certainty that what they had just heard was "probably a hundred percent false, probably started by a pissed-off competitor who lost a contract to Channing-Mills."

"Yes, Cal, I know how rumors get started in business," she had interrupted him.

Regan had considered for a moment asking her whether her dismissive tone indicated displeasure with him or with someone else, but he decided to continue with his caution.

"I'm sure you get that the *rumor* is probably bullshit. Even if it isn't complete bullshit, it's still probably not that big a deal. A guy broke the law when he worked for another company, but not when he worked for Morrison. The most important thing to understand is that while it won't be a problem for Morrison, it could be a problem for us if a reporter ever thought we were pushing it. So we don't want anything we just heard and don't know is true getting around the campaign. Okay?"

"Okay, boss," she had replied while snapping a salute that made Cal Regan wonder for the second time if she was making fun of him.

A waste of time, Regan thought, when he asked Mick Lowe if he could think of anyone who worked at Justice or had worked there in the last administration, and could be discreetly tasked with finding out if there had ever been an investigation or even a discussion about investigating anyone associated with Channing-Mills. "I suppose I can find someone," Lowe replied. Regan mentioned a young partner at Hanson, Strong with whom he was friendly, and who had worked at Justice in the late 1990s and early 2000s—a deputy assistant attorney general in the Criminal division—and still had lots of friends there. "Hopefully, one or two in the Fraud section," he speculated. "I'll give him a call next week."

Left unsaid, because it was unnecessary for Regan and Lowe to caution each other not to get carried away, was the importance of keeping their inquiries discreet and as vague as possible. Neither expected to find anything the campaign could use against Morrison, and they both knew to be careful not to convey a sense of urgency or an intention to do anything but put to rest a rumor they believed was untrue. They were just doing due diligence.

"Are you going to bring it up with Samuelson?" Lowe asked.

"No," Regan answered. "Not yet, anyway." It was also unnecessary for Regan to explain to Lowe his reasons for not informing Samuelson. It would be reckless to risk a story that a senior White House official had discussed with the president's campaign staff malicious gossip about the president's opponent, and that after that discussion, questions had been put to certain Justice Department attorneys, one of whom had mentioned it to a reporter who happened to be his neighbor or college buddy or whose kids attended the same grade school.

At two o'clock that afternoon, the chairman of the Democratic National Committee would gavel the convention to order. The First Lady would speak in prime time tonight. She would arrive at noon, and Regan would be waiting to greet her at her suite in the same hotel where he was lodged. He would brief her on the events of the day and gossip with her a little about a few of the personalities who were also scheduled to speak that evening. He would accompany her to the hall at five o'clock, when she would rehearse her speech, or rather, read a few lines from it to make sure the teleprompters were placed where she preferred them. The following day would feature the keynote speaker, a fresh face who had won the governorship of a red state, a lucky survivor of the Republican tidal wave in the last election. On Wednesday, the president would arrive in town, and he and the vice president would be renominated and briefly appear with their families onstage. They would give their acceptance speeches on Thursday.

Regan would make sure these events occurred without problem, to the thunderous acclaim of delegates, the general approval of the press, and the satisfaction of the president. He would spend countless hours repeating the convention's theme and setting up the campaign's fall message to reporters, staff, speechwriters, surrogate speakers, donors, and delegations.

Although the managing of the convention had been delegated to two experienced hands from conventions past, he would oversee every aspect of it. His schedule would be crowded with a succession of meetings with people from all the convention's operations. He would meet twice daily with the various communications shops: television, print, national, regional, local, radio, and online. He'd meet with the people who ran the whip operation and made sure delegates were in their seats for prime-time speeches and applauding at the right times. He'd meet with the technicians in charge of the lighting, teleprompters, sight lines, and the pictures that would appear on the immense video screen behind every speaker.

He'd commiserate with the speechwriters who would write or revise most of the speeches that would be delivered at the convention, most of them not in prime time and limited to a few minutes. Almost all the speakers with a three-minute slot arrived at the convention clutching draft remarks that had been lovingly prepared and repeatedly revised to their satisfaction and would take twenty minutes to deliver without applause, of which there would be little after the speechwriters had tossed it in the trash and hastily pounded out a much shorter version.

He'd help soothe egos upset over the pettiest of concerns. Donors who didn't like the seats they had been given for the president's acceptance speech. Party grandees who felt their counsel had been ignored and their influence underutilized. The former vice president whose wife had not received an invitation to sit in the box reserved for the president's family when her husband gave a speech Tuesday night that would be remembered only for its bombast and the deafening volume with which he would deliver even the most pedestrian of its passages. The Senate committee chairman who had forgotten his credentials and been prevented from joining his state's delegation on the floor by a twenty-year-old volunteer who did not know and did not care who he was. Delegates who threatened to walk out when a certain pro-life senator took the stage to give a speech that wouldn't mention abortion.

All these things and more would occupy Cal Regan's time and mind for the next four days. By the end of the convention, he would almost have forgotten about Allen Knowles's tip, and that he and Lowe had decided to make a discreet call or two just to satisfy themselves that they had not missed an opportunity to embarrass Tom Morrison, and force him to spend part, perhaps as much as a week, of the precious time that remained before the election defending his reputation.

He would not get to sleep before two o'clock in the morning any night of the convention. He would not attend any of the most exclusive parties that convened each night as soon as the last speaker strode reluctantly off the stage to applause he or she had hoped would be more sustained. Until midnight or later, he would still have calls that had to be returned or instructions to give for the following day that he might forget if he waited until morning. When at last he could safely retire for the evening, he would limit himself to a single drink with Mick Lowe before enjoying the four hours of sleep he required. If a few reporters, knowing his habit, were waiting in the bar of his hotel in the hope he might divulge something of interest while in a state of relaxation that he would not share with them in an interview, he would accept the drink they would list on their expense accounts, chat amiably with them for a half hour, and leave them disappointed they had learned nothing they could not have found in the talking points repeated in dozens of press releases issued and interviews given that day.

He remembered fondly the conventions he had attended as a younger man with fewer responsibilities. He had enjoyed them like an undergraduate on spring break. He hadn't needed four hours of sleep then.

Drunk and disorderly in New Orleans's French Quarter. Four years later on Beale Street in Memphis. Nearly incarcerated when he and his fellow youthful revelers were discovered at three thirty in the morning stripped to their underwear or less, wading up to their thighs in the warm, lapping tide of Tampa Bay. The crashed parties, the unplanned encounters with celebrities who acquiesced to drunken appeals for photographs or autographs scrawled with a marker on various body parts, or with the occasional prominent elected official, much friendlier in private than he appeared to be in public or when accompanied by the wife who was nowhere in evidence that evening. Each night ending in satisfaction with a different companion than the one he had woken up with that morning. He couldn't help feeling a little envious, even now that he had attained his own celebrity status, of the young staffers who had no duties so onerous that they couldn't be performed satisfactorily despite the hangovers and fatigue that afflicted them.

Tess Gilchrest was of an age and disposition to spend late nights in rowdy excesses that were for her and her cohort the primary attraction of the convention. She was the acknowledged social leader of her circle of junior staff, volunteers, and the dozen or so reporters of like age and inclinations who avoided spending their nights drinking in the company of veteran journalists, listening to their not terribly interesting tales from the campaign trails of decades past.

She was the one they relied on to secure invitations or talk her way past security for parties where their names were not found on the official guest list. It was she who convinced the middle-aged lobbyist or the business associate of her father's with whom she was on a first-name basis to pay for the drinks they upgraded at his expense. It was she who found the name and address of the all-night establishment with the sickest band or most hilarious karaoke scene or best barbecue, known only to the most knowledgeable locals, in exotically run-down parts of town where cab-drivers had to be excessively tipped to take them.

She couldn't help but take an interest in people, she said, who seemed to her "a little lonely" or "could stand a little cheering up." She made it her responsibility to cultivate friendships with these unfortunates, and always to include one or more in their nights on the town. That is how Walter Lafontaine came to enjoy himself more than he had in a very long while, bouncing from one party to another late on the second night of the convention in taxicabs crowded with kids whom he knew only casually, and a few he didn't know at all, but whose exuberance was a tonic for the sadness that afflicted him.

Long before the convention, Tess had introduced herself to Walter and made a point of learning the general details of his background. She had noticed him often hustling past the area where she worked, and she thought him cute in a childish way, with his slight build, brisk gait, and fidgety manner, his voice growing a little squeaky when he spoke hurriedly, as he always seemed to. He was always nicely but rather primly attired, suit coat always on and buttoned, tie never loosened, shoes always polished. More intriguing was the unease she detected, the aimlessness his hustling and exuberance did not disguise. She had pressed a senior staffer with whom she was friendly for information about him and learned of his long association with the president—"his gopher slash protégé in the early days," she was informed. "The president's got a soft spot for him." She had also been told he "didn't make the cut for the White House. Kind of a legacy cost now, or maybe a good-luck charm," confirming her impression the campaign was more of a haunt for him than a job.

Walter had been effusively courteous to her and very charming in his childish way when she had introduced herself, asking her questions about her family, where she'd grown up and gone to school, and if she had ever met the president. "Next time he's here, I'll introduce you to him," he promised. "He and I go way back." She knew, too, about his mother (many people in the campaign did), that she was suffering from an incurable disease and that he was devoted to her. "Just breaks your heart, doesn't it," she had remarked many times to coworkers.

She had spotted him that afternoon walking down a hallway past the warren of temporary offices beneath the podium and had shouted out his name. He had turned around abruptly and given her his nicest smile as he shouted her name in return. "I just got here," he explained, as he tried to rebuff politely her invitation to "come out with us tonight."

"Well, you're just in time, then," she insisted. "Meet me right here at ten. We're ducking out early tonight. Got us invited to the Creative Coalition party."

Walter tried to explain again that he had just arrived and had a number of things to attend to, and it probably wasn't a good idea to make it a long night, but she interrupted him, telling him affectionately, "Come off it, Walter. You're coming out with us. No excuses!"

Walter liked Tess. But the thought of spending the night crashing parties with kids who were nearly twenty years his junior had little appeal, and it only reminded him again how unimportant he had become to the campaign, and to the president. He had been assigned no responsibilities at the convention. He hadn't been asked to attend any of the planning discussions. No one had even thought to inquire when or whether he was coming. He had had to ask for hotel accommodations and convention credentials.

He had made up his mind not to come, but Geraldine had kept talking about it, assuring him she would manage without him for a few days, and saying she couldn't wait to hear all about it when he got back. "You tell the president," she kept reminding him, "how proud we are of him, how proud we are on the South Side, all us old women. We knew when we first laid eyes on him he was going to make us proud."

He had come to the convention because he feared he would disappoint his mother if he didn't return with stories of how busy he had been, of the famous people he had seen, how he had talked to the president and First Lady, and how they had asked after her and sent her their love. He had booked a return flight at six o'clock Friday morning and would be back at Geraldine's bedside by ten. There was no reason to leave later. He wasn't interested in attending any parties. The president was leaving right after his speech, with most of the senior campaign staff traveling with him. Walter hadn't been asked to join them.

Quite a surprise it was to find himself drunk and thoroughly enjoying a night on the town with a group of kids he hardly knew. They had made a circuit of the night's parties and were now on their way in a caravan of five taxicabs to a bar his companions had patronized the night before and had looked forward to revisiting. He was riding in the backseat of a cab with two others, wedged between Tess and a reporter for a news website who looked like he wasn't old enough to have a driver's license and wore rectangular eyeglasses too big for his face.

Everyone had been so nice to him, so welcoming and solicitous, treating him as if he were kind of a big shot, asking questions about the old days, when he and the president had been inseparable. He was becoming very fond of Tess. Walter did not have confidants, except for Geraldine, and there were many things he couldn't share with her. But Tess made him imagine what it would have been like if he hadn't been an only child, if he'd had a little sister, someone he could confide in, some-one he could trust with the entire truth of his life, his disappointments as well as his hopes.

"What do you think about him?" she'd asked Walter, nodding her head in the direction of a boy who was fetching her a beer at the other end of the bar, and who had been the fourth passenger in the cab.

"What about him?" he asked.

"Worth a hookup, you think? Or too preppie?"

"Why are you asking me? I'm not your matchmaker."

"C'mon, pretend you're my big brother. Would you let me leave with him?"

"If I was your big brother, I'd make sure you had already gone home—alone. But, no, I think you could do better."

"Thanks, bro. That's what I think, too."

From that moment on, Walter would always call Tess "little sis." And she would continue to call him "bro."

★ CHAPTER 17 ★

At this point four years ago, O had begun to dislike almost everything about campaigning. He felt different this time. There was the satisfaction of having been proved right, of others realizing they had underestimated him. He had not let their alarm infect him. He had taken the longer view. He had known what he was doing. He hadn't panicked when it had become a contagion, spreading its bilious fever to people who weren't in normal circumstances passionate about politics.

It had all passed as he alone, he sometimes thought, had known it would. The growing economy had persuaded the persuadable that life had returned to normal. Politics was assigned again its minor importance. The chronically disaffected returned again to the margins of society, where they could be mostly avoided by people who had better things to do with their time than shout out their frustrations in public.

As a child he had resented the separateness his circumstances had imposed on him, the alienation from many of the conventions and conceits of American life. But he knew now it had been a path to wisdom. He had an anthropologist's detachment, scrutinizing without experiencing the behavioral psychology of American society. The satisfaction he gained from having anticipated this change in the public's attitude and his political fortunes was richer than the pleasure he took in proving his judgment superior to the opinions of the manipulated press, his nervous fellow Democrats, his emboldened Republican adversaries. Not many politicians would ever experience it. It was the satisfaction of knowing he understood the people he governed more completely than they understood him.

He could tolerate the drudgery and absurdities of the next two months, not always with good humor, but not with as much resentment as he had the last time. So much had been accomplished, so much proved. He had begun to change the country, and the country, after a difficult period of adjustment, had begun to accept it. In two months' time, his last campaign behind him, he would bring more change, which Americans would learn to accept, and for which he would be remembered.

The convention had been as successful as expected. His acceptance speech had been enthusiastically received, and, in his opinion, as memorable as any he had ever given; not just for the excitement it had caused in the hall among people who were there to be excited, but for the subtlety with which he had communicated truths that in the past would have been considered impolitic to mention. He would never claim it publicly, but he believed his gift as a public speaker was greater and rarer than the one commonly attributed to him, his ability to inspire people. He enlightened them. He made them understand, without making them feel threatened, that America could be a better society, that Americans could be more just, braver, wiser than they had been. Their nationalism, their pride in themselves was justified only if it was not meant to disguise their fears but to aspire to the more perfect union they had yet to achieve.

He had not felt it necessary to attack his opponent vigorously. He had barely mentioned Morrison by name. Instead, he had let people draw the obvious inference: that Morrison led the reactionary forces he disparaged. The unspoken implication, conveyed without malice, was plain. For all his valiant service to the country, Tom Morrison didn't have as much faith in Americans as O did.

The weekend after next, they would begin debate prep at Camp David, the first of many sessions that would consume far more of his time than necessary, becoming so tedious and redundant he would at times have to struggle to control his temper. He would object to the number of events on his schedule that had no other purpose than to serve as backdrops for pictures of him in various poses meant to convince voters that despite the demands and privileges and trappings of his office, the president was still gratifyingly normal. "Tell me," he would ask his staff on numerous occasions, "do you think anyone has ever voted for some-one for president because they saw a picture of him eating a corn dog at the state fair?" He would become exasperated by the press's attempts to contrive controversies, nitpicking small oversights and misjudgments, misinterpreting a casual remark, trying to start a fight about something insignificant so they could relieve their boredom.

These frustrations were inevitable, and he was resigned to them. His anticipation of them did not spoil the contentment he felt this day and was certain he would feel four years hence when he left office. He had convinced Americans to accept his expectations of them, and he would exceed their expectations of him.

He was satisfied, too, with the work of his campaign staff, the cool-ness with which they pursued their objectives, leaving nothing to chance, adjusting tactics when necessary, but not letting themselves be bullied into doubting their strategy. They were confident, hard to distract, deter-mined, a campaign that reflected the qualities he prided himself on.

On the flight leaving the convention, he had invited Cal Regan to his cabin, where he, the First Lady, Rick Noth, and Avi Samuelson had gathered.

"I thought it went as well as we could have wanted, didn't you?"

"Yes, sir, I do. That was a hell of a speech."

"You've done a hell of a job, too, Cal. And I want you to know how grateful I am to you, and all the staff. You've got us in position to win as long as I don't blow it. It's all I could ask from you. Thank you."

"Thank you, Mr. President. There's still a lot of game left to play, though. We'll try not to give you a reason to reconsider your opinion."

The talk turned to other subjects, none of them particularly impor-tant, before Regan tried to excuse himself to keep a commitment he had made to answer a few questions from the reporters who were traveling on *Air Force One.*

"Let them wait a few minutes," the president instructed. "What do you think you'd be doing if you were in their place; if you were managing Morrison's campaign," he asked him, "to try to get the ball back?"

Regan sat back in his seat and thought for a moment before answering. "I'd be hoping we'd make a serious mistake. I don't know what else they can do. There isn't a strategy or message that would work any better than what they have. They've made their best case. You have a stronger one. They probably think the debates are their last chance to turn it around, and they'll spend a lot of time trying to figure out ways to trip you up, throw something unexpected at you. But they're smart enough to know it probably won't work."

The president reflected on how they might have found themselves in a different position had the economy taken another downturn. "We'd be praying for him to make a mistake," he observed.

"I'm not sure we would, Mr. President," Regan disagreed.

"Why?"

"We know how to score points from whatever the defense gives us. Our candidate taught us how to do that."

The president smiled his appreciation and nodded. The First Lady smiled at him also. Samuelson told him good-naturedly, "Try not to get too cocky until after the election." Rick Noth patted his arm. "Okay, now you can go tell the press what a genius you are."

Regan left their company as pleased with himself as the president was with him. He was smiling still when he greeted the reporters who had been waiting for him, since Rick Noth had refused their request for a few minutes with the president and told them they would have to entertain themselves by "badgering Cal Regan." Maddy Cohan was the first reporter to return his smile, which she mistakenly believed was intended for her.

Sandy Stilwell had just finished taking questions from reporters assigned to the Morrison campaign, who had dutifully recorded his assurance that General Morrison was eager to begin the fall campaign and looking forward to the debates, "which would give the American people their best chance to see past the attack ads and compare the real records and visions of the candidates."

No one had asked Stilwell a question he hadn't expected, and the reporters could have written his answers themselves. Stilwell did his best to disguise his boredom. Reporters hardly bothered to hide theirs.

"How do you plan to answer the criticism that the governor's election would put at risk the progress the administration's made on the economy, health care, et cetera?"

"An economy that's not quite back to where it was over four years ago. Millions still out of work. Personal income flat. Home values still not recovered. Is that what the president calls progress? Americans call it unacceptable."

The reporters had made a few weak attempts to knock Stilwell off his stride, but with little hope of success. Stilwell smiled through their provocations and repeated his message until boredom and fatigue resigned them to accepting it, and parroting it intact for the viewers and readers.

"They inherited the deepest recession in memory," the reporter for *The New York Times* contended, "and they argue that Republicans, had they been able to, would have prevented what progress there has been."

Stilwell didn't want his candidate to be lumped in with Republicans in Washington. He didn't like to have Morrison associated with anyone or any institution located in Washington save for the men and women of the armed forces who were stationed there. And he did not like having to make at least an implicit defense of congressional Republicans part of his rebuttal.

"Look, it might have been the deepest recession in memory. It also happens to be the longest in memory. When was the last time, under Democrat or Republican administrations, that even during a severe recession it took almost four years before Americans saw the first real glimpse of a recovery? Never, that's when."

Most of the reporters present weren't inclined to dispute the opinions Stilwell asserted as economic facts, preferring instead to take advantage of his brief availability to get a sense of how the Morrison campaign would frame their message for the fall campaign and try to argue their way out of the hole they were in. He left after answering a few more questions on the same subject, having exhausted the possible variations on the campaign's message: it isn't progress if the country is only back to where it was four years ago. But reporters knew, as did he, that it's hard to persuade a majority of voters to take that long a view.

O

They could only hope voters would not firmly make up their minds until after the last debate, and that they were still open to persuasion should something unexpected happen. None of the senior staff of the Morrison campaign would concede it was their opponent's race to lose, not to one another, not to their spouses, not to their candidate. But not one of them believed any differently.

Several of them had gathered in Morrison's office to watch the president give his acceptance speech, the speech they knew he would give, the speech they would have written for their candidate were he the incumbent.

Sandy Stilwell knew his most important job for the next week or so would be to persuade the Morrison campaign staff that, as he confidently insisted to a skeptical press, the country deserved better and expected better and would vote for better if they all did their jobs right.

Tom and Margaret Morrison and their children watched it in the family room of their home, mostly in silence. "What did you think?" Morrison asked his wife afterward. "Well, he didn't attack you personally as much as I thought he might," she answered.

"No, he didn't, not by name anyway," he agreed.

He had spoken to Stilwell several times that day. In their last conversation, he had signed off on their response to the president's speech. He hadn't planned to call him again that night, but he decided to do so on the pretense of asking Stilwell's opinion of the speech. He knew what Stilwell would say: the president had done no worse and no better than they had expected, and elections aren't won at conventions. Voters would now give their full attention to the campaign, and that would be as much an opportunity for them as for O.

His real purpose was to tell his campaign manager he wanted to say a few words to the staff early tomorrow morning, before he left for his first event of the fall campaign in a small town in central Missouri, an outdoor event in the center of town, which was every bit as picturesque as the location where O would campaign an hour earlier.

All staff, from Stilwell to the summer interns who answered phones and restocked supply shelves, were assembled and scattered among the desks in the largest space in the headquarters, where partitions had been removed to give them an unobstructed view of their candidate. For many junior staff it would be their longest personal encounter with Morrison, and there was palpable excitement among them as they jostled for positions close to Morrison, where he might notice them. They had been told Morrison wanted to thank them for their hard work and fire them up for the fall campaign. They had been expecting a rousing call to arms, and when Morrison began his remarks by professing his affection for golf, several of them exchanged quick and confused looks.

"I like to play golf," he began. "And I like to watch the major golf tournaments on TV whenever I can. I like to see people who are the best at what they do compete against each other. You learn something every time you study someone try to achieve perfection. You might not learn how to do it as well as they do, but you know what it takes, you know how to get better, and you know something else, something very important to people in any walk of life who really try hard to succeed.

"In every major, the commentators always make the same observation on the last day of play, when the first golfer gets to the back nine. They always say, 'Now the tournament begins.' What they mean by that is after four days, sixty-three holes, it's still anyone's tournament to win; anyone who's put themselves in a position to win. Anyone who's no more than three or four strokes off the lead."

Morrison could see and was unconcerned that many in his audience seemed puzzled over his pedestrian opening attempt to boost their morale. He paused for a moment, smiled broadly, and, looking from his right to his left, made eye contact with a half dozen young staffers. *They'll get the drift in a second,* he assured himself.

"Well, friends, we've got nine holes left to play. The tournament starts today. And we're not four strokes off the lead. We might be a stroke behind, maybe two. But we're in a position to win. And we're in that position because of you. You got us here. And I'm deeply grateful. Now I've got to play my very best game. I know *you* will. If I do, too, we'll win. And I will. I know what it takes. I know I've got that game in me. And I promise you, I'll play it. You deserve it. You deserve a candidate that gives it everything he's got just like you have given it everything you've got. Because you know, and I know, the people of this country deserve better leadership than they've had for the last four years. And they're going to get it just as soon as we win this thing."

Sandy Stilwell led the applause when he had finished, thankful that Morrison had relieved him of the task of boosting their confidence when his own was ebbing. The rest of them exceeded his example, clapping more vigorously and chanting "Mor-is-son, Mor-is-son" as the object of their exaltation smiled his thanks and gave them a salute before leaving with Stilwell for the airport.

"The golf speech," as it would be remembered by those who heard it and those who heard about it, might not have provided the Churchillian inspiration many of them had expected that morning. But it served its purpose. He convinced them they could win, and that they would win if they did their jobs right.

A few of the campaign's seasoned professionals still thought it an odd choice of metaphor, and the speech would have been more encouraging had Morrison given them examples of military battles where outgunned but brave and scrappy soldiers had vanquished their more numerous enemy. One of them whispered conspiratorially to a colleague as Morrison was leaving, "What do we do if O plays his best nine, too?" But even they appreciated the heartfelt sentiment and graciousness the analogy had conveyed.

For the younger staff, those who were working on their first presidential campaign, it was a moment they could imagine themselves recalling with reverence to friends and acquaintances after the election. Most had been elated at the end of their convention, thrilled by Morrison's acceptance speech and the reception it received, and convinced by four days of congratulations and encouragement that they were working for the next president of the United States.

But it had all dissolved when their opponent's convention commenced and was, they could not help acknowledging, at least to themselves, as successful, probably more so, than theirs. It was then they realized a convention was a false measure of success. It was the only major event in a campaign that was almost entirely within your control. Your opponent need only control his convention as well as you had controlled yours to deprive you of any lasting advantage.

Morrison had not restored their sense of triumph. But he had reassured them their destiny was still theirs to control. Nothing had ended. It had only begun. A man of stature, a general of the army, a man of great accomplishments and proven courage believed in them, had thanked them and told them they deserved to win. Most of them imagined they had witnessed a subtly inspirational speech, intended to encourage them without resorting to the demagoguery that a man of his stature would find undignified. They believed Tom Morrison was as wise and good a person as they would ever have the privilege of working for. They would do all within their ability to repay his trust in them.

Morrison had thought it nothing more than an ordinary responsibility of command, to see to the morale of your troops on the eve of battle. You needn't tell them only what you knew for certain to be true. You needn't tell them the entire truth. You had to make certain they would fight for you. The truth, a half-truth, or a lie could be employed, whichever served best in the circumstances. Perhaps he had encouraged them to believe their prospects were better than they were. Perhaps they now believed he held them in higher esteem than was accurate. But he did not believe he had lied to them. He did appreciate their efforts on his behalf. And they could still win. They weren't more than a couple of strokes behind. But he, too, knew, as Sandy Stilwell, his senior aides, and the press knew, he could play his best game, and still O would have to shank a drive and blow a couple of putts for them to win.

★ CHAPTER 18 ★

Cal Regan, looking dapper and in high spirits as he returned from the morning staff meeting, tossed an empty water bottle at his assistant, who caught it one-handed and deposited it in the recycling bin she kept next to her desk.

"There's a Tim Henderson on the phone," she informed him. "He says you know what it's about."

Fifteen minutes later, he called Mick Lowe into his office and asked him to close the door behind him.

"There is an investigation," he told Lowe, "or was. Unclear if it's still ongoing."

Two weeks before, Regan had called Henderson, his former partner at Hanson, Strong, and asked him if he had any friends at Justice who might tell him "whether there is or ever was an FCPA investigation of a former VP at Channing-Mills named Victor Salazar." "Possibly," Henderson had answered. "How hard do you want me to push?"

"Not hard," Regan instructed. "I got a heads-up there might be one. But I don't know if there's anything to it, or, if there is, whether it's something we could use."

Left unsaid was who *we* referred to or why Regan hadn't asked the White House to inquire about it. Henderson didn't need to be told why the president's campaign would be interested in a corrupt executive at Tom Morrison's former company or why the White House wouldn't be asked to look into the matter. Any communication from the White House to a federal agency, no matter how informal and discreet, is an official communication, unprotected by executive privilege, subject to all laws and regulations governing official communications, including the Freedom of Information Act, unless it is classified for national security reasons or to protect the integrity of an ongoing investigation. It would be well within the purview of a curious member of Congress who might have learned of it and expressed an official interest in knowing who had made the inquiry and why.

Henderson had lunched with a former colleague who still worked in the Criminal Division, although not in the Fraud section. "He remembers hearing something about it more than a year ago, maybe two years ago," Henderson recounted, "but nothing since then."

"Does he remember hearing specifically that Salazar was the target?" Regan had asked.

"He thinks that was the guy. He's definitely sure it was an executive at Channing-Mills, and he thought there might have been more than one guy they were looking at."

"He remember any of the other names?"

"No. You said not to push too hard, so I didn't."

"How much can you trust him?"

"Enough. He's a good friend. Our wives are close, too. He asked why I was interested. I told him I was just curious about a rumor I'd heard, but it wasn't something I could or would use publicly. He probably thinks I have a client interest. He seemed a little wary but not too much."

"Do you think he would look into it if you asked him to?"

"I don't know. He might. But probably not unless I told him why I wanted the information, and who I would be sharing it with."

"Let's hold off for now," Regan had told him. "I might come back to you later for a little more information if you think your friend could find it without making a fuss. We might need to know the status of the investigation, if it's closed or still active, and if anybody might be indicted this year."

Mick Lowe hadn't managed to find anyone who could corroborate or expand on the information Henderson had relayed.

"All we know, then," Regan summarized, "is there was an investigation of someone. We don't know if Morrison knew about it. And we don't know if we can find out what we don't know."

After raising and quickly rejecting several people they might ask for help, Regan agreed with Lowe's suggestion that they task the campaign's private investigator with looking into Salazar's present situation. All they knew about him was that he had left Channing-Mills. They didn't know where or if he was presently employed. They didn't know where he lived. They also didn't know, but very much wanted to, if at any point in the last several years Victor Salazar had incurred large legal bills.

For appearances' sake the private investigator, Carl Barstow, was kept on retainer to the campaign's chief legal counsel, whose own retainer from the campaign included, in addition to his compensation, sufficient sums to pay whatever work he thought it appropriate to subcontract. Normally, when they needed Carl Barstow's services, Lowe would first inform the chief legal counsel. On occasion, Lowe would tell the lawyer what he wanted Barstow to do, but more often he gave the instructions directly to Barstow, who did not need to be reminded to report his findings directly to Lowe and not to the attorney who paid his retainer.

On this occasion, Lowe would not inform counsel they had a job for Barstow. Regan and Lowe both knew that while it would have been prudent to brief their lawyer on their interest in Victor Salazar, the lawyer, a painstakingly cautious man, would react with demonstrable apprehension.

Lowe left to call Carl Barstow, and Regan went to a meeting, for which he was now fifteen minutes late. Both men were satisfied they were handling the matter responsibly. They had not ignored an opportunity to improve their candidate's chances for reelection, but their attention to it had been cautious. They had not, as far as they knew, violated any laws or unwritten standards of their profession. Whatever anxiety their actions might have induced in the chronically anxious lawyer whom they had kept in the dark, they were confident their purpose could be fairly described as due diligence. If nothing came of it, so be it.

On Friday, Regan would fly to Washington for a meeting at the Democratic National Committee. Later that afternoon, he would join a few White House staffers and members of the president's debate prep team, who would travel by bus to Camp David, where a second full weekend of debate prep was planned. He had never been there before. He had grumbled to Mick Lowe about being held captive in the woods and forced to suffer forty-eight hours of mind-numbing tedium, but he was quietly thrilled by the privilege of visiting the presidential retreat. He also managed to contain his excitement when Avi Samuelson called him on Thursday to inform him the president had invited him to travel to Camp David on the president's helicopter, along with the First Lady, their children and their dog, and Samuelson.

Such marks of presidential favor are the highest denomination of Washington currency. They distinguish the recipients as people of unique influence, who can dispense prized favors of their own, and whose counsel to clients is as invaluable as it is expensive. Their proximity to the center of executive power ends with the term of the administration, but their influence endures, often outlasting the retired president's. They have attained the distinction of elder statesmen in their party, a status that doesn't require the age or the high-minded patriotism it suggests.

They are consulted by future presidents of their party, given prestigious political assignments as the heads of transition teams and vice presidential search committees. They are tasked with more discreet missions as well: the placating emissary to primary rivals who refuse to accept their defeat; the bearer of bad news to unwelcome aspirants to high appointed office; the brisk messenger of doom to the party's national chairman, who has embarrassed his president once too often.

They are fixers of difficult problems, finders of hidden remedies, minders of troublesome ingrates, conduits of patronage. They are the A-list guests at the most exclusive Washington gatherings; the chairpersons of the most august Washington philanthropies; the inhabitants of the president's box at the Kennedy Center when the president is somewhere else, and sometimes when he's not. When they reach their golden years, some will be called upon by presidents of the other party to tender their offers of legislative compromise to the leaders of their party, or to serve on bipartisan commissions when the president needs to smother the stench of a scandal or abdicate an impossible responsibility to distinguished worthies who do not have to run for reelection. They are the eminences of the permanent political class.

This was the future Cal Regan beheld when he rested his mind for a moment from his labors. An offer would be made once the president was safely returned to office. Perhaps the tired Avi Samuelson would return to his beloved home city, and the office of senior advisor, its political power second only to the president's, would be offered. Party chairman was a possibility, though he would prefer a White House office. Even chief of staff wasn't out of the question. The president would ask for him. The two of them would confer alone for a few minutes. The offer would be made. Samuelson would arrive to offer congratulations. Regan would accept with gratitude and sincere, if temporary, humility. The joy in having reached the summit that would make permanent his exalted station in Washington would have that brief effect on him.

Two years. That's all he would stay. He would want to have occupied well in advance of the end of the president's reign the lucrative position from which he would make the transition from staffer to statesman. No one would begrudge him that. It would be expected. A privileged future. A deserved reward.

The pride he felt in anticipation of his coming fortune was not a possessive pride. He was not proud of his power, privileges, influence, and wealth, but of the fact he had earned them. The distinction was an important one to him. Up the greasy pole in record time, and hardly a single false step. He had been mentored and promoted by patrons, but he had exceeded expectations. He had been given important responsibilities, and he had managed them better than his peers, better, perhaps, than his patrons could have. He owned his successes. His hard work, intelligence, and nerve had purchased them. Anyone would be proud who could honestly make such a claim.

A family, too, would come when he left office, to take the place of the family that had been left behind in the town of his childhood. They would be proud of him, too, as was the family of his past, even though the favored son and brother of memory had begun to disappear, a familiar presence at the odd birthday and anniversary and wedding, but supplanted most days by the gleaming success, the public man in his prime, the handsome face in news magazines and on television.

Sometimes in his reveries, he could imagine the faces and personalities of the family that was to come. Three children: the two eldest, boys, handsome athletes, quick-witted, self-starters; the youngest, a dark-haired and perfect girl, a little brash, a bit of a smart-ass, her acerbic wit softened by a capacity for graciousness and kindness, and encouraged in the security of exclusive schools and the protection of her father and brothers. The imagined wife bore a resemblance to Maddy Cohan, their daughter's panache, virtues, and talent for coloring her legacy.

She was not often on his mind, not as much as she had been, preoccupied as he was with the campaign. She had been on *Air Force One*. He had known she would be, having seen the passenger manifest in advance. But, still, when he had come to the back of the plane and hers was the first face he noticed, he had felt something like surprise, a flash of unexpected gladness. Her questions and his replies had had a bantering quality, a mutual enjoyment plain to all who witnessed it. He had thought of calling her after they had checked into their hotel and suggesting a drink. But considering the lateness of the hour and the early start the next day, he realized the proposal might have led her to think he had been encouraged by their conviviality to assume an invitation she had not intended to offer.

Perhaps, next year, after the president was inaugurated a second time, and they were settled into their new situations, he would propose dinner. He would wait for a chance encounter, a party they both attended, where he would prolong their exchange of greetings. He would ask whether she was enjoying the new job Janssen would have given her or whether she had left the paper for one of the broadcast or cable networks, as most people assumed she eventually would, and how her transition to television was going. She would ask about his new job, probably make a joke about it, nothing offensive, a little teasing about learning to live on a government salary again.

He might offer to fetch her another drink as he was heading to the bar to refill his own, and she would say, "I'll come with you." Their conversation would turn more personal, just a little, though, nothing too suggestive of their past. He might ask after her mother and sister and nieces. She might tell him how well he seemed, how his new responsibilities seemed to agree with him. He would make the invitation seem offhand, as if it had just occurred to him, a way of ending their conversation. "Look, why don't we have dinner sometime, catch up." If she were receptive, he would say as he left, "Great. I'll call you next week or maybe the week after." He wouldn't want to appear too eager.

Were things to develop between them again, naturally progressing from the repair of their friendship to a mutual admission that they missed their former intimacy, they would agree there was no longer a need to conceal their relationship. They had attained a status where attempts at deception could only prove embarrassing and raise questions of compromised professional integrity. Washington wouldn't just accept an admitted relationship. It would celebrate it. It wouldn't even be necessary to insist they avoid professional interaction. Such discretion would be assumed. There were many popular Washington couples who had once been reporter and source. Their adversarial professions gave their union a cachet others envied. Their names were always prominent in harmless, gossipy articles about Washington's power couples, with an accompanying attractive photograph.

Regan could picture them in situations that displayed their social prominence: hand-in-hand at state dinners—arriving late at exclusive after-parties as photographers and a relieved host welcomed them—occasionally sharing a dinner date with the president and First Lady.

He imagined them as they prepared for these evenings. He saw her seated at her vanity, finishing her hair and makeup while he beheld her beauty and received a welcoming smile in return. They kissed their young children good night and implored their obedience to the au pair, the children excited by the radiant beauty and vivacity of their parents. He held the door for her and made a funny face to the children to leave them laughing as the elegant couple slipped into the night.

But she was on his mind only in his rare idle moments, when images of his privileged, contented future drifted into view. She was not on his mind now as he attended to the work that would make his dreams possible.

Seated around him at a conference table were pollsters, media people, the political director, his deputy, the communications director, and
the head of the scheduling team. Regional political directors were con-
ferenced in by phone from their various headquarters.

They started with a discussion of the latest national tracking poll
numbers, and all agreed the race was stable and no adjustment in their
national message was needed. They turned to the cross tabs of battleground polls, detecting small shifts in voters' attitudes here and there,
among under-forty-five working mothers in Michigan who had a college
education, second-generation Hispanic heads of household in Nevada
with annual incomes below forty-five thousand dollars, Jewish retirees
in Dade County, and unaffiliated voters living in Denver exurbs and
employed in service industries.

Remedies were discussed; either support for the president had
declined among these and other groups, or they had indicated an ambiv-
alence not evident in last week's polls. "Let's see if we can fix it with mail,"
Regan usually instructed. Within a week, targeted subgroups of voters
would receive in their mail glossy, double-sided ten-by-twelve cards with
bullet-point lists of three to five statements, reminding them of the president's efforts to reform public education and the generous increases he
had made in college tuition grant programs; or his agreement to respect
the right of Catholic hospitals not to perform abortions; or his support for Israel; or the various tax breaks he had given families with joint
incomes below $150,000 a year. Many of them would be thrown away
with the rest of the day's junk mail. But enough of them would be read
and absorbed by wavering voters to assure the campaign's pollsters they
had correctly identified a problem in time to address it effectively.

States where the president's support had fallen off by a statistically
significant number were marked for an imminent presidential or vice
presidential appearance in the cities and counties where the drop was
most pronounced. The campaign schedulers would identify dates and
times that had been purposely left available for contingency scheduling, or would determine that a previously scheduled visit was probably
unnecessary for now and could be postponed. Regan would instruct

them to run the dates by their liaison with White House schedulers. If they met resistance, he would explain to Avi Samuelson, in one of several phone conversations they had every day, why the added stops were necessary.

"Are you sure they're necessary?" Samuelson would invariably ask. "He won't like it."

"I wouldn't recommend it if it weren't," Regan would invariably answer.

"He's still bitching about the extra stops last week."

"They helped. You can see it in the tracking."

Samuelson usually conceded the point by sighing, and threatening Regan with the prospect that the president would call him personally to complain, which he occasionally did.

Various local issues that were influencing voters in these places were discussed, and talking points for the president were conceived and later sent to the policy team to be vetted, which would promise specific action by the federal government, or at least the president's intention to work with state and local leaders to find a satisfactory solution. They would send out mailings to reinforce the president's commitment. If one of the regional political directors expressed significant alarm at how much an issue was driving voters' attitudes, Regan would ask, "Is it worth doing some local radio or TV on?" The head of the media team would promise to get back to him by the end of the day with a draft script and a description of the size and cost of the buy.

Their attention then turned to ads in other regions, states, and specific communities that might need to be revised or increased, or their rotation with other ads reconfigured, or that had burned in enough in their respective markets to come off the air. They took some time discussing their Spanish-language ads, because earlier in the meeting, their lead pollster had emphasized a softening of intensity in Hispanic voters nationwide.

Fifteen minutes after the meeting adjourned, a second one convened, with the heads of voter identification and turnout operations. Regan would take a more granular interest in their discussion than he had in the polling and advertising discussions. A bad poll or an ineffective ad was easier to address than a systemic problem in voter ID and turnout, and he was constantly pressing his subordinates for evidence the campaign was meeting, and preferably exceeding, its targets.

In the last election, the O campaign had built the greatest voter turnout operation in American political history, a civic infrastructure that exceeded the most ambitious plans of previously successful presidential campaigns. At every moment of every day, the O campaign knew almost exactly where it stood in every battleground state, and how much more progress they would have to make before they could be certain of success. Everyone who worked in the last campaign, including O, was enormously proud of the sophistication and scale of the operation, and was convinced it, more than any other investment, had overwhelmed their opposition and made it possible for the first African American to take the oath of office as president of the United States.

For four years, Republicans had studied the Democrats' success in '08 and invested heavily in assembling a comparably expansive and sophisticated turnout operation. The GOP's success in the midterm elections had convinced Democrats they would have to build an even bigger one. Regan was atypically anxious and humorless and obsessed with small details in meetings convened to measure their progress. No other responsibility given him was more important to the White House or to his own future. The president himself had made that clear.

"Johnson County seems a little soft to me," he suggested to Regan after reviewing the latest phone bank results for Iowa.

"That's Iowa City," Cal reminded him. "Where the University of Iowa is. Students aren't back yet."

"I know it's Iowa City, Cal," O snapped. "You might recall we spent some time there four years ago."

"Of course. I just meant we won't have a clear picture of the situation there until we start calling students."

"Most of whom," O reminded him, "are registered to vote in their home counties, not Iowa City."

O, the former political organizer, took a detailed interest in campaign functions of which most candidates had only a notional understanding.

Candidates typically asserted themselves in scheduling, money, and messaging decisions but trusted most other decisions to their staff. O received regular briefings on the progress of voter targeting and turnout operations, and made it clear he would have the final say in major decisions related to them.

He could be abrupt with Regan in these discussions, but Regan knew O wouldn't have offered him the job if he hadn't thought him competent to manage the basic operations of the campaign. Regan knew also that when it came to shaping and communicating the campaign's strategic message, O's circle of trusted advisors was much smaller, and he was not among them. Samuelson was probably the only person whose counsel influenced O's views on messaging, and even his advice was superfluous because they were usually in agreement on the subject.

So often had Regan said "not good enough" after listening to reports about the hundreds of offices that had been opened in battleground states, the thousands of organizers hired, the tens of thousands of local volunteers recruited, that participants in the meetings referred to them as NGEs. "Don't schedule anything before noon," the political director had told his personal assistant that morning. "I'm not sure how long the NGEs are going to last today."

Regan insisted paid organizers provide him with the lists of names and brief biographical descriptions of the well-liked and influential local figures they used to help assemble and lead the teams of volunteers in their communities. He stressed repeatedly how important it was for volunteers to be recruited from the precincts where they would work, although he was quick to authorize the dispatch of thousands of out-of-state volunteers to territories that had not yielded enough local ones.

Team leaders were responsible for voter contact and turnout in eight to twelve precincts in and around their own neighborhoods. Regan had helped design the multiple training sessions for them, which emphasized the importance of repeated face-to-face contact with undecided and first-time voters, and coached them on how to interpret from the verbal and physical cues of voters when their visits had probably achieved their purpose and when their persistence had begun to annoy. He reviewed much of the consumer data the campaign had mined to identify persuadable voters in every contested precinct. He barraged volunteers with e-mails in his name, exhorting them to redouble their efforts and reinforcing the specific and coordinated messages they were to give voters.

Every team leader was given a specified quota of contacts their teams had to make, and had to report their progress regularly to the paid organizers, who reported the figures in turn to the state political director, who reported them to the regional director, who gave them to Chicago and the DNC. Regan had often talked on the phone to the state directors before they made their reports to the regional director.

On Election Day, the team leaders would know how many O voters their precincts must produce. Each of them was made to feel personally responsible for the outcome of the election. "No excuses," Regan declared to the state directors. "Tell them, anybody who's short more than ten votes is gonna explain to me why they let the president down."

The participants in the meeting Regan had just convened examined the progress made to date. They went over again the latest numbers for several bellwether counties where other evidence, some of it merely anecdotal, indicated declining enthusiasm for the president's reelection, and they considered the various possible reasons for it. They discussed problems the campaign had with a few state party organizations: the truculent Michigan chairman who had taken offense at being "bossed around by a kid from California" the campaign had hired to run its operations there, infighting among Iowa county leaders, a haphazardly organized and spendthrift New Mexico party.

One regional political director reiterated a concern he had expressed in the previous meeting about a recent TV ad whose message was alienating some voters while appealing to others. Others complained about inadequate support from the DNC. Regan listened impatiently before curtly dismissing some with a promise to "give it more thought," and dispatching others with a nod to Mick Lowe and an instruction to "get on it."

Regan would have several more meetings that day in the same conference room. He had a finance meeting scheduled for two o'clock, and a budget meeting right after that. The rest of his day would be spent in dozens of telephone conversations. He would talk with Samuelson before his next meeting, and twice more before the end of the day. In their final call, Samuelson would pass the phone to the president, who wanted Regan to explain why he needed to make another appearance in Reno, Nevada, when he had just been there a week ago.

He would talk to the chairman of the DNC, and two state party chairmen who felt they were being ignored by the campaign's top operatives in their states. He would personally apologize to a major donor who had been inadvertently left off a list inviting a small group of donors to have a drink with the president in Chicago next week. He would return a call he had been putting off for several days to someone whom he had promised a job he had recently assigned to someone else. He would call the political director into his office and tell him to discourage one of the regional directors from chronically complaining about the failings of others "and start concentrating on his own job," which Regan, after talking to Mick Lowe, wasn't convinced he was doing satisfactorily.

He would return a number of press calls, some at the behest of the press office. The deputy press secretary had volunteered to sit in his office while he made them. Several others he decided to return on his own and didn't feel it was necessary to inform the press office about in advance.

If nothing unexpected happened between now and then, he would leave the campaign headquarters around eight thirty that evening to get a quick drink and dinner with Lowe before going home. He preferred, whenever it was possible, not to eat his evening meal at the campaign, and to be in his apartment no later than eleven o'clock. Before he went to bed, he would read the last of the day's press clips, and a summary of Tom Morrison's remarks and activities that day that had also been prepared for him. He would take a last look at his own schedule for tomorrow, as well as the latest draft of the president's and Tom Morrison's schedules. Then he would go to bed. He would almost always manage to fall asleep as soon as he lay down, attributing the facility to an easy conscience, to the knowledge he had again done his best to exceed expectations of him.

If the weather permitted, he would go for a run along the lakefront at five the next morning. There wouldn't be many mornings left in the campaign when he would have time to indulge his enjoyment of running outdoors, a deprivation he would regret. Getting in a run always made him less uneasy about the bad diet and other unhealthy practices unavoidable in the last months of a presidential campaign. And it was usually the only time when he could spare a few minutes to imagine his life after the campaign and allow Maddy Cohan to capture his thoughts again.

The last call he made before he and Mick Lowe left for dinner was to Tim Henderson, who had sent an e-mail to him several hours earlier. "Call me, I've got an update for you," it had instructed.

★ CHAPTER 19 ★

Tom Morrison was on time. That in itself was unusual. Maddy had never begun an interview with a presidential candidate at exactly the time it had been scheduled. They were always late. Tom Morrison surprised her when he entered the hotel suite at precisely two twenty, with a smile, and an arm outstretched to shake her hand. She had been reading her e-mail. Her recorder and notebook were still in her bag. She stood up abruptly and banged her knee on a coffee table. Clumsily, she later recalled with embarrassment, she tried to take his hand while crouching to rub the knee she had hurt.

"Are you okay?" Morrison asked sympathetically.

"I'm fine. Klutzy me. I didn't expect you to be so . . . um . . . punctual."

"Well, we only have a half hour, so I thought we should start on time," Morrison explained, perplexed by her presumption that he couldn't manage a simple task like showing up on time.

Taking a cue from Morrison's down-to-business attitude, she quickly retrieved her recorder and notebook, and asked her first question: a three-part, open-ended invitation for Morrison to methodically deliver the campaign's talking points.

"How do you think the fall campaign is shaping up; are you where you expected to be after the conventions; and what issues do you think will define the race from here until November?"

As she expected, Morrison assured her he was "very pleased" with where they were, and confident the election would be won by the candidate who persuaded voters he "would restore competence and accountability to Washington." He then ticked off a half dozen issues where the president's competence and accountability were plainly lacking.

"According to most polls, you're behind. That doesn't concern you?"

"No, the general election is just getting under way. We had our say at our convention, and the president had his. And now we've got the debates and a lot of campaigning ahead of us. Lots of people haven't made up their minds yet because they're only now starting to pay close attention."

Maddy was never aggressively contentious in an interview. Her preferred style was to spend the first half of it putting the candidate at ease by asking predictable questions that begged rote responses. She wanted her subject to become almost uninterested in the exchange before she started asking questions they might not have prepared for; the ones she hoped would elicit a little unexpected candor, a misstatement, a false assertion, a display of emotion; something that would distinguish the interview from the dozen others reported that week.

She asked the question she hoped would provoke an unexpected answer in the manner of an anthropology graduate student trying to clear up some misperceptions that had contaminated previous research.

"Governor, I wonder if you have an opinion on something I'm not sure we in the press understand as well as we should. Why do you think many conservatives, many people associated with the tea parties, people supporting you, believe there's something foreign about the president? The 'otherness factor,' I guess you could call it, that makes people think he's a Muslim or foreign-born, not like the rest of us in some way."

A pause ensued as Morrison considered his response, a long pause compared with how briskly the interview had proceeded until then.

The tea parties, flush with their midterm success in electing a good number of their preferred candidates, had looked for a while as if they would be the dominant force in the selection of a Republican presidential nominee. But Morrison had met with the leaders of the most prominent groups and assured them he was as ardent a proponent of smaller government as were they. He discovered, though, that meeting with the leadership of one group excited the suspicions of others, as tea partiers started to focus much of their energy and anger on purging people from their own ranks rather than weeding out insufficiently conservative candidates from Republican primaries.

Morrison also appreciated that political activism was an alien and not entirely enjoyable experience for middle-class, independent voters, and many of them had started drifting away from Tea Party rallies and meetings as the economy improved, old attitudes returned, and an episodic interest in the political affairs of the country was considered an appropriate civic commitment when you're busy making a living and raising a family.

Morrison expected his résumé would attract the admiration of many Tea Party rank-and-file. He could be a George Washington for our times, a patriot whose allegiance was to the country, and not to the bewildering array of special interests and Ivy League elitists who were ruining it. They would vote for the uniform. So he complimented their patriotism and energy, and stayed clear of their squabbles and public events.

At Sandy Stilwell's recommendation, he had asked to meet with the woman who, for reasons he didn't quite understand, still retained the affections of many Republican activists and tea partiers of various ideological stripes. He assumed her pugnacious antielitism struck a chord that still reverberated with people who even in good times couldn't shake their sense of persecution.

She had, after a period of reflection that lasted until the end of her third very profitable book tour, decided not to run for president. "But I'm not going away," she promised her admirers. "I'll be keepin' an eye on our candidates. I still got your back."

She had sat there quietly smiling as he explained his reasons for wanting to meet her, twisting her wedding ring around her finger and nodding as he spoke. Unexpectedly, she impressed him as a more reserved, even shy, personality than she appeared in public.

"Just to be clear, I'm not asking for your endorsement today. If you decide to endorse someone, I hope you'll consider me, but what I wanted to do today is get your advice on issues you believe the candidates should be talking about. You've been active longer than I have in terms of communicating with the grass roots, and I was hoping you wouldn't mind sharing with me your sense of their priorities."

"They want to hear the candidates talk about them," she offered.

Morrison had thought this rather general though not bad advice, and he waited for her to elaborate. But she didn't.

"Well, what exactly is it about them they want candidates to address?"

"Their values; American values, commonsense American values."

"I see. And how do you think I could best do that?"

"Open your heart to them. They want to hear your heart. They wanna know you got their backs."

"And what would convince them that I have their 'backs'?"

"Tell them how you're gonna get their country back for them. Tell them, not the media."

"Well, that's what I intend to do, ma'am. You can count on it."

Get their country back. *To its rightful owners,* Morrison added silently. Their grievances, their feelings of deprivation and persecution, their anger, burned. You could feel the heat as it cooked up conspiracy theories about O's secret birthplace and secret allegiances. All of it nonsense, of course, and distasteful to Morrison, who thought people who couldn't govern their emotions in public had weak characters.

But he thought he understood why they believed these things. They felt mocked or patronized or ignored or victimized by Washington, by the media, by a culture they thought scorned them and their traditions. Morrison believed O bore some of the responsibility for it. Telling Americans, in effect, you won't make this country better. You're too unreasonable, too self-interested. I'll have to make you do it. So O became the Other, un-American, a Muslim, a Kenyan, whatever. He understood the grievance even though he objected to its expressions. He believed O treated flag officers—intelligent, well-educated, battle-tested men—as his inferiors in intellect and judgment. His arrogance was an irritant to Morrison, but a disciplined man knew how to keep the injury hidden as he plotted to avenge it.

Genially and with a vaguely distracted air, as if he were still considering the question, Morrison suggested to Maddy, "Oh, I don't know, I guess when some people get riled up, Democrats or Republicans, conservatives or liberals, they can say a lot of intemperate things. Maybe they don't mean them. Maybe some of them do. It's regrettable, and I wish it didn't happen. It's a big quilt, America. Lots of people from lots of different backgrounds with lots of interests and opinions. The president is as American as the rest of us. We have our disagreements but I'm sure he's a patriot."

He paused to let his generosity, which he assumed would impress her, sink in before continuing.

But if Maddy was impressed, she didn't show it, and she preempted the rest of his answer with a follow-up. She leaned forward, as if to engage him physically, pushing a lock of hair behind her ear.

"But why do you think they believe these things about the president? They're just getting a little carried away because they're 'riled up'? Riled up about what?"

He considered venturing an insight or two, just this side of excusing the behavior, that hinted at O's culpability in his own vilification, but he thought better of it. He leaned back in his chair to reestablish an appropriate distance from Maddy and folded his hands in front of his chest.

"I don't know that there's a general answer to that question. What I do know is both the president and I should object to behavior that coarsens the debate. I think we can agree there's much too much anger and . . . I suppose *incivility* is the right word . . . in our politics already. Certainly a majority of Americans believe that."

Maddy thought she heard a hint of an indictment in his answer, beneath the platitudes he offered her. "Do you think the president has, even inadvertently, helped create an environment that encourages this kind of extreme reaction to him? His policies? Something about his personality?"

Perceptive young woman. Yes, I think the president pushes people's buttons, condescending to them the way he does, that self-regard of his, too smart for the rest of us to keep up with. Morrison believed himself admirably free of such pretensions. His character and judgment had been formed by experiences that proved their merit. He was certain self-

212

knowledge and not vanity guided him. He would have been confounded and wounded by the knowledge that some people, including Maddy, suspected that a vein of self-righteousness ran beneath the surface of his public persona, an imperiousness disguised by his elaborate courteousness but hinted at by his detached formality.

"I can't read their minds. I don't know why they say the things they do," he protested.

"Do you think it's possible the president brings some of this on himself?"

"No, that would be unfair to him."

"So, do you think the people who say these things about him are being malicious or self-deluding or what?"

She's as overbearing as she is perceptive. "I think they're wrong. You'll have to ask them why they say those things."

"So you have no opinion? Not even an educated guess?"

"Asked and answered, Maddy," Morrison's press secretary intervened.

She's quite attractive, though. Too bad her manner doesn't complement her looks. "No, I disagree with it. That's all."

Pretending to move on to another subject, she asked, "Governor, you have a reputation, and it's not meant as a criticism, of being sort of a technocrat, an executive type, not especially ideological. And your message of competence and responsibility is meant to emphasize it. Do you agree with that assessment?"

Now what's she driving at? That I don't have ideals? That I'm faking my political values? "No, not entirely. My ideals are important to me, as they are to Americans generally. That's why I'm running. And I think my message is one of competent leadership in service of traditional American ideals."

"What do you mean by *traditional*?"

Look it up in the dictionary. Traditional, time-honored, tested, cherished. "The values we believe distinguish America from other countries. Freedom, personal responsibility, respect for families, community standards, faith."

"Do you believe those values are under assault today?"

Pretty obvious that they are, isn't it? Turn on your television set. Do you see them fairly represented? Do you think Washington does them credit? Do you think O puts his faith in the freedom and responsibility and values of Americans? "Yes, in some places they are."

"In what places?"

"In some aspects of popular culture. Goodness knows, standards have slipped in the arts and popular entertainment since I was a boy. I think on some of our college campuses there's a prevalent view that values aren't absolute, they're relative, and no culture's are intrinsically more valuable than another's. I think, too often, they get short shrift in Washington. And I think a lot of folks, who still believe our political and cultural ideals are superior to those in societies with less freedom, would like to see them given greater respect in our society."

"You were a boy in the 1960s. Do you believe those traditional values, as you describe them, have lost the respect they had then, in popular culture or academia or politics?"

She thinks she's trapped me in something? What? That I respect our values? Guilty. "I think this is becoming a little philosophical for an old soldier, and our time is running out. Suffice it to say, I think we'd all be better off if our values were . . . well . . . more valued . . . in Washington, Hollywood, Wall Street, and everywhere else. I think most Americans would be relieved if they were."

"Okay. Thank you. I appreciate it. Sorry, I do have an annoying attraction to academic discussions. I hope you don't think I wasted your time."

"Not at all. It was a pleasure to meet you."

"Just one more, sir, if I could, to conclude our philosophizing." Not waiting for his consent, she asked, "Do you think some of the people who say the things about O you object to don't believe he shares their values, and maybe that's why they say them?"

"I'm sure he does share them. And I'm sure he can explain that to them himself," Morrison rebuffed her, more curtly than he intended. *And they'll laugh in his face when he does.*

★ CHAPTER 20 ★

"The guy he talked to at Justice called him," Regan informed Lowe, recounting the conversation he had just concluded with Tim Henderson. "He said he had asked a friend in the Fraud section if he knew anything about the case, and he did. He wasn't working on it himself, but he knew the people who were."

"And?"

"And they still are. The case is ongoing."

Regan had learned Salazar and two associates who worked for him at Shield Holdings were the only subjects of the investigation, and only for their activities before Channing-Mills had acquired the company. But the investigation was launched when Morrison was still CEO. For two years, Tom Morrison had employed the target of a criminal investigation. Henderson had asked his source if Morrison had been aware of the investigation. He thought it was unlikely but didn't know for certain. Henderson offered to go back to his source and put the question to him directly, but warned Regan the inquiry could look suspicious, especially if any information he learned about Morrison became public soon after. Regan had told him not to bother.

"Well, it adds a couple of pieces to the puzzle," Lowe observed. "It's an active investigation. Morrison and Channing aren't suspected of anything. Nothing there to kill him with. But it would be an embarrassment. Keeping a guy with Salazar's reputation on the payroll for two years."

"Piss-poor judgment," Regan added. "Indifference to possible improprieties. Lack of due diligence."

"Not exactly his message, is it?" Lowe suggested. "Not an example of executive competence from the guy who says he can run the government better, the guy who wants voters to think he's untainted by the kind of screwups that make them hate politicians."

"No, it's not," Regan agreed. "But we wouldn't get a lot of mileage out of it. He'll say he ran a clean company, and if Justice had shared their suspicions with him, he'd have fired the guy. We could knock him off his message for a couple of days. But the press won't stay interested much longer than that unless he gave them a reason to. He's smart enough not to do that."

"Two days is better than nothing, though. He doesn't have enough days left to lose a couple explaining why he kept a crook on the payroll."

Regan remembered another piece of information Henderson had given him.

"Oh, almost forgot the fun item. Apparently, about about a month ago, they reached out to one of the other guys they're looking at, who worked for Salazar, to see if he'd cooperate. Henderson's guy wasn't sure, but he thought they might have been trying to set up some kind of sting. Four days after that, Salazar left the country and hasn't come back. He owns some property in Costa Rica, where they think he's hiding."

Over dinner they discussed whether it was worth the trouble of sharing the information with a reporter. Would it excite enough interest to trouble the Morrison campaign for more than a day or two? They thought Salazar's flight to Costa Rica was the kind of juicy detail that would intrigue reporters and their editors, and might keep their interest alive after it was clear the case could only be tangentially connected to the Republican nominee.

If they decided to pass on the information, who should they give it to? It had to be a reporter who they were certain would source the story so vaguely that it didn't establish an explicit connection to the campaign, and who wouldn't subsequently implicate them when he appeared on several cable shows and was asked directly and repeatedly by the hosts if the O campaign had given it to him. The reporter would probably have to be young, someone covering his first presidential campaign, who hadn't made much of a professional reputation, was eager to do so, and would push harder and longer on the story than veteran reporters would have thought worth their while. A few names were considered, but the pool of prospects was a small one. Not many reporters met all their qualifications. Younger reporters, even the most ambitious ones, weren't usually the ones you could rely on to keep the affiliations of their sources absolutely confidential.

Only seven weeks remained in the campaign, but neither of them felt a particular urgency to dispose of the matter. If they chose to give the information to a reporter, the middle of October would be the best time to do so. By then, each hour of a candidate's time would become precious. Their schedules were constantly revised, their planes diverted, additional events crowded into working days that already ran eighteen hours or more, because slight changes in polling data identified a possible opportunity to close the gap in Florida or firm up a small lead in Missouri.

Morrison couldn't afford to waste ten minutes trying to disassociate himself from a scandal in which he was not implicated. His campaign would attempt to deal with it by releasing a written statement, denying his knowledge of or involvement in the investigation. Justice attorneys working on the investigation would be angry it had leaked, and would probably agree to release a statement that Tom Morrison was not now nor had he ever been a target of their investigation, which would be quoted in the campaign's release. Any press availabilities the Morrison campaign had scheduled before the story appeared would be postponed for twenty-four hours in the hope that interest in it had already peaked by then. Morrison wouldn't want to seem as if he had been forced to defend himself on television.

But if Regan and Lowe chose the right reporter, he or she would write the story to suggest the question they wanted to force Morrison to answer: how competent is a chief executive who didn't know what a good many people in his industry and in the Justice Department knew, that he had put on his payroll a person who used bribes to win business? Reporters would insist Morrison answer that question personally.

Forcing him to answer that question in October would give voters less time to forget it had ever been asked. It would only be a brief embarrassment, a hiccup in Morrison's message. But it would occur at the point of maximum interest in the campaign, when voters who hadn't yet made up their minds were beginning to do so.

Regan and Lowe had plenty of time before they had to decide what, if anything, to do with the "Salazar thing." Though they did not discuss keeping the information private, both knew they might ultimately decide to do just that. They were ahead, after all. They might decide, as they would put it, to cut the bastard a break and, not incidentally, avoid any risk of being exposed for making public an investigation that the Department of Justice preferred remain a secret.

The next morning, Carl Barstow called Mick Lowe to confirm what Lowe had already learned. "I don't have much for you on his finances yet, other than his credit history and property records," the investigator conceded. "But I have some news I think will interest you." Barstow proceeded to explain that the spacious five-bedroom colonial Salazar still owned in an expensive suburb of Atlanta, where Shield Holdings had been headquartered, and his condominium in the northeastern city where Channing-Mills's corporate offices were located had not been occupied by Salazar or his wife for almost a month. They had left the country for Costa Rica and were staying in the large coastal property he had purchased several years ago as a winter vacation home. The Salazars' two adult children, one son in Atlanta and the other in Los Angeles, were assumed to be in regular communication with their parents. Barstow didn't know whether the Salazars spoke frequently with anyone else who might know why they had relocated and when, if ever, the Salazars planned to return to the United States.

Lowe thanked Barstow for the information and told him he didn't need to continue his investigation. They knew all they needed to know for now about Victor Salazar.

As he hung up with Barstow, Lowe noticed Walter Lafontaine hustle past his door. "Hey, Walter," he called after him. Walter turned around and stuck his head inside Lowe's office. "How's your mother doing?" Lowe asked him.

"She was having a pretty bad time a week ago, but she seems to be doing better now," Walter replied. "She started the chemo again and it's hard to get used to in the beginning."

"Tell her to hang in there," Lowe said. "And you hang in there, too, Walter," he added.

"We will. Thanks for asking."

Geraldine had withstood the six months of chemotherapy, as Walter had assured her doctor she would. The disease's progress had been checked, and she had been allowed to go home. Walter had moved in with her, ignoring her protest that he had his own life to live and she could manage on her own. She felt just fine, she assured him, now that she was finally back in her own home. But he had insisted. "I got to keep an eye on you, Mama," he had joked, "or you'll get up to your old tricks again, running around all hours with those friends of yours, chasing after poor Reverend Martin."

For three months after she had returned home, weekly blood tests confirmed her MDS remained in check, and she encouraged Walter to spend more time at the campaign. By May, he was working forty hours a week, taking up again his modest responsibilities, which others had easily managed in his absence. But the first week of June had brought discouraging news: a blood test confirming what Geraldine and Walter had suspected when she had awakened one night frightened because her breathing had suddenly become very difficult again. The disease had resumed its progress and would likely soon become acute leukemia if they didn't begin another course of treatment immediately.

This time, Walter had let himself be persuaded to wait and see if supportive care and a less toxic drug therapy would work to relieve her symptoms and slow the disease. Her doctor had again thought it the best course considering her age and frailty. Geraldine had pleaded with Walter to let her stay in her own home, which she would not have been allowed to do if she had to endure another six-month regime of aggressive chemotherapy. Walter could take her to the hospital for her weekly injections, and a visiting nurse could be arranged to look after her while Walter worked.

Reluctantly, he had agreed, although he would not consider spending as many hours on the campaign as he lately had been. Visiting nurse or not, Walter would be in charge of supervising his mother's care. He would make certain she limited her activities and conserved her strength to battle the disease, allowing her only the pleasure she took from preparing his supper.

In August, Geraldine's doctor told them what they both knew. Her new treatment had not succeeded. Her latest blood test confirmed a diagnosis of leukemia. He had described various treatment options, including radiation, transfusions, and more toxic chemotherapy, but his words and tone had suggested their odds of success weren't good enough to warrant the suffering the treatments would cause her. Better they focus on improving the quality of the life she had remaining, and not intentionally worsen it by resorting to therapies that could kill her before the disease would. Another combination of drugs with less severe side effects could be tried that wouldn't require her hospitalization. Steroids to help her breathe more easily would be administered as well, and palliatives given for her pain. They could reduce her suffering, give her as many good days as bad for a while.

Geraldine accepted the diagnosis calmly and agreed with the recommended course of treatment. Walter didn't say anything until, following his mother's example, he thanked the doctor as they left. But the following day he had waited in the hospital until her doctor finished his rounds. "We talked about it some more," he told the doctor, "and decided she should be on the high-dose chemo. It worked before, and you saw how strong a woman she is. She can handle it." The doctor had argued with him, careful to show sympathy at first for the desperation that had caused the change of heart. But after fifteen minutes he had become impatient, recognizing that it was only the son who refused to accept his diagnosis. The patient had done so with admirable grace and wisdom.

"Look, Walter, you shouldn't encourage your mother to endure unnecessary pain and suffering, not when the final outcome is unlikely to be any different," he had urged him. Before Walter could respond, he added, "You need to ask yourself if this is really in your mother's best interests or if it's just going to make you feel better."

"I'm offended by that question, doctor," Walter had angrily replied. "It's my mother's life we're talking about. Not mine. The last treatment worked. It stopped the MDS, and she got her normal life back until now. She could do the things she liked to do, and do them by herself. You don't think she's strong enough to go through it again, to do what she has to do to stay alive, but you're wrong. She *is* strong enough. You have no idea how strong that woman is. I know her better than you." It was much the same argument Walter had made to Geraldine twelve hours earlier, but without the hurt and resentment that now fed its angry tone.

The doctor, attempting to placate him, said he wanted to hear from Geraldine before he could agree to Walter's request. Walter took offense at that, too, though none had been intended. "I'm not a liar. She wants to do it. We talked it over."

"Still, I'll need to talk with her, Walter," he calmly insisted.

"Okay, I'll have her call you today."

"I'd rather talk to her in person."

Walter spent that evening convincing his mother to stand by his decision. "I know you can beat this," he repeated again and again. Geraldine, who knew something different, gently tried to make him understand she wasn't as frightened of her fate as Walter thought she was. But he was adamant. And in the end, for the sake of her boy, she agreed.

The next morning she told her doctor she had decided she wanted the "stronger treatment." She could put up with its side effects and stay in the hospital another six months as long as there was a chance she could beat the disease. "We talked it over, like Walter told you yesterday, and decided that's the best thing for me to do."

The doctor reminded her there was no guarantee of a cure, no matter what they did; "in fact, there's not a very good chance we would get as good a result as we did last time." And as tactfully as he could, he warned her again, "The treatment could hurt you more than it helps." She replied that she understood, but her mind was made up. "Geraldine, I can't even promise you that you'll ever go home again," he sadly observed, causing Walter to wince. She stoically accepted the warning and said she thought that she would. And the doctor, as Geraldine had, finally acquiesced to Walter's will.

Walter spent little time at the campaign now. The three days at the convention had been a mistake. When he got back to Chicago, he had taken a cab directly from O'Hare to the hospital. He was shocked by how feeble and small she had looked, as if she were dissolving in the spread of her disease and the toxic wash of chemicals used to treat it. A terrible guilt had possessed him then and still did: guilt for having enjoyed himself while she suffered, guilt for having convinced her to endure what she did not want to endure, guilt for lying about a strength she no longer possessed and never again would.

She had been so sick the previous week that he had seldom left her side, going home to shower and change clothes at four in the morning, hoping to be back before she woke up. Her condition slightly improved now, Geraldine had started to badger him again to go to the campaign for at least a few hours a day. He usually turned aside her entreaties with a joke or an assurance he was keeping in touch by phone and e-mail.

That morning he had preempted her with a declaration that he would be spending a couple of hours at the campaign attending to a few matters, but would be back before three that afternoon. His only purpose in going there was to keep a promised lunch date with Tess Gilchrest. That was the reason he had walked past Mick Lowe's office at eleven forty-five that morning.

Tess Gilchrest knew she had a talent for forming close friendships with people she had only just met or who had been no more than a recognizable face until a shared experience brought them briefly under the spell of her beguiling gregariousness. People often commented on how she needed less than an hour to make someone feel he or she was a lifelong friend.

That Cal Regan had been a rare exception intrigued her, especially since she had granted him a privilege that, despite the casual attitude she affected about sex, she did not extend indiscriminately. Since the Knowles dinner, he had made obvious his intention to refuse the familiarity there had been between them. Their few exchanges had been brief and, on his part, curt. A teasing remark, a hand placed briefly on his arm in greeting, a flirting wink and smile, all discreetly offered, and meant only to convey a secret acknowledgment of intimacy, had received only indifferent responses, typically no more than a "Hi, Tess," although once he had added, "How's it going?"

His aloofness was little more than intriguing, however, although it was perhaps a small disappointment. It did not disturb her faith in the winsomeness she took for granted being irresistible. No more than an anomaly, she decided, an exception that proved the rule. The ease with which she quickly captured the affections of others assured her the fault was in Regan's personality, not hers.

By the end of their first shared evening at the convention, Walter considered Tess Gilchrest to be his closest friend on the campaign, the nearest thing to a confidante he had. They had made, and kept, plans to meet at least once a week for lunch or drinks, except last week when he couldn't leave Geraldine for even an hour. Tess had sent an arrangement of flowers to his mother's room then, the second time she had made such a gesture. On the first occasion, Walter had to explain to Geraldine they were from a friend of his, whom she hadn't met yet. "One of my best friends on the campaign," he had called her, and not, as Geraldine had assumed, someone's secretary who had been assigned the task on behalf of the campaign. "I'll bring her for a visit when you feel stronger," he had promised.

He had come to rely on Tess's thoughtfulness, on the consoling sincerity of her concern expressed in phone calls and e-mails and face-to-face when they met. He had come to rely on her most of all because there was no one else on whom he could rely, no one else he could go to for comfort and encouragement. Geraldine made an effort, of course, and his heart hurt to see her refuse to let her failing health silence her devotion to him. But their roles had been reversed by her disease. He must comfort her as best he could, ease her fears and not let her trouble with his. Tess filled that need for him now.

Although he didn't dwell on it with her, she could tell he resented some of the senior staff, those he saw as professional mercenaries who didn't share his history with and personal commitment to the president. And she often targeted their self-importance and other foibles for abuse, knowing it was the quickest way to cheer up her friend.

Several times she had made fun of something Cal Regan had said or done, which Walter had clearly enjoyed. "God, he's full of himself, isn't he?" she often observed, and Walter would laugh in agreement.

"He's a Ken doll come to life. And just as stiff. Everything pressed, plastered, and primped. You ever notice the way he always raises one of his bushy eyebrows when he thinks he's said something funny in an all-staff meeting? The only thing that makes me laugh is the eyebrow. The fucking thing looks like a hairy caterpillar."

"Aw, he's cool," Walter pretended to protest, "in his own way. A Ken-doll, made-for-TV, with-caterpillars-for-eyebrows kinda cool."

Once, she had recounted the dinner she and Regan had had with Allen Knowles, and how it had been hard to tell between the two of them "who was more desperate to be the alpha male." She had confessed, "for your ears only, bro," to having slept with Regan the night before, to explain how she had come to accompany him to the dinner, adding how uncomfortable about it he had been afterward, and laughing as she joked, "He really didn't need to be worried about it. He didn't make a big enough impression for me to remember it long enough to tell somebody about it."

She described, too, how nervous Regan had been because Knowles "started to talk trash in front of me about some guy who works for Morrison" and how patronizing he had been after that. "Really annoying," she had called it, "but kind of funny, too, unintentionally, like someone's dad explaining the facts of life to his little kid who'd just seen two animals copulating."

Had she mentioned to Walter the name of the guy who worked for Morrison or the misconduct Knowles had alleged? She couldn't remember, not with any certainty, but she would guess she probably had not. She couldn't remember Walter asking for those details. Why would he be interested in them? He didn't even know Allen Knowles, lucky him, and she was sure he didn't know whomever the hell it was Knowles had been talking about. She would only recall having briefly referred to the incident "in a general way, as part of a conversation we were having on another topic." "Just a funny anecdote," she would explain, "to make a point about something unrelated." She would remember the jokes she had made at Regan's expense but would keep them between her and Walter.

She would also remember her last comment to Walter about the conversation that had made Regan behave in so officious a manner toward her, twenty-four hours after they had slept together. "I've known Allen Knowles for a long time," she had said. "And I know not to pay attention to anything the asshole says. There's almost no chance it wouldn't be a lie." She would share that recollection, in an attempt to allay concerns about her innocent indiscretion, when Lowe, whose displeasure she feared a lot more than Regan's, called her into his office, where Regan would be waiting.

They would bark their questions at her. "Who did you talk to about it?" "What did you say?" "Why can't you remember?" "Are you lying?" Lowe would threaten to fire her. "I don't give a flying fuck who your daddy is; if you don't tell us exactly who you talked to and what you said, I'll shit-can your ass right now."

She would just shake her head and say she'd told them all she remembered. She knew Lowe had the balls to make good on his threat, but Regan was too much of a weasel to risk pissing off Hank Gilchrest, whose goodwill he might need someday.

They would make her cry anyway. The fuckers. But not until they had let her go and went looking for someone else to yell at, which she hoped wouldn't be Walter.

CHAPTER 21

O watched the cable anchor laugh again as the video clip ran for the third time that morning. Above a Chyron that read "Was he or wasn't he?" the president appeared to glance at the shapely backside of a young woman speaking from the podium at one of his campaign events. "The Leer," as the anchor had cheerfully pronounced it, dropping his voice an octave for comedic effect, had happened two weeks ago. But it hadn't been noticed until yesterday, when an intern at the cable network, tasked with finding video for a weekly wrap-up, excitedly brought it to the attention of his producer.

"And what if I was? So what!" O shouted at Rick Noth and Samuelson. "Jesus Christ, do they expect you to be castrated by this fucking job?"

Samuelson, although he regretted the distraction the president's intact manhood would create, knew better than to give an answer to a rhetorical question that could incite an argument. Noth offered the observation that declining ratings had turned the cable network in question "into a whorehouse for perverts," and then excused himself so he could repeat the insult and several others to the president of the network.

There were reporters who impressed O, including a handful of conservative columnists, whom he believed kept sensibly aloof from the puerile excesses of politics. But he disdained most of them as imitative, frivolous, and tactless. And he often complained to aides about their gullibility for story lines hand-fed to them by the campaigns, which revealed an intellectual laziness that would not be tolerated in other professions. He was just as derisive privately when reporters uncritically embraced his campaign's narrative, although he never complained about it.

He rarely conveyed his scorn to an offending reporter with anything more pointed than a brief, cold stare or an audible sigh as he shook his head. But once in a while, he tired of the effort of restraining himself and became more demonstrative. If the culprit wasn't at hand, he ordered Rick Noth to convey his displeasure.

O had just returned to the White House after four days of campaigning in the Pacific Northwest, Colorado, and Nevada. Most of his weekend would be spent in debate prep, before he returned to the campaign trail Monday morning. He had been irritable for much of the week, which he often became when deprived of the company of his wife and daughters for an extended period. They would have dinner together tonight and watch a movie in the White House theater; no invited guests, just the four of them.

Now, thanks to the juvenile sensibilities of cable news producers, he knew he would endure his wife's silent disinterest in him tonight, the punishment she reserved for those of his offenses that, while not very serious, had embarrassed her as well as him. Theirs was a strong marriage. He genuinely admired his wife's strength and independence. But was it such an imposition, he lamented to himself, to expect her to understand how absurd his predicament was, to be subjected to public ridicule for such a human instinct?

She found the manic intrusiveness of the press and the preposterous expectations imposed on the First Family as maddening as he did. But she often assigned him some degree of culpability for his humiliation. Or so it seemed to him when she responded to his grievances with her I-want-you-to-know-I'm-biting-my-tongue-through-another-of-your-self-pitying-jags look—eyebrows arched, head tilted to the right, the corners of her mouth turned down a little, not a scowl exactly, but not a smile either. He read in that look the accusation he tried to repress in his own thoughts: his ambition had put them in this predicament, and he should accept general responsibility for the impositions, stress, and humiliation that followed.

"I couldn't do this without you," he often told her.

"I wish you could," she often replied.

In less agitated moments, he was able to admire the honesty in her lack of sympathy. She had a finely tuned bullshit detector, the quality that had turned his attraction to the beautiful, vivacious, and confident young woman into love.

He had been taken with her instantly when a fellow summer associate at their Chicago law firm introduced him to her. She had initially been friendly but indifferent to his interest in her. He was unaccustomed to that. He knew he was attractive to women: good-looking enough, thoughtful, quick-witted, well-spoken, and ambitious. He had been marked for distinction in law school. His classmates admired him. He had acquired a number of influential benefactors. Obviously, he would be a good provider for his family, when he decided to acquire one.

He took the blow graciously when he heard from his friend she wasn't interested.

"She said you were 'cute' but a little full of yourself."

"Yeah? Well, tell her I resent being called cute. Puppies are cute. Most people consider me handsome. Dashing—I've been called dashing as well. Tell her she might need glasses."

Their first dinner date occurred a week later. They were a couple by the end of the month and engaged to be married a year later. From the getting-to-know-each-other to the imagining-their-future-together stage of their relationship, she had listened to his career plans with an attitude that suggested she might tolerate the concessions his political ambitions would require but he shouldn't expect her enthusiastic approval. Nor should he assume she would modify her personality or relinquish her ambitions or homogenize her views to conform to the stereotype of a candidate's spouse.

"I want to change politics," he grandly promised.

"Good for you," she said. "But you'd be the first politician who didn't let it change you."

Less than two decades after they were married, they were living in the White House. His swift and spectacular ascent had entailed a great many concessions both had once believed they would never accept. She didn't resent it. They were making history together. The prize was worth the price. But she didn't pretend to him they had remained perfectly faithful to the

innocent convictions of their youth or that their triumph was an unquali-
fied blessing. Although he chafed at times at her uncomforting honesty, he
knew it was the thing—sometimes the only thing—that kept them from
losing forever the authenticity they had once believed incorruptible.

O calmed down after venting his anger to Samuelson and Noth,
and recognized he was, despite his wife's certain displeasure, still looking forward to an evening alone with his family. *I'm letting it get to me,*
he rebuked himself, and resolved to summon a stouter fortitude for the
degradations he would have to suffer to remain in office.

The last campaign had tested his self-control. The eighteen-hour days,
the frenetic travel, the bad food, the loss of autonomy, and the silly expectations imposed on him. The ersatz patriotism. The feigned conviviality
with strangers who asked him outlandish questions. Suffering the predictable whining of reporters who swooned to his message of change but were
themselves averse to change. You dropped two points in a poll or said
something obviously true but too blunt for ears trained to detect danger in
honesty and they were at your throat. People crowding you every waking
minute. Take a few days to recharge or a couple of hours to shoot some
hoops or take your wife out, and you're cocky or lackadaisical.

But he had kept it together, mostly. In private, he could become
cross when mistakes occurred or when assurances proved false or when
pressed to conform to campaign orthodoxies he thought stupid. But staff
who had experienced his displeasure marveled at his ability to appear
unbothered and focused in public. He didn't overreact to unexpected
setbacks. He never acted impulsively when surprised. Never let his
instincts, which were as insistent as any politician's, overcome his reason. Never seemed to give a shit when reporters or griping party insiders
were concerned he wasn't hustling enough, responding to attacks quickly
enough, worrying enough. He never appeared anxious over the outcome
or desperate for the office. He told his story. He was different and he
would make the stupid, maddening business of Washington politics different. He paid the same quiet, careful attention to his showmanship that
he paid to his message. He spent prodigiously to drive up his opponent's
negatives. And he let the country come to him.

The White House had proved a bigger challenge. Staff were always orbiting him, hustling their plans and whispering their worries to one another, trying not to disturb him or take their eyes off him either. Reporters at his heels, importuning him, goading him, trying to steal his secrets, wandering in the Rose Garden, craning their necks to catch a glimpse of him behind his office drapes, with his feet on his desk and his tie loosened. Foreign leaders courted his favor and scoffed at him, lectured him, and whimpered like petulant adolescents when he treated them as heads of state rather than his new best friend. He worked and lived in a museum. He had little privacy and yet felt isolated.

In Washington all calamities, and the opportunities they offered for social progress, were absorbed by its rituals and reconstituted into scale weights in hourly recalculations of power's dispersal, which obsessed its every constituent part. Little distinction was made between appearance and fact or the trivial and the significant. Paradoxes threatened to suffocate every initiative. Everything mattered and nothing mattered. Everything was urgent and nothing had priority. Hurry up! Not so fast! You forgot about this! You're attempting too much! All his efforts to encourage a more reasonable governing environment were met with hostility from the opposition and indifference from his supporters, and his failures were grist for the media's constant grind of hyperbole, conflict, and agitprop. And every day the final measure of everything was attributed to him, personally. Did *he* succeed or fail? Did *he* keep his promise or break it? *Christ, was there ever a less self-reflective place?* Despite universal protestations to the contrary, no one here really wanted him to change Washington, only to preside over it more successfully than the last guy had.

O had misinterpreted his mandate, one pundit after another alleged in the months preceding the midterms, hurrying to explain the seismic political reversal for Democrats the polls were predicting. Voters had given him a personal mandate, not a policy one. They trusted his promises of bipartisanship, his reasonableness to work cooperatively with Republicans and Democrats in Congress to fix the economy. They hadn't signed on for these huge, divisive battles on health care and climate change, or the massive spending.

What a crock. I didn't run on health care? I forgot to mention I wanted to do something about climate change? No one thought the government would have to intervene when businesses everywhere were downsizing their inventories and laying off millions and the banks wouldn't lend money? And what if we hadn't done it? How would they explain the country's mood then? They'd accuse me of thinking small, squandering a mandate for change that had a short political shelf life. Here you go, Mr. President, a big, fat, catastrophic, global recession, courtesy of your predecessor, now go dig us out of it overnight, will you, by playing small ball. And remember to play nice with Republicans while you do it.

He had tried to play nice. He waited on, implored, and flattered the shrinking cohort of Republicans who had greeted his landslide by pledging their cooperation in a national emergency. They were problem solvers first, they insisted, partisans second. He listened to their ideas, pushed Democrats to accept as many of them as they could, solicited their advice, shoveled money to their constituents, invited them to the White House for the goddamn Super Bowl, and called them on their birthdays.

And what did it get me? Complaints about exceeding my mandate. I'm spending too much. I'm taxing too much. I'm destroying the finest health care system in the world, which unfortunately isn't available to about fifty million Americans. I'm not taking them seriously as they piss themselves in terror stoked by those pompous, opportunistic multimillionaires Glenn Beck and Rush Limbaugh, and the Ward and June Cleavers in Minuteman costumes; as they Photoshop Hitler mustaches on my picture and wait for orders from their Calamity Jane of the North, who is still too pig-in-shit happy with her seven-figure book deals and reality TV politics to give in to their fevered desire that she lead them on a righteous crusade to take the White House from the Ivy League elitists and their enablers in the "Lamestream Media."

The Tea Party movement. A movement? Are you kidding me? A disorganized mob of conspiracy nuts, immigrant haters, vengeful Old Testament types, publicity hustlers, and people who just have way too much time on their hands. The only thing that unites them is their sneering self-righteousness and burning hatred for me.

After the midterms, he had briefly and unhappily bowed to Washington's expectation that he would have to find some way to cooperate with Republican leaders on something, anything, to show voters he got their message. He had to save himself, the pundits insisted. Congressional Democrats are on life support. He needs a "big government is over" moment. He'll find an issue like Clinton did with welfare reform on which Republicans can't refuse to work with him. *Just like Clinton, right. Good old Elvis, everybody's favorite country slicker, grabbin' ass and cuttin' deals, his big paw resting on the shoulders of unfortunates, whispering his sympathies and promises in their ears two minutes before he threw them to the wolves to save his own ass.*

He had summoned the Republican leaders in the House and Senate to the White House.

Even that had met with resistance. He had invited only the two men for drinks in the family residence. The other members of the leadership, distrustful of their leaders' fortitude in the face of a presidential charm offensive, and goaded by the militant backbenchers in their caucus, protested their exclusion. "We'd like to bring the entire leadership and staff," the chief of staff to the Senate Republican leader informed the head of the White House Office of Legislative Affairs. "And we'd rather the meeting took place in the Cabinet Room and not the residence."

"Tell them he wants to make them an offer on the tax cuts," Samuelson instructed his deputy. "And if they're too afraid to come here without bringing the Village People with them, he'll announce it in the Rose Garden."

When the two men arrived unaccompanied two days later, O told them he would agree to extend all the cuts for two years only, postponing a final resolution until after the next election.

"I won't extend the upper income cut after that. But I'll have to get reelected to stop you from doing it."

While waiting for a response neither Republican seemed eager to give, O floated his alternative compromise. "Or you can agree to extending all of them now except the top bracket, and I'll agree to a ten percent cut in the corporate tax rate."

Either deal would be portrayed by the press and furious liberals as a huge concession to the right. The cut in corporate taxes had been a core issue for Republicans and their corporate benefactors in several election cycles. O knew businesses didn't care that much about keeping their income tax cut. But they squawked constantly about the corporate rate, *along with whining about how mean I am to them. Thanks for raiding the Treasury to save our asses, but don't dare try to prevent us from blowing up the economy again.*

"Well, Mr. President, I'd like to thank you for having us here," the Senate Republican leader began his response. "These are the kinds of discussions we should be having, and I hope we'll have more of them. And we'll certainly take these ideas to our caucus. But I'm not sure a majority of our members will accept them."

The House leader was more certain about his caucus's reaction. "We want to make them all permanent. But we could discuss a five-year extension and the corporate cut in exchange for raising the debt ceiling."

"But you've been suggesting to us for months that you could live with a two-year extension," O plaintively reminded them. He added, more angrily, "Now, I'm offering it to you in good faith, and you're making new demands? Raise the debt ceiling? How big of you. You're prepared to let the country default on its debts, are you? Unbelievable."

Dutifully, and a little sheepishly, the Senate leader conceded the deal might have been good enough in the last Congress, "but all the new energy in our caucus has created a new dynamic."

"A new what?" O asked.

"A new dynamic."

"Is that code for 'Sorry, but screw you and your concession, Mr. President'?"

"It's not personal, sir. Elections have consequences, as you often remind us."

"Does the 'new energy' in your caucus understand we have to govern the country together? For at least two more years. Americans don't expect much from us, but I think they might still assume we could manage not to push the country into receivership."

Voters possessed as little self-awareness as the politicians they reviled and regularly reelected. Some had voted for O because he flattered their enlightened worldview. Others had voted against him because he personified their fears. Those who had decided the election, the independents, had voted for him because they were so upset over the downturn in their fortunes that they were willing to risk a greater presidential disappointment to rebuke the last one. Their conflicting demands and expectations of him were similar only in their lack of patience. Nothing he did could prove them right fast enough. He couldn't succeed fast enough. He couldn't fail fast enough. In that way he was often a disappointment to all of them.

He had given a speech late in the first year of his presidency, when he was still trying to get health care reform passed. Republicans were calling him a socialist. Liberals were denouncing him as a sellout. That was the first time he saw one of the signs that soon became popular bumper stickers in the gentrified working-class neighborhoods where the newest generation of overeducated, underemployed, and uncompromising progressives lived in a state of perpetual agitation.

He spotted it as soon as the kid stood up to wave it above the heads of the seated audience. No doubt the kid believed he had personally won the last election for O and now got to decide how he should govern a country divided on almost every major issue. He was one of the Letdowns. They were let down when he didn't immediately let gays serve openly in the military. And after he did, they were let down because he didn't nominate a lesbian to be chairman of the Joint Chiefs the next day. They were let down every time an American soldier fired his weapon in another country. Let down every day the CIA still existed or the former vice president wasn't in jail. Let down because his government wouldn't hand out free abortions and houses and electric cars.

WHERE'S THE CHANGE, BROTHER? it read, and O smiled when he saw it. He wouldn't let a childish attempt at impudence crack his composure, and he imagined his unspoken response.

I am all the change you're going to get. Brother.

★ CHAPTER 22 ★

The Morrison campaign planned to roll out large policy pronounce-
ments every week for the duration of the campaign. They would do so
even during the weeks when the three presidential debates were scheduled. Stilwell had conceived the plan to have Morrison give a big policy
speech on the day before each of the three debates, to rattle the O team a
little, who would have to rush to prepare something and brief the president on Morrison's proposal, adding to the stress and irritation candidates battled in the hours before their debates.

The most controversial policy speech would occur ahead of the first
debate. Morrison had agreed to it very reluctantly. He had rejected it
out of hand when Sandy Stilwell had first raised the idea with him two
weeks before their convention. Stilwell had brought it up again during
the week of O's convention and pleaded with Morrison to "at least give
it more careful consideration." But weeks of debate and argument had
followed, and many phone calls were placed to seek the quiet counsel of
army friends, counsel that Morrison hadn't shared with Stilwell or anyone else on the campaign.

Morrison had not been surprised when the president's timetable for
the withdrawal of American forces from Afghanistan had missed one
deadline after another. He had followed the progress of the war closely.
He had stayed in frequent touch with several former subordinates, who
were now flag officers themselves and were willing to share information he couldn't find in press coverage of the war. The enemy had been
dislodged from most of its strongholds, and the general in command
of allied forces had pronounced Afghanistan free of significant enemy

activity. But less progress could be claimed for the political and economic reconstruction of the country.

Afghanistan was still stubbornly divided into tribal fiefdoms, under the control of various warlords. Their support for assistance by the central government and the West to build the local economic, political, and security infrastructures required to prevent a return of hostilities was unreliable at best, and was conditioned on how much of it could be diverted to their own purposes. Neither had much progress been made through the tangle of competing self-interests that defined Afghan politics to convince sizable numbers of Taliban to forswear violence in favor of a political role in the country's future.

Morrison knew all the achievements made at great cost and sacrifice to the United States and its allies were tenuous, and the Taliban, damaged and diminished, had not yet given up the ghost. They were lurking in sanctuaries on both sides of Afghanistan's border with Pakistan, biding their time until events turned in a more favorable direction for them, new recruits would enter their camps, and new offensives would be launched to retake some of their recently lost territory. In the meantime, they planned and executed what attacks they could to remind Afghans living in the remote towns and villages of their fractured civilization that they were as they had been for centuries, prey for various predatory forces that fought eternally for control of their benighted country. Morrison had never declared during the campaign that he believed it would take two or three more years before the Afghanistan government and military would be strong enough to defend the country on their own. But he had little doubt that even that was an optimistic timetable.

Working with a team of advisors recruited for the task because of their reputations for discretion, Stilwell had prepared for Morrison a policy proposal that called for the withdrawal of all U.S. ground forces from Afghanistan by the end of his first year in office. U.S. military advisors would remain in Kabul to encourage Afghanistan's armed forces in their duty, and a large CIA station would continue to operate there. U.S. warplanes would operate from a base in another Central Asian country, from where they could support Afghanistan military operations, when necessary, as would a fleet of predator drones under the control of the CIA station in Kabul. The number of American civilians involved in economic reconstruction efforts in Afghanistan would have to be significantly reduced because they could not be protected by the U.S. military. But more than a token presence would stay, composed of young civil servants, most of whom did not have spouses or children.

Public opinion polls were showing a marked increase in the number and intensity of Americans who wanted the United States to end the longest war in its history. While the issue was hardly voters' biggest priority, its salience had grown as the public's economic anxiety had decreased. Who better, Stilwell reasoned, to give voice to their demands than a decorated four-star general? They could open a whole new line of attack against the administration on an issue where Morrison had unimpeachable credentials, and catch the O campaign completely unprepared for a debate they would not have expected.

"No," Morrison said, and repeated it for emphasis when Stilwell approached him with the proposal. "There are some things, Sandy, that are too important for politics. Not losing a war that we can win is one of them."

Stilwell, repeating the question he had raised with the policy team, asked Morrison how long he could envision "keeping tens of thousands of American soldiers hostage to the corruption and incompetence of the Afghan government and the centuries of tribal politics that have kept that country in the dark ages."

Morrison hadn't placed much trust in the advice of Stilwell's team. Nor did he trust Stilwell's own counsel on the subject. On the contrary, he resented it. He liked Stilwell, and thought him a reliable man with mature judgment when it came to running a political campaign. That he presumed to offer advice on a military campaign showed the detestable ignorant arrogance common in Stilwell's profession.

But Morrison was surprised to find Stilwell's advice echoed by a few fellow retired officers whose counsel he did respect, as well as one active-duty major general, who had once served as his executive officer and whose career Morrison had greatly helped to advance. "General, I think we've probably achieved all we can reasonably expect to achieve in that screwed-up country," he had calmly asserted. "And I don't know how much longer the army can afford to keep an occupying force of that size there," he had added.

Still, Morrison had continued to resist taking the controversial position. "I would squander the best advantage I have over the president," he insisted to Stilwell, "by letting him appear tougher on an important national security issue."

Stilwell had responded by comparing Morrison's situation to Eisenhower's when he ran for president at the height of the Korean War. "When Eisenhower was a candidate, he promised to end the war, and it didn't diminish his credibility with voters," he had argued. "On the contrary, voters automatically believed he could do what Adlai Stevenson and Harry Truman couldn't do: relieve them of the sad duty of reading about American casualties in their newspapers every day."

It was this final argument of Stilwell's that had proven decisive in convincing his candidate to run as the peacemaker his opponent could no longer credibly claim to be. It did not erase from Morrison's conscience the knowledge of falseness. Nor did it mollify the resentment Morrison had felt when Stilwell had first broached the idea with him. But despite his pretensions, Morrison knew he had to rely, as candidates usually do, on rationalizations of worthy ends and false means. Unavoidable, really, he reassured himself when a quiet conscience said otherwise.

Anticipating the shock to the O campaign gave Stilwell, for the first time in weeks, a reason to feel encouraged the race hadn't slipped entirely beyond their ability to influence it. They did not have to wait and hope for their opponent to screw up or some other deus ex machina to give them an opportunity to win the thing. With a little daring, they could still make their own luck.

Unlike his candidate, Stilwell was less concerned with the soundness of the policies Morrison advocated. Presidential candidates promised many things that they could not make good on in office. In the last campaign, O had offered voters quite a grandiose vision: an era of peace and goodwill among nations and individuals, when reason ruled, rich and poor prospered alike, technology saved man from the defects of his nature, the oceans receded, and fatal diseases were cured.

That they could not keep all the promises they had made as candidates didn't trouble the consciences of most presidents, immersed as they were in the daily management of the politics and responsibilities of their office, and constantly reminded of the limits of democratic government. You got what you could, much less than you promised. And if the country wasn't blown up because of your obvious negligence and voters had more disposable income than they had at the beginning of your presidency, you would probably be reelected.

Tom Morrison possessed a little of the reformer's zeal about government, and a great deal of confidence in his own competence. But he had enough experience with the sluggish bureaucracies to appreciate the limits of even the most competent executive's ability to achieve more than incremental improvements.

Still, a promise to end a war was not one a man of his background and probity could backslide on without doing considerable damage to his self-esteem, which he had a hard time distinguishing from his public reputation. And were he to keep his promise, and Afghanistan fall apart, that, too, would threaten his pride. "If I commit to it," he had insisted to Stilwell, "I'll have to do it even if I shouldn't. I try to avoid getting myself into predicaments like that, when going forward is a mistake and so is retreating."

"The country's already in that predicament," Stilwell had responded. "Just like it was in Korea. And the only pertinent question is: who's the better choice to get us out of it, you or the president?"

Morrison knew better than to make pretentious claims for his candidacy, to offer himself as the nation's savior rather than its chief executive. O had been guilty of such arrogance in the last campaign, Morrison believed, and still was at times. Only to himself would Morrison confess he felt called to the presidency by something grander than opportunity or ideology or the conviction he could govern better than the incumbent. Something essential to the country was in danger of being lost.

The standards of excellence that Americans had always created on their own initiative had been consigned to the past. Progress now was defined for the nation as the future the government would create. Government would now decide standards of excellence and make sure they were in almost any person's reach. Problems Americans had created for themselves would be solved for them by a government that believed itself enlightened on a scale that could not be achieved by individuals. Everyone would be safer, healthier, happier. Everything would be fairer.

It is desirable, Morrison supposed, for people to trust their government. But Americans often did not and had managed to race through history without worrying about it much. It is essential that government trust the people. That's what was lost in the president's vision of progress. His government expected less of Americans than had governments in the past. It assumed more of their responsibilities for them because it didn't believe people were capable of meeting them without doing terrible injury to one another. It did not trust the people it governed. The restoration of that trust was essential for the nation to make any progress worthy of the name. That was the cause that Morrison believed called him to the presidency.

Morrison's first major policy speech of the fall campaign had been given in a Denver hotel to a local association of small-business owners, where he announced what his campaign called "the first serious and comprehensive plan in over twenty-five years to revolutionize, modernize, shrink, and simplify the federal tax code." The redundant verbs chosen to describe it were meant to emphasize a boldness not normally found in the abstruse language employed by the economists and corporate leaders whom the campaign had recruited to help put together the proposal.

No outside advisor, however, had been more involved in its development than Morrison himself. He had spent more time than Sandy Stilwell thought necessary discussing and debating the provisions highlighted in the speech, which were emphasized again in a flurry of e-mailed summaries, talking points, and endorsements from various chambers of commerce, trade associations, small-business coalitions, taxpayer advocacy groups, economists, and a half dozen individuals with no public affiliations who shared a basic profile: heads of household, annual income between forty-five thousand and seventy-five thousand dollars.

There had been no disagreement between Morrison and his advisors about the centerpiece of the plan: eliminating scores of corporate tax loopholes and replacing them with a reduction of the corporate tax rate from thirty-five to twenty percent. Stilwell had hinted more than once to Morrison that he could trust his advisors to work out the smaller details. His time was better spent concentrating on the politics of the issue than sitting for hours at a conference table examining and reexamining the possible implications of every proposed change in the tax code. But Morrison, who, Stilwell often observed, occasionally indulged a professorial inclination to "beat a dead horse to life," clearly enjoyed the exercise and refused to be excluded.

In the Denver speech, greater emphasis and a distinctly populist gloss had been placed on the loopholes to be closed. The following day, Morrison's visit to the midwestern farm implement manufacturing plant that for sixty years had provided a livelihood to several thousand local families was intended to defend the corporate rate cut. His seven minutes of remarks to the plant's assembled workers and the pictures of him walking the factory floor, asking questions and listening sympathetically, were intended to emphasize that working people and not the wealthy were the real victims of the second-highest corporate tax rate in the world.

The DNC and the president's campaign had denounced the idea thirty seconds after Morrison had finished his Denver speech as "a corporate giveaway of staggering proportions that will result in a windfall to special interests, bigger bonuses for billionaires, and more of the nation's tax burden falling squarely on the back of the middle class."

The next day, Morrison explained, in words and images, that the primary purpose of the proposal was to save American jobs. In the depth of the last recession, the plant had barely escaped being selected for closure by corporate headquarters. It had survived, but the workers employed there lived in fear of their future, with the dreaded certainty that the aging and exhausted engine of their community's prosperity was on borrowed time.

"Here's what's happening," Morrison explained. "Washington takes a disproportionate share of your earnings, the money your company would use to modernize your plants, expand your operations, build new products, sell more products, create new jobs, and pay higher wages so that every bureaucrat there can build his or her little piece of our massive, heavily leveraged federal government bigger than their wildest dreams. Meanwhile companies in China, Germany, Brazil, Zambia, and other countries whose names I can't even pronounce are taking your business and your jobs away.

"It's just one idiotic provision in the federal tax code," he added, "seventy thousand pages filled with the most complicated, unintelligible, counterproductive, and grossly unfair schemes ever devised by the minds of people who've never run a business, sold a product, met a payroll, or built anything useful in their lives."

As the employees cheered the universal sentiment of chronic government malfeasance, Morrison offered his remedy. "We need to throw this ridiculous monstrosity into a trash can big enough to hold it, the whole darn thing, and start over. And that's only going to happen if we change management in the White House. In four years, the president hasn't removed a single provision from the tax code. Not one. But he has added several hundred more. That's the kind of progress that can kill an economy."

With a trace of anger that didn't sound affected, he closed by warning his audience, "So don't pay any attention to all that nonsense you hear from the president's people about how it's going to billionaires and special interests. You know where those earnings would go if they didn't disappear into the black hole of Washington. They would go to you. To your families. To your town and your neighborhoods. And that's exactly where they belong."

Morrison had not taken any questions from the press in Denver. His campaign wanted the speech to be reported without being diluted by back-and-forth exchanges between the candidate and reporters. The campaign had agreed to reporters' demands that he answer their questions after the plant tour, knowing it would ensure Morrison's tax reform proposal would receive prominent coverage for the balance of the week.

For two consecutive days it would be featured on the front page of every leading newspaper and near the top of the evening news broadcasts, recycled every half hour on cable, and would continue to be discussed at length on the Sunday shows.

The sky was overcast, and the first of autumn's leaves tumbled in sudden gusts of wind as Morrison walked toward the waiting reporters, lending an incongruous melancholy to the businesslike atmosphere. The advance staffer in charge of the audio worried a gust would be picked up by the microphone and drown out Morrison as he gave an answer the campaign would want broadcast intelligibly on television. A small paperweight had been placed on the podium to secure a card on which the names of reporters were typed in the order he had been advised to call on them. When Morrison reached the podium, he glanced at the card before putting it in the inside pocket of his jacket. Morrison's press secretary stood ten feet to the right of the podium, out of camera shot, facing reporters as if prepared to caution them should they become unruly or confrontational. Four senior staffers, including Stilwell, stood next to the camera riser behind the seated reporters. They were more interested in observing their candidate's deportment than the reporters' manners.

After he answered eight questions from the wires, networks, and national dailies, all of them predictable and easily answered, he took a couple of questions from local reporters, as he had been reminded to do by his press secretary.

When he finished with them, his press secretary was prepared to announce the press conference had ended by shouting "Thank you." Morrison had told him to wait for his signal, a quick nod, before doing so. "If there's time, I might let one or two of the folks who never get called on ask a question." His press secretary had thought that would be fine but recommended Morrison not call on someone he didn't recognize. "They might be hostile or kinda crazy and ask you something way off topic. It could be someone who's there to embarrass you. You could get a question you can't answer."

As it happened, he did not give the agreed signal to his press secretary after he had finished his answer to a second local reporter. Instead, he announced he had time for one more, and after a quick survey of faces, he pointed to a reporter whose face he recognized but whose name he had never bothered to learn. He had seen him at previous press conferences and OTRs, staged photo ops that were not, as the acronym suggested, off-the-record.

Once, as his motorcade drove onto the tarmac of the Jacksonville airport, Morrison had noticed the reporter waiting in line to board the second press plane, which the campaign had leased after the convention to accommodate the larger press contingent that now traveled with Morrison. Reporters called it "the ass plane," as did the junior campaign staffers assigned to their care and feeding, an appellation meant to recognize not only that the plane invariably took off and landed after the candidate's plane, but also the stigma associated with traveling in the much smaller aircraft without the larger plane's amenities of hot food and drinkable wine. Reporters assigned to it were considered too unimportant to merit a seat on the candidate's plane, those who were never given interviews with the candidate or called on at press conferences. They were handed a bottle of water, a soggy sandwich wrapped in cellophane, and a bag of chips as they boarded.

"He's hard not to notice," Morrison explained later. "He's such a funny-looking little fellow." He was short, barely five and a half feet, and slightly built, with a haphazardly barbered mop of curly dark hair, a disheveled appearance, and black-rimmed glasses too large for his face.

"He's one of Bianca Stefani's baby bloggers; 'citizen journalists,' she calls them, so she doesn't have to pay them a living wage," his press secretary replied. "Terence Haley. He's English or Irish maybe, I don't know."

"Why do we have a Stefani reporter traveling with us?" Stilwell asked incredulously.

"Well, in hindsight, it probably wasn't a good idea to let him on the plane," the press secretary conceded. "But we have empty seats, and the press are bitching about their share of the charter we're billing them for, and he'd just fly commercial if we didn't give him one. He'd still show up at our events."

No one had yet discussed the question that had precipitated the conversation. When Stilwell had asked Morrison if he had "any idea what the kid was talking about," Morrison had only replied, "I don't think it's something we have to worry about."

Stilwell doubted that. Other reporters would be as curious about it as he was, and would soon be quietly talking to their editors and fishing around for an explanation from Terence Haley, from the campaign, from reporters covering Justice and the defense industry. The campaign needed to know what it was they would be looking for. In another minute or two, Stilwell would ask the other staffers to leave Morrison's cabin, so he could have a private word with the candidate.

Considering the source, it was almost certainly a question based on a rumor picked up from some obscure left-wing blog, or a supposition made from a misunderstood fact, and was asked to raise a false suspicion or elicit an unusual response that would intrigue the other reporters who witnessed it. The question had, in fact, succeeded in achieving the latter effect. Morrison had paused and stared at the kid for what had seemed like an unusually long time before responding. Of course, it would have been easy to dismiss. The question had obviously come out of left field, a ridiculous rumor no one but a Stefani reporter would have paid any attention to. Morrison was unsure of how to respond. But he had responded, and the response had been so cryptic that it made the pause preceding it seem almost menacing.

Haley had not looked surprised when Morrison called on him. Nor had he needed a moment to collect his thoughts and formulate his question. He had fired it off the instant Morrison had pointed at him and said, "You."

"Governor, would you care to comment on the fact that an employee of yours when you were CEO of Channing-Mills is the subject of a federal investigation for bribery?"

Morrison had turned his head for an instant, in the direction of his press secretary, as if he was looking for guidance about how to answer a question he didn't understand. Then he turned back to face the reporter, straightened his shoulders, and stared at him for at least ten seconds, his lips pressed firmly together, standing perfectly still until he allowed a small smile to soften his appearance. He said, "Son, I'm afraid you're asking something you really wouldn't want to hear the answer to."

That was it. That was all he said. When Haley had responded that he "would, in fact, like to hear the answer," Morrison had simply walked away from the podium toward his motorcade, as his aides and Secret Service detail scrambled to catch up to him.

"That was weird," the AP reporter observed to the Reuters reporter sitting next to him, which was exactly what Avi Samuelson had said to himself as he watched the end of the Morrison press conference on the television in his White House office, wondering if he had missed something in Morrison's response because of the gust of wind that had garbled the sound. "Yeah, it sure was," the Reuters reporter had agreed.

The audio problem was one of the reasons cable producers didn't include the response in the clip they ran of the press conference, and was why the networks didn't use it in the nightly campaign wrap-ups on their news broadcasts. It hadn't been necessary for producers of the cable and broadcast news shows to explain their main reason for excluding it. Neither they nor any of their reporters covering the Morrison campaign knew what the hell it was about.

After Sandy Stilwell had dismissed him from Morrison's cabin, the campaign's press secretary walked to the back of the plane where the press were seated. "Just coming to say hi," he announced, "not to gaggle," which meant he wouldn't answer any of their questions on the record. He had come to gauge their interest in the curious question and the more curious response that had brought the press conference to its rather sudden conclusion. The reporters did ask him questions, and he did respond to them. But most of them either were of a social nature or were concerned with incidental matters: questions about the schedule, mild complaints about the inadequate time they were given to file their stories. A few questions addressed more serious issues: the debates and the subjects of future policy speeches, one "to clear up some confusion" about a provision in Morrison's tax reform proposal. No one appeared to be in a hurry to ask him about Terence Haley's question. Only when the press secretary appeared to be leaving did one of the reporters ask him about the subject that was on all their minds. "Your guy seemed a little pissed by that last question," he observed, as every reporter within earshot looked up to catch the press secretary's response.

"Wouldn't you be?" he shot back. "He gives the kid a break, a shot at prime time, and what's the kid do with it? He asks about whatever Roswell sighting Bianca's worked up about today. He just won the record for the shortest career ever as a political reporter." His answer was greeted with smiles and laughter, and when the press secretary had walked through the curtains separating them from campaign staff, the reporters were still smiling as they scribbled down his response word for word.

Sandy Stilwell was still in Morrison's cabin, listening to the candidate brief him on the issue he had declined to discuss at the press conference, and caution him somewhat severely that he wasn't to discuss it with anyone else on the campaign, and certainly not with anyone in the press.

At the same moment, in Chicago, Mick Lowe was leaving a voice-mail message on Cal Regan's phone, while Regan was on a plane to Washington.

"Call me as soon as you land."

CHAPTER 23

"Someone asked Morrison about the Salazar thing at his press conference in Wisconsin," Lowe informed him, his matter-of-fact delivery indicating he thought this development, while curious, was not something to get too excited about, just as their discovery of the "Salazar thing" hadn't warranted overexcitement.

"Who asked him?" Regan asked.

"One of Bianca's little dirt diggers," Lowe replied. "Terence Haley. That British kid with the funny glasses."

Regan didn't recognize the name or recall the funny glasses. "How did Morrison respond?"

"I e-mailed you the transcript. Basically, I can't tell if he didn't know what the guy was talking about or if the question freaked him out and kind of paralyzed him. He said something like 'You don't want the answer,' which I guess could be interpreted as an accusation that the question was just a political statement and Haley didn't expect Morrison to answer it, or Morrison didn't have an answer because he wasn't sure what Haley was talking about, or that he could answer but didn't want to."

"Has Stefani posted a story yet?"

"Nope."

"Huh. Let me know as soon as she does. Any idea where Bianca might have heard about this?"

"Your guess is as good as mine."

"We should probably try to find out. Maybe I should call her and ask what it's about, if it's something we should be interested in."

"I'd probably hold off on that for a while. If she's sure she's onto something, she'll yak about it in front of every camera she can find."

"Yeah, and I'd like to know what she knows, and whether she knows what we know before she posts something or talks about it. I'll hold off for now, though."

"By the way," Lowe continued, "the transcript I sent you doesn't give the full flavor of the thing. It was weird. Morrison gave the guy a real death stare before he said that thing about not wanting the answer, and then sort of marched off suddenly while the kid was responding to him. Took everybody by surprise, including his staff and Secret Service. Stilwell was there, and you can see him run to catch his candidate. The cameras followed him, and no one said anything, all you could hear was the wind blowing. The whole thing looked very weird."

Regan had other voice-mail messages waiting for him when he landed, and in the town car on his way to the DNC he listened to Bianca Stefani implore him to call her immediately.

"Cal, it's Bianca. Am I your favorite person today? We must talk as soon as possible to discuss the follow-up to the favor we did you today. We can't let the old media and Morrison ignore this. But I need some facts, darling, which I know you have. Call me back. Ciao."

The purpose of the call to Bianca Stefani, he had suggested to Mick Lowe, would be to find out who had told her about the investigation, and whether she knew the campaign was aware of it. Her message had answered the second question. She obviously believed or suspected the campaign had been told about it. If her source was someone associated with the campaign, then she had more than a suspicion.

The list of suspects was a short one. Only two names were on it: Allen Knowles and Tess Gilchrest. He and Lowe hadn't discussed the matter with anyone except Carl Barstow, whose reputation for reliable discretion was much deserved and a point of professional pride. He briefly considered the possibility that Knowles's assistant, the statuesque Scandinavian, might be the source, before dismissing it when he remembered her complete lack of interest in the matter when Knowles had discussed it.

Stefani's timing, as usual, was lousy, Regan mused, lousy for the campaign, anyway. He hadn't taken seriously her talk of doing the campaign a favor. She had a story, however tenuously sourced or incomplete, that no one else in the media had. She intended to publish it before anyone else could. Her only interest was the glorification of *The Stefani Report,* the new media, and Bianca Stefani. She had sent her reporter out to get a reaction from Morrison, knowing how unlikely it was Morrison would call on him or answer a shouted question after the press conference was over. She would have done that only to alert the rest of the press that she knew something they didn't. And she would have never done that if she wasn't ready to publish with or without Regan's cooperation.

When his meeting at the DNC concluded, Regan asked for the loan of an office where he could return some calls before he went to the White House. *The Stefani Report* still hadn't posted the story, and it was now nearly three o'clock.

He placed his first call to Allen Knowles, expecting to be told that Mr. Knowles was in a meeting or traveling but would return the call when he was free. Regan would not have thought anything of it. It was always difficult to get Knowles on the phone on the first try. To his surprise he was put right through.

"My man," Knowles boomed into the phone. "What can I do for you?"

"Nothing much. I'm trying to get a handle on something you might or might not be able to help me with."

"Sure. What do you need?"

"How well do you know Bianca Stefani?"

"Hardly know her at all. Seen her at parties here and there. Why do you ask?"

"Just a shot in the dark. I don't know if you saw Morrison's press conference today, but one of her reporters asked him about the Salazar investigation."

"I heard. You're calling to see if I told her about it."

"No, not really. I was hoping to find out where she might have heard about it, though. Have you ever discussed it with anyone else?"

"Like I told you, there was a lot of chatter about it in the industry, and I took part in some of those conversations. But I haven't said a word about it to anyone since I left the thing in your capable hands. I assumed you guys had given it to the reporter."

"No. We didn't. Tell you the truth, we don't know if it's really that big of a deal."

"But you've looked into it, right?"

"Yeah, indirectly."

"And from whom did you find what . . . indirectly?"

"Allen, it's probably better if we didn't discuss that in detail."

"Okay. But you confirmed there is an investigation?"

"There appears to be one, yes. But we have no information that Morrison is implicated, and he probably isn't."

"Still, that's not good news for him, is it?"

Regan was beginning to be irritated by Knowles's obtuseness. "If he didn't know what Salazar was doing before the acquisition, it won't hurt him that much."

Knowles, who was growing frustrated with Regan's lack of imagination, wondered whether he had overestimated his cunning. "Buddy, if Salazar was dirty, and he was, there's no way Tom Morrison wouldn't have known that before he bought the company. He's very thorough about information gathering before he does a deal. Part of his military training, I guess. Situational awareness, they call it. And, believe me, he is very inquisitive and very attentive to getting an advantage from everything he learns from whatever source, balance sheets, transaction records, or back-channel gossip. He doesn't miss much."

Regan didn't need a lecture on their opponent's attentiveness and instructed Knowles on the situation Morrison was in. "Unless there's hard evidence he knew about Salazar and kept quiet, the most this could do is knock him off message for a news cycle or two. And we're in good enough shape without this story."

"Well, all I can tell you, buddy, is that if Bianca Stefani has the story, she didn't get it from me. Anything else I can do for you?"

"Nope. Thanks for taking the call."

You can never tell, Regan thought to himself, *when Knowles is on the level and when he's not.* It didn't matter to Knowles whom he did a favor for, whether they were business clients or philanthropies or political candidates. What mattered to him was the transaction. A favor given in the expectation of a favor returned.

The post on *The Stefani Report* read:

> For several years the Justice Department has been investigating a senior executive at Channing-Mills Corporation for violating the Foreign Corrupt Practices Act, and is believed to be close to issuing an indictment, sources familiar with the investigation have confirmed to *The Stefani Report.* Victor J. Salazar was vice president for international sales for a small defense contractor, Shield Holdings, headquartered in Atlanta, Georgia. In 2003, Channing-Mills bought Shield Holdings, an acquisition engineered by then Channing-Mills CEO and current GOP presidential nominee Thomas Morrison. Mr. Salazar was kept in his position by Morrison after the acquisition and did not leave the company until Morrison retired in 2005 to run for governor.

The story went on to describe the nature of Shield Holdings' overseas trade, and the countries in which it did business, and that "some of those contracts are believed to have been won as the result of bribes Salazar made to local government officials," although it did not identify in which of the countries the alleged bribery occurred. The story concluded after noting, "When asked at his press conference today to comment on the investigation, Morrison declined to do so and abruptly ended the press conference."

That's going to piss them off, Regan thought, referring to the comment about abruptly ending the press conference. As it was written, the story didn't worry him, although he still wished it had not been published now. The "sources familiar with the investigation" was nicely vague. It could be a reference to sources at Justice, but he doubted reporters would believe it plausible that someone working for Bianca would have sources involved in the investigation.

Of course, the press would still be intrigued by the possibility that someone in the White House had learned about the investigation and passed the information to the campaign. That kind of discovery was front-page news.

Regan expected he would have his first conversation with a White House official that weekend. Someone, probably Avi Samuelson, would mention the story as a curiosity, suspecting that Regan knew more about it than the White House did, and that he might also know how it had come to Bianca Stefani's attention.

When Regan arrived at the White House, he had only a few minutes alone with Avi Samuelson, barely time to exchange greetings, before they were told to board *Marine One* in advance of the First Family. It wasn't until Friday night, after they had finished supper with the president and First Lady, and the members of the debate prep team who had arrived by bus, that Samuelson brought up the *Stefani Report* story as he and Regan walked to the cabin they were to share.

"What do you know about it?" he asked.

"I got a tip about it at the convention," Regan answered. "But I haven't done anything with it. Mick Lowe and I are the only people who know much about it, and we didn't give it to Bianca."

"Who tipped you?"

"A donor who does some business with a defense contractor."

Samuelson almost asked for the donor's name, but he decided it was better if Regan retained sole custody of that information, for the time being, anyway, until Samuelson had satisfied himself that the man he had recommended to manage the campaign was not involved in any mischief that might embarrass the president. He did want to know if Regan had planted the question at Morrison's press conference. If he had, Samuelson would curtly instruct him not to do something like that again. It was the kind of prank you expected College Democrats to pull, not the president's campaign manager. It would offend Samuelson's and the president's dignity, which the campaign was expected to reflect, and it wasn't necessary.

"Did you know her guy was going to ask Morrison about it today?"

"No, we were surprised."

"So was Morrison. Do you know if it's true?"

"I believe there is an investigation of Salazar. No idea if he's going to be indicted soon or ever."

"Did your donor tell you that?"

"No. A friend who used to work at Justice."

Samuelson suppressed an urge to ask for the name of Regan's friend. "Do you think Morrison has much exposure on this?"

"No. He kept the guy on after the acquisition. That would be a minor embarrassment for him. But I don't think Salazar is being investigated for anything he did at Channing while Morrison was CEO."

Samuelson didn't ask Regan if he had talked to anyone currently working at Justice to confirm the tip. Regan would have known better than to have done that, and so, Samuelson hopefully assumed, would anyone at Justice.

"It was weird, huh, Morrison's no comment?" Samuelson observed.

"Yeah, it was strange. We're getting some press calls on it."

"I heard."

"We're just telling them we don't have anything to give them. Is the White House getting any?"

"Noth said he got a few, nothing direct, just fishing."

The conversation turned to other campaign matters before both men retired to their rooms for the night. Debate prep was scheduled to begin at eight o'clock the next morning, last until a noon lunch break, and then continue until five that afternoon. They both knew they would need a good night's rest if they were to avoid falling asleep in the president's presence. They wouldn't discuss the *Stefani Report* story that night or the next day. Neither of them would feel a need to discuss it again until they had to.

The need arose Sunday morning. A three-hour debate prep session had been scheduled before buses returned everyone to Washington except the First Family, who would spend a few private hours at the presidential retreat, already showing its autumn colors. They were two hours into the session when Regan received the e-mail he had been expecting.

"Hello, Cal," the president summoned the attention of his distracted campaign manager. "Are we boring you?"

"No, sir," Regan assured him. "I'm sorry. I just got an alert I was waiting for."

"Something urgent?"

"No, sir. Not really."

"Good. Then maybe you can take a minute to answer the question I asked you."

Regan smiled sheepishly but did not otherwise respond.

"Well?" O prompted him.

"Could you repeat the question, Mr. President?"

"Cal?"

"Yes, sir?"

"Turn your BlackBerry off, please."

One of the Sunday morning news shows had invited Bianca Stefani to the roundtable discussion that concluded the show. It was her first television appearance since her website had broken the news about the investigation.

She appeared often on the show, and the story was not one of the topics the host would invite his guests to discuss. But the host expected Bianca to blurt out something about it at some point and was quite content that she should. Regan, too, expected her to raise it, as did the campaigns of both candidates, and the entire political and media establishment. The show was not often the ratings leader on Sunday mornings, but it would be that day, in Washington, at least. Regan had told the campaign's press office to e-mail a rushed transcript to him as soon as it was available.

"What I would like to know, Jim," Bianca interjected in the middle of a discussion of Morrison's tax reform speech, "is why the best minds and vast resources of the old media failed to uncover and continue to ignore the criminal investigation of a Channing-Mills executive who was employed by the Republican nominee for president." And with that she combined abuse of Republican politicians and the entire Washington establishment that tolerated their existence with her unique mix of affected aristocratic politesse and unblinking belligerence.

Defensively, the host and his other guests, without putting too fine a point on it, suggested it might have something to do with the fact that no respectable member of the old media was irresponsible enough to assume the story was credible on her say-so alone.

"The Justice Department hasn't confirmed the story's accuracy," the host observed. "No one—including you, Bianca—has published anything that suggests Tom Morrison is implicated in the investigation, if there is an investigation," one guest argued. "The campaigns haven't made an issue of it," another explained, "and you would think the president's would have if they believed there was something to it." The last guest to speak on the subject, who was once considered a close friend of Stefani's but was now widely known to detest her, as many of her former friends did, was the bluntest. "Frankly, Bianca, no experienced reporter is going to accept at face value the credibility of an anonymous source to *The Stefani Report*."

Stefani never seemed to take offense at being insulted or even to notice that she had been insulted. If she felt injured, she concealed it lest its public acknowledgment impose on her a humility she wasn't as a rule inclined to extend to her adversaries. "Frankly," she shot back, "what concerns me is that no experienced reporter, including you, wants to bother with challenging Morrison's credibility as the paragon of virtue he pretends to be."

"And why is it then, Bianca," came her former friend's sharp retort, "that the president's campaign, which stands to gain most from your story if it's true, hasn't touched it? Perhaps they have doubts about its accuracy, too."

"Trust me, they don't have any doubts," Bianca countered. This caused a considerable stir among the other guests, all of whom importuned her to reveal whether she had discussed the story with people in the O campaign or, more to the point, whether someone in the campaign leaked the story to her.

"We don't reveal the identity of confidential sources," she admonished them. "Even under pressure, which is more than I can say for every member of the old media. But suffice it to say that this is something people in the O campaign and many other people have known about for quite some time."

"Then why aren't they talking about it?" was shouted almost in unison.

"Why don't you ask them?" she dismissively replied. "That would at least be closer to actual journalism than this code of silence you're obeying."

They soon would. As he left to call Mick Lowe, Regan was formulating a response in his mind.

"We're already getting calls," Lowe told him.

"I think we say that while we won't have any comment on the story, we deny anyone at the campaign talked to anyone associated with *The Stefani Report* about any Justice Department investigation," Regan advised him.

"She didn't say we talked to her," Lowe observed. "She said we knew about it. And we did. Know about the investigation, I mean."

"I know, but they'll think she talked to us, and I want to make it clear she didn't."

"Can we say no one on the campaign talked?" Lowe asked, knowing the answer to be negative.

Regan told Lowe he planned to interrogate Tess Gilchrest the next morning. He rejected Lowe's suggestion they call her that afternoon before they gave any response to the press, insisting he wanted to confront her in person. "I want to watch her reaction," he explained, which, as it turned out, would be nothing more than her usual flippant disregard for his authority. Even Lowe wouldn't be able to scare her, although he would get her to allow she might have said something about it to Walter Lafontaine, and that she knew Terence Haley and had introduced him to Walter.

In the meantime, they agreed on a response to reporters that would buy them time to determine whether they could confidently assert their innocence. "Tell them off the record that we didn't take her call," Regan proposed, "and had we talked to her we would have told her we won't comment on a rumor."

Samuelson sat next to Regan on the bus ride back to Washington. "Knock it down somehow," he instructed him, referring to Bianca's assertion that the campaign was aware of the investigation. "We don't need this."

Regan wasn't yet sure he could truthfully assert that no one on the campaign had disclosed the investigation to *The Stefani Report*. Nor could he truthfully deny knowledge of the investigation. But he understood his instruction. He was to keep the campaign out of the story without lying to the press, if that was possible. If he couldn't, he would need to take care that his dishonesty wasn't subsequently exposed.

★ CHAPTER 24 ★

Walter had spent three nights in Geraldine's hospital room. Her condition had stabilized, and he had thought he might sleep in his own bed that last night. But he had dozed off in his chair a little before ten o'clock, and when he awoke it was after two in the morning. Eleven past two, to be precise, the exact moment Geraldine's heart stopped beating and her soul departed her body to meet the God she had believed in all her life.

The sympathy the nurses offered him was sincere. He had been a nuisance, but they couldn't help but be touched by his devotion. Geraldine's doctor didn't resent being roused from his sleep with the news. He, too, felt a duty to come to the hospital to offer his condolences, and to gently suggest it was a mercy she had slipped away before she had suffered the worst agonies her disease often inflicted on its victims in their final days.

Walter mumbled his appreciation and asked to be alone with his mother's body for a few minutes before they took her away. Standing next to her bedside, holding her lifeless hand, he felt the first hard blow strike him. His chest heaved and he tried to swallow the sobs that escaped him in gasps. Here was finality unlike the end of other experiences, beyond the sad, foolish hopes of recovery that ease the pain of other losses. Gone forever was the life that had been lived for his happiness, the reassurance that had always been there and would never be replaced by another's. Gone, too, was the life she had cherished, the dreams she had cheered, the disappointments she had consoled. He was alone and would always be alone. Memories would take the place of dreams, remembrances of happiness and disappointment, never again to be experienced as they had been when his dreams had led him to them.

He would sell his apartment and most of its furnishings and live in the house he had bought for Geraldine. It was to her house he went when he left the hospital to call the funeral home in Englewood. He called his aunt Mary, too, the widow of the brother who had invited Geraldine and her infant son to Chicago. She and two of his cousins would come right over, she promised. "Good, kind woman," she said on the phone. "God bless her soul."

In years to come, Walter wouldn't remember the preliminaries to his mother's funeral and interment. Nor would he remember much of the services or the reception in Geraldine's house. He hadn't paid much attention to any of it.

The only event he would remember in detail was the phone call he received from Cal Regan around three o'clock in the afternoon of the day his mother had died. Walter hadn't thought to inform anyone at the campaign that Geraldine had passed. Neither had it yet occurred to his aunt Mary to suggest he do so, the necessity slipping her preoccupied mind. Regan was unaware of the loss when he instructed Walter to come to the campaign: "I need to talk with you about something."

When he did not immediately reply, Regan added, "Today, Walter."

"I don't think I can," Walter finally responded. "My mother died this morning."

Taken by surprise, Regan had stuttered his condolences. The information presented him with a predicament. He wanted to determine immediately how exposed the campaign was before Bianca Stefani implicated them further, which he was certain she soon would. Obviously he could not have this conversation with Walter on the day his mother died. He would have to wait several days, maybe even a week. Conceding the present impropriety of his purpose, he repeated again how sorry he was for Walter's loss, and that the reason for his call could wait until he felt "up to coming back to work."

"Take your time, Walter," he thoughtfully added, "and please let us know if there's anything we can do. I'll let people here know your mother passed away. They'll want to offer their sympathies, too. I'm very sorry for your loss."

He was about to hang up when Walter interrupted him.

"Cal."

"Yes?"

"We can talk now if you want. My aunt and cousins are here, and they're taking care of things."

Regan repeated it could wait. But when Walter insisted again that he didn't mind, that it would give him "something else to think about for a while," Regan, more delicately than he had initially intended to, raised the matter of the Salazar investigation, the *Stefani Report* story, and whether Walter, with the best of intentions, had shared what he had learned from Tess Gilchrest with Terence Haley.

"I understand you guys hung out a couple of nights at the convention with Terence Haley. If you mentioned something to him, I'd like to know what it was, just to get a handle on what they know about this thing."

"Nah, I didn't talk to him about it."

"Are you sure? 'Cause it's no big deal if you did. Have you heard from him since the convention?"

"No."

Walter was about to hang up and told himself this was the last time he'd ever have to talk to this asshole. Cal considered whether it was worth pressing him more even if it crossed the line to impropriety. He didn't know when he would have a chance to continue the interrogation.

"Walter, really, I don't care if you did. I just need to know."

"Cal."

"Yeah?"

"I didn't talk to the reporter or any reporter about any investigation. Okay?"

"Okay. You let me know if there's anything we can do for you, Walter. You're in our prayers, and your mom."

Walter didn't respond to his last condolence. "Fuck you" was all he said, but after he had hung up, and not loud enough for his aunt and cousins to hear him.

Regan recounted the conversation to Mick Lowe. "Do you believe him?" Lowe asked.

"No. I think either he or Tess said something to Haley. Stu Trask told me Walter tried to get his hands on the DNC's research book last year. Told them Trask had authorized it. I think he imagines himself as an oppo guy, the guy who single-handedly drives the stake into the enemy's heart. He's probably our leak, and there's not a goddamn thing I can do about it now."

"Why not?" Lowe asked.

"Because his mother just died, you heartless fuck. It's Tess Gilchrest's fault, anyway, for telling him about it. And I can't do anything to her, either."

"And whose fault is that?"

"Shut up."

It was almost eleven o'clock that night when the president had finished his discussion with Rick Noth. "One more thing: Walter Lafontaine's mother died today," Noth told him. "Regan talked to him."

O sighed and looked down at his desk for a moment before remarking, "Walter will take that hard."

"You'll want to call him, then?" Noth suggested. "Or write him a note?"

"Both. Has the campaign been keeping him busy?"

"I don't think he's been around much. He's been looking after his mother most of the year."

"Make sure they do now."

When Noth left, O asked a White House operator to get Walter Lafontaine on the phone for him. He waited for ten minutes, until the operator apologetically informed him she had tried Walter's home, his cell phone, and his mother's home. No one had answered any of the calls.

"Would you like me to try again, Mr. President?" she asked. "Or call someone at the campaign who might know where to reach him?"

"No, thank you. Just give me his cell number. I'll try him myself in the morning."

The next morning began early. O left the White House at six o'clock to fly to Denver for a town hall meeting. He would spend the night in Los Angeles, after speaking at a dinner of California donors, attended by a considerable number of Hollywood celebrities, whose red-carpet arrival would attract the attention of entertainment news reporters feigning excitement for their viewers, as they called out the names of movie stars they mostly detested while the pool of starstruck political reporters pretended not to be thrilled to be there. The next day, he would appear at rallies in Tucson, Albuquerque, and Las Vegas before he returned to the White House. His daily national security briefing and all other official White House business would be conducted in the air as he traveled from one city to the next. In the press of all this activity and the strain to stay as little behind schedule as possible, it was understandable that his intention to call Walter had slipped O's mind.

"Shit, I forgot to call him," he reprimanded himself when told on the morning after he had returned to the White House that several campaign staffers were at that moment attending the funeral services for Walter's mother.

"We sent flowers from you and the First Lady," his secretary reassured him, "and we gave Jim Curtis a condolence note from you. He's going to hand it to Walter after the funeral."

"Find out when I can call him today, and make sure I do," he ordered her. "And tell Avi to tell Regan to put Walter on the manifest for the Friday trip. He can meet us in Cedar Rapids and travel with us to Wisconsin."

O's second campaign trip of the week would take him to several midwestern cities and, on Saturday afternoon, to Chicago, where his wife and daughters would join him. It would be his last return to Chicago until Election Day. He and the First Lady would have dinner with old friends Saturday night. And another debate prep session was scheduled for Sunday morning at the campaign headquarters.

His first thought when he had remembered his intention to call Walter was to meet with him in Chicago. But his time there would be brief and had been scheduled to the minute. Walter had never been on *Air Force One*. Inviting him on the Midwest swing would be a nice gesture, reassurance that O still cared about him. O would invite him to sit in his cabin on one of the legs. They would talk about old times, and about his mother; what a fine woman she had been and what a fine son she had raised. He would tell Walter he wanted him in Washington after the election. And this time he would mean it.

Walter drifted through the funeral and burial, and the reception at his mother's house, in the same barely comprehending state he had been in the afternoon after she had died. The funeral drew a capacity crowd of mourners to the small church, mostly his mother's friends from her Englewood and Chatham neighborhoods. A long-retired alderman for the Seventeenth Ward had attended. The incumbent had dropped by the wake. Two elderly nuns from the Catholic elementary school Walter had attended came. They remembered Geraldine fondly from the days when she had conspired with them to keep her son out of trouble. Several associates from his former law firm were there. Eleven campaign staffers, led by Curtis, the political director, came, too. Several others had come to the visitation. Tess Gilchrest and two other junior staffers attended the reception as well. The floral tribute from the president and First Lady of the United States had been placed in front of the altar.

Walter said little more than "Thank you for coming" to any of them, including Tess. He would nod his head in agreement as one after another mourner told him how special Geraldine had been and how proud her son had made her, give a "yes, ma'am" or "yes, sir," and wait for each of them to move on. "You know, Walter, your mama would want you to get over your grieving as soon as you can. She lived her life for you, son," more than one reminded him. He nodded at this, too.

He hadn't spoken at the service. He knew he wouldn't have been able to get through it, and his aunt had been right: Geraldine would have wanted a dignified funeral. Tess had asked him when he would come back to the campaign. He shook his head and turned to another person waiting to have a word with him. He was relieved when it was over, when his aunt and other relatives had cleaned up, collected the dishes, and told him to get some rest, and that they would check in on him tomorrow. "You're going to be okay, Walter," his aunt insisted again as she left. "She did everything she could to make sure you would always be all right. Don't you let her down."

The phone in his mother's house rang several times that night, but he didn't answer it. His cell phone would have rung, too, but he had turned it off days ago. E-mails, some offering condolences, others imploring him to contact the campaign, were never read.

"You're going to have to send somebody to his place," Regan told Jim Curtis the next day. "Tell him to answer his phone and return the president's call, and get his ass to Cedar Rapids tomorrow morning."

"I'll go find him myself," Curtis offered.

"No, never mind. Send Tess Gilchrest. She'll know where to find him. They're friends."

Tess tried his cell phone to no avail. She sent him an e-mail. "Dude, answer your phone. Everybody's trying to reach you, including POTUS. They're sending me to find you. On my way." She received no response. She took a cab to his mother's house and asked the driver to wait. No one answered the door, and there were no signs anyone was in the house. She went to his apartment building. He wasn't there either. Or if he was, he didn't answer the buzzer she pressed insistently. She tried his phone again, and on her way back to the campaign, she sent him another e-mail.

"Where are you? How are you? ANSWER YOUR PHONE. PLEASE."

The president arrived in his hometown on Saturday afternoon a half hour ahead of schedule. He couldn't remember the last time he had arrived somewhere early. The trip, from Cedar Rapids to Chicago, had run smoothly. Every event had started and ended on time. No surprises. No problems. The crowds at each of the rallies had been large and exuberant. The campaign's event turnout operation, like all of its operations, was running at peak performance.

You could feel it. The entire campaign had shifted into gear for the final stretch, setting a new standard for proficiency that exceeded the exceptional competence of his last campaign. Schedules were kept. His appearances were well staged and photographed beautifully. The images they were intended to produce were inescapable to anyone with a television or a newspaper subscription. Each day's message was reported exactly as they wished it to be, because the press and everyone who spoke in an official or unofficial capacity were kept on message by an almost hourly barrage of e-mailed talking points and telephone calls from press staff. They were outbuying Morrison's advertising in every state and district that mattered. Unseen, but just as proficient, was their voter ID and contact operation. Every new report boasted targets met early. Everything looked good, felt good, was good. O hadn't lost a point off his lead in any public or private poll. He, too, felt he was in his prime as a campaigner. Elegant and inspirational. Relaxed, confident, and in command.

He enjoyed the feeling of being in command, of knowing he and his campaign appeared to everyone—to the voters, to the press, even, O imagined, to his opponent—as an incomparable political force, a resolute, relentless juggernaut. Running the government, by nature a less coherent and controllable enterprise, would never be as satisfying to his self-regard as this. He *should* enjoy it, he told himself. This is who he had always expected to be, this competent, cool, commanding leader who was always a step ahead of his rivals, a step ahead of the country, if truth be told.

However, for all of its evident competence, his campaign could not manage to locate a missing staffer, a grieving, motherless son and long acquaintance of the president, whose whereabouts had eluded discovery by the best-run campaign in history and White House operators who were legendary for their ability to find on a moment's notice any person to whom the president wished to speak. Walter Lafontaine was the only person on the planet who had not returned a call from the president of the United States. The unaccountable failure needled O as he landed in Chicago and noticed again he had not been able to give comfort and encouragement, as he had planned to, to a friend from his past for whom he still felt affection. The disappointment aggravated the little kernel of guilt he felt for abandoning Walter.

Cal Regan had joined the welcoming party at the airport, and O invited him to ride in his limousine. As Regan started to talk about how good the day's events had looked on television, O interrupted him.

"Cal, have you located Walter yet?"

"No, sir," Regan conceded, "and I'm sorry. It's the damnedest thing. We've sent people to his apartment, to his mother's house. We've called and e-mailed him a hundred times. We talked to his relatives. No one knows where he is and it seems he doesn't want anyone to know. His closest friend on the campaign is Hank Gilchrest's daughter, and he's not responding to her, either."

"Why don't you call the mayor's office, then? Tell them I'm worried about a friend who disappeared after his mother's funeral, and would appreciate it if they'd ask the police to look into it. It's just ridiculous that it's taken three days and you still can't track him down. He's on our payroll, for chrissakes."

Fucking Walter, Regan thought to himself. *The first time I've ever been criticized by the president, and it's because you won't answer your goddamn phone.*

"I'm sorry, Mr. President," Regan repeated. "I know it's ridiculous. But the guy really doesn't want to be found. We think he's probably just taken off somewhere for a few days, you know, to come to terms with his loss or something, and turned off his phone. I wasn't at the funeral, but I talked to staff who were, and they said he was pretty uncommunicative, obviously, you know, distraught. I know you know how close he was to his mom."

"Yes, I do. That's why I wanted to see him and why I still want to see him before I leave Sunday."

"We're trying. I'll call the mayor's office myself and relay your message."

"Is there any reason he might be mad at the campaign? Was he being treated well? People stay in touch with him while his mother was sick? I've known the guy a long time, and I can't imagine him intentionally refusing to talk to me."

Regan hesitated before answering, not sure he should mention the situation that might explain Walter's absence. O could tell he was withholding something and wondered if Regan was being evasive out of self-interest or exercising discretion in order to spare the president embarrassment. "What is it?" he asked, not bothering to hide his irritation.

"I don't know, Mr. President. I think he's probably just distraught and wants to be alone for a while. But he might think he's in trouble."

"In trouble, what kind of trouble? With whom?"

"With us, the campaign."

"Why?"

"It's kind of a long story. He's not in trouble. And no one wants him to think he's in trouble. You remember that weird press conference Morrison did the other week? When he got that question about a Justice investigation of one of his former employees?"

"Yes."

"Well, we knew about the investigation."

"How?"

Clearly uncomfortable now, Regan hesitated again. The details of how the president's campaign had come into possession of a potentially embarrassing episode from their opponent's business career was not something a campaign manager should discuss with his candidate. The first rule of campaign management was to keep your candidate in the dark about whatever mischief you got up to. Should it seriously backfire, the candidate had to be unencumbered by even a trace of culpability so he could condemn it and fire your ass without fear of being proven a hypocrite. This was all the more important if your candidate was chief executive of the federal government and ultimately responsible for the actions of any government employees who had collaborated in his campaign's misadventure.

"Sir, it's probably better we don't get into that."

O now hesitated before responding and stared at Regan for a moment, as if he was trying to read in his campaign manager's facial expression how serious a warning he had just received. His curiosity got the better of him.

"Go on," he instructed.

"We got a tip from a donor, Allen Knowles. He said it was a well-trafficked rumor in the defense industry."

"Did you check it out?"

"Discreetly and at a distance." Regan did not elaborate further and would refuse to do so if O pressed him, which he did not.

"And it's true?"

"I believe so. But we didn't use it. We're not sure how big a problem it is for Morrison and, as things are, we don't think we need to use it."

"What does any of this have to do with Walter?"

"Well, we think the reporter who asked Morrison about it—he works for Bianca Stefani—might have heard something from someone at the campaign. We're not positive, but Bianca sort of half-assed implied the other day that they got it from us. This young staffer, Tess Gilchrest, Walter's friend, knows Knowles, and Knowles told her about it."

"Why would he do that?"

"That's a longer story, sir, which I'm positive I shouldn't go into. The upshot is, she told Walter about it, and they both know the reporter."

"And you think one of them gave it to him?"

"They both deny it. But it's possible."

"So you asked Walter about it? And that's why he might think he's in trouble?"

"Yes."

"When?"

"Sir?"

"When did you ask Walter about it?"

"The day his mother died. But I didn't know. I didn't know she had died when I called him."

The motorcade arrived at the president's house, where his wife and daughters were waiting for him. He didn't immediately leave the limousine but sat in silence next to Regan for a moment, deciding if he needed to say what was obvious, that Regan had been, inadvertently or not, an insensitive son of a bitch. Then he gave a nod to a Secret Service agent, who opened his car door. Turning to Regan as he was about to leave, he said, "I'll see you tomorrow, Cal. In the meantime, find Walter. And when you do, apologize, and make sure you tell him yourself he's not in any trouble with you or me."

Regan made his way to another car, which would take him back to the campaign. When he had settled himself in the backseat, he said to no one in particular, "Fuck me." He said it again when he arrived at his office and had seated himself behind his desk. Only Mick Lowe was there to hear it.

On Sunday, the president arrived for debate prep. Regan had not apologized to Walter. He had not found him. He had called a friend in the mayor's office and asked for the favor on the president's behalf. The police hadn't found him yet either.

A few facts would be established later and passed to Regan by his friend in the mayor's office. The morning after his mother's funeral, Walter had purchased an airline ticket to New Orleans. Hotel and restaurant charges to his credit card confirmed his continued presence in and around the Crescent City. Messages left with hotel operators were not returned.

Mick Lowe called Walter's aunt. She had not heard from Walter either. "Could he be visiting relatives in Louisiana?" Lowe asked her. "He wouldn't know anyone there," she told him. "Geraldine never took him back home." The absent father had died more than a decade ago, having never made contact with his wife and son since the day he had deserted them.

On the day of the first presidential debate, Regan learned Walter had checked into a motel on the outskirts of Mobile, Alabama. He thanked his friend for the information and conveyed the president's appreciation for the mayor's helpfulness. No further inquiries would be necessary. It was clear that Walter Lafontaine had come to no harm and did not want to be contacted.

October 3, 2012

★ CHAPTER 25 ★

Little more than a month remained before the election. The president still enjoyed a comfortable lead in all public and private polls, and Morrison had few opportunities left to cut into it. Barring a major mistake by the president's campaign, the debates were his only chance to change enough voters' minds to put O's reelection in doubt. But he couldn't be too aggressive. Voters would see it as desperation and the press would encourage that view. He needed to force, without seeming to have done so unfairly, an error on the president's part—a flash of temper that appeared unprovoked, a sullen admission of a mistake, an obviously inaccurate assertion, a boast that could be immediately exposed as fanciful—that might raise questions about O's judgment, honesty, or temperament. It was a difficult task, and he had not accomplished it that night in the opinion of most observers.

The debate, their first, had been, for the most part, quite civil. Both candidates lived up to their reputations as intelligent, capable men who disdained the histrionics produced by presidential debates in the past. Neither appeared too aggressive or passive. They were engaging and quick on their feet, but neither seemed interested in exaggerating or contriving a confrontation. Most reporters thought that was a mistake on Morrison's part, though they admired the sensibility it suggested.

A half hour of the debate had been consumed by the candidates' argument over Morrison's surprising proposal to withdraw American combat troops from Afghanistan, made in a speech the day before, which the press had anticipated would provoke the night's most contentious exchange. But that, too, failed to incite a heated confrontation.

O had confessed his frustration that the original timetable he had proposed in good faith had not been met. "Believe me, no one is more disappointed about it than I am," he assured the forty million people watching, and explained with an air of dignified solemnity how heavily the responsibilities of command weighed on him. He reminded the viewers how often he called families who had lost loved ones in Afghanistan, and how keenly he appreciated their grief. "I very much hope I won't have reason to do that so often in the future."

But he reminded Americans he couldn't make military decisions based on compassion and sympathy alone. He couldn't risk the progress Americans had sacrificed their lives for by withdrawing from Afghanistan, not before he was certain the country would not revert to the control of the Taliban and their al Qaeda allies after we left.

As Morrison listened to O's defense, his disdain reinforced his conviction that the president was wholly unsuited to the office of commander in chief. *So, you had to make a few bereavement calls, did you? How noble of you. I've watched men die as a result of my decisions. I've seen terror in their eyes, heard them scream for their wives and mothers. What do you think that feels like, Mr. President? I'll tell you what it feels like. It feels like shame: deep, deep shame and remorse. And you can't get rid of it by making a phone call. It doesn't go away. It's still there, a poison in your gut, when the next day you have to order more men to their deaths.* But he struggled imperceptibly and successfully to keep his contempt out of his response.

"It's not a perfect situation," he conceded, "but the Afghani government and military can stand on their own feet now, with our assistance, but without so many Americans still in harm's way over a decade after we first sent them there."

His scorn for the president's playacting temporarily allayed his fears that the policy he had advocated was, as O had intimated, as dangerous as it was expedient.

It was a curious thing to the Washington establishment, considering the different backgrounds and worldviews of the candidates, that each of them should so completely embrace a view that would more naturally belong to the other. But both men appeared to have made the transition smoothly, even if neither seemed to be enthusiastic about it. Both offered similar qualifications to their positions. "It's not a view I take lightly," was repeated often. And both promised they would reconsider their position "if facts on the ground were to change."

Disappointing to Morrison's people, O seemed to win the argument on points when he mused, "I find it a little surprising to be accused by Republicans of being too big a hawk, since they normally like to run me down for not being tough enough with our adversaries."

Morrison hadn't pressed him as vigorously as Stilwell had warned him he might have to. And O never seemed to take genuine offense at the criticism Morrison did offer. Neither man's heart seemed to be in it, which accurately described the entire ninety-minute debate.

"No runs, no hits, no errors," was how one pundit, appearing on a panel of reporters, columnists, and retired political consultants assembled by one of the cable networks, described the first presidential debate moments after it had concluded. His fellow panelists concurred. "By my count," another observed with disappointment, "there was just one moment of real tension and it was over as quickly as it began." Before the debate had started, the consensus view among the political cognoscenti was that a tie would be scored as a victory for the president. And that was how it was scored in the instant analysis that issued from the mouths of commentators on every news show seconds after the president and First Lady and Governor and Mrs. Morrison had smilingly shaken one another's hand, and given a last wave to their cheering supporters in the audience.

Spokespeople for the campaigns who appeared on television after the debate offered a different view, insisting their candidate had clearly routed the other, and had it been a prizefight, it would have been stopped by the referee in the early rounds. But the boasts weren't taken seriously by the reporters who solicited them or the people who made them.

Most of these comically exaggerated claims were made in the spin room, where within minutes of the debate's conclusion a constellation of senior campaign officials and surrogates gathered, standing beneath signs bearing their names held aloft by volunteers, and attracting solar systems of reporters, who jostled to hold their orbit and thrust digital recorders toward the open mouths of their sources. Spin rooms were a tired convention that had little real value anymore. They rarely occasioned more than a little half-in-jest preening by spinners and reporters alike, and comments so predictable they hardly needed to be spoken to be recorded. They were good for a few filler quotes for the stories reporters had already written in their heads. They were still a mildly entertaining ritual, though, which most of the participants indulged with good humor. They were more social occasion than a serious exercise in political communication.

Curious to see what all the fuss was about, Alex Morrison asked Sandy Stilwell if he could accompany him to the spin room as an observer. "Sure," Stilwell agreed. "Come see the circus. But I wouldn't say anything. They'll try to get something out of you they can twist around and use to embarrass your dad. So leave the talking to the professional bullshitters. We know all their tricks."

The brief moment of "real tension" referred to by more than one pundit that night had occurred in an exchange between the candidates an hour into the debate. The moderator had asked how each of them would improve ethical standards in his administration. Both candidates insisted their administrations would be models of public integrity, surpassing the rectitude of any government theretofore known to man. O had bragged about the "new levels of transparency and accountability" he had already established in his administration. "A vast improvement," he added, "over the record of the previous administration."

In rebuttal, Morrison, as genially as he could, mentioned the names of three minor administration officials, an assistant secretary of defense and two program directors in the Department of Housing and Urban Development, who had involuntarily resigned their offices after having been accused of at least appearing to transgress the ethical standards O had proclaimed inviolate.

The merest trace of anger flashed in O's eyes in reaction to Morrison's taunt, and no more than a couple of seconds elapsed as he considered his response. He looked directly into the camera when he did.

"A president makes thousands of appointments to the government, and as hard as you try to avoid it, a few of them won't work out. The important thing is, do you hold them responsible for their mistakes? And I held the individuals you mentioned responsible. They are no longer in my administration. That is what I mean by real accountability; accountability some of my predecessors couldn't claim to have enforced as strictly as we have."

Turning away from the camera to look directly at his opponent, he added, "There will always be people who let us down, who don't live up to our standards. I'm sure that's happened to you, Tom. Did you do something about it? Because that's what a president should be judged on."

The moderator along with the camera turned to Morrison, assuming he would claim a minute to offer a response to the president. Instead, he let a silence last long enough to become uncomfortable and suggest the anger it restrained. He stared hard at O, and O stared right back at him. It continued no more than five seconds until the moderator cleared his throat and began to ask his next question. But the reporters and campaign officials, who were scrutinizing the candidates' every gesture and utterance with an intensity few voters would think necessary, felt as if they had just held their breaths for five minutes.

The charged atmosphere left behind a residue of foreboding in the minds of a few aides, and a trace of curiosity in the minds of more than a few reporters. Cal Regan and Mick Lowe had exchanged a wide-eyed glance when O had asked Morrison the question, which had not sounded to them as if it was meant to be strictly rhetorical. Sandy Stilwell had bent forward in the chair he was slumping in and briefly felt a surge of alarm. Several reporters notionally formulated questions they might later decide to pose to campaign officials in the hope of determining whether the president had intimated an accusation he did not want to make explicit. But soon enough they all returned to carefully observing the back-and-forth in the last half hour of the debate.

Afterward, Regan teased and joked with reporters in the spin room, giving no sign that the small disruption in the otherwise unremarkable debate had engaged his interest. A wire service reporter asked him directly about it. "Was the president referring to a specific incident when he asked Morrison how he had handled misconduct by his personnel?"

"Huh?" Regan dismissively responded. "Did the president mention a specific incident? Because if he had one in mind, I'm sure he would have said so. Otherwise, I think you can assume it was a rhetorical question."

"It didn't sound rhetorical."

"Really? It did to me."

"Well, it just seemed as if he had something in mind. Maybe it was more his body language, I guess, than his words, that gave that impression. And Morrison's body language seemed to suggest he interpreted it that way."

"Their body language? C'mon, we've just watched two experienced candidates, both with a good command of English, debate nonstop for ninety minutes. If they had something to say in response to the questions they were asked, they said it. Let's just focus on that, okay? I don't think any of us are qualified to deduce some subliminal message from their postures."

Less than forty feet from where Regan displayed his talent for nimble evasion, a knot of a dozen or more reporters had surrounded Sandy Stilwell. Their manner was more serious and they pressed their questions more insistently, not because Stilwell was less practiced than Regan at sloughing them off, although he was, but because the reporters were certain that Stilwell and his candidate had to be disappointed the debate had not changed the direction of the race.

"You need to shake up the race," one of them declared. "Do you think you did that without a clear-cut victory tonight?"

"We did have a clear-cut win," Stilwell insisted. "It's always a win for a challenger if he goes toe-to-toe with the president of the United States and appears just as presidential."

Alex Morrison was standing a few feet to Stilwell's left, sipping Coca-Cola from a plastic bottle and listening as Stilwell labored to persuade reporters without success that their eyes had deceived them and Morrison had scored a resounding victory. Several reporters approached him for a comment, which he declined with a shake of his head and a barely audible "I'm just here to watch."

Eventually reporters began to ask Stilwell questions about matters other than the debate. The subject that most interested them was the Morrison campaign's plans to begin pulling out of states they no longer had any hope of winning. There comes a point in all losing presidential campaigns when they must accept the necessity of triage. The battleground begins to shrink, one reluctantly surrendered state at a time, until there remain only the bare minimum needed to produce 271 electoral college votes. All resources are then focused on the nearly, but not quite, hopeless task of threading a needle's eye that is no wider than the thread.

It is a painful, dispiriting process, and Sandy Stilwell dreaded it. Party officials in abandoned states would plead for mercy to him and to anyone in the campaign who would listen. They would demand to talk to the regional political director; then the national political director; then the chief strategist; then the campaign manager; and then finally they would press into service the party's most senior elected officials in the state, who would soon place urgent phone calls to Stilwell and the candidate. When all their pleas had been rebuffed, sympathetically in the beginning and abruptly near the end, they would start accepting the phone calls of national political reporters, who would invite them to savage the decision.

And the press would pile on, painting a picture of a luckless, incapacitated campaign, powerless to avoid its approaching doom. Every day would bring fresh accounts of a dying cause, filled with colorful and mostly anonymous criticism from aggrieved fellow partisans, assailing not only the campaign's withdrawal from their states but its every function, strategy, message, all political operations, advertising, personnel, scheduling, and the hapless candidate, who never found his footing or who blew a good chance of success when he veered off message, or was lulled into a false sense of security and stopped fighting as hard as he had been, or who put his foot in his mouth one too many times.

Then vulture time arrived, and the quotes weren't anonymous any longer. People put their names to them because they no longer feared they would be making an enemy of the next president and his vengeful aides. It was time to protect their reputations for political sagacity by dissociating themselves on the record from the ineptitude of their nominee's campaign.

One pundit in particular usually led the charge: a bald and cadaverous former political strategist who hadn't been involved with a campaign in thirty years and now published a newsletter that offered subscribers his best guess about election outcomes and helped shape whatever conventional wisdom held sway at various points in an election cycle. But his real career was appearing almost nightly on broadcast and cable news shows, where his opinions were prized mostly for the entertainingly morbid metaphors he employed to express them. Candidates who were behind late in a campaign were "bloodless cadavers," "kneeling before the ax," "practically stiff with rigor mortis," "sleeping with the fishes," "death-rattling invalids receiving the last rites."

On several occasions, the "bloodless cadaver" had gotten off the table and managed to pull off an upset win. Accuracy wasn't his first objective, however; notoriety was, along with the lecture fees it brought. Whatever talents he had as a political prognosticator, his most profitable skill was his thorough understanding of the media and its insatiable appetite for glib, provocative insults. That evening, he was nearly bursting with impatience for the Morrison campaign or anyone loosely associated with it to acknowledge even on background it was withdrawing its resources from an erstwhile battleground state. It didn't matter to him which state, any one of them would do. All he needed was a nod and a wink and off he'd trundle to the nearest camera and pronounce the Morrison campaign "deader than Saddam Hussein."

Sandy Stilwell had no intention of acknowledging anything of the kind less than an hour after the first presidential debate. An aide had just whispered to him the results of the instant polls that cable networks had commissioned. In two of the three polls, voters thought Morrison had narrowly edged the president. It was unexpected good news, though hardly scientific, since viewers had been invited to phone an 800 number or send an e-mail to give their verdict rather than being randomly selected. But still, it was a talking point in their favor he did not think they would have when he first arrived in the spin room, and he would make the most of it.

"Sandy, can you confirm reports that the campaign has made the decision to pull out of New Mexico?" a reporter asked him immediately after he had cited the cable polls as evidence of a clear-cut Morrison victory, and the harbinger of a Morrison surge in the real polls.

"No, I cannot," he replied testily. "We're fully organized in New Mexico. We're running ads there. We see a lot of room for movement."

"So, you're saying you're committed to staying in New Mexico," another reporter followed up.

"I'm saying New Mexico is very important to us," Stilwell repeated. "Nowhere is the American Dream in greater danger than there."

"Brother," one reporter whispered in the ear of another, "laying it on a little thick, isn't he? He sounds like a candidate."

Stilwell didn't notice the diminutive reporter with the thick, dark-rimmed glasses squeeze between two other reporters, raise his left arm, and point another recorder at Stilwell's head. Had he seen him, he would have announced, "Last question, I've got a plane to catch," to avoid yet another off-the-wall question from Bianca Stefani's baby-faced troublemaker.

The reporters encircling Stilwell were packed three deep, and Terence Haley had only managed to penetrate the outer ring. He would have to shout to be heard, although it wasn't necessary to bark his question quite as loudly as he did, startling into silence the other reporters and causing Stilwell's head to jerk, as if he was snapping to attention. Alex Morrison, who a moment before had considered leaving the room, having lost interest in the experience, was startled as well, and now fixed Haley with a hard glare that, had anyone noticed it, might have been described as angry. The question hung in the air for a moment, as every head turned to see who had asked it and saw an otherwise impassive Haley blink rapidly behind his thick lenses as he waited for an answer.

"Pardon me?" was all Stilwell managed to produce in response.

"I said, why didn't Governor Morrison respond when the president raised the criminal activity of one of his employees at Channing-Mills?" Haley repeated.

"I'm sorry, Haley, is it? Do I have your name right?"

"Yes, with *The Stefani Report.*"

"I know who you're with," Stilwell said with noticeable contempt. "Did we watch the same debate? Because nobody said anything of the kind in the debate I watched."

The other reporters began to shift their positions slightly, clearing a small space around Haley so they could watch both men simultaneously as whatever was about to happen happened. They gave the appearance, though, of people recoiling in embarrassment from an unseemly confrontation that had suddenly upset the normally placid environment of their workplace.

"Clearly," Haley pressed on, "the president was referring to Channing-Mills's vice president, Victor Salazar, when he asked your candidate if he held his people accountable for their misconduct."

"Clearly?" Stilwell snorted incredulously. "Is that right? Or was he asking a rhetorical question, which is what most of us who don't have such vivid imaginations assumed he was doing?" Looking at the other reporters, he pleaded, "Look, people, can we just stick to fact-based questions? I don't think there's enough time to get into whatever conspiracy *The Stefani Report* is fixated on today." The other reporters, however, were not yet willing to relinquish their role as spectators, and none of them asked a question to change the subject.

"Fact," Haley shouted as loudly as he had asked his initial question, startling them all again: "your candidate employed an individual who is now under investigation for bribery. Fact: your candidate kept that individual on his payroll while he was being investigated. Fact: the individual was not asked to leave Channing-Mills until your candidate retired as CEO to run for governor. Fact: the individual has now fled the country. And fact: your candidate boasts he has always upheld the highest ethical standards and criticized the president in the debate tonight and previously for the misconduct of a few of his appointments, and yet refuses, repeatedly refuses, to explain, defend, or even acknowledge the criminal behavior of an employee at Channing-Mills; criminal behavior, I might add, that was committed to sell weapons to Third World dictatorships that used them against their own people."

A visibly angry Stilwell began to respond when Haley cut him off. "So, sir, would you please care to comment on the fact of your candidate's hypocrisy?"

"That's enough, young man," Stilwell cautioned, struggling to control himself. "You're wasting my time, you're wasting their time"—he nodded toward the other reporters—"and you're wasting your time. If you think you're onto something, then go with it, although I'd advise you to find a source to go on the record this time, just one source who actually knows what they're talking about if you want anyone to pay any attention to you. Don't expect the rest of us to take seriously some wild accusation you probably heard about from a commenter on your website, who heard a rumor at his neighborhood coffee shop or that someone sent him through the fillings in his teeth. Go peddle this crap somewhere else, okay, and let the adults here get back to work."

"You deny it, then?" Haley asked, as calmly as if he had just asked Stilwell for the time. "Is that the official Morrison campaign response? You're denying there is an investigation or that Morrison knew there was an investigation or that Morrison employed the subject of a criminal investigation? Or are you denying that Morrison's ethical standards apply to everybody but himself?"

"I am denying," Stilwell countered, "that you and your employer live on the same planet as the rest of us. Now, I'm sorry to say, I'm out of time. I apologize that we've wasted the last five minutes on this . . . whatever it was."

Had matters ended there, the interest of the reporters who had silently observed the exchange and been fascinated by it, although they would never admit it, would have ended as well. No one would have included it in their stories. Stilwell had their sympathy. Haley was an oddball, chasing a poorly sourced story that experienced reporters had been unable to confirm. He had crossed the line from provocation to disrespect, more intent on insulting Stilwell than getting an answer to his question. Stilwell had a reason to be pissed off. If it were them, they would have been pissed off, too. And he had appropriately put the *Stefani* reporter, who none of them considered a real reporter, in his place.

But it did not end there. As Stilwell turned to walk away, Alex Morrison approached Terence Haley, stopped less than a foot in front of him, vigorously shook the plastic bottle of Coke he was holding, released his thumb from the bottle's opening, and sprayed its contents in Haley's face, while shouting "You asshole" at his victim.

"Hey!" the reporters who witnessed the assault yelled in unison, followed by a "Whoa." Stilwell turned around and froze as he tried to process what had just happened. Haley looked confused. His mouth hung open, his arms raised in a position of tardy self-defense, his vision impaired by the sticky film that coated his glasses.

It took a few seconds for the witnesses to notice that Alex Morrison was trembling, "shaking almost violently," a reporter would later recall, boiling with indignation as he began shouting more abuse at Haley.

"Who the fuck do you think you are?" he demanded of the mute Haley, who began to backpedal away from his assailant, his arms still in the air, the palms of his hands exposed in supplication. "You're not fit to carry my father's mess kit, you little fucking worm, you fucking low-life scum," he screamed, his face almost scarlet with anger and noticeably flooded with tears.

Stilwell stepped forward to put a hand on Alex's shoulder, and in a surprisingly calm voice tried to reason with him. "C'mon, Alex, that's enough. It's time to go, son. It's time to go." It seemed as if Alex was about to comply with the instruction when Terence Haley finally found his voice, although it was a considerably quieter voice than the one he had used to bark his questions at Stilwell. "It's my job. It's just my job," he muttered weakly.

"Your job?" Alex screamed back at him. "It's your job to be a fucking asshole and insult people you don't even deserve to know? That's your fucking job?" As if to emphasize his disgust with such a base occupation, Alex shook off Stilwell's hand, and with both his arms shoved Haley in the chest. Haley stumbled backward but somehow kept on his feet until Alex shoved him again and sent him tumbling to the floor.

Finally stirred to action, the mesmerized reporters rushed to help Stilwell restrain Alex, who was now hovering over Haley with his fists clenched.

"Enough, Alex!" Stilwell shouted into Alex's ear as he gripped the boy by both arms. "Goddammit! Enough! We're leaving. Right now." The volunteer who had been holding the sign with Stilwell's name dropped it and helped the older man drag Alex from the scene as quickly as they could.

Two Morrison press aides hustled over to get an account of what had just occurred from the reporters who had been questioning Stilwell, and who were just now noticing that all activity and conversation in the spin room, a space as large as two basketball courts side by side, had ceased, and every person in the room was staring in their direction.

More than two dozen individual press conferences with the senior leadership of both campaigns and various eminences of both political parties had halted abruptly when Alex had bellowed his first obscenity at Haley. The outburst had been so loud it had been heard in the farthest corner of the room, where the governor of Pennsylvania had stopped insisting to a group of bored reporters that the president's debate performance had exceeded his most optimistic expectations, and asked the press aide accompanying him, "What the fuck was that?" Several hundred people who had been completely occupied with their own purposes, and oblivious to the other conversations in the room, had frozen in place, moving no more than it took to get a better view of the confrontation, and remained that way for the duration—except the still photographers and TV camera operators, who, after of brief moment of indecision, started shooting it. Everyone had watched it mostly in silence, although "Jesus Christ" and "Holy shit" and other expletives had been uttered in amazement when the confrontation had turned physical.

Cal Regan was so close to the spectacle that he ducked as if someone had thrown something at him when Alex screamed "You asshole." When

Stilwell had started to pull Alex away, Regan had to resist the natural impulse to come to his counterpart's aid. Mick Lowe had turned his head too sharply toward the sudden commotion and strained a muscle in his neck, which he fussily rubbed and stretched for the rest of the evening. Maddy Cohan, who had just asked Avi Samuelson a question, caught her heel when she tried to step around another reporter who was blocking her view. Samuelson caught her as she pitched forward, and she watched the rest of the confrontation absently holding on to his left arm. The room remained silent for nearly a minute after Alex Morrison had left it before finally stirring back to life. "Could've heard a fucking pin drop," Mick Lowe recounted several times later that night.

The reporters who had been questioning Stilwell felt genuinely sorry for Alex Morrison. The kid was a little high-strung, and obviously not used to the abuse candidates have to take from reporters and all sorts of people. He had behaved as a kid would do if a playground rival had insulted his father's reputation. But it hadn't happened on a playground, and it was a pity his demonstration of filial loyalty would only serve to embarrass his father. Colleagues who queried them for details of the exchange that had ignited Alex Morrison's temper shared the sentiment.

None of them, however, would think to spare Tom or Alex Morrison any embarrassment. Print reporters included an account of the confrontation in the postdebate analysis they hurriedly posted on the websites of their newspapers and magazines. Several paragraphs would be devoted to it in the morning editions. Television reporters mentioned it in their stand-ups, unnecessarily describing details plainly visible on the video clip that played while they talked, the expletives bleeped out. Reporters with the wire services all filed separate stories about it, in addition to their debate stories, which included a reference to it. Late-night comedians made fun of it throughout the following week and would often return to it for the rest of the campaign because it never failed to get a good laugh.

Every mention of the incident included a reference to the still-unconfirmed "story" that had provoked Alex Morrison, rekindling the press's curiosity about it, which had until then begun to wane.

The spin room began to empty twenty minutes after the incident ended. It was unlikely anything more interesting would occur there that evening. Quite a few reporters remained, still gathering details about what had caused it. Terence Haley was approached repeatedly for his side of the story. For several minutes following his assailant's departure, he had remained seated on the floor, still looking quite confused. Eventually, another reporter, after thinking twice about it, had extended a hand and helped him to his feet, and then wandered off without asking him if we was okay. When Maddy Cohan reached him, she noticed his hand trembling as he wiped his glasses with his shirttail.

Tom Morrison was talking on the telephone in a hotel suite when a Secret Service agent opened the door to admit his son and campaign manager. Both looked bedraggled. The few long strands of hair that covered Stilwell's bald pate were flapping in the air, and part of his shirttail was untucked. Alex was holding his jacket and tie, and he had a look of almost bitter determination on his face, rather than the sheepish countenance he usually presented to his father.

Aiming for a calm and understanding tone despite the aggravation his appearance suggested, Stilwell announced, "We had an incident after the debate, in the spin room." He went on to describe the details, and to note, "Pretty much the entire press corps witnessed it. There's probably video of it running right now, if you want to see it for yourself."

Morrison listened without comment or visible irritation. When Stilwell had finished, and began to suggest an official comment from the campaign, Morrison cut him off. "Sandy, I'd like to talk to Alex alone for a few minutes. Stick around, would you, and we'll discuss what we're going to say about this in a bit."

Alone in one of the suite's bedrooms, Morrison told his son that nothing that happened in campaigns was ever as serious as it might appear at the time.

"It's not like the army. It's not a war. People who work in this business, including the press, just act like it is because they've never been in an actual war. There's no good reason to let any of this crap get to you. You gave that reporter more than he ever hoped he would get from badgering Sandy or me. But, and this is important, it doesn't matter. For a day or two, they'll make a big deal about it, and then they'll move on. They always do. So don't beat yourself up. I know you were trying to defend me. And that's all it is, really, a son defending his father, no matter what anyone tries to make of it. Sandy will suggest we send you home for a while for your sake, to keep you out of the spotlight. But I don't want you to go home. I want you to stay with us and keep doing what you're doing. Tomorrow, everyone will see you doing your job, and acting like you don't have a care in the world. But, Alex, I don't want you to talk to a reporter, any reporter, for the rest of this campaign."

Other than a few attempts at explaining why the reporter had deserved the abuse he had received, which his father waved off, Alex accepted his father's advice and instruction. He promised he would not lose control of himself again and would never, "as long as I live, say anything to another reporter."

When he had finished with Alex, Morrison asked Sandy Stilwell to come into the bedroom. "We're not going to say anything about it," he told him, "not officially, not unofficially, not tonight and probably not tomorrow. Not a word."

Stilwell protested halfheartedly. "We should probably at least try to shame the press into being sensitive that Alex is a kid, who loves his dad. Maybe they'll let it go after tomorrow."

"No. It won't be necessary. We'll have something to say, but not what they expect, and not when they expect it. It will take a couple of days to set up." Morrison proceeded to share his plans with his campaign manager. When he finished, he asked Stilwell to get Andy McDonald, his personal attorney, on the phone. It was late, and Stilwell pointed out that McDonald would almost certainly be asleep when he got the call. But Morrison had a task for McDonald he needed done the next morning. "They won't give Andy an answer right away," he explained to Stilwell, "and I don't want to wait more than a day for one. So I want to start the clock on this first thing tomorrow morning."

★ CHAPTER 26 ★

At eight thirty Monday morning, two days after the debate, Morrison campaign volunteers had finished hanging a blue sheet on the wall of the otherwise drab conference room of a precision tool company in Columbus, Ohio, and were moving two flags and stanchions into place. In a half hour, Morrison would stand behind a podium in front of the flags and blue backdrop and read a statement to an invited group of reporters. He would not answer any questions after he read the statement, although reporters would shout questions at him as he left the room. He would then proceed to his only other campaign event of the day, a tour of the company's factory floor, where the noise would be too loud and the press pool kept at too great a distance from the candidate to have any hope their questions would be heard by him. To their chagrin, the event would only produce pictures of Morrison talking earnestly with workers, pointing at machinery, and asking questions and nodding in satisfaction with the answers he received, which is all his campaign wanted from the event.

The campaign's public schedule indicated Morrison would spend the rest of the day in debate prep at a Columbus hotel, which was partially true. Morrison's debate team had assembled in Columbus, carting boxes that contained dozens of overstuffed black binders. They would spend three hours with Morrison that day, going over the comprehensive list of questions that might be asked at the next debate, which would focus exclusively on domestic policy, the likely positions and lines of attack O would take, and the arguments they recommended Morrison make on offense and in rebuttal. After the session ended, the candidate and his staff would spend the seven hours before they flew to Florida for campaign appearances the next day watching the television coverage and reading news clips of the statement he had made at nine o'clock that morning, and whatever response, if any, the O campaign had.

Morrison had told Stilwell they all needed "to take a little breather"; this was the reason he gave for clearing his schedule for much of the day a month out from the election. Had Morrison not beaten him to it, Stilwell would have proposed the idea. The candidate and his staff knew it was important they avoid making any other news that day. The statement was the only news they wanted voters to hear.

Morrison had written it himself. Stilwell had reviewed it and, after consulting with two other senior aides, had proposed only minor alterations. The reporters who had been invited to witness it represented all the broadcast and cable networks, the wire services, four newspapers with national readerships, and the Columbus, Cincinnati, and Cleveland papers. The government officials Morrison had instructed Andy McDonald to contact on his behalf had not yet agreed to substantiate the claim that he would make that morning, and Morrison decided he would wait no longer for it. Eventually, they would have to comply with his wishes. It would be politically unavoidable. "The man has been the subject of a completely dishonest attack," Andy McDonald had argued to the head of the Justice Department's Fraud section. "He's got a right and an obligation to defend himself."

No decision had been made that weekend by the attorneys involved in the Salazar investigation, or by their superiors, about how or if the Department of Justice would respond to the statement that McDonald assured them the Morrison campaign would soon issue. But it had been the subject of extensive discussion among them, working up their chain of command to various assistant attorneys general, deputy attorneys general, and finally, the attorney general himself. After deliberating most of Sunday, the attorney general had thought it appropriate to inform the White House legal counsel that a fraud investigation that had been the subject of recent press speculation was about to be confirmed, probably the very next day, by the Republican candidate for president, and that he and other Justice officials were still considering the department's official response to the disclosure.

When the Morrison campaign released on Sunday afternoon their candidate's schedule for the next day, Cal Regan and Mick Lowe believed they knew the subject Morrison would address in his statement. Even if Avi Samuelson hadn't called Regan on Sunday night to give him a heads-up, both he and Lowe would have presumed Morrison's statement would address in some way the investigation of his former employee.

Alex Morrison's confrontation with Terence Haley had dominated the political news through the weekend and triggered frenetic activity by the press to get to the bottom of the alleged scandal. They couldn't be sure what Morrison would say beyond decrying the politics of personal destruction, the typical response of candidates under attack, and implicitly defending his son. But he couldn't possibly refuse to comment on the extent of his knowledge of Salazar's activities and the investigation, having convened a press pool for the purpose, they assumed, of putting the controversy behind him. They expected he would deny all knowledge and express his disappointment if a former Channing-Mills employee had, as alleged, engaged in fraudulent activity when he had worked for another company. They also assumed that no matter what Morrison would likely say or how persuasively he said it, Morrison's implicit admission of an employee's criminal behavior would, after all was said and done, benefit the O campaign.

Maddy Cohan spent most of her Sunday pleading with Morrison's press office for an invitation to Monday's event. She was repeatedly rebuffed and was told the room simply wasn't large enough to accommodate more reporters. She left several messages on Sandy Stilwell's voice mail that were not returned. Exasperated by her persistence, Morrison's communications director had finally barked, "There's no way we're letting in any so-called *news* websites, Maddy, so they can continue the scandal-mongering that got us into this ridiculous situation." She protested that *Body Politic* did not, like *The Stefani Report,* practice "advocacy journalism; we're a real newspaper, a widely read real newspaper, I might add," which, she pointed out, "does in fact publish a daily print edition."

"Maddy, relax," he told her, signaling the end of their conversation. "You're just going to have to do what other reporters who weren't invited are going to do. Watch it on television. We'll release the statement right after he makes it, so you won't have to bother recording it. You're not going to miss anything. He's not going to take any questions." *Probably not,* she thought, *but I'd like to ask him one or two anyway.*

The reporters had been in place for twenty minutes when Morrison arrived at precisely nine o'clock. There would be no preliminaries, no "Good morning," no "Hey, how are you" brief banter between candidate and reporters. Morrison was all business. He wasn't agitated. He didn't appear to be anything other than calm and purposeful as he stepped to the podium.

"Thank you for coming on short notice," he began. "Let me say at the outset I regret the necessity of this statement. It had been my intention to keep a confidence I was asked to keep over seven years ago by the Department of Justice, before the current administration took office. Unfortunately, I can no longer honor the agreement, because the subject of that confidence has become an issue in this campaign, and the basis for an intentionally dishonest attack on my character."

Everyone who watched Morrison on television that morning, nearly the entire press corps and every person involved or interested in national politics, knew the moment Morrison made his opening declaration, intimating his cooperation with the government, that their presumptions about what he would say had been wrong. They knew they were about to be surprised. And no one was more certain of it than Cal Regan and Mick Lowe, who did not like to be surprised, because in their businesses being surprised was evidence of incompetence.

"In the spring of 2005, as CEO of Channing-Mills, I authorized the acquisition of Shield Holdings, a defense contractor in Atlanta, Georgia, which specialized in the manufacture of body armor and small arms. In our review of Shield's financial records, and in discussions with their competitors, which our executives initiated as part of our due diligence in advance of the acquisition, it became increasingly clear there were reasons to suspect irregularities in some of their overseas sales. Let me be blunt: we suspected that some of Shield's overseas contracts might have been the result of illegal gratuities, bribes, given to government officials and the relatives of government officials in the countries concerned.

"At my instruction, Channing-Mills's attorneys contacted attorneys in the Fraud section of the United States Department of Justice to alert them to our concerns and share with them the documentary evidence that had raised our suspicions.

"Over a period of approximately one month, our lawyers had numerous discussions with the Justice Department. I received a call from John Hazelton, who was at that time the head of the Fraud section, in which he first asked me if I would consider keeping Shield's vice president for international sales, Mr. Victor Salazar, in Channing-Mills's employ after the acquisition. They believed him to be responsible for violations of the Foreign Corrupt Practices Act, and, at that time, they were considering organizing a sting operation to catch him in the act. I agreed. I do not know if a sting operation was attempted. I do know he was under surveillance, and the subject of a continuing investigation.

"More than two years later, as I was preparing to leave Channing-Mills, I instructed our lawyers to discuss with the Justice Department allowing us to terminate Mr. Salazar's employment with us. I cannot say with certainty that Mr. Salazar is guilty of the crimes he is suspected of, but we did not believe it was in the interest or consistent with the practices of Channing-Mills to continue employing an executive suspected of unethical and possibly unlawful activities. Justice had spent over two years looking into the matter, and we felt we could not risk further our company's reputation for integrity. So, one of my last official acts as CEO of Channing-Mills was to order Mr. Salazar's termination.

"That is all I know about the investigation that has become an issue in this campaign. I do not know if Mr. Salazar is still under investigation. I had my attorney inform the Justice Department of my intention to disclose these facts. I did not ask for their approval. I did ask if they would consider corroborating what I have told you if they were asked for a comment by the press. As of now, they have not given us an answer. Perhaps you in the press will have better luck getting a response than I have.

"As you can see, regarding my role in the criminal investigation of a Channing-Mills executive, which a rather disreputable and openly partisan news organization has tried to use to falsely imply impropriety on my part, I behaved at all times in accordance with the laws of this country, with respect for the government's efforts to enforce them, and out of concern for the integrity of the company I had the privilege to lead. As I said, I regret I had to make this statement, and any difficulty it might cause the Justice Department. But I do not believe I had an alternative."

Had he ended his statement there, it would have been considered by the press, the political establishment, and the voters to be an impressive performance, quite a surprise so late in the campaign. Morrison had been dignified, to the point, and authoritative. Most alarming to Cal Regan, he had managed to pull off a rarely successful feat in politics: to appear the victim of an unscrupulous attack without seeming pathetic.

Voters are usually repelled by candidates they perceive as whiners. They don't really care if their grievances are legitimate. Elections are about the voters' grievances, not the candidates'. But Morrison had not appeared to be a whiner, complaining about typical campaign mischief on his way to losing an election. On the contrary, he had surely earned as much admiration from the voters for his apparent forthrightness and restraint under duress as he had sympathy for being falsely accused. In fact, his no-nonsense, just-the-facts response to an unfair attack, his seeming to abstain from posturing or from milking it for maximum advantage, would encourage undecided voters, and a number of voters who thought they had made up their minds, to object more than they typically would to another instance of political chicanery. He had certainly helped himself. No one in the O campaign could think of a single reason to believe otherwise.

But Morrison did not end his statement there. After a brief pause, he looked squarely into a camera, and without seeming to read from his prepared statement, said, "Now, if you'll allow me a brief personal comment.

"I'm not particularly surprised or upset by the false implication that my conduct in this matter was inappropriate. Before I got into politics, I knew how things were done in campaigns. I knew the civility and mutual respect most people show each other in everyday interactions aren't exactly the norm in political campaigns. I don't like it, but I'm a big boy, and I've been in tougher situations than this. So I'm not going to make a big deal about it.

"I would like to observe, not just for politicians to consider but for the American people to consider as well, that maybe the failings they find in politics and politicians generally have something to do with our country's acceptance that normal rules of decency don't always apply in this business. Maybe we've all become a little too jaded to see that the abuses and excesses in politics we find distasteful continue because we don't expect anything better.

"Sometimes I think it would be a good thing for our country if we could look at the world through the eyes of young people, who haven't experienced so many disappointments that they've become used to it. If we did, maybe we would expect more from the people we elect to office, and maybe they would learn to respect the decency and fair play that most people believe ought to exist in any walk of life.

"The other day, my son, who is new to the world of politics, acted as many sons would when he heard someone malign his father's character. He became upset and felt a personal responsibility to respond. He's a teenager, and self-control . . . well, let's just say that's something most teenagers have to work on.

"He had been taught that all people deserve respect for their honesty, for their character, unless they give you an actual reason to doubt it. He didn't understand the lesson doesn't apply in politics. You might say he's a little naïve, I suppose. But that's hardly uncommon among teenagers. You might also argue that maybe we could all benefit from that kind of naïveté from time to time.

"And because he believed these things, naïvely, he's had a rather unusual experience for a young person who is not a politician or a celebrity of any kind. He has been embarrassed on national television and in newspapers around the country. Obviously, that's kind of a tough thing to take at that age. But you know what's harder? It's harder for a father to figure out some way to explain to his son why, of all things, our country's leaders, the men and women who are responsible for protecting our security and enforcing our laws, for ensuring justice is done and the peace is kept, are exempt from the standards of honor and decency that are so common everywhere else in this great country. I haven't done a very good job explaining that to him. And if any of you have an idea how I could do it better, please let me know. I'm all ears.

"Thank you all for coming."

He nodded at his staff, grabbed his statement from the podium, and departed the room as briskly as he had entered it. The reporters were too dazed by what they all would concede had been a stunningly effective performance to make more than halfhearted attempts to detain him. They really had only one question for him. Did he mean to imply his opponent's campaign had been responsible for leaking the story to *The Stefani Report*?

There were a few reporters and more than a few operatives, having acquired a durable cynicism from many years of exposure to the contrivances and subterfuge of candidates, who detected in Morrison's straight-from-the-heart appeal a welcome and reassuring note of hypocrisy. After all, they couldn't resist observing, hadn't Morrison, in his plaintive and public objection to the exploitation of his son's innocence, done the same thing? Hadn't he, too, taken advantage of his son's embarrassment to advance his ambitions? One veteran political reporter, much loved by his colleagues for his sardonic wit and curmudgeonly manner, repeatedly referred to Alex Morrison, although only in private conversations, as "Morrison's cocker spaniel," a reference to the "Checkers speech" that had kept Nixon on Eisenhower's ticket.

So, too, did a few reporters take note of the conduct of Morrison aides, who were privately intimating the president's campaign might have had a hand in the attempted disgrace of their candidate without sharing much in the way of evidence to justify their suspicions. Wasn't that an example of the degradation of our politics Morrison had decried? Unless, of course, those suspicions proved to be true.

But in the current of excitement that coursed through the journalistic establishment and the profession of politics it viewed with suspicion and affection, little attention was paid to these discordant thoughts. In the immediate coverage of the Morrison statement, no doubts or alternative interpretations were presented for the public's consideration. Voters heard nothing but general acclaim for the evident sincerity and political effectiveness of Morrison's performance, which all but the president's most committed supporters welcomed as an affirmation of their own opinion.

Even Bianca Stefani, who had seemed to appear on every cable news network minutes after Morrison had finished his statement, did not express much skepticism about what she called "Morrison's version of events." Betraying not a trace of embarrassment, she seized the opportunity to salute the brave new journalism practiced most bravely by the underpaid reporters for her eponymous website.

"What we've seen, yet again," she informed each of her interviewers, "is another example of the new media picking up the fallen standard of bold, unafraid, and unbought investigative reporting from the clammy dead hands of the old media. Were it not for our reporter, who endured physical assault to find the truth that no one in the old media thought they had a responsibility to uncover, the Morrison campaign would never have been compelled to finally address these allegations. I think we deserve to be commended, especially Terence Haley, who could have been seriously hurt in the violence he was subjected to for his persistent search for the truth."

"So you aren't skeptical about Governor Morrison's explanation of his role in this investigation?" every interviewer asked her.

"Of course, I'm a journalist," she reminded them, "and a good journalist is always skeptical, even if that virtue has fallen out of favor with the old media. We will, of course, continue looking into the matter to make sure all the facts are presented to the public. Maybe now other news organizations will do the same."

"Okay. Well, keep us posted on whatever you find," one cable anchor said to her.

★ CHAPTER 27 ★

Maddy had just finished reading it when her agitated executive editor, Will Janssen, slapped on her desk another copy of the statement by a spokesperson for the Department of Justice that confirmed, without elaboration, "Counsel for Channing-Mills Incorporated informed the Department in 2005 that executives at Channing-Mills suspected they had found evidence of unlawful activity in the records of Shield Holdings."

"Looks like the fucker was telling the truth," Janssen acknowledged with a note of disappointment.

Long ago Maddy had worked out a formula for keeping unpleasant encounters with Janssen as brief as possible. Pretend to take no notice of him and he'll erupt right away, his anger will be spent in seconds, and he'll leave you be in a minute or two. If you engaged him immediately, his anger built, as he seemed to entertain himself by finding more ways to express his displeasure, and the whole damn thing could go on for ten or fifteen minutes.

"Well, goddammit, Maddy, I don't want to interrupt you, but maybe you could answer one question for me?"

"Okay."

"How many people have that story?"

"What story?"

"Justice confirms Morrison account. That story."

"Will, it was a public statement. Everyone has the story."

"That's right. Everyone has the story. And why does everyone have the story? Not because it was a public statement, Maddy. But because Justice had to make a public statement. And why did they have to make it?"

298

"Because it was politically impossible not to?"

"Right. And do you know why they couldn't politically avoid it?"

"Because of Morrison's statement yesterday?"

"Wrong. Wrong. Wrong. Because somebody who doesn't work for *Body Politic* wrote another story. And that story forced Morrison to make his statement, which then made it politically impossible for the Justice Department to not confirm it."

"Yes, Will, but that story turned out to be wrong."

"Oh, really. And in which of its particulars was it wrong? Was there not a criminal investigation of an executive at Channing-Mills? Did that executive not remain on Channing-Mills's payroll until after Morrison left the company?"

"You know perfectly well it was wrong in its implication that Morrison was either negligent in his management of the company or an accessory to bribery."

"Of course it was wrong in its implications. It's the fucking *Stefani Report,* for chrissakes. That's what they're in business for, to make accusations. But it was not wrong in its facts. No, Maddy, it was not wrong in its facts. And those facts were exclusively reported by a midget teenager from Bianca Stefani's posse of minimum-wage interns, who despite his complete lack of journalistic experience and reputation has managed to shake up a presidential election that was on the verge of being over. Am I unhappy, Maddy?"

"You appear to be, Will."

"Yes, I'm unhappy. I'm unhappy because I didn't pay a teenage midget blogger minimum wage to get the one story everybody in this business would kill to have gotten first. I paid a rising star of journalism a rather handsome salary to use her wealth of experience, her expensive education, and her dozens and dozens of contacts—in both campaigns, in the White House, on the Hill, and every other place where such a story might be found—with whom she has famously cultivated close, personal relationships, to get that fucking story. But she didn't get it. She couldn't even confirm it. The midget who isn't a real reporter, who doesn't have any experience or contacts, who lives on the birdseed he's paid with, got it.

And you know who gets the credit for making all this happen, all this drama, all this fucking news? That fucking dilettante Bianca Stefani. That's who. Not us, Maddy, not us. And that has made me very unhappy. So, if you could please finish the story I don't give a shit about and start working on getting us the story I do give a shit about, the story all the other boy and girl reporters are busy trying to get, I would really fucking appreciate it."

"Will."

"What?"

"Fuck you."

"Fuck you, too, Maddy. Go get the story."

"What fucking story, Will?"

"What story? The only fucking story. The story I want first. The story of who the fuck gave the midget the other fucking story. That fucking story. Go get it. Now. Please."

Across the Potomac River from the Arlington office tower where *Body Politic* leased its headquarters, another chief executive was expressing his displeasure in less offensive language.

The O campaign's overnight tracking poll had recorded a huge bump for Morrison. It was only one night, and one-night tracking samples were very small, with a high margin of error. It would probably be smaller in tonight's track, and they wouldn't have a clear picture of how big a boost Morrison had received until tomorrow night, when they averaged the three nights' results. But, still, last night's numbers were eye popping. The average of all last week's polls, public and private, showed Morrison stuck eleven points behind them. In last night's track, he was two points down.

No one was panicked. There was no reason to panic. Bumps like that fluctuate a great deal night to night and are almost always temporary. They had to stay on their message but get the initiative back by adding a new line of attack to their "keep going forward, not backward" message, using an attack on Morrison's energy policy they hadn't planned to make until the second debate. O would argue Morrison's policy favored big oil with tax incentives for new exploration and licenses for new offshore drilling that would inevitably lead to new oil spills that would threaten the livelihood of Americans living on the Gulf Coast, rather than promote the development of alternative energy sources certain to create new economic growth and jobs, and free the country from dependence on OPEC.

O would make the charge at two massive rallies, the biggest of the campaign to date, scheduled for tomorrow and the day after. They would have to make sure their crowds were bigger and more energized than Morrison's. It was eleven o'clock in the morning in Washington. Two hours later, at noon central time, Morrison would appear at a rally at a Florida fairground. Chicago had just relayed to the White House a report from the trackers they had dispatched to the event, who described the crowd that had already arrived as "probably the biggest one Morrison's had so far."

Their candidate was stuck in Washington today for a teleconference with his commanders in Afghanistan that had been scheduled to counter Morrison's argument that O had taken his eye off the ball and let progress there stall. He had a bill-signing ceremony that afternoon, too, which would make some news, but not much. It had been postponed a week because Congress hadn't passed it until the final hours before adjournment, nine days later than congressional leaders had assured him it would. Tomorrow, he would return to the campaign trail, where, but for a night here and there, he would remain until Election Day. Tomorrow they would get back on offense and wait for the favorable impression Morrison had obviously made with his statement to recede a little from the voters' minds.

O tried to concentrate on memorizing the talking points staff had prepared for the bill-signing ceremony. Grabbing a red pen, he began to strike off every second or third line and scribble revisions in the margins. Normally, he wouldn't bother to rewrite boilerplate remarks for an event no one would remember in a week. It wasn't a valuable use of the president's time. But the exercise relieved some of the tension he was feeling and helped him compose the calm, self-possessed image he wanted to portray on camera.

Everyone was on edge, including the candidate, anticipating the next numbers and worrying they would confirm the campaign's fear that the race was no longer stable. Morrison had energized his voters, and others who had thought they had made up their minds were possibly taking another look at him.

This late in a campaign, shaken complacency brought weariness with it, similar, O thought, to the fatigue that affects a basketball team that had a lead throughout the game only to have the other team tie it at the buzzer and send the game into overtime. Panic brought energy with it. But a panicked team rushed its shots and swore the rims had gotten tighter as the ball started clanging off the back iron. They weren't panicked. *Thwarted* would be the best way to describe their emotions. Their instincts told them they needed a breather, but they knew they couldn't take one. They would have to count on their professionalism, their know-how, and money to overcome the lassitude they felt creeping into their bones.

If tonight's and tomorrow's tracks showed Morrison's bump rapidly receding, on its way to vanishing, and the national polls showed little change in O's net favorable, their energy would return naturally as fresh confidence quickened their step and sharpened their wits. But if they didn't, they would have to manufacture vitality by reinforcing discipline and taking new actions: sharpening their message, changing ads and increasing their media buys, adding stops to the candidate's schedule, dazzling the press with the theatrics of their public events.

That morning, after Justice had backed up Morrison's account as grudgingly and tersely as it could, O betrayed the anxiety caused by the uncertainties that suddenly confronted his campaign, and which, as a matter of pride, he would not admit were bothering him. Instead, he was unusually animated in his irritation over the written reaction to Morrison's statement, issued in Cal Regan's name, which had not been shown to O before it was released.

"We could have been a little more generous, and not so goddamn defensive," he complained to Samuelson, Noth, and Regan, who was on speaker.

"With respect, Mr. President, I don't think it was ungenerous," Regan argued, feeling a little aggrieved at the criticism of a statement he had dictated himself.

"No?" O remarked as he picked up the release and began to read from it. "Do you think this sounds generous? 'While we respect the governor's desire to put the issue behind him personally, we hope his campaign doesn't use it to distract Americans from the issues that are at stake in this election.'"

"Sir, the statement began by acknowledging your sympathy for Morrison, as a father yourself, for how tough campaigns can be on a candidate's children. We thought that was generous."

"That was unavoidable. If we hadn't said at least that, I would have looked like a complete asshole."

"With respect, Morrison *is* going to use this to avoid campaigning on issues he knows he's losing on. We have four weeks to go. I don't think it will, but if it turns out this thing does change the dynamics of the race, we need that argument to get it back, back on our ground, and that means we need to plant the seeds for it right away. Voters who might be reconsidering their impressions of the race, who might be more open-minded than they were last week, are in a receiving mood. Their minds are open to all sorts of information. We have to feed them our stuff, too, before they close their minds again, and Morrison starts to walk off with some of them."

Although Regan's last point had been too alarmist for the others, who, like the president, insisted they never let Washington's frequent mood swings disturb their self-assurance, Samuelson agreed with him.

"Cal's right," he contended. "There isn't enough time left for us to be too generous. They wouldn't be if the roles were reversed."

"Well, I think we could have waited a day or two to start this shit," O insisted. "We've got to be careful that my negatives don't creep up. That ought to worry us a lot more than a one-night track."

"Right," Samuelson acknowledged. "And they'll use this stupid fucking story to try to drive them up."

"And this statement will help them do that," O persisted. "It makes us look immediately political while he looks like America's dad."

"He did that. Not our reaction," Samuelson corrected. "And he'll keep doing that for as long as we let him."

"We should have just sympathized with his complaints about the press," he offered. "First, because he's right, and second, because it would show people we can't stand this crap either."

"Okay," Samuelson said, to bring the largely pointless discussion to an end. "We get your point."

"From now on, I'd like to see these things before they go out," O demanded.

"Okay," Samuelson repeated, smiling at the thought of bringing to the president of the United States the dozens of press statements his campaign released every day. "Your Afghanistan briefing starts in fifteen minutes, so we should probably wrap this up."

"How was he?" asked Mick Lowe, who had been sitting in Regan's office during the conference call with the White House but had heard only Regan's end of the discussion.

"Pissy," Regan answered. "Very pissy. He wants to review our releases before they go out. Apparently, I wasn't nice enough to Tom Terrific yesterday. For fuck's sake, you'd think this was his first campaign."

People who don't work in politics, and have no knowledge of the norms that govern the relationships between reporters and their sources, would have a difficult time understanding why a pollster or a media advisor would share a confidence to a reporter that would embarrass his or her party's presidential candidate. But all well-established consultants had several reporters to whom they owed a favor, reporters who in one campaign or another had written stories that flattered the consultant's candidate or distressed the opponent, using information the consultant had provided them. On other occasions, they had written stories that exalted the role the consultant had played in a successful campaign or downplayed an embarrassing mistake he or she had made. Those favors had to be returned. No one ever put it as bluntly as that, but you knew when reporters were calling in their markers: when the story was an important one, and the competition to break it first was fierce. You didn't always cough up when you had something they wanted. But you had better do it once in a while.

Regan and Lowe knew reporters would be under terrific pressure from their editors to find out who had tried to implicate Morrison in the scandal he had disclosed to the authorities, and they would be casting their nets widely in desperation to dredge up some bit of useful intelligence. They would read Haley's other stories to see if they could detect his usual sources in the O campaign, and they would talk among themselves to see if any of them knew the kid well enough to ascertain any friendships he might have on the campaign.

Regan told Mick Lowe to have another conversation with Tess Gilchrest. "She'll take it more seriously coming from you," he explained. "Tell her she should expect to get calls from reporters she's never met. They might even bump into her at the bar she and her friends hang out in, introduce themselves and buy her a drink. They might offer to take her to lunch or dinner. But if they ask her anything about Morrison, Victor Salazar, Allen Knowles, me, you, Walter Lafontaine, or Terence fucking Haley, she better have nothing more to say than fuck off."

As he issued the instruction to Lowe, Regan was still bothered, as he had been since Morrison had made his statement, by the feeling he was somehow responsible for the interruption in the campaign's progress. That was not a reasonable or a fair judgment, he told himself. He had only checked out the information Knowles had passed to him. It would have been negligent not to. Anyone in his place who deserved to be there would have done the same.

But, still, he was nagged by self-recrimination he couldn't explain or define, though a distinction he recalled from his Catholic grade school education, between sins of commission and omission, had occurred to him. But that, too, was unfair. He didn't know what Morrison's involvement had been until Morrison explained it. Surely, it isn't the job or moral obligation of the manager of a political campaign to defend the reputation of his candidate's opponent. *That's Sandy Stilwell's fucking job*, he insisted to himself.

Whatever it was that bothered him, rational or not, wouldn't go away, he knew, until Tom Morrison's sudden bump in the polls disappeared.

CHAPTER 28

The second debate ended as indecisively as the first. The candidates spent most of the first half of it contending over whose economic policies would bankrupt the country and whose would ensure its prosperity. Most of the second half was spent, as the O campaign had hoped it would be, in a lengthy back-and-forth over energy policy. It had become heated at times, but only the tight-lipped, finger-wagging kind of heat, nothing over-the-top to cause voters to wonder about the temperament of either candidate.

The confrontation the press had hoped would occur hadn't. The moderator, an amiable and well-liked veteran television reporter, had given it a shot. He had asked Morrison if he believed "the president's campaign was responsible for spreading misinformation about your involvement in a federal investigation." Morrison had replied ambiguously. "It's always hard, Jim, to know how these things get started," he conceded, and then made a joke, or what most viewers assumed was a joke. "I'm sure the president didn't start it himself."

"I'd like to thank Tom for giving me the benefit of the doubt," O had interrupted with his own attempt at humor.

"But, I do think," Morrison continued, "it's important for us to step back and think about how our political process could better serve the interests and values of our country, if we all wouldn't be a lot better off without the kind of excesses—the mudslinging, the duplicity, the constant personal attacks—that seem to have dominated our elections in recent years and demean us all."

O had nodded throughout most of Morrison's answer, hoping the cameras would pick it up. He knew his only play was to endorse whole-heartedly Morrison's appeal. That Americans should begin demanding better from politicians was the very message O had used to withstand Republican attacks and win the White House four years ago.

"I agree with Tom. Americans *do* deserve better," he said as he began a familiar litany of his attempts to improve public discourse and over-come the obstinate forces that resisted them. Asking for an additional thirty seconds, O appended to his response a note of sympathy for his opponent to make it appear more gracious and less self-interested.

"I just wanted to say, I thought Tom's statement the other day about this whole matter was appropriate under the circumstances, and certainly something I think was important for the press to hear. Maybe it will give them a little pause the next time they're tempted to jump to conclusions, as they often do. It was also, I think, an important reminder of how tough campaigns can be on our families. That's something I've struggled with since my daughters were little, and that Tom has had to struggle with in this campaign. We're fathers first, candidates second."

It was Morrison's turn to nod his head in agreement with his oppo-nent. Some reporters, however, took offense at being implicated in the intrigue of a partisan website, which they did not consider a member in good standing of their profession. They resented O's response even more because it signaled the end of discussion on the subject, and the end of their hopes for the angry confrontation that would have enlivened the debate and their coverage of it.

Morrison's bump in the polls had receded, although not in the sec-ond and third nights' tracking polls, where Morrison had stayed within a couple of points of the president's lead. The bump hadn't begun to decline appreciably until two days before the debate, six days after Morrison had made his statement. It had not disappeared entirely as the president's aides had tried to reassure themselves it would, but enough to prevent panic from seizing them just before the debate.

The last two nights had O four points in the lead. The new Gallup poll showed him ahead five points. It wasn't enough to restore their for-mer confidence, but it settled their nerves and convinced the press that

Morrison hadn't been able to hold on to the initiative, and that the race was beginning to recover its old, predictable direction.

The scene in the spin room after the debate had been indistinguishable from the previous debate's, except no one assaulted Terence Haley, who wasn't there. Predictable questions. Scripted answers. No news, just filler.

Cal Regan saw Maddy Cohan edge to the front of the scrum of reporters encircling him. She didn't ask him a question, which surprised him. She had left a half dozen messages for him that week, none of which he had returned. She obviously had something to ask him. When he called for a last question and nobody asked one, he said, "Okay, we'll see you at the next one, then," and started to leave. Maddy walked a dozen paces behind him until he had nearly reached an exit her press credentials did not entitle her to use. "Cal, you have a minute?" she shouted at him. He didn't answer but stopped and waited for her to reach him. They were out of earshot of other reporters, most of whom were starting to leave by the exit on the other side of the room.

"You need to return my call."

"I'm sorry, Maddy. But as you can guess, we've been a little busy, what with the election three weeks away."

"I need to talk to you, Cal. I want to hear your side. Otherwise, I'm going to have to file and say you were unavailable for comment, which I don't want to do, and I don't think you'd want me to either."

"My side of what? Why don't you ask your question now? I can give you a couple of minutes."

"Not here. Tomorrow. Whatever time tomorrow works for you, but the earlier the better. Will's on my ass."

"What's it about, Maddy?"

"Give me your word you'll talk to me tomorrow."

"Okay, we can talk first thing after the senior staff meeting. Call my cell at eight thirty."

"I'd rather do it in person."

"I'm going back to Chicago tonight, Maddy."

"I know. I can get an early flight out in the morning, and be there by ten or ten thirty."

"Alright, ten thirty, then, at the campaign. Now, what's it about?"

"Allen Knowles."

At 10:32, the morning after the debate, Cal Regan showed Maddy Cohan into his office. He had had only a couple hours' sleep the night before, and his fatigue showed in the purplish half moons beneath his eyes. Normally fastidious about his attire, even when casually dressed, he looked a little disheveled in a wrinkled button-down shirt and jeans. "You look tired," she observed when they exchanged greetings.

"End of the campaign, Maddy. No rest for the wicked," he responded with a weak smile.

"I don't suppose so," she agreed.

He and Lowe had spent the hourlong charter flight to Chicago speculating about what she might have learned. In the car ride from the airport, he had called Allen Knowles at home, waking him, and insisted he tell him with whom else he had discussed the Salazar investigation. "A reporter is coming to see me tomorrow to ask me about you," he had informed him. "I can't think of any reason why she would unless she's found out about our conversation."

"Cal, relax, buddy. I told you it was an open secret that Salazar had a problem. I've heard it mentioned in a lot of conversations over the years. But I haven't said anything about it to anyone since I gave it to you. Your reporter probably ran into someone in the business who's heard the same thing and is guessing I did, too."

"Not this reporter," Regan had wearily corrected him. "She wouldn't ask to talk to me if she didn't have something concrete. I need to ask you again, Allen, did you give Bianca Stefani this story?"

"No, goddammit, I told you. I hardly know the woman."

"I don't want to be surprised tomorrow when I talk to her, Allen. So I need to know tonight what she has. I'm not going to give her anything if I don't have to. But if she knows you told us about it, I can't afford to bullshit her. She'll think I have something to hide when I don't. I never used the information, thank God, because you didn't really have the whole story, did you? But if *you* did, if you told Bianca what you told me, or if you told anyone else, I need to know it."

"Why do you need to talk to her at all?" Knowles asked.

"I'm not going to bullshit you either, Allen. If you're the source for this story, and she knows it, which I suspect she does, we're going to have to distance ourselves from you. That might be a little embarrassing for you and for the campaign. But trust me, it will be a much bigger problem for you if it turns out you lied to us."

"Take it easy, Cal. You shouldn't threaten friends," Knowles responded coolly, and added with just a hint of belligerence, "Maybe someone in your shop told her I talked to you. I might have to distance myself from you."

"It's not a threat," Regan replied curtly. "It's an unavoidable consequence when friends don't tell us the truth."

"One last time: I didn't talk to anybody about Salazar after I told you. You can call me tomorrow if you want, after you've talked to your reporter. I'm going back to bed now."

"He's lying," Regan said after he hung up with Knowles.

"Well, then fuck him," Lowe suggested. "Tell her he talked to us, but we didn't believe him and sent him packing. And if he gave it to *The Stefani Report,* shame on him and shame on them."

"Yeah? And what will that get us? A story that one of the president's biggest financial supporters started the false rumor about Morrison, a supporter who's raised, what, more than a million for us? She'll have the number to the last cent. A supporter who's a former client of the president's campaign manager, to whom he gave the information, and which we neglected to mention when we were busy sympathizing with Morrison over the unfair attack on his reputation, and his poor kid, who took it personally."

"It's Maddy," Lowe reminded him. "We don't know for sure what she has. But if she knows Knowles talked to you, you can ask for some consideration given your, uh, personal situation. She doesn't have to write the story like that."

"We don't have a personal situation anymore. And anyway, once she writes it, the rest of the herd will fill in any missing details."

Regan looked out the window as the car drove down Lakeshore Drive toward his apartment building.

"Let's go up to my place and call Samuelson."

The conversation with Samuelson had been brief. Regan told him about his pending appointment with Maddy Cohan, and his suspicion she knew Knowles was the source for the Stefani story or that Knowles had talked to him about the investigation or both. He wanted advice from Samuelson about how forthcoming he should be in his answers.

Samuelson resented being asked for advice. Regan, unintentionally perhaps, had gotten himself into a predicament, and Regan should be able to come up with a plan to get himself and the campaign out of it. Samuelson thought it inconsiderate of Regan to expect a senior White House staffer to advise him how to deceive a reporter. Considering that Regan didn't seem to have a firm grasp on which of his associates was leaking to the press, it was possible their conversation would be shared with a reporter, and Samuelson would then be harassed with questions he'd rather not answer. But he kept these thoughts to himself.

"Don't tell her anything she doesn't know," he recommended. "See what she has. If it's a hunch she's working, make her prove it."

Wow, great advice, Regan thought to himself. *Don't answer any questions I'm not asked. I'd have never thought of that.* When Regan asked what he should say if Knowles had told Maddy he was Stefani's source, Samuelson, irritably, Regan thought, reminded him Knowles wasn't on the campaign's payroll and was not his or the White House's responsibility. "If Knowles is the idiot who leaked this, we'll cut our ties to him. Let's hope we don't have to return any checks except his. He's raised a lot for us."

Samuelson had tried to bring the conversation to an abrupt end by telling Regan to use his best judgment. "You know her pretty well, don't you? You'll know if she's fishing."

It wasn't really a question, but an acknowledgment of an intimacy Regan had thought he had managed to keep private. "I didn't get the feeling last night that she was fishing," he responded without bothering to deny or confirm Samuelson's observation. "She said she was ready to file."

"They always say that. I don't think she'd come to Chicago if she already had it."

"You want me to deny it, then?"

"I want you to use your . . . *experience,* I guess is the best word . . . *familiarity,* that's probably a better one . . . with her to find out what she knows. If you really think she's going to write that Knowles came to you first, then blow it off. Tell her off the record that campaign donors are a constant source of conspiracy theories, crap advice, and all kinds of useless fucking information, and you didn't pay any attention to him or any of the other rich dilettantes who pester you daily with garbage like this. We had nothing to do with the story getting out, and if Knowles did, then, on the record, the president deplores it, and we won't have anything to do with him in the future."

Moments after Maddy Cohan had identified herself to the receptionist, the campaign's communications director called Regan to ask if he wanted someone from press to sit in on the interview. "Not necessary," Regan had curtly responded. The communications director, no wiser for his inquiry, reminded Regan he should let the press office know when he scheduled his own interviews. At this point in a campaign, when the chief preoccupation of every staffer was to avoid making a mistake, interviews with the campaign's senior leadership were granted only after the reporter was judged to be friendly, or at least not overtly hostile; the reporter had disclosed the issue or issues he or she wished to discuss and agreed not to raise any others; the communications team had agreed there was value in discussing those issues with the reporter; and the interviewee had been coached on how to respond. Regan had simply hung up without responding to the reminder and told Lowe to tell the communications director "to mind his own fucking business unless I tell him otherwise."

"Okay, what do you want to know about Allen Knowles?" he asked to indicate the let's-get-this-over-with-quickly attitude he thought appropriate for the situation.

"I'm well, Cal. Thanks for asking. And how are you?" she responded in the hope she could humor him into the easy rapport they had always had, before and during their brief affair, which she thought more conducive to accomplishing her purpose.

"I'm sorry, Maddy. I've got twenty hours' worth of shit to get done today and twelve hours to do it." He had planned to say this, to establish at the outset he didn't have time for a lengthy interview, in the event he needed an excuse to end it abruptly.

"Okay, okay. You do look tired, though. Hope you're planning a long vacation after the election."

"I haven't had time to plan anything after the election. Thanks for your concern, though."

"Right. Down to business. I know Knowles was a client of yours."

"A Hanson, Strong client, but I worked on the account, yes."

"How much did you know about his business?"

"How much? I knew what I had to know about his business. I knew what he needed us to help him with. What part of his business are you interested in?" Knowles's business ventures weren't the subject he had assumed she wanted to discuss. He had never considered the possibility she was here to discuss something other than the Salazar thing. He felt himself relax a little before realizing it was possible there was a problem with Allen Knowles he didn't know about, a problem worse than the one he did know about.

"Did he ever need your help with Gabriel Tech's joint venture with a defense contractor, Integrated Security Systems? Specifically, with a procurement bid to develop new cybersecurity software for the Pentagon?"

"No, he didn't. I knew he was considering entering that market, but it's not something we had been involved with. Can you get to the point, Maddy? Why are you interested in Gabriel Tech's contract bids?"

"Knowles is one of your biggest bundlers. There's always the potential for an apparent conflict when a major donor does business with the government."

"Half our major donors have probably run businesses that at one time or another have bid on government contracts. And I guarantee you at least half of Morrison's donors have as well. That's not why you're here."

"No, not exactly. I'm trying to find out if you knew Knowles had a conflict when he told you about the Salazar investigation."

"Back up. You just alleged something you don't know."

"That Knowles had a conflict? I do know. His biggest competitor for the Pentagon contract is Channing-Mills. In fact, sources inside the industry and the Pentagon are pretty certain Channing-Mills is going to get it. They're the bigger player, and a lot more experienced with the ins and outs of the Pentagon procurement system. It's not exactly a leap to think Knowles was trying to embarrass Channing-Mills and maybe hurt their prospects by making the investigation an issue in the presidential campaign."

"That's not what I was referring to. I didn't know Channing-Mills and Knowles were competing for the same contract, but I'll take your word for it. I don't really give a shit either. It's your other allegation that concerns me. Who said Knowles knew anything about the investigation, and, more important, who said he told me about it?"

A long but not noticeably tense silence held while each studied the other's face. She looked for something, a restrained smile, a raised eyebrow, a tilt of his head, something that indicated he was just playing the game, waiting for her to show her premise wasn't a hunch disguised as an assertion she was trying to dupe him into confirming. She hoped he didn't intend to lie blatantly to her.

He looked in her eyes for a trace of benevolence, a willingness to be dissuaded from hurting him. He looked for the Maddy he had fallen in love with, the one who cared that he looked tired and needed a vacation, which would be a very good idea, he thought, if she were to accompany him. But he didn't see anything but the reporter, intent on breaking her story at his expense. And he became angry; angry he had to put up with this bullshit just three weeks before he never had to work another campaign in his life; angry she had surprised him with information he didn't know, and had him frantically calculating how it would make him look; angry she didn't care how bad it made him look as long as she got her story; and angry most of all that he hadn't done a goddamn thing wrong, and yet he was starting to look and feel like he had.

Finally, she said in a tone that didn't conceal her disappointment, "I have it from a reliable source that Knowles told you about the investigation during the convention. Do you want to deny that on the record?"

"Who told you that, Maddy?"

"I'm not going to tell you that. You know that. But it's solid, Cal. There's no reason my source would make it up."

"Everyone has a reason to make shit up in this business. *You* know *that.* To throw you off someone else's trail. To cause problems for an opponent. Personal grudges. And just plain fucking showing off to a reporter by retailing second-, third-, fourthhand rumors to make themselves look like they're something bigger than the ignorant fucker no one ever pays attention to."

"Cal, stop. It's firsthand. I got it from someone in the room. I should never have told you that, because I just broke my word to my source. And I sure won't source it that way in the story. So, can we please get past this now? I'm not out to get you, okay? Tell me you didn't do anything with it, and I'll write it to give you every benefit of the doubt."

Stunned, he considered the list of suspects. *Tess Gilchrest.* He paused to consider whether Knowles himself might be her source. He couldn't see the angle Knowles might have thought he was playing. However the story was written, it wouldn't be good for Knowles. He decided on the default defense he had discussed with Samuelson. Dismiss it. Claim that a donor pestering him with unsolicited tips and rumors was such an ordinary occurrence that he habitually ignored it.

"Off the record, do you know how often donors bug me with shit like this? Every time I talk to one. I thank them for it, change the subject, and forget it. If I paid attention to every rumor and half-baked conspiracy theory some mouth-breathing donor pushed on me, I wouldn't have time to do anything else. I tune it all out, Maddy. If I didn't, I'd go crazy. If Knowles mentioned something to me in passing about Morrison's business affairs, believe me, I only pretended to listen."

"That's kinda hard to believe. I don't think he mentioned it to you in passing, did he? He made a point of taking you aside and discussing it at length. I don't know if you did anything with it, Cal. Tell me you didn't, and I'll write there's no evidence the campaign gave it to a reporter or used it to embarrass Morrison. But don't play dumb. Help me help you."

She was offering him a way out. It wasn't a graceful exit from his predicament. At best, he would look like an unwitting accomplice in Knowles's scheme to embarrass a business competitor. Moreover, no matter how emphatically he insisted neither he nor anyone in the campaign had tried to implicate Morrison in the controversy, or done anything to bring the investigation to public attention, he would not escape the presumption of guilt the public believed every politician caught keeping the wrong company deserved. But it was an exit. If he cooperated, she would write a story that would blaze through the news cycle, consume a twenty-four-hour supply of oxygen, be brought under control by a couple of days of steady damage control—denouncing Knowles, severing his ties to the campaign, and protesting their ignorance of his conniving. After the Sunday shows, only a few faintly glowing coals would remain, soon to be extinguished as air drafted toward some other news, unless another unexpected development revived them.

It was an exit, but because he was angry and because he resented insinuations that he had ever been neglectful or played for a fool, he stubbornly refused to take it.

"I'm sorry, Maddy, I can't help you. If he mentioned it to me, I didn't take it seriously enough to remember it."

"Do you remember discussing the investigation with the White House?"

"No. I remember not discussing it with anyone in the White House. Because there wasn't anything to discuss."

"Even after the *Stefani Report* story? After Morrison's statement?"

"Of course we discussed it after Morrison's press conference. How could we not? It was the only campaign news that day. But it wasn't anything more nefarious than a 'What the fuck was that all about?' conversation."

"Who's we?"

"Huh?"

"You said *we* discussed it. Who at the White House did you discuss it with?"

"I don't really remember. It was inconsequential. Like I said, it wasn't like we had to strategize about it or anything. The campaign put out a reaction in the president's name, and that was all we did."

"Did you talk with the president about it?"

"No."

"You didn't talk to him at any point about it? After the Stefani story? After the first debate? When you put together his statement?"

"No. Look, Maddy, I'm sorry. I can't make it easier for you to write your story. I don't know what I don't know. And I can't spend an entire day trying to convince you."

She thought it possible, even likely, he wouldn't have discussed it with O. Others surely had. Samuelson, most likely. And Regan would have certainly discussed it with him. She didn't expect him to share those conversations with her. But she had nursed a small hope he would believe she wasn't trying to hurt him and would dispense with the aggressive I'll-pretend-you're-an-idiot pose he used on reporters with whom he hadn't had an affair. Her disappointment in him made her as eager as he was to finish the interview.

She had one question left to ask: had he talked to anyone in the Justice Department about the investigation? She was still trying to help him lay the groundwork for the damage control he would have to do after her story ran. She wanted to get his on-record denials to obvious questions others would surely raise. But to Regan, her last questions were a threat. She suspected he or someone had conducted an investigation and crossed the line from due diligence to impropriety. He would be fired and disgraced. Disgraced at the hands of a woman for whom he had once had great affection. Now she wanted to be the agent of his destruction.

"No, I did not."

He didn't want to be in her presence for another minute. She would write her story and hurt him, make a round of cable appearances to promote the injury, enhance her reputation, and then, he hoped, he would never again have to acknowledge the existence of the woman who had had such a perplexing hold on his imagination.

"Maddy, I've got to get back to work. I've told you all I know, which isn't much. I hope you'll write the story fairly. But there's nothing I can trade you for fair treatment."

"You know I'll write it fairly. That's why I came here."

"You came here to do what reporters do. Get a story. I don't have one for you that would interest you or your editors. If it turns out Knowles has spread this rumor, then we'll be as offended by it as anyone else, and we'll end the minor association he had with the campaign. But we're not going to cop to doing something we didn't do or to hiding something we didn't hide just so *Body Politic* can win this week's buzz contest."

Her disappointment and weariness vanished. She was angry now and wanted him to know it, but not at the cost of revealing his insult had hurt her. *Treat a fool's abuse with polite indifference,* she reminded herself. *There's no worse affront to his ego.*

"I'm sorry you feel I'm out to get you. I asked to see you for professional and personal reasons, out of friendship as much as anything else. But I can see you don't believe that."

"I don't believe or disbelieve anything. I just have to get back to running the president's reelection campaign. Do you want me to walk you out or do you know the way?"

"I can find my way. Thanks for seeing me."

"You bet."

"Cal, one last thing. The person or persons you probably suspect are my source aren't. So don't go on a jihad. I know who was in Knowles's suite that night. Only one of them talked to me, and it wasn't who you think it was."

Stupid bastard. Stupid lying bastard, she thought as she waited for the elevator, her emotions a mix of regret, sympathy, and contempt. Years later, when she'd think of him, which wouldn't be often, she would remember him with more kindness, her disdain for his pitiful dissembling no longer diluting the memory of her attraction to the man she had once found unexpectedly hard to resist.

★   CHAPTER 29   ★

The night before the Democratic National Convention began, Allen C. Knowles, CEO of Los Angeles–based software manufacturer Gabriel Tech, appointed by President O to the National Security Telecommunications Advisory Committee and a prominent financial supporter of the president's reelection campaign, arranged a private meeting with campaign manager Caleb Regan to discuss information Knowles had obtained about the Justice Department's investigation of Victor L. Salazar, former vice president for international sales at Shield Holdings, a subsidiary of defense industry giant Channing-Mills, Inc., a source with firsthand knowledge of the discussion has told *Body Politic*.

The Republican presidential nominee, Governor Tom Morrison, was CEO of Channing-Mills at the time the company acquired Shield Holdings, and had been accused of turning a blind eye to Salazar's alleged criminal activity in the wake of a story published by the liberal news website *The Stefani Report*, which first disclosed the investigation three weeks after Knowles had discussed it with Regan.

Those questions were put to rest recently by Morrison himself, in a dramatic press conference in which he revealed he had informed the Justice Department of his concern that Salazar had on numerous occasions violated the Foreign Corrupt Practices Act. According to Morrison, and confirmed by the Justice Department, Morrison was asked by officials not to take any action that might alert Salazar he was under investigation.

Knowledgeable sources have also confirmed to *Body Politic* that

Knowles told *The Stefani Report* about the investigation and his conversation with Regan. What was not known to either Regan or *The Stefani Report* at the time Knowles informed them of the investigation was that his company, Gabriel Tech, had entered into a joint venture with defense contractor Integrated Security Systems to bid on a contract to develop cybersecurity software for the U.S. military. Their biggest competitor for the Pentagon contract was Channing-Mills.

Knowles is reported to have urged Regan to leak news of the classified investigation to the press in an effort to embarrass Morrison and Channing-Mills. *Body Politic* has uncovered no evidence indicating Regan or someone else in the O campaign made any effort to publicize the information or attempted to influence officials in the Justice Department to publicly disclose the investigation.

Neither does it appear the president's senior White House aides or the president was aware of the investigation until after it was revealed by *The Stefani Report* and confirmed by Morrison. Nor were they informed of Knowles's conversation with Regan.

In an interview with *Body Politic,* Regan claimed he couldn't recall the conversation with Knowles, and noted that the campaign's major donors often give him unsolicited advice and inaccurate information about their opponent, which he routinely disregards. "I tune it all out. If I didn't, I'd go crazy," he explained.

Maddy Cohan's story continued for another thousand words and included a colorful account of Knowles's rise to prominence as a software developer, his Hollywood associations, his ostentatious displays of wealth, the esteem he enjoyed in some quarters, and the envy and disdain he provoked in others. It also briefly recounted Alex Morrison's assault of Terence Haley and noted the political effect of Morrison's statement.

Cal Regan read it on his BlackBerry and was infuriated by the lede, depicting a dinner as an arranged private meeting to discuss the investigation, as if he had known in advance what Knowles was going to tell him and had agreed to plot with Knowles how to use it against Morrison. His anger didn't subside when he read the paragraph that seemed to absolve him of impropriety and any responsibility for publicizing the investigation.

"She screwed me. She made me look like a coconspirator in the lede," he complained to Mick Lowe.

"Yeah, she might have worded that better," Lowe conceded. "But I don't think she tried to screw you. I think she was pretty generous with us otherwise. She made it clear you didn't do anything wrong."

"Grudgingly, grudgingly, five or six graphs into it. She didn't uncover any evidence—*yet*—that I did anything wrong. But she sure makes me look like I might have."

"Dude, she gave you a pass. She gave us all a pass. No White House knowledge. No contact with Justice. No evidence of anything worse than associating with an asshole like Knowles. It could have been a lot worse."

"Jesus, stop digging for the fucking pony. I just got lumped into a scandal that, at best, will turn into days of who-did-what-when-to-whom process stories one week before the last debate and three weeks before the fucking election. Could have been worse? I suppose the feds could show up today and handcuff me, but other than that I don't really see how much worse it could be."

"She didn't have to put that 'no evidence' graph in there," Lowe argued. "I'm sure that asshole Janssen didn't tell her to put it in there. She probably suspects, with reason, we would have tried to check out Knowles's information. And I doubt very much she believes you never said a word about it to Avi. Let's be thankful for small mercies, huh?"

In fact, Will Janssen hadn't told her to put it in the story. On the contrary, he had struck it from the story himself. When Maddy had argued for it to be put back in, he had refused.

"He stonewalled you, Maddy. You don't owe him a fucking thing," he'd said.

"I want it back in, Will. I gave you the story you wanted me to get. Knowles was impatient. He leaked the story before anyone in the campaign figured out what to do with it. Maybe Regan would've used it, and maybe he wouldn't have. But he didn't. I'm sure of it. And the story has to say that."

In the end, Maddy had had to demand he take her byline off the story if it ran without the exoneration. And when that didn't work, she had threatened to quit. "Goddamn you, Maddy," was all he said as he relented.

Though he refused to concede it, Regan recognized the story could have been worse. And he knew the time he spent resenting it would be better used planning the campaign's response. Samuelson was traveling with the president, but he had sent an e-mail to Regan from *Air Force One* that morning with a copy of the story and the message "Not good. Will call when we land." He and Lowe needed to sit down with the communications director and press secretary and start working up a statement so he would have something that looked like a plan to show Samuelson. But when Lowe suggested they do so, Regan had looked at him and asked, "Who do you think gave it to her?"

"I don't know. We can worry about that later."

"She told me it was someone in the room," Regan said, ignoring the suggestion to postpone speculating about Maddy's source. "It wasn't me. I can't believe it was Knowles. It had to be Tess, right?"

"I suppose so. But we'll take care of it later. Whose name do you think it should go out under?"

"What?"

"The statement. It can't be in your name."

"But she said something weird before she left. She said it wasn't who I would think it was. Who else could it be? No one else was there. Maybe she was lying about it being someone in the room."

"Dude, you gotta get your head back in the game here. It's gonna be a busy day."

Maddy Cohan had not lied to him. And Tess Gilchrest wasn't her source. Nor was Allen Knowles her source, although she had tried repeatedly to talk to him. She needed to get information from Terence Haley.

Maddy had begun by checking with the campaigns' press advance staffers. Both were women about her age, with whom she was on friendly terms, having expensed their meals and drinks to *Body Politic* so often that the paper's bean counters had complained to Janssen. "We won't even credential that little shit for our events anymore," Morrison's press advance told her. "Much less let him fly with us."

The staffer for the O campaign told her, "He's not traveling with us, but we just credentialed him for the town hall in Raleigh tomorrow night." She booked a flight for Raleigh. She got to the site in advance of the campaign and the press who were covering O that day, and waited to take a seat until Haley arrived; then she took the seat next to his.

She asked him if he was flying with the campaign to Cleveland that night. "No, I have to fly to L.A. in the morning," he told her. "Me, too," she said, appearing delighted by the discovery. "Let's get dinner." When Haley agreed, she suggested a barbecue place she had eaten at the last time she had been in Raleigh. "Great," Haley responded, appearing delighted at the prospect of sharing a meal with a widely respected colleague who had never spoken to him before.

Over ribs slow-cooked in a mustard-based sauce, and three pitchers of beer, Terence Haley poured out his tale of woe to Maddy Cohan. He had gone to Northwestern University's Medill School of Journalism, written a popular column in the school newspaper, and won a coveted summer internship at *The Washington Post*. He had graduated with aspirations to return to Washington or maybe New York and begin his career in the world of big-time journalism. "I used to think by this time I would have gotten my first foreign assignment," he told her.

But journalism had disappointed him. A year after graduation, he was still living with his parents in Boston and working at an entry-level job in the corporate communications office of an insurance company. He had applied to dozens of newspapers and three weekly magazines. The only offer he had received was from a weekly in upstate New York, a job he hadn't even sought. "My uncle was best man at the publisher's wedding," he explained. He had turned it down.

Out of boredom, he had started a blog. "*Haley's Comet*. Pretty pretentious, huh?"

"No, it's cute. I like it," Maddy assured him.

"I wrote a lot on national security; that's where my main interest is."

To his surprise, his blog had gained favorable notice in certain circles.

Several celebrated left-wing blogs often linked to him, in appreciation for what one pundit turned blogger called the "acid wit behind his trenchant criticism of the dick wagging the Bush administration calls statecraft."

"That's how she found me," he explained.

"How who found you?"

"Bianca. She called me out of the blue and said, 'Dahling, I love your blog. You're just who we're looking for. Come to Los Angeles. We'll make you famous,'" he recounted, imperfectly mimicking his employer.

"And?"

"And I went to L.A."

His complaints were many: the subsistence salary he was paid, an expense account that rarely afforded travel on campaign planes or accommodation in hotels where other reporters stayed, the constant abuse Bianca screamed at him.

"I know this isn't journalism, Maddy," he lamented. "But I thought it was a way in. I was so excited when she told me she wanted me to cover the campaigns. I thought if I just wrote some decent copy, broke some minor news once or twice, editors might notice me. Instead, she sends me out with that fucking question for Morrison, and then tells me to get in Stilwell's face after the debate. Now no one in either campaign will talk to me, and reporters treat me like I've got a communicable disease. And Morrison makes me look like a dick on national TV. I got death threats after his press conference. When I showed some of them to Bianca, you know what she said?"

"What?"

"'Why don't you change your e-mail address.'"

She knew it was her opening. The smarter play would have been to keep circling her quarry for a while, drawing him further and further into the false sense of intimacy in which she was enveloping him. But, Jesus, the thought of another hour of poor Terence Haley crying on her shoulder depressed her. So Maddy decided to take her shot. Shaking her head in commiseration with her suffering colleague, and as casually as she could, she asked, "Whoever gave her the story anyway? Didn't she check it out first?"

"Her? Check something out? That's 'old media, dahling.'"

"Oh yeah, I forgot."

"Some bundler for O she hangs out with. Knowles. Allen Knowles. He told her he had already given it to Regan at the convention, and the campaign had probably already given it to the *Times* or *Post*. He said he was doing her a favor."

"Some favor," Maddy remarked, still maintaining an attitude of casual interest, although she was excited to start working the story now that she had gotten the lede. "What do you know about Knowles?"

Haley suddenly gave her a more alert look.

Idiot. Stupid, greedy idiot, she thought. *Why did you ask a follow-up? You could have googled his fucking name. He knows you're after the story now.*

After a pause, during which she assumed he was considering whether he had just been taken advantage of, he said, "A software billionaire, in L.A. Don't really know him."

"Hmm. Never heard of him," she said, hoping to signal she had merely been curious and not working on a story. But she knew her impatience had obliged her to give Terence Haley another hour's worth of sympathy.

"Now, why don't we talk about how we're going to get you out of Bianca's sweatshop and into a sweatshop like mine," she invited him, without betraying her regret that she wasn't running to her hotel to start working her phone.

The rest had been easy. The guest list for the Knowles dinner. Seven unproductive calls, until number eight told her he hadn't heard any discussion about an investigation, "but Knowles and Regan and their dates went up to Knowles's suite for a nightcap. Maybe they talked about it there."

"You wouldn't know who their dates were, would you?"

"Oh, that Swedish girl, maybe she's Norwegian, I don't know. She's Allen's 'personal assistant.' I don't know her name. And Hank Gilchrest's daughter, Tess. She works on the campaign and is dating the boss, I guess. Par for the course for Tess."

Knowles wouldn't return Maddy's calls. She tried various ruses to get him to respond. She mentioned to another bundler for the O campaign, whom she had gotten to know, that she had heard the campaign and the president himself were very impressed with Knowles. She had a feeling they were starting to look at him as a prospect for a big job in the second term. "Maybe commerce secretary," she speculated. She wanted to start building a relationship with him. He could be important to know. "Do you think you could introduce me?" she asked. "Or get him to return my call, and I'll introduce myself."

Word came back a day later that Knowles didn't talk to political reporters. "Just a rule he has," her acquaintance explained. "He thinks the president appreciates that kind of discretion."

Tess Gilchrest made the most sense. She didn't know her. But she knew the bar the kids on the campaign frequented. She could have walked into it any night and recognized someone; introduced herself to Tess; bought a few rounds; complimented her clothes, her jewelry, her hair; laughed at her jokes and made a few of her own about Regan or Jake Collias, Tess's boss.

Then, in a voice too quiet to be heard by the others but not so quiet she appeared disingenuous, she would tell Tess she knew that she and Regan had had "a little fling," and confess, conspiratorially, "Between us, we have a history, too. Thank God, it *is* history. He can be a bit much, can't he?" And when Tess laughed and gave an acknowledging response—"You think?"—Maddy would mention in passing, "I heard about the dinner with Allen Knowles. He's some piece of work, too, isn't he? I would've loved to have seen Cal freak when Knowles told him about the 'secret investigation' in front of you. Did he put his hands over your ears?"

"Just about," Tess would have merrily agreed. And then they both would have laughed at how ridiculous the "boys" looked now that their big Morrison scandal had turned out to be anything but.

She couldn't bring herself to do it. She didn't really know why. If Tess Gilchrest wanted to play with the grown-ups, she shouldn't expect them to make allowances for her age and gullibility. It would teach her a lesson about the dangers of trying to fuck her way into the spotlight. Why should she care if it humiliated Regan, knowing Tess's indiscretion was the price he had paid for his own indiscretion? *Serves him right,* she thought. *She's a kid, for chrissakes.*

But Regan would have known Tess had been his source. He wouldn't have any other suspects, and he would have Lowe get rid of her. It wouldn't matter who her daddy was. He'd have her fired or exiled to Idaho or some other state the campaign couldn't care less about, after Lowe had reduced her to tears for betraying them. And Maddy wouldn't have escaped the knowledge she had been cruel in taking advantage of her, too cruel. Maybe too cruel to Regan as well, she supposed. Her story would cause him enough aggravation, without wounding his pride. Although it was well past time he stopped taking pride in running up his score of sexual conquests.

She decided to deceive Tess only if she had to, if no other witness would confirm the conversation. She had already gotten Bianca Stefani to acknowledge that Knowles had told her about the investigation. She had called Bianca's office and learned she was in D.C. Bianca never came to D.C. without scheduling a round of appearances on the cable shows. Maddy had called a booker for one of them and gotten herself invited for the same segment. She pulled Bianca aside in the greenroom before they went on. "Did Knowles tell you he and Channing-Mills were bidding on the same government contract?" she asked. She had discovered the fact, or rather, a researcher she had called to do a quick search of Allen Knowles and his business had discovered it the morning after Maddy had wheedled the self-pitying Terence Haley's cooperation.

"Why should he have?" Bianca had asked in response, without betraying any surprise that Maddy had learned the identity of her source. "Because when he gave you the tip, he should have told you he had a conflict," Maddy argued. Bianca had looked at her quizzically for a moment before replying, "Doesn't everyone, dahling?"

But Maddy wanted an eyewitness to the conversation. She kept trying to reach Knowles to no avail. She decided to call his Scandinavian personal assistant and tell her she was writing a story identifying Knowles as *The Stefani Report*'s source unless he returned her call to deny it. She was informed Maja Almquist was no longer employed at Gabriel Tech. She sent an e-mail to the address the receptionist provided, and waited for a reply.

Maja Almquist did not share with Maddy the circumstances of her unexpected departure from Gabriel Tech. But it was clear she had a grievance with her former employer she had yet to satisfy. "Yes, I remember the dinner. I remember Allen telling him about the investigation. Allen never worried what I heard. He thought I was too bored or stupid to pay attention to his little secrets."

"But you obviously did," Maddy remarked. "Do you remember exactly what he said?"

"He tried to convince him he was giving him a big gift. But I have to say, I don't think Regan believed it. Or if he did, he didn't care very much about it."

"Well, thank you. I appreciate it, and, of course, I won't use your name in my story," Maddy promised.

"Of course," Maja repeated. "Will your story get Allen in trouble?"

"Maybe a little," Maddy confessed.

"The more the better." Maja laughed before hanging up.

Maybe the bitch will divorce him anyway, Maja thought after hanging up with the reporter, the epithet referring to Mrs. Knowles, who had informed her husband she was no longer prepared to tolerate his infidelity with his assistant, whom she had seen in one too many magazine photographs, looking stunning and smiling charmingly in his company. It was time to start up with a new one, she implied, unless Knowles was prepared to relinquish half his estate again to another ex–Mrs. Knowles, which Knowles was not yet of a mind to do. So, on a Monday morning he had matter-of-factly informed Maja it was time to move on. "She's got her war paint on over it," he explained. "Nothing I can do about it." And off Maja went, with a generous severance, her rent paid through the year, the diamond studs and bracelet Knowles had given her, and drawers full of expensively slutty lingerie he had acquired on her behalf.

She thought she would go back to modeling when the severance ran out, the profession where she had been moderately successful before Allen Knowles had noticed her. *I'm still young enough,* she reassured herself. *Still young enough to get into the movies, too,* she added. That was the dream that had led her to California in the first place. She decided to resume her acting lessons and begin making herself conspicuous again, conspicuously unattached, at clubs and restaurants frequented by producers and bankable stars.

She did return to modeling, and for a time again enjoyed moderate success. Some years later she managed to land small parts in a few movies, although no one would have described her acting career as successful, moderately or otherwise. When modeling offers became fewer, and acting jobs that promised more than a few seconds of nudity in films that catered to the tastes of college fraternities disappeared entirely, she followed a boyfriend to New York. When the boyfriend followed a younger and more than moderately successful model to Milan, she went home to Stockholm, which she often regretted ever leaving.

None of the movies in which Maja Almquist would speak her few lines, as alluringly as she could in just a few takes, would be produced by Allen Knowles. An hour after Maddy's story appeared, he was notified in a phone call from someone he'd never heard of, and by a faxed letter some hours later, that his involvement in the president's reelection campaign had ended. A day later, he received another faxed letter from the White House Office of Personnel Management, informing him he was no longer a member of the President's National Security Telecommunications Advisory Committee. *Who gives a shit,* he said to himself. *The thing was a fucking waste of time anyway.* Two weeks later he received a check refunding the money he had personally donated to the campaign, though not the millions he had raised for the president from others.

A month later, executives at Channing-Mills, Inc., modestly celebrated the Pentagon's announcement that their company had been awarded the contract to secure the military's communications networks from cyberattack. "Ah, we weren't going to get it anyway," Knowles volunteered to one of his vice presidents, and insisted it had been "worth a shot. We're no worse off than we were." The announcement marked an end to Knowles's aspirations to enter the lucrative world of defense contracts.

He soured on politics, too. He never again gave another dollar to a politician who hadn't done him a favor first. On the whole, though, he took the experience in stride. He certainly didn't feel embarrassed, and laughed at the notion he had disgraced himself. He didn't believe anyone worth more than a billion dollars could be disgraced. And no one had ever found out, not even that nosy reporter, that he had reached out to Victor Salazar, indirectly, of course, to let him know the investigation Salazar had been sweating out was about to be leaked to the press to embarrass the former employer who had fingered him. "If I were you," Knowles's agent had advised Salazar, "I'd get my ass out of the country until it blows over." A few weeks after he had been exposed as the person who had tried to smear Tom Morrison, Knowles realized he was actually enjoying his new notoriety, believing it added another little mystery to his public image as a bit of a buccaneer.

He did, however, soon tire of running a software company and eventually began producing movies. "There's not as much money in it," he conceded to an entertainment reporter, "but it's a lot more fun. I mean, how much fucking money do you need anyway?" When some years later he accepted the Academy Award for Best Picture, swaying a little from the effects of an anticipatory celebration earlier that afternoon, he ended a rambling speech with a declaration of his patriotism, which the censors had barely caught in time. "God, isn't this a great country?" he shouted. "Even the politicians can't completely fuck it up."

CHAPTER 30

"Fucking unbelievable," Cal Regan repeated for the third time, not trying hard enough to adjust to the new reality the numbers represented. Morrison was making up ground in almost every battleground state according to their tracking polls. A new Gallup national poll had the head-to-head at O 51 percent and Morrison 49 percent. The media was burbling with excited speculation that the race had fundamentally changed and was now hurtling toward the destination that reporters, wherever their personal political sympathies lay, longed for it to reach: the State of Too Close to Call, the City of Dead Heat, the Valley of Sudden Death.

Mick Lowe tried to revive his friend's flagging confidence by arguing that the change in the candidates' net favorables represented nothing more than right-leaning independents and wavering Republican moderates returning to the Republican candidate, as they usually did in the last weeks of an election, and Morrison's surge in the battleground states would prove to be too little, too late. "He needs two- to three-point leads, not deficits," he explained.

Their better ground game was the main talking point the campaign used to counter speculation Morrison had closed the gap in the nick of time. With one reporter, Lowe had used the argument that it was worth two or three points, and regretted doing so when he began to worry polls might soon show Morrison with a two- to three-point lead in some of the battlegrounds. And ground games, even those with a resource disadvantage, can be infused with new energy by shifts in momentum. Supporters who have lost heart are revitalized by the sudden change in fortunes and begin flooding local campaign offices with offers to help get out the vote.

Regan and Lowe worried most about the debilitating effect Morrison's momentum had on the health and psyche of the O campaign staffers. The indigestion and irritability they suffered was mostly caused by poor diet, extreme fatigue, and the constant scrutiny even the lowliest staffer experienced as a personal affliction. All campaigns endured these complaints in the final, frenzied weeks of an election. Now O's staff was burdened with the added strain of trying not to panic. Only campaigns that were expected to win and were suddenly confronted with a late reversal of fortune knew what that felt like. Losing campaigns usually had plenty of time to become accustomed to their fate, and they lumbered toward Election Day thinking mostly of the relief they would feel when their suffering was finally at an end.

Regan knew that panic sharpens the senses and makes a campaign more alert to danger and quicker to respond. But it's hell on your concentration. It disrupts the strict attention to assigned responsibilities and a winning campaign's steady, grinding progress toward the scores of individual goals staff have been assigned, which cumulatively assure victory. Panic breeds a sense of urgency that can overwhelm judgment. Panic produces mistakes. And in a tight race, the campaign that makes the last mistake loses.

Slugging down his second Diet Coke of the morning, which had begun at four thirty when he had awakened from, or, more accurately, given up on two and a half hours of restless sleep, Regan tasted the bile rising in his throat and recognized it as panic's calling card.

Most surprising to the staff of the O campaign and to the candidate was how often they were now surprised. O thought he had disarmed the controversy in the last debate, so effortlessly had he escaped the character contrast Morrison had wanted to present. But as their polls indicated, his relief had been premature.

When the moderator had asked him to "explain your campaign's involvement, if any, in disseminating the rumor that Governor Morrison might be the subject of a criminal investigation," he resisted the impulse to point out that Morrison's former employee, not Morrison, was the rumored subject of the rumored investigation. He knew that regardless of any pedagogical satisfaction he might derive from correcting another reporter who couldn't keep his facts straight, it wasn't a message that would earn any credit from voters.

Instead, he gave an artful and persuasive response they all thought had effectively placed the blame where it belonged, away from his campaign.

"Campaigns are magnets for all kinds of rumors, as anyone who's ever been in one knows, from all kinds of people, who have their own agendas or who don't know any better than to believe the latest conspiracy making the rounds. I'm sure your staff has heard some doozies about me, Tom."

"None that we ever used," Sandy Stilwell whispered to himself.

"Now, let me be clear about one thing," O continued. "No one in my campaign paid any attention to or took any advantage of the false rumor that one of our donors was apparently trying to spread. And when we learned about it, we told that person we no longer wanted his support. My staff are professionals, and good people, who work as hard as they do because they care about their country. Just as I'm sure your staff does, Tom. They know better than to listen to that kind of . . . stuff." He paused to appear as if he were considering using stronger language that might not be suitable for a general viewing audience.

When Morrison was invited to respond, he said, "I accept that," and for a moment it seemed as if he wouldn't have any other comment. But he continued and made what O and his delighted aides considered a serious mistake.

"You know, you could have called me yourself, Mr. President, and asked me about the investigation. I think you have the clearance to hear about it. Or you might have called your own attorney general. He could have answered any questions about my role in it, and then you could have had your staff let your donor know that he had been mistaken, if he wasn't already aware of that."

O hesitated for a moment, and looked at Morrison as if he was confused or surprised that a nominee for president didn't know the rules that prevented a president from involving a cabinet official in a campaign matter.

"I didn't have any questions about your role in the investigation, Tom," he responded in the gentle tone one would use for correcting a child who suffers from low self-esteem. "Because I didn't know there was an investigation.

"And as for calling the attorney general, Tom, even if I had heard about the investigation, you should know I couldn't do that. I would be accused of politicizing a federal investigation, and rightfully so. It's against the law, which I'm sure my attorney general would immediately remind me of before having me arraigned."

It had been perfect. O had convincingly argued their innocence, appearing not just sympathetic to Morrison but on the same side, and then made Morrison look like an idiot. In the room where his senior campaign staff were watching the debate, it was all smiles and backslapping.

But four days later, the numbers were still moving in the wrong direction. And the only jokes to be heard in the O campaign were starting to sound like gallows humor.

A car had been dispatched to collect Avi Samuelson and two other White House staffers, who had just arrived at O'Hare for the meeting that would convene in an hour to assess their situation and plot tactics to improve it, or rescue it, some might say, depending on whether they assessed the situation as merely distressing or dire. Attendance would be restricted to the three White House advisors and the most senior members of the campaign staff: Regan, Lowe, the lead pollster, the political director, the head of the media team, and the communications director. The president would join by telephone an hour after the meeting began, when he was between campaign stops.

They would decide to reallocate assets from states they could no longer afford to contest to states they could not afford to lose. They would leave ads up in some states they didn't believe they could win to deny the press the confirmation they frantically desired: that circumstances had changed so much that they had forced the very rich O campaign to make very difficult choices. They would take their ads down only in states that they had long ago conceded, on background, would take a national landslide to win, to show they were adjusting to realities they had always been prepared for.

They would try to surreptitiously move money and operatives from states they didn't want to admit they were abandoning to states they couldn't abandon. The risk of discovery, however, was high, as party leaders in states on the wrong side of the reallocation would likely denounce the insult to any reporters willing to listen.

Samuelson would handle the elected officials in the affected states. Lowe would call the state party chairmen and executive directors, and the campaign's chairmen in each of the states. Their message would be pointed and unambiguous: if word leaks out, we will hold you accountable, and our justice will be swift and harsh.

They would somehow squeeze as many as ten additional appearances into the president's congested schedule, some of them in states that less than two weeks ago the campaign had decided were safe enough to be spared another presidential visit. They would do so knowing the president would make it unmistakably clear how displeased he was that they had let things deteriorate to the point where they had to risk his "public collapse from exhaustion" to salvage the campaign. "You do realize," he would remind them, "you can gallop a horse only so far before its lungs give out?"

They would bounce around a few ideas for making news that might distract the media for an hour or two from their obsession with Morrison's rise. "Could we announce something on Afghanistan," Regan asked Samuelson, "like the situation has improved enough that we're going to bring more troops home sooner than planned?" Samuelson rejected the idea. "It would look like Morrison scared us into doing it."

"Well, could we announce anything that looks like good news to somebody?" Regan somewhat peevishly replied. "We need to get Morrison to engage in a debate on something," Lowe argued, "so the press can take a breather from kissing his ass all day long."

Finally, before the president joined them, they discussed the dilemma that would be preoccupying other Democrats on the ballot that election, who were beginning to sense there could be danger in appearing too closely associated with a president the voters might be preparing to turn out of office, but whose resources they coveted and whose appearances in their states and districts would energize volunteers and base voters. They did so more for their amusement than to devise an effective plan to dissuade nervous members of Congress from criticizing O if they thought it would spare them their own defeat.

Regan would volunteer to play the role of enforcer, but he knew, as they all did, that politicians would risk whatever vengeance he threatened them with if it meant the difference between remaining in office or returning to East Jesus, where they would endure all the inconveniences of public life—Rotary Club invitations, civic association requests, commencement addresses to graduating eighth-graders—without any of the privileges. They would risk it more readily if they thought O might not be in a position to exact retribution.

How did this happen? Regan kept asking himself. *It's ridiculous. A rich prick plants a bullshit story on a website nobody takes seriously. Big fucking deal. Morrison gets a little scratch, and he comes off looking like Joan of Arc. We didn't have anything to do with it. We didn't do a goddamn thing wrong. We ran a near perfect campaign. The fucking press got bored. That's what happened. They don't like it when everything goes according to plan. So he gets a scratch, and we get gangrene.*

Watching Samuelson strain to conceal his anxiety with his "we're going to straighten out your mess" attitude, Regan knew he had been effectively demoted. Through no fault of his own, he had lost Samuelson's confidence, and no doubt the president's as well. He hadn't done anything they wouldn't have done had they been in his position. And he knew they would agree. But in the protocols of O's world, anything that threatened the equanimity of the enterprise, the imperturbable self-assurance they insisted was their authentic and enlightened disposition, was a grave and inexcusable injury. Theirs was a culture in which bad luck was as unacceptable as bad judgment.

He should have recognized Knowles for what he was: arrogant, self-interested, and as ignorant of the rules of politics as he was cynical about its purposes. He should have anticipated Knowles would do something like this and taken immediate steps to prevent it or shelter them from collateral damage. You have to have a sixth sense about these things to play the game on this level. Didn't he recruit Knowles as a donor? Hadn't he recommended Knowles be appointed to that commission? Would they be in this predicament if he hadn't opened doors for a troublemaker? Bad judgment precipitates bad luck.

No one would bother to explain this to Regan. No one needed to. He had been admitted into their culture. He knew their rules. No action would be taken to punish him. No one would do anything that would appear reactive and self-incriminating. He wouldn't be fired or demoted. They would not distance themselves from him. They wouldn't utter a word of criticism of him, on or off the record. Were they to do anything other than sneer at such suggestions, it would appear as if they had sacrificed him in supplication to the frivolous, excitable Washington culture they disdained. Worse, it would be regarded as a concession they were in some way to blame for slandering Morrison. They would dismiss as preposterous any insinuation that his conduct had been less than exemplary. They would make a show of their confidence in him, and the loyalty to their own that Washington could never appreciate but they would never relinquish. When this was over, and, knock wood, the president was safely reelected, no doors would be shut in his face. No one would have him embarrassed. And none of them would trust him with anything important ever again.

So it was that Cal Regan's future was altered by a small misadventure for which he was, for the most part, blameless, and which would not have occurred but for unpredictable, unpreventable events that had created it and shaped its fanciful appearance. The alteration was not drastic or even noticeable to anyone but him. The life he had imagined for himself had been his private entertainment. No one would know what objects had escaped his grasp. In time, he would appreciate what good fortune he had enjoyed. Though less enviable than the influence he had hoped to possess, he would have wealth and respect and work that was usually more interesting than dull. He would marry a beautiful wife, and they would have beautiful children who rarely disappointed him. His friends would be accomplished and good company. Mick Lowe, who would be best man at his wedding, would remain his closest friend, counselor, and confidant.

What of the heights he would not ascend? The powerful who would not rely on his counsel, the accounts he would lose to competitors who had attained greater prestige or were thought to have a reasonable chance of attaining it, the parties that would be notable for reasons other than his presence? Well, contentment could be had with less. It wasn't worth complaining about, really.

Such was the profession he had chosen, and the city that existed to worship it, where the incompetent and unlucky, villain and victim were all marked with stigmata, none more noticeable than another.

★ CHAPTER 31 ★

"Ready, Mr. President." *Was it a question or an announcement?* he won-dered. *Am I ready? Are they ready? Ready for it to be over, to know how it ends? Not like the last time, is it?*

"Give me five minutes."

"Yes, sir."

On the morning of the day before the people in their constitutionally anointed sovereign majesty would decide his future, O sat quietly behind the stage of a college auditorium in a holding room indistinguishable from the countless other small, windowless cells provided for his private preparation before a public address: unadorned walls thickly painted in yellowing white, a few pieces of inexpensive furniture, the inescapable fruit plate, a coffee urn and plastic cups and saucers. Agents guarded the door and settled into their watch in the auditorium. His personal aide, having delivered his reminder, now leaned against a wall, hands in pockets, looking at the ground. Other aides roamed subterranean halls, staring at BlackBerries and iPhones, cursing a weak signal. The advance team that had busied themselves for hours—checking sight lines and mult boxes, repeating stage directions to the starstruck locals who would share the dais, measuring the distance between the holding room couch and coffee table to make certain the president could cross one leg over the other without incident—now stood idle and anxious. The press rustled in their pen behind the last row of seats on the main floor, affect-ing fatigued indifference. Behind them a riser sagged from the weight of forty television cameras and their fussing operators. And the crowd had begun to chant: "O . . . O . . . O . . ."

He opens the door and nods. Everyone falls into formation and marches with him for seventy-two feet to the stage. As he starts to ascend its four stairs, they all disperse to assigned seats or to lean against the auditorium walls, except two agents who remain no farther from him than the distance they can lunge in an instant. The crowd rises and roars. He lets them go on for a moment before acknowledging the local some-bodies who are sitting to his right, applauding vigorously and blinking in the glare of television lights. He starts slow. He wants to be a little personal about what they all mean to him. He builds a rhythm when he gets to the either/ors. *You can either help pull the wagon or just sit in it. Just don't get in its way. You can either lend a hand or take a hand. But don't bite the hands that are busy rebuilding our country. You can believe America's best days are still ahead or worry they're not. But don't make it harder for our children to follow their dreams.* He paints them a picture of the America they're building together. *It's not easy. I told you it couldn't be done in a day. But it will be done. So help me, God.* He leaves them thrilled. They'll work for him tomorrow.

He would give the same speech four times in four different states, and then once more late in the evening back home in Chicago. On the flight to the next rally and on each flight to each rally that day, he asks to be left alone in his compartment. "I need to rest," he politely explains, "to get through today without making a fool of myself."

Tom Morrison and his Secret Service detail marched briskly to the hangar where fifteen thousand supporters had been screaming themselves hoarse since his campaign plane had landed and rolled slowly to a stop on the tarmac a hundred yards from them. Several thousand more were lined five and six deep on the other side of the security fence, turned away from the magnetometers at the entrance to the hangar when the Secret Service informed the organizers the facility had been filled to capacity.

He clutched a note card bearing the names of the local Republican candidates he would recognize and thank at his first rally of the day, which, he was pleased to note, would start precisely on time, thirty minutes after the president finished his first event. He did not carry any notes for the rest of his twenty minutes of remarks, a condensed version of his stump speech, which he had committed to memory. He wouldn't deviate from it by a word in any of his six rallies that day.

A sudden screech of feedback that made Morrison wince erupted from the amplifier of the lead guitarist in the band that heralded his arrival with a spirited—and a little grating to the ears of a traditionalist—interpretation of "The Caissons Go Rolling Along." He reminded himself to relax and enjoy the day, as he had been advised to by Sandy Stilwell. "It'll be a long day, but try to have fun. Be upbeat. Excited. Confident," Stilwell had urged.

Familiar with the conviction common to military minds that outcomes could be anticipated from personal observations of opposing forces on the eve of battle, Stilwell thought it prudent to caution his candidate against such speculation. "Don't try to interpret anything from the size and enthusiasm of the crowds," Stilwell had counseled. "They're all big and crazy today. O's, too. Fire 'em up and enjoy it. We need the pictures."

He wished Margaret and all his children were there. He could enjoy himself more if they were. Only Alex would accompany him to all but the last event. He looked to see if his son was trailing behind him. An agent touched his shoulder and nodded toward the hangar, which Alex had already entered, heedless of the body man's responsibility to stay in close proximity to the candidate. He was standing in front of the stage with a camera, shooting pictures of the crowd and smiling.

Margaret and the girls had been dispatched to several media markets Morrison wouldn't visit today, where they would describe him as a loving and sympathetic husband and father in dozens of interviews with local reporters. The anecdotes they told to suggest his tenderness toward them were unpretentious, the affection behind them genuine and obvious, and their effect, it was hoped, would soften the hearts of the persuadable women voters who, Morrison's last poll indicated, still suspected his reserved manner concealed an unsympathetic austerity.

They would join him at the homecoming rally and accompany him to their polling place tomorrow morning. It would be their last public appearance of the campaign, after which they would retire to their weekend retreat to wait for the returns. It would be over soon, the campaign that had lasted longer than many of his overseas deployments. He was certain he was prepared for any outcome, and he kept himself from imagining a final scene of triumph or disappointment. In either event, he would be proud of what he had done, and of Margaret and the girls, and of Alex, too. The Morrisons had acquitted themselves with distinction in challenging circumstances. If the achievement proved to be a consolation, so be it. It was a good one. If fortune favored them tomorrow, he was certain they had proved themselves worthy of the office he would enter. *Sleep soundly,* he would tell himself tonight. *You earned it.*

That night, O's two-minute address to the voters would air on all the broadcast and cable networks, right after his opponent had concluded his. Could he talk his way over the finish line? It was the only question the press had. They knew words were his art. With words he had made history four years ago, history none of them had expected to see in their lifetime. He had a gift. He used it to persuade Americans to believe not just in him but in themselves; not in who they were, but who they could be. Almost like Lincoln, some had suggested then.

But his speeches alone couldn't close the deal. They were fine for dewy-eyed kids and paunchy, middle-aged liberals to whom his biography was a lure and not a problem. But there weren't enough of them.

It was his equanimity that had suggested to voters he wasn't merely a man of words but a man of parts. His every attribute had seemed to accentuate his promise: his elegant comportment, his coolness under assault, the way he worked his audiences into a kind of rapture without getting carried away with himself, without shouting or surrendering his detachment. That's what made his oratory so beguiling, even its occasional overstatements and hazier appeals.

Cal Regan and Mick Lowe were not their usual selves. They dispensed with their habitual teasing and brashness as they concentrated on supervising operations that would not add huge numbers of voters to the president's total, but perhaps enough in a close election to make the differ-ence. Both were on the phone much of the day. They discussed with the campaign's regional and state political directors the results of last night's phone banks. They identified counties where the president's support had softened or worse. They tried to anticipate problems they could still address and others—forecasts of inclement weather in swing districts, for instance—they could only pray would not prove accurate. They talked separately to the head of the DNC's legal team to satisfy themselves that they had capable lawyers who were briefed and prepared to file peti-tions to keep polls open past their closing times in precincts where the president's support was strong and where, they hoped, the lines of voters would be very long.

As they performed these and other responsibilities, they spoke in clipped sentences and soft voices, avoided making jokes or extraneous observations or otherwise digressing from the task at hand. They were intent on acquiring the information they needed as completely and as quickly as they could. They needed time to make last-minute decisions and prepare the briefing Regan would give the president and Samuelson when they arrived in Chicago tonight.

The nervousness that would have afflicted them tomorrow, even if the last polls hadn't been so close, had arrived days earlier. The campaign seemed edgy but muted. The headquarters buzzed with the intensity of scores of purposeful people drilling hurriedly through their checklists, but was quieter than it should have been. No one yelled or complained or spoke in a loud voice. No one joked. No one argued. No one threw anything at a wall. People looked busy in a strangely practiced, almost robotic way.

The "tight lips and tight sphincters," as Lowe described it, were a symptom of uncertainty. No one knew which candidate would win, and no one asserted in private the confidence they boasted in public. Many told their spouses and lovers in quick phone calls that they just couldn't get a feel for how this one would turn out.

The day before, O had curtly informed Regan that the script for his televised address, which everyone agreed had the right mix of becoming humility and inspirational self-promotion, "isn't what I wanted." When Regan had asked him what changes he wanted made, O told him, "Don't bother, I took care of it." That made Regan worry. "He's been acting kind of squirrelly lately," he observed to Lowe. They trusted O's instincts, and they took his irritable if inexpressive disposition in the last days of the campaign, which seemed uncharacteristically similar to their own, as a sign the president's instincts were worried.

No drama, their tight little mantra. It had made O laugh to witness its uneasy adaptation by the anxious, suspicious, unsleeping overachievers who worked for him. For the campaign's graybeards, the attitude was a discipline, a concentration on strategy and not the occasionally unpredictable tactics of their opponent, often enforced with outbursts of anger. For him, it was the face he had always shown the world, the grace that made him.

Now they were all at pains to maintain their cool. Cal Regan had the look of a man who had gambled his inheritance on the stock market and then watched helplessly as it plummeted several hundred points in a single day's trading because a stupid computer glitch had started a panic. And O, too, had lost his balance when his performance in the last debate hadn't given them enough of a boost to recover their advantage. He had been angry and had let it show in public last week. A television reporter asked him if he was worried his campaign had been too negative, and that his personal attacks on Morrison were causing voters to sympathize with him.

"What personal attacks?" he had asked testily, and not waiting for an answer demanded she identify "just one of my speeches or one of our ads that made a personal attack on Governor Morrison."

"Well, sir, you recently said his energy speech could have been written by OPEC—"

"That's an argument, a policy argument, not a personal attack."

"With respect, sir, I don't think I'm the first person to think your campaign has been negative. Look at the polls, they seem to indicate—"

"Why don't you look at the record?" he interrupted her again. "Why don't you take the time to look at what we've been saying, instead of asking uninformed questions."

When he had seen the look on his press secretary's face after he finished the interview, he held a hand up and said, "Not a word. I know I shouldn't have, but I'm getting tired of this crap." But the lapse made him angrier with himself than he had been with the reporter; he knew his outburst would be replayed constantly on every news show, with pundit after pundit delightedly agreeing it was a sign O was struggling to keep his composure in the unexpectedly tight race.

Maddy Cohan began the day with a quick phone call to her mother before boarding the Morrison campaign plane. She answered questions about her eating and sleeping habits between gulps of coffee. "Giant bags under my eyes, Mommy, and I'm so fat I can't button my jeans," she confessed. "But I'm off to rehab after tomorrow, so you'll recognize me when I come home for Thanksgiving," she promised. "Who do you think will win?" her mother asked her after she said she had to go. "I don't know, Mom. No one does," she answered.

Had she been confident in the outcome, she would have chosen to spend today and tomorrow with the winning campaign. Morrison might win, but that wasn't why she decided to cover him at the end. O's campaign hadn't made her feel very welcome lately. She hadn't dared ask to interview Cal Regan. But she had asked to talk with Samuelson and had never received a response. She didn't get an answer from Mick Lowe either. The campaign's press secretary had rebuffed her plea to intervene on her behalf. So she called Morrison's press secretary and was promised an interview with Sandy Stilwell after the last event of the day.

She had mixed feelings, anyway, about covering the O campaign on Election Day. If he won, she would probably regret not being there. A celebration was a better story than a concession. Who knows, Cal might stop acting like such a dick. He would be so excited and pleased with himself that he might forget to remind her how much he resented her. But if O lost, seeing Cal would be torture. He'd either fix her with an are-you-happy-now glare that would make her angry, or he would look so lost and broken that she would, quite undeservedly, feel pangs of remorse. Better not risk it, she told herself.

0

• • •

It was always going to be hard, delicate work to convince Americans they needed government to protect them from themselves and not just criminals and natural calamities and foreign enemies. There had been times when O thought he was the only person who remembered that; when he wished he still smoked a pack a day.

Would anyone ever appreciate just how great a triumph it was to remain composed and intent amid all this discord and folly? He had managed it with few nearby examples to encourage him. His chief political advisor was steady but cheerless. His budget director seemed flustered. The members of his national security council squabbled and leaked their disagreements to the press. Young aides, once ebullient and confident, were now disheveled and tired, burdened with insistent responsibilities, and harassed by history.

Little wonder, then, that he had come to feel a kinship with his Secret Service detail. No president since Lincoln had been the subject of more death threats. The service had required a large increase in its operating budget to stay on top of the daily deluge of letters, faxes, phone calls, and e-mails threatening the "Kenyan," "Communist," "Muslim" in the White House. Of course, almost all these would-be Lee Harveys turned out to be misfits fantasizing a place in history they had no more intention or means of achieving than they had of escaping the failures of their dreary lives. Still, you would think men and women who were expected to overcome their instinct for self-preservation might have betrayed during his public appearances a little anxiety over the unprecedented volume of deranged musings about his violent death. Yet they never did.

Once, while working a rope line outside a steel plant, he had noticed the head of his detail shoot his right hand toward the midsection of a grinning, gray-haired man in Carhartts to remove the utility knife holstered on the old guy's work belt and casually hand it to the agent behind him. The unwitting offender hadn't noticed a thing. O stopped his progress for a moment to look to the agent for guidance and received a quick nod of the head to indicate he should proceed. He admired the neatness of it. Precise, and just as cool as you please; a hard discipline to maintain in the charged atmosphere of the White House.

Walter had never seen O in the White House. He pictured him as president as he had known him in Chicago: the unflappable, approachable political organizer; the baller with great court vision who didn't talk trash, who didn't want his points more than he wanted to win.

Ten days ago, Walter had come home to Chicago. He called Tess to let her know he was fine. "Are you coming back to the campaign?" she asked. "No," he quickly answered, and gave a little laugh she mistook as scornful, although he hadn't meant it to be. "I'm retiring from politics," he explained. "Before I'm too old to do something else."

Six hours after he ended the call with Tess with a promise to meet for a drink after the election, the president called him. Their exchange was brief. O was late for the next rally. "How are you, Walter? I'd like to see you. I'd like you to come out on the road with me."

"Thank you, Mr. President, but that's not necessary. I'm doing fine."

"I didn't say you weren't. Walter, if the president says he needs you, it's necessary. I told Cal to get you on a plane to Denver tomorrow. I scared them into giving me a few hours of downtime there. I'm spending at least an hour of it playing some ball. So are you. Pack a bag for the week."

Walter got on a plane for Denver with an overnight bag and a return ticket for the next day that he had purchased himself.

"If I don't get beat next week, I want you in the White House with me," O informed him.

"Thank you, Mr. President. But that's not necessary."

"Walter, you gotta quit telling me what's not necessary. I get to decide that. I'm sorry. I'm sorry for how you were treated. I'm sorry for a lot of things."

"You don't owe me an apology, but I accept it."

"Yes, I do, and thank you. So, if I've still got a job next week, we'll discuss how you'll spend the next four years experiencing the majesty and misery of the White House. And if I lose, we can both figure out what we're going to do for a living."

"I appreciate the gesture, but I don't want to go to Washington."

"It's not a gesture, Walter. I wish I'd had you there the last four years. I might have done a better job. I definitely would have enjoyed it more."

"You did fine, Mr. President, and you'll do even better next time. But I've got other plans. You told me politics shouldn't be my only career."

"What are your other plans?"

"I spent some time in Mobile, Alabama. I liked it there. And I'll like it even better in the winter. I'll probably practice law if I can. But I thought I'd look into teaching eventually. I might be good at it."

"What do you think your mother would want you to do?"

"She'd want me to be happy, Mr. President. That's all she ever wanted me to be."

Walter rode in the presidential limousine to the gym where he and O, O's body man, Eddie, two Secret Service agents, and a local pol, who had played on the Stanford varsity team, spent an hour playing three-on-three, like they were doing what they always did on a weekend afternoon.

"Pick your team, Walter."

He picked the local pol and one of the agents. Eddie inbounded to O to start the game. O passed to his agent, who brought it down court and passed it back to O, who put the ball on the floor to drive and pulled up when his defender kept backing up. Walter quickly rotated from defending Eddie to get a hand in the president's face before he took a shot. O took advantage of the mistake and threw a behind-the-back pass to the unguarded Eddie, who took it to the hoop. O raised his eyebrows at Walter in chastisement. *You should've known that would happen,* it communicated.

The game was one-sided. Eddie was the best player on the court, and O was better than the former Stanford starter, who had gotten paunchy in middle age and complained his knees were bothering him. The agent playing with Walter was decent, and the youngest man on the court. But he wasn't any better than the agent playing with O. And Walter, who never had much game, was the worst of them. He was quick but heady. He wasn't a playmaker. He didn't see the play.

He overplayed on defense and got burned. He forced his shots. He drove the lane in traffic and got stuffed or lost his handle. There wasn't any trash talking. There wasn't much talking at all. But O twice counseled him, "You had a man open. Drive and dish."

They were down twelve with only a few minutes left to play. Walter told the agent guarding O to switch with him and guard Eddie.

"Why?" the agent, who didn't believe Walter could defend O any better than he had Eddie, asked.

"'Cause I can't guard Eddie."

The agent shrugged and did what he was told.

The other agent brought the ball up and passed it to O, who was waiting at the top of the key. Eddie was fighting for position on the low post. O dribbled the ball but didn't move, waiting for Walter to try to ball-hawk him. But Walter kept waving his arms without reaching in. O smiled at him just before he started the move Walter had seen him do a hundred times: fake right, drive left. Walter dropped back, slid to his right, and planted his feet. O drove into him as he tried to lay it up. But rather than fall down and argue a charge, which no one calls in a pickup game, Walter spun around to play for the rebound, keeping in front of O. Everyone heard the president grunt as Walter slammed his left elbow into his stomach.

Eddie called foul. "It's up to him to call it," Walter corrected, nodding at O. "You were on my back, Mr. President."

O laughed. "You were under my feet, shorty. No foul."

"You coming with us?" O asked as he and Walter walked toward his motorcade later that afternoon.

"No, sir. I got a flight back to Chicago tonight."

"Will I see you election night?"

"I'll be at the party."

"It might be a wake."

"It won't be."

"Make sure you come see me then. Even if you don't change your mind about the job."

As Walter began to walk away, O called out to him.

"Walter."

"Yes, sir?"

"You'll make a good teacher. Your mother deserves the credit for that, too."

"You do, too, Mr. President." Walter did go to the election night party, where O would thank his campaign staff and friends. But the party would begin much later than planned, nearly one o'clock in the morning, and would last only an hour. Walter had a couple of drinks with Tess and a few other junior staffers before he went home. He didn't work his way through the circle of people surrounding the president. He didn't try. He never talked to O again.

He knew it had been a mistake to expect a politician to be responsible for his happiness. Successful politicians, especially presidents, learn to regard people as part of a demographic or as means or obstacles to their progress. Friendship and its responsibilities require more of their attention than they have to spare. Even their families must go begging sometimes. It's not a character flaw necessarily. For the best of them, it's a sacrifice. They regret it and hope the service they gave was worth it. O had been a friend and mentor to Walter. The president of the United States couldn't have that privilege even if he wanted it.

The president opened the door of his cabin and invited Avi Samuelson and Rick Noth to join him. "Anyone want to play a hunch?" he asked them. He didn't believe they had a better idea what tomorrow would hold than he did, but he knew they would welcome an opportunity to reassure him.

"A little closer than last time, but you're going to be stuck with this job for another four years," Samuelson declared. "Tell him, Rick." Noth agreed with the assessment.

"I'd say you can sleep like a baby tonight, but if I were you, I'd cry like one. I don't know why anyone would want the fucking job." They all laughed at that, without any of them believing a word of it.

On the flight home, O looked out on a landscape ablaze with man-made light. As the lights of one city or town began to fade behind him, the flickering lights of highways and airports pointed like signal fires toward the next brilliant illumination just coming into view. He saw the lights of cars beetling their way through the night in numberless, rushing caravans bringing his countrymen to homes and families and jobs on the third shift and the promise of a new start in some other well-lit town that would replace the one that had disappointed. Americans let no darkness impede their progress or hide their creations.

What a curious people. Their mania for self-improvement encompassed everything that touched them, and they resented the cost of every change. They were proudly self-reliant and quick to assign blame to others for their disappointments. They were certain theirs was the most enlightened and envied society on earth, that human history was mostly a chronicle of their achievements, and were convinced, too, that their country was constantly in need of repair. Everything they had was better than what any other people had, including their form of government, and nothing was good enough. They believed in themselves and distrusted the leaders they elected. They admired the candidates they voted for and believed politics was a profession for double dealers, cheats, and frauds. They relied on government for justice, security, and order, and believed it was run by incompetents who coveted their liberty.

O had been watchful all his life. He had the distance to see the whole. He thought he saw a nation uncertain how to live up to its promise. For all its power and influence, its abundance and enterprise, it was still an immature society: impatient, demanding, not comfortable with introspection, frivolous and audacious. He had wanted to inspire Americans, reason with them, set them an example, and, if necessary, beguile them into maturity, into recognizing they weren't the world's only makers of history, and they would have to change themselves if they wanted to remain preeminent.

But it had been a foolish conceit to think he could float above them all and direct their raucous enterprise. Americans won't be led from a distance. They let their presidents live in a mansion, but it's their mansion. You are their servant. Their wants are your work. They are freer than you.

Was he wiser now that he recognized the humbleness of his occupation, that his pride, his insistent self-respect had convinced him to be a subject and not autonomous? Or was he overdrawing the lesson? Would he find a better balance between the two? Would he have that chance?

America would let him know tomorrow. And if it rejected him, what would he be then? America's youngest ex-president. Is that all? What was it that he feared? That he would be rich, bored, without purpose, without an occupation? Surely not. In a country where people were always reinventing themselves, reimagining themselves, wouldn't he, too? What would he be? He would be one of them.

When the plane landed and came to a stop near his idling motorcade, he saw his wife and daughters waiting to greet him. They rode in the limousine with him to the final rally. When the agents closed the doors of the car, his wife kissed him, not like she had a moment before for the cameras. It was a lingering kiss, one hand stroking the back of his head, causing their daughters to giggle. Then she smiled at the girls and at him. *It's good to be home.*

He had rejected the script for the recording that would air that night and rewritten it himself. He wanted Americans to know he recognized he had made them a promise he couldn't keep. He couldn't change politics, because it required self-denial; it required a change in himself, in other politicians, in Washington, and in voters that none of the parties were selfless enough to make.

He didn't put it that way. He simply conceded campaigns would not ever be completely free of the superficial and discreditable, of deliberate misrepresentations and exaggerated disagreements, of all the things voters detested and responded to in the ways campaigns presumed they would. It was worth trying to improve them, but no one should promise a transformation that human nature itself resisted.

After he voted tomorrow, he would go to the gym and shoot some hoops. He would take a nap that afternoon. And before the returns started to come in, he would take his wife and daughters out to dinner at their favorite neighborhood restaurant. His staff would spend the day pestering reporters for exit poll results, monitoring the turnout in bellwether counties, staring at numbers for key precincts, worrying about the weather, trying to discover as soon as they could his future and theirs. He was going to relax. The voters had made up their minds, and he would know their decision soon enough.

Americans would make their history, and his too, in the bargain. He and the country were theirs to do with as they wished, at the service of these restless, discontented dreamers.